Map

To Miami 74 miles
Tavernier 3 ½ miles

North

Quarry

Camp 1

Islamorada Train Station

Hotel (FERA HQ)

Florida Bay

Atlantic Ocean

Camp 5

Alligator Reef Light

Camp 3 & Ferry Landing

Veterans Camps, 1935

Bridge Construction

0   2   4 miles
Scale

To Key West 67 miles
Marathon 24 miles

*Veterans Key (24° 51' 3" N, 80° 44' 41" W) :
USGS entry February 23, 2006

Contents

Title Page

Copyright

Map

1	The Forgotten Man	1
2	Pay Day	9
3	Havana Special	17
4	One For All . . . All for One	22
5	The Bower	25
6	Introductions	36
7	Date Night	49
8	Sunrise	57
9	Outbound	62
10	Havana	71
11	Bank Job	80
12	On the Run	91
13	Montreal	105
14	The Law of Storms	109
15	Southernmost Charm	123
16	Late Night	132
17	Manhattan Weekend	138
18	On the Job	150
19	A Walk in the Park	156
20	The Bremen	163
21	One Day More	175
22	The Ballad of Goldy and Dixie	196
23	The Night Before	204
24	The Game is Afoot	226
25	Hotel Matecumbe	255
26	Picnic	269
27	Inquiries	276

28	The Last Raid	282
29	The Wave	290
30	Relief	306
31	Verrat (Betrayal)	331
32	The Survivor	339
33	Miami	351
	Historical Notes	368
	Sources and Acknowledgements	374
	About the Author	381

Chapter 1

Sunday, August 4, 1935 – The Forgotten Man

"Who's the bum?"

The deputy whacked the desk with his copy of True Detective Magazine. "Says his name is Fred Dunn, Sheriff. He's got his Army discharge. Works at one of those vet camps." He flicked the mashed horsefly onto the floor.

Karl O. Thompson, Sheriff of Monroe County, Florida, let the screen door slam behind him. He sized up Dunn, itemizing his unshaven face, unkempt hair, frayed shirt, tattered trousers, muddy boots, and a bindle stick leaning against the wall. He took the discharge paper handed him, quickly scanned it and gave it back. "Could've fooled me. So, the Veterans Work Program, eh? Why aren't you working?"

"Sunday, Sheriff," replied Dunn, cap in hand.

"Off Saturdays, too?"

"Forty-hour work week, it's the law, Sheriff."

"And Federal holidays?"

"Yes, sir."

"And half days on pay days?"

"Pretty much so, Sheriff, sir."

"Well, no days off in law enforcement. So, what brings you to Tavernier?"

"Recreation, Sheriff. I hike the tracks every Sunday, usually out to Craig Key. Today, I thought I'd visit Key Largo."

"Just can't have that, Mr. Dunn. Around these parts we get a mite anxious when there's some stranger snooping around dressed like you. If I let one hobo stroll through my county all devil-may-care, word will get around and soon there'll be a swarm of bums, looking for hand-outs, stealing what's not nailed down, and squatting wherever, like a pack of mongrel dogs. Even the blacks know better than to shit where folks walk. Say, you aren't one of those Reds who torched Washington back in '32?"

"Weren't no Reds. Was the Army done that, Sheriff."

"Proximate cause, Mr. Dunn, *proxi-mate* cause. Wouldn't have been any fracas if y'all hadn't made that fool march, set up shanties all over town and started pestering Congress about your damn war bonus. Gave veterans a bad name. Able bodied men demanding a cut while decent families lose their homes, shameful."

"We have families, too, Sheriff."

"Then you should've gotten jobs to support them!"

"Weren't none, Sheriff. Only the President's relief camps."

"Playgrounds for derelicts, more like it! Roosevelt just wanted to get you bums out of Washington before the next election. Couldn't count the number of times I've seen your crowd laying back with a smoke and a beer while honest folks were working up a sweat. Even the blacks work harder. I should lock you up on general principles but it wouldn't sit right with the taxpayers, accommodating a vagrant for the night when you're already gettin' free room and board from the Government. Now, get your ass over Snake Creek and don't come back acting like no hobo!"

"Can I have my belongings back, Sheriff?"

Thompson glanced at the deputy. "Checked for stolen property?"

"Yes, Sheriff."

"Well let's just see what a working stiff packs in his bindle." The Sheriff dumped the contents of a cardboard box onto a table: a church key, pocketknife, a half-filled glass hip flask, some coins, a laundry ticket, a sandwich wrapped in newspaper, and a tin snuff box. Its contents rattled. He opened it, looked inside and held up a small cross-shaped object on a piece of blue ribbon. "What have we here?"

"The Distinguished Service Cross, Sheriff."

"I know that. Question is, did you earn it?"

"So they told me, Sheriff. Killed some krauts. Had the citation once but lost it."

"Probably the last thing you earned."

"Meaning no disrespect, Sheriff, but I've worked plenty. And I ain't never stole nothing from nobody, ever."

"Sure, sure, and now you're relaxing on the public's dime while regular folks go hungry. Take your stuff and git before I change my mind." Thompson tossed the medal onto the table.

"Thank you kindly, Sheriff." Fred repacked his things in the flour sack bindle and tied it to the stick, then tipped his cap and headed out the door. He took care to close it gently. Two steps away he let rip a resounding fart. "Well, still early, guess I'll just about face and hike on down to Camp 3."

* * *

Camp 3 was on Lower Matecumbe Key, some 12 miles altogether. Fred crossed the wood trestle bridge spanning Snake Creek to Windley Key, passing by Camp 1 on the beach where he bunked. He hiked the half-mile Whale Harbor Fill to Upper Matecumbe Key, entering and leaving the tiny tank town of Islamorada. You could walk from end to end in the time it took to hawk back and spit. The Hotel Matecumbe was about a mile beyond the train depot. It was rented out to the State of Florida for the camp headquarters.

Indian Key Fill linked Upper and Lower Matecumbe Key. Fred stopped there for lunch, a swallow of rum from his hip flask followed by the fried baloney and cheese sandwich he'd saved from breakfast. About four miles offshore boats were fishing for tarpon and dorado around the iron pilings of Alligator Reef Light. Indian Key itself was visible just a little offshore. The Seminoles had massacred the white settlers there almost a century before, as the story goes. They won the battle but lost the war.

Fred walked past Camp 5 on the eastern tip of Lower Matecumbe. 195 men were bunked here. They slept in wood plank shacks on rickety platforms, set up so near the ocean they might float away with the next high tide. There weren't many around this afternoon, just a bunch playing ball. One guy sat on the beach his back resting against a coconut palm, drawing on a sketch pad.

A frigate bird hovered about 30 feet above Fred. Its wings were motionless, but with only an occasional flick of its pencil thin tail it kept pace with him. It was a good companion, silent and alert. He sang the bird a verse of the song he'd been humming,

The punk rolled up his big blue eyes,
And said to the jocker, "Sandy,
I've hiked and hiked and wandered too,
But ain't never seen no candy."

* * *

Fred was about a mile from the ferry landing near Camp 3. It had gotten very hot. He lay down the bindle stick and wiped his face with a bandana. He wringed out the sweat and then tied it loosely around his deeply tanned neck. The key here was only 200 yards wide. A spur from the main line ran to a siding at the bridge construction site. It was a short cut to the camp canteen and some cold beers. He thought he might follow it. On his right, parallel to the base of the grade ran State Road 4A. There hadn't been any traffic for a while. The road was an option, but a few feet higher on the Florida East Coast Railway's right-of-way there seemed to be a bit more breeze and fewer mosquitoes. Also, the crib ballast was almost level with the tops of the ties, allowing a natural stride.

Out of the blue a hobo's itch wanted scratching. By old habit Fred bent down and grasped the rail. It burned his hand in the afternoon heat.

The steel faintly hummed. He placed his ear against it, ignoring the pain. "Strange, the train from Key West never comes this early."

The shimmering rails converged in the west, then, nothing. A whistle sounded a ways off. He stood up, turned east and looked up the track. The whistle blew again, this time closer. Two more short blasts and one of FEC's 4-8-2 oil-burner locomotives appeared, blasting towards Key West. "Must be doing about sixty, a real cannonballer, looks to be half a mile. That gives me 30 seconds to decide whether to risk it."

The engineer leaned out the cab window and waved his arm. He blew the whistle again and opened the cylinder cocks. White clouds of steam erupted from either side of the engine. Fred nimbly hopped off the tracks and waved back.

Long Chain Charlie used to take bets in the jungle. He'd offer odds figured on the length of the margin. The smaller it was, the bigger the payoff. Charlie was good, he'd made a study of it. Most any bum can run eight feet, the length of a tie, in a second or so. But the rules said, standing start. Not many could jump that in a single leap, and even if they could it wouldn't necessarily be the fastest way. Charlie did it in two steps. He'd stand on the end of a tie waiting for the train to get close enough to make the bet interesting, then push off with his right foot, landing on the tie midway between the rails with his left, push off again and land on the opposite end of the tie with his right foot. The rails themselves were standard gauge, 4 feet 8 ½ inches apart and about seven inches high so you had to take that into account. But of course, it wasn't just practice, it was nerve that made a winner.

In '31 Charlie got the Jake leg. They said he was crazy to go track jumping after that. When the train hit him, he burst like a rotten pumpkin and greased the rails for a quarter mile. They tried hosing down the locomotive, but it took high pressure steam to do the trick. The word on the road was that the engineer found poor old Charlie's jawbone wedged up in the pilot, pried out a tooth, boiled it, and glued it beside the throttle. It wasn't the only one.

Fred picked out the joint bar two 39-foot rail sections up the line. Charlie had paced twelve feet back from the nearer joint. Fred took only six just to keep it fair and tossed his bindle across the track. The engineer saw and waved him back. Fred smiled and gave an answering wave.

The locomotive roared over the farther joint, the rail flexing beneath its massive weight, cylinder cocks wide open again, bellowing clouds of steam. Fred pressed his right toe against the tie. *Now!* He jumped over the first rail, landing on the tie midway. Less than four feet to go. He'd be clear with his next bound.

Perhaps he'd misjudged the train's distance or speed. Perhaps the second rail caught his toe. There was a flash and an impossibly loud bang. He was blinded and deafened. He smelled the mud of France, reeking of death and mustard gas, and tasted blood. The world seemed to jump, and he felt a brutal kick in the ass. A blast of air sent him tumbling into the ditch at the bottom of the embankment.

Flat on his back Fred looked up at the pale faces of boy soldiers whipping past. One of them leaned far out a window, laughed and tossed him a can. It landed in the weeds nearby. Fred got back up, shook himself and noticed nothing missing. "God damn it!"

As the last car sped by, he saw a banner tied across the rear platform, *265th Regiment, Florida National Guard.* From his hip pocket a sticky wetness began spreading across the seat of his pants and down his leg. Reaching behind he felt shards of glass and cut his finger. "Son of a bitch."

Brakes squealing, the train slowed to a stop, the last car about 200 yards past Fred. The conductor came out on the observation platform and looked back along the tracks. He jumped off and started walking towards Fred. A group of Guardsmen followed, shouting and pointing. One of them waved at Fred. "Must be the kid who tossed me the can."

It was lying nearby. He held it up. The conductor stopped half-way and pointed.

"Is that the drunk?"

"Yep, he was lying in the ditch," replied the Guardsman.

"What's your name?" the conductor shouted at Fred.

"Huey Long," Fred shouted back.

"A wisenheimer, eh? Well now, *Senator Long*, the Sheriff will hear about this, you goddamn crazy ass mother fucking son of a bitch!"

Several vets watching the show hooted him down. The conductor glared at them, "No-account hooligans!" He checked his pocket watch, grimaced and hurried back to the train. The Guardsmen followed at a slower pace.

A curious vet walked up to Fred. "Hey, Hooey, what camp ya' from?"

"One, and it's Fred."

"Damnedest thing I ever saw. Thought sure the train got ya'. Didn't nick ya' none, did it?"

"Nope, nothing broke but this," Fred held up the neck of the flask. "And that I fell on."

"Hoo boy! You sho got a pair! Next time you try that stunt give me a heads up and we'll make a killing."

"Oh, wasn't planning that. Just seemed the thing to do."

"Hah! You sure some crazy ass mother fucker!"

The train started up again and the vet wandered off. Fred looked at the can he was still holding, Krueger's Special Beer. Passing a hand through his shock of dark brown hair he grinned, "Beer in a can, complete with instructions. Gee, that's peachy. Hmm . . . Nope, Stoopnocracy is peachy!" He stuffed the can in the bindle, got back up on the tracks and started off again toward Camp 3.

His last bet with Charlie was for a quart of hooch. This round was a net loss, a newfangled tin of beer for a pint of un-taxed Havana Club.

"But maybe I'll have to wait a mite. No rule says it has to come just now. The dead are in no hurry to pay up. They have plenty of time. I expect a lot, though. Big fucking deal to bet your life. Maybe on payday. Yeah, I can wait that long."

Fred noticed a shadow on the ground and looked up. The bird had circled back. He sang,

I've hiked and hiked till my feet are sore
And I'll be damned if I hike any more
To be buggered sore like a hobo's whore
In the Big Rock Candy Mountains.

Chapter 2

Friday, August 30, 1935 – Payday

Fred paused on the back stroke of the cross-cut saw. "Want a drink?" he called to his partner on the other end. Razor Blade let loose a long stream of brown tobacco juice. It made a nasty puddle on the quarry floor.

"Yeah, sure. Teeth starting to get dull, anyway."

The 20-man crew working in pairs had begun work at 7 a.m. By mid-morning their bare torsos were covered in a pink paste of coral dust, sweat, mashed mosquitoes and blood. The quota was 8 blocks of keystone a day. Each weighed about ten tons. The saw blades wore out quickly.

While Mr. Blade exchanged the saw for a sharpened one, Fred visited the cooler of limeade. He drank two cups, filled them again and started back.

"Break!" shouted Sergeant Hank Morgan, the foreman. The men looked up from their work. Hank removed a sweat stained pith helmet and wiped his bald head with a towel, "Gotta make a run to the warehouse. Who's coming?"

The men returned blank stares.

"We'll stop at the depot for a drink." Several now mumbled approval. "OK, get on the truck, and put your shirts on. There might be ladies present."

The highway ran beside the railway tracks and the men could see the train chasing them. Hank drove faster to stay ahead, bouncing over the wood trestle bridge at Snake Creek. It was about 2 miles to Islamorada. When they arrived, the locomotive was still a distance from the depot. Inside a waiting room was provided for whites, and a ticket booth and telegraphy office for the agent. In the back were two restrooms marked WHITE and COLORED. This was progress. *Separate but equal* they called it.

The gang bought their beers and smokes at the little general store, beside the post office, and then went around to the depot platform to see what fun they could have with whomever might step off the train. This is what passed for live entertainment on Matecumbe.

Fred was last in line. Minding the store was a cute teenager, one of Henry and Ruby Russell's nine kids, aged 15 to one. And maybe one more on the way. The old goat was wearing out that pretty little wife of his. Bernice Mae was their second. There were about fifty members of the Russell clan on Matecumbe. With little urging she'd rattle off all their names in twenty seconds, 40 seconds if she included their middle names. When she finished, she'd wipe her brow and exclaim, "Whew!"

Her uncle, John Russell, was Islamorada's postmaster. Fred suddenly felt a pang of guilt, he still hadn't opened that damn letter. He'd found it under his pillow the Sunday he tried to hike to Key Largo. Someone must have tossed it on his bunk the day before. The return address was familiar, he guessed the contents. The business always made his head ache. He'd swallowed a handful of aspirins with a gulp of stale beer from the open bottle on the floor. He ignored the dead bug floating inside. *Why don't they just leave me alone?*

Had John known he might think Fred was disrespecting the U.S. Mail. Not many vets were getting typed letters from New York City. He would remember. He might ask about the letter and the one that came before if he saw Fred. Why, John could come walking through that door right now to chat with his niece. *All that effort gittin' it here through gloom of night, hell, and high water and ya haven't the common decency to even open it!* This needled. He'd just have to do it. Wouldn't have to read it, though. The first one he did, all the way through. It was at the end that it hit him. He retched until there was nothing wet to throw up, then heaved some more. They docked him three days' pay after Doctor

Dan said there was nothing wrong with him, just a batch of bad moonshine. No pay for drunk days. He didn't dare open the one that followed. He slid five pennies across the counter.

"Beer's a dime, Fred, you know that."

"Swore off."

"Really?"

"Sober for 25 days. Just a coke, please."

"Well, good for you. How about a Nehi, instead? We have orange, grape and peach."

"You're a peach, Bernice Mae. But I'll still have the coke."

"Thought you'd like to try something fresh and juicy. It's what I like." She smiled a little sideways and handed him the soda bottle.

"Thanks, sugar." He popped the top with the rusty bottle opener tied with a cord to the big red and white cooler.

"Coming back later?"

"Dunno."

"Isn't it payday? There's a swell new picture show in Tavernier, with Gable and Harlow. You like Jean, don't ya?"

"Sure, but Tavernier? I don't cross Snake Creek 'cepting to work. I bet you've plenty of friends who'd go with you."

"Ah gee, Fred, you know . . ."

"Yeah, I guess I do, but I'm not crossing that line neither. Here's two bits. Go have some fun."

She glanced at the quarter he'd placed before her, then looked up to his face and grinned. "Oh, boy! Thanks!"

He smiled back and headed out. The girl placed her elbows on the counter, rested her chin in her hands, and watched his walk.

"Don't work too hard."

Fred glanced back over his shoulder. "Ha! Not a chance." The screen door slammed behind him.

* * *

Bernice Mae sighed and slipped the coin into a small leather pouch tied to a strap around her neck. Her father had made it for her when she was little. She looked in the mirror on the wall, fussed with her cropped raven hair and tried to picture it after a soaking in ammonia, Clorox and Lux soap flakes. Just like Harlow. "Now Fred is about Mr. Gable's age, and if he grew a pencil mustache . . . yeah, that would work."

She made a funny face and laughed. Under the counter she felt for the wad of bubble gum she'd stuck there when the vets came in. It hadn't hardened much. She popped it in her mouth and chewed.

On the shelf below the cash register was her new copy of Photoplay, with Kay Francis on the cover. The feature story, though, was *The Private Life of Ginger Rogers*. She'd read it through three times already. She began again.

* * *

Fred ambled to where his buddies were loitering. Beside the platform the engine hissed. The fireman had swung out the spigot arm from the water tank and was filling the tender. Going around the opposite side of the depot building was John Russell carrying a mail bag over his shoulder. He hadn't seen Fred and kept on to the post office. *Well now, that was close.* Putting the bottle to his mouth he leaned his head back, closed his eyes and took a swig. After a moment he noticed that the idle chatter of his pals had stopped. There were now wolf howls, whistles, lip smacks, catcalls:

"Hot damn! Fill a bucket, let's see how she looks wet!"

"My, my, my! Oh, baby, come to Papa!"

"Hey Jane, wanna go for a swim with Tarzan?"

"Pussy, pussy, sweet little pussy!"

"Show some leg, doll! Smile!"

Fred opened his eyes to see who had caught their attention. He swallowed the coke in a hard gulp that hurt his throat. Standing beside the nearest passenger car not more than four steps away was a dazzling dream of a girl, about 5 and a half feet, all in white, brilliant in the morning sunlight. The sleeveless dress fitted her very closely and came to mid-calf. Sleek as an otter, 20, maybe 21, he thought. She had a blue silk scarf with white polka dots around her neck, white pumps, and wore a wide brimmed beribboned sun hat cocked to one side revealing short, wavy platinum blonde hair. Nonchalantly she removed her sunglasses, placing a temple tip between her teeth. Bright blue eyes regarded him. Then a coy half smile curved her slightly parted, ruby lips.

"Want a sip, miss?" Fred offered the bottle, stepping forward.

The platform suddenly became very quiet. This was a show the vets hadn't expected.

"Gee, mister, that would be swell!" She said it like one of those sassy gold diggers in the Warner Brothers musicals, *Yeah, sure brother, that's just what I need.* Taking the bottle without bothering to wipe its mouth she closed her eyes, threw her head back and took a long drink. He gawked at her slender throat, pulsing with each swallow. She drained the bottle, spit some back in, then delicately ran the tip of her moist pink tongue around the lip. Grinning, she gave it back to Fred, their hands briefly touching. That merest contact was like an electric shock, unleashing a torrent of emotions. He was speechless. Maybe he would come up with something clever by tomorrow. She seemed about to say something when the conductor shouted, "All aboard!"

Another girl came up and grasped the blonde by her arm. "Come on Cindy. The train won't wait, not even for you."

Cindy, that fits, he thought. Her friend was younger, hardly older than Bernice Mae, but poised and confident, a glossy bob, black bangs crisply cut, a stylish two-piece frock. For an instant their eyes met. There was an appealing archness about her and something foreign, maybe German in her voice. If he hadn't seen the blonde first, he'd have been more interested. Both girls turned and started walking away. The fabric accented Cindy's every movement, her weight gracefully shifting from hip to hip as each step fell nearly in line with the preceding one. Great butt. *Wonder if she's wearing anything underneath . . . no, she isn't.*

Abruptly, Cindy stopped and reached into the small reddish-brown purse she was carrying. She pulled out a penny postcard, fumbled some more and found a stubby yellow pencil. Holding the bag on its side in her left hand, she laid the card on it and scribbled something. Then she spun around and jogged back to Fred. She took his right hand and pressed the postcard into his palm. For a moment her fingers played with his wrist.

"Gotta go, now." She grinned, turned and walked smartly to the car steps where the other girl stood shaking her head.

Fred watched them climb aboard and disappear inside. The conductor snapped shut his pocket watch and frowned at Fred before signaling the engineer. Cindy did not appear at any of the windows. But as the train began pulling away a hand holding a scarf reached out and waved in Fred's direction. He tapped the brim of his cap. His hand still tingled where she had touched it. He finished the coke.

With smoke and steam and much clatter the train headed down the line. "Yeehaw!" exclaimed Hank who was standing closest to him. "What did she say?" The other men gathered around eagerly.

Fred only now looked at the postcard in his hand. The picture was the railroad's emblem, a view of the Havana Special crossing the Long Key viaduct. He turned the card over. It read, *Casa Marina tonight. No kidding! Cindy.* Without expression he folded it in half and shoved it in his dungaree pocket.

"Well, what did she say?" Hank asked again.

"Oh, nothing much, just thanked me for the coke," Fred replied. "Really. . . no kidding."

"Yeah, couldn't be anything serious. Just a sweet kid, I say. Freddie, you can feed the other guys that line of horse shit but I've known you since Vittel. Come on, level with me. I'm only looking after your best interests, wouldn't want you to get your heart broken again like with that cutie Army nurse . . . now you've took the pledge and all."

"OK, OK, just between you and me, she asked me to come to her hotel tonight."

"Ooh la la!" the men chorused.

"How about her friend?" one of them asked.

"I don't think she approves. Besides I haven't decided whether I'm going. There's the ball game in Ojus on Sunday."

Razor Blade spoke up. "Think you'll get more than one night with her? I can loan ya some, I'm staying in camp."

"Thanks, but my good clothes are at the Miramar."

Hank draped his arm over Fred's shoulders. "Hey, buddy, when a classy doll like that grabs your coke by the neck, sucks it dry and then rims it with her tongue a man, a real man, a decorated hero of the Great War doesn't need an order. He fixes bayonet, charges up the hill and shoves it right in that fur-lined fox hole! I'm going to the game myself and you know how loud I razz the other team so no one will miss you, and some of the guys have clean duds that will fit. Ain't that right fellas?" Several of the men nodded in agreement. "And I'll even give you a lift to the ferry. You see Freddie? If you won't go for yourself then go for us poor slobs who get by knowing their buddy is gettin' laid!"

Fred thought a few moments. "I dunno. There's maybe a one in a hundred chance she's on the level. I'll think about it after I cash my check."

"Maybe Dunno just likes them younger." Fred looked up.

"What's that, Skeeter?"

"Spent an awful long time in the store alone with that little piece of jailbait. Did she lick your lolly? No? Oh, I get it, you only had a nickel and she's a two-bit cocksucker." That got some nervous laughter from the men.

Fred walked coolly up to him and stopped within an inch of his chest. Skeeter took a firm grip on the empty beer bottle in his right hand.

Razor Blade stayed close to Skeeter's side. "Better watch your mouth, the Russells won't let that slide."

"You got a hard-on for her, too? Fuck off!"

Fred looked over his shoulder at Hank and winked. Suddenly he whipped around and drove his right fist low into Skeeter's gut. "I'll kill anyone, anyone who messes with that girl!" Skeeter stumbled back gasping, unable to breathe.

Hank laughed. "You had that coming, Skeeter. Walk it off. Captain Hard-ass says all Conch cunts are off limits, get caught and it's either vamoose or the hoosegow, dependin'. OK, you flabby-assed goldbricks, show's over. If you wanna get paid today, back on the truck!"

Clutching his belly, Skeeter spit out some pinkish bile. His grimace shifted into a thin smile.

Chapter 3

Friday, August 30, 1935 – Havana Special

"What were you thinking? The conductor warned you not to get off the train!"

"Don't I always get off and take a brisk walk when the train stops? It's good for your circulation, helps keep your derrière firm . . . saw it in a movie. You should try it."

"Not at that stop. Didn't you see Time Magazine this week?" Cindy's friend demanded, producing the issue from her travel bag. She flipped quickly through the pages, folded the magazine, and held it up to Cindy. "*Playgrounds for derelicts*, that's what it says! *Shell-shocked, whiskey-shocked, depression-shocked, psychopaths!* They were staring at your breasts, seeing you naked, getting hard. The filthy things they said! And you, shamelessly flirting with that man."

"Ella, please. I'm playing a hunch. I think he's the right guy."

"Right for what, a scavenger hunt? The only place he belongs is skid row. So, what was on that postcard you gave Mr. Shirtless?"

"He was wearing an athletic undershirt, very sexy. You could see his nipples."

"You invited him, didn't you? I knew it! It'll serve you right if he does come, and you see what a worthless derelict he is."

"Derelict? You know Riverside Drive, uptown along the Hudson?"

"No, never been there. Why?"

"Sure, you have. The Central's tracks go right by."

"That hardly counts."

"Just listen for a sec! Back in '32 a bunch of homeless, jobless, *derelict* veterans built a shanty town, between the tracks and the river. The city was OK with it because nobody complained. Then some dried-up old biddy complained to the police that the shanties were unsightly.

They had to come down. You know what? Some of those vets were *Croix de Guerre* men. You know what that means? What they did to earn it, what it meant to them? They hocked their medals to eat! Can you imagine how low you'd have to go to do that? It would be like me pawning my mom's purse or you that necklace with the whatchamacallit."

"It's called a *hamsa*, it's a good luck charm." Ella placed the magazine on her lap.

"Daddy helped find them work. He says the only difference between a derelict and a man is a job. Well, my forgotten man has a job, building bridges, or something. And he was polite, sorta sweet, even. Not much hair on his chest, I like them smooth. And you couldn't have missed those arms and shoulders. He could be on varsity crew, show up those impossible frat boys."

Ella harrumphed. "Well, a boy he's not. He's probably old enough to be your father."

"Hardly. If he was 18 when the war ended, that would make him 35, maybe even younger. You know some of those boys lied about their ages to enlist."

"I don't know about your uptown vets, but *these* men are broken. The war ruined them. They can't hold a job. They're a demoralized *lumpenproletariat* begging the government to transport them to *konzentrationslager* where, if they work at all, it's only to get enough money to get drunk."

"*Lumpenproletariat*? Where did *that* come from?"

"Marx, Karl Marx. You've heard of him? Those men are dirty, rude, vulgar and pee in public. I don't know how you could possibly drink from the same bottle. There are plenty of decent, responsible, clean young men back in New York, and you go vamping in a relief camp for broken-down drunks!"

"I felt safer than at the riot you took us to last month. I bet you're sweet on that Red who grabbed the swastika. What was his name? Billy?"

Ella sat up straight. "Bill Bailey is a true comrade, not afraid to risk his life for the Party. What he did took real courage! You heard him speak at the anti-Nazi rally, up there on the podium in front of 20,000 people in Madison Square Garden! Wasn't he wonderful?"

"He said he was Catholic. I was just wondering . . ."

"You mean can a good Catholic be a Communist? Well, there's considerable debate about that, but it is essentially a political question. You see . . ."

"No, not that. I was wondering if a Catholic cock is any different from a Jewish cock, appearances aside, of course. You know, performance wise."

"You're so shallow, Cindy! Can't you ever be serious?"

"I am being serious. Cocks come in all shapes, sizes and colors, or so I've heard. It's a subject close to my heart. They should have a catalog for them, like for mushrooms. Now your professor has that wild hair, genius look. You follow him all over campus like his pet schnauzer. How does he look without his pants?"

"Really!"

"So, just talking?"

"We enjoy speaking German."

"And that's all you do?"

"We walked together under the stars that last night in Ithaca. The moon was nearly full."

"The moon in June, that's original. I bet he turned it into a physics lecture."

"You laugh but he knows why the stars shine, the only one who really knows, with equations and everything! It's all about Coulomb repulsion and the proton-proton reaction. You know, hydrogen fusing into helium."

"Oh, Ella, how romantic! He'll win a Nobel one day or maybe fill up zeppelins."

"He said I was . . . that everything was made of *star dust*. It was the most beautiful thing I've ever heard."

"Yeah, I like Hoagy, too. But for you it was the equation part, wasn't it? He has a formula for making whoopee, definitely get the Nobel for that."

"Stop teasing! I told you; he respects my father. Peter is very proper with me. And we're both concerned about what's happening in Germany. The SA is back on the streets. Goebbels is making speeches again. I haven't heard from *papi* and *mutti* in a month."

"Oh, they can't think about you all the time, they're probably on vacation."

"There's to be an important announcement at the *Parteitag* in September."

"Another speech by *him*?" Cindy rolled her eyes.

"Yes, and they say he'll proclaim the final solution to the Jewish question."

"Don't be such a worry-wart. So, Ella, what is Prof Pete, 20 years older than you?"

"Eleven."

"Well, our tastes aren't that different. Anyway, this is our last chance to have fun before classes start. Maybe you'll find someone."

"You do this every time, Cindy, picking up strays! This was supposed to be just you and me. Can't we just go somewhere by ourselves for once? Now what am I supposed to do? I should have just stayed in New York. Bill's court date is next Friday. I should be there with him for the verdict. Solidarity!"

"Oh, he'll get off. Daddy knows the judge, he hates Nazis."

"Then they'll be a big party to celebrate . . . and I'll miss it."

"Hey, Emilio will keep you busy. He can rumba, mix cocktails, and he's planning something special for us. And just think, you may get to see Hemingway! His house is in the city tour guide. He's another geezer you're sweet on. You read all his stories, even the fish tales."

"That's the point, Mr. Ernest Hemingway is successful. Your Mr. Shirtless is a bum."

Cindy didn't reply.

"Well . . . anything to say?"

Cindy shrugged and looked out the open window, studying a close formation of brown pelicans keeping pace with the train. Ella took note, too, leaned around Cindy and took a snapshot with her new Leica camera. She returned it to its leather case and then began reading an old Cosmopolitan, April '34. The pretty girl on the cover looked a lot like her, black penciled eyebrows, blue eyes, long lashes, a perky nose, and alabaster skin. Only the hair was different. Earlier that summer, Ella had bobbed her school girl braids. Inside was a complete short novel by Hemingway, *One Trip Across*. Cindy didn't find the characters very sympathetic. Ella likely brought it hoping she could get it autographed.

* * *

When Ella spoke again Cindy strained to listen.

"*Wenn die Soldaten* . . . when the soldiers came home from the war, they were missing . . . eyes, arms, legs, faces . . . their manhood. Some were missing parts inside you couldn't see, holes in their souls, what they saw, what they did. Some had . . . *granaten* inside. You never know when they will explode." Ella covered her face with her hands and wiped the tears away. "Cindy, this man, be careful."

Cindy wrapped her arms around her friend and hugged her hard. "I will, Ella, I will," she whispered, ". . . remember my forgotten man".

Chapter 4

Friday, August 30, 1935 - One for All . . . All for One

The windows were all open and the electric fans running but it was still stifling in the mess hall. Outside, Bonus Bill roused the waiting men with his stammering sing-a-long:

K-K-K-Katy, beautiful Katy,
You're the only G-G-G-Girl that I adore,
When C-C-C-Congress pays me the bonus,
I'm not coming round to see you anymore.

"Akers, E. H.," the paymaster shouted. The singing stopped. He waited impatiently for Akers to make his way to the table and get his check.

Akers gave it a double take. "Only $25? That's a mistake, should be 30."

"Take it up with the time keeper. You want the 25 or not? You're holding up the line."

"Fuck it." Akers signed the check and gave it back. The paymaster counted out $25, 2 tens, and five ones. This would take a while, there were 253 other checks.

Frederick Poock, headquarters office manager, had set up shop on a table near the mess hall exit. He was trustee of the veterans' trust fund. He'd volunteered for the job as an additional duty, handling deposits as a convenience for those who didn't want to squander their pay as soon as they received it. He was scrupulously honest and was easily the most trusted man in the camps. Fred planned to open his own account with him today. He'd saved some cash since he quit drinking.

Jimmie Conway, a muscular mug, came up behind Fred and tapped him on the shoulder. Jimmie's fist swung around and stopped just short of Fred's jaw. "Working out this afternoon?"

"Ya punch-drunk palooka, what're ya trying to do? Mess up my purty face before my big night out? Got me a date in Key West with a looker! Going anywhere yourself?"

"Naw, I'm in training for my big comeback! No temptations for me. Remember to keep your guard up and lay off the booze."

"Sure thing, Champ."

An hour later Tongue-tied and Frisco Red gave Fred their Sunday best. He retreated to his shack and tried them on. There were a shirt and pair of pants that fit pretty well. Fred did have a jacket of his own that nothing had nested in. The cuffs were just a little frayed. Then he took a salt water shower in the bathhouse, buffed his low-quarters and dressed. He was about to step out the door to meet Hank when he remembered the letter. It was in the cigar box atop his bunk-side orange crate. He took it out and debated whether to just open it then and there and be done with it. No, not now, later. He'd just take it along with his discharge papers and DSC. Those he always carried on trips to Key West. They could be helpful with a sympathetic judge.

Hank was waiting in the truck beside the mess hall, motor running. The others bound for the ferry had already climbed aboard. Fred rode shotgun. Nearby, leaning against a shack, Skeeter watched. He cursed, bent over and vomited on the ground. There was blood.

The stake body made it to Camp 3 a little past two o'clock. As they neared the ferry landing the boys in the truck bed began singing:

Cap'n Hard-on made a big talk, Parlee voo.
Said all bad vets will have to walk, Parlee voo.
But Cap'n please, when I get high,
Remember you're the same as I. Hinkey dinky, parlee voo!

I Dunno went to Key West, Parlee voo.
He said he was going to get some rest, Parlee voo.
He met a dame who knocked him cold,
And when he woke up, he had been rolled, Hinkey dinky, parlee voo!

Hank laughed and turned to Fred. "Got your own verse! When you get back you can change the ending."

"Fuck you. Now I'll have that in the back of my head all weekend."

The last car was just being loaded on the *Monroe County*. Fred and ten other vets jumped off the truck and dashed for the ferry.

"I'll see you all back in camp Monday," Hank shouted.

Chapter 5

Friday, August 30, 1935 – The Bower

After getting paid Skeeter hitched a ride into town. He bought a beer at the store from the little Russell bitch. She barely noticed him. There were others in the store. He waited outside until they left.

When he came back in, she was reading a magazine. He let the screen door slam behind him. She looked up and smiled. "Hi, Skeeter. Can I help you?"

He leaned on the counter. "I hear you're sweet on Fred Dunn. Wasting your time on that bum. Just saw him on the way to Key West. Got himself a date with some hot blonde. Beats me how. Don't expect he'll be coming back anytime soon, if ever."

Bernice Mae frowned then wiped her nose with the back of her hand.

Skeeter reached in his pocket, pulled out a ten spot and placed it on the counter. "If you're interested, I'll be down on the beach around six." He turned and left.

* * *

Bernice Mae looked at the bill, held it up to the light, and whistled. She was innocent but not ignorant. She'd seen Pa and Ma at it often enough. Couldn't but, they all slept in the same room. He'd get on top and they'd roll about the bed grunting. Then they'd cuddle close, laugh a mite and start to whispering. And every year or so she'd have a new baby sister or brother. Cathy had stories to tell, too. Only a year older she'd been with a few fellas. Now Skeeter was a big man, bigger than Fred, biggest she'd ever seen on Matecumbe. How would it go? Would he squish her flat like a bug? Hah! Some bug. Someone was opening the door. Quickly she hid the money under the counter.

"Hello, Aunt Charlotte."

"Working hard today, Bernice Mae?"

"Not too much, ma'am."

"Those veterans not bothering you, are they child?"

"Oh, no ma'am, they're perfect gentlemen."

Aunt Charlotte raised an eyebrow. "I should . . ."

"Yes, ma'am?"

"Nothing child. Just remember why these men are here. Uncle John sent some mail over. Here's your wish book!" She plopped the big Montgomery Ward catalog on the counter.

"Thanks. Ma was expecting that, I would've picked it up."

"No bother. I was coming here anyway to ask if you're free this evening to stay with Jimmy."

"Um . . ." She placed her forefinger against her cheek and squinted. Everyone knew she was good with kids, plenty of practice at home. And she loved holding and fondling them. Jimmy was a doll. "Sorry, ma'am, but the girls are all going to the Keys Theater tonight. I promised I'd go with."

"Well, never you mind dear. We'll make do. You have fun now, you hear? And remember to take care. It's payday at the camps."

"Yes'm."

* * *

Skeeter had been leaning up against a palm tree for some time. He'd come early for no particular reason, just bored maybe by the carryings on at camp on payday. For once he hadn't been looking for a fight and no one was offering one. The girl would show, he was sure of that, a sawbuck in this dump meant a lot. He figured he'd have to pay her more when he was finished, just to keep her quiet. There'd be hints though, he'd have to be careful. The Conchs were no better than saltwater hillbillies. They'd be up for a feud. He wanted no part of that. In two months, the camps would close and he'd be gone, long before she began to show, if he'd knocked her up. He still hadn't figured out just how to let Fred know. "Fucking shame if the bastard got shipped out without knowing."

He saw her skipping up the beach, barefoot, chasing the plovers and white ibis feeding in the tidal pools, tossing stones out into the water. "Just like some damn kid. And she's carrying a big basket for Christ's sake. Does she think this is some fucking picnic?" When she saw him, she waved and came running.

"Skeeter! I knew you'd be here." Bernice Mae took his hand. "Come with me, there's a place back in the woods. Nobody will bother us."

She sure was making this easy. Had she done this before? Never heard any talk back in camp despite what he'd said to Dunn. There had been some shit about other Matecumbe girls. There'd be trouble for sure if the bosses found out. Getting caught copping Conch cunt meant the boot or worse, depending if she was legal or not.

She led him down some trails, then some fainter paths through thickening growth. "What is this, some kinda maze?"

"Aw, come on, almost there. Gotta be careful." Another turn and they stood in a cool, shady bower, the trees joining above in a leafy ceiling. Butterflies flitted through errant rays penetrating the woods from the sun now low in the west. Birds sang. The grass was matted flat. She put down the basket, jumped up and hugged him.

"Nice, huh? We have it all night if we want."

He grasped her in his big hands. She felt firm and solid. He lifted her up to his mouth. They kissed. Her lips were soft and eager. He liked the heft of her. She wouldn't break.

"Lie down."

"Just a sec." She took a blanket from the basket, shook it out and spread it neatly on the ground. "This is Cathy's idea. It's soft so your knees and my heinie don't get sore. Ya know? And look." From the basket she took some bottles and something wrapped in a dish cloth. "Grape Nehis for me and Wagner's for you." She unwrapped two sandwiches. "Fried conch, Ma made 'em. Told her they were for the picture show tonight."

"Conch? Those big ass sea snails? You can eat them?"

"Sure thing! You'll love 'em. And here for dessert some pie made with limes off our own trees. I made it! Ya wanna eat first or fuck?"

He laughed. "Shouldn't be talking that way, kid. Put that stuff away from the ants. Then take your clothes off."

In a few moments she was naked before him, eyes locked with his, lips parted in the coyest of smiles. He couldn't help but grin back. Someone had taught her how to pose, feet together like a T, right pointed forward, the left to the side, with a bend of the right knee, hands on hips. Her breasts were ripe, she curved nicely, a dark curly patch in her crotch, and tan all over. She was far more than he had imagined. He forgot all about Dunn.

Around her neck was a slender strap with a small leather pouch attached. "What's that?"

"This? Just a bag for my little money."

"Take it off."

"Sure, Skeeter." She slipped it over her head and placed it atop her dress on the blanket. "I showed you mine, now you show me yours."

He un-buckled his belt and dropped his pants and underwear. They bunched on top of his boots. Then he knelt before her, grabbed her butt and pressed his face between her thighs. She smelled fresh and clean. He tasted the salt of her sweat and the musky flux of her sex. She hugged his neck and kissed the hair on his head. She gasped when he laid her down on the blanket. He stretched out on top of her, belly to belly.

"Careful there, Skeeter! I ain't no bug."

"What?"

"Don't be squishing me none, just stick it in."

He glared at her. She looked back. Something didn't feel right. With his right hand he checked himself. It was limp. There was a faint sound of crunching leaves behind him. He froze. In his pocket was the switchblade. He slowly reached for it, felt the shape but fumbled for the pocket opening. The girl was gazing off to the left, smiling. He looked. Two skinny dogs, no, tiny deer were watching them. He rolled off the girl and got up on his knees. "What the fuck? Scat!"

"No, no, Skeeter. They're pets, Rosey and Snowy. Must have followed us. They're always turning up." She reached over and scratched behind their ears. "Good girls!"

He glanced down at himself. "Well, that just about ruined it."

"Pa found them beside the road on Big Pine, orphans. Someone had run over their mama. He brought them home for me and Cathy. We named them Rose Red and Snow White, like in the fairy tale, you know?"

"No, I don't."

"They were sisters, made friends with an enchanted bear. They tried to help a dwarf who kept getting into trouble. He was very ungrateful. Finally, the bear kills him and like magic the bear, not the dwarf, turns into a handsome prince. And they all, except the dwarf, live happily ever after. Never heard that?"

"No." He stroked himself but nothing.

She looked, wide eyed. "Why, I never! Ain't that supposed to get bigger? I've seen the little winkies on baby boys, for sure. Thought men folk had bigger ones."

"Shit!" He stood and pulled his pants up. "Listen, you never, ever tell anyone about this! *You hear?*" He took a crumpled fiver from his pocket and tossed it at her.

"Cross my heart and hope to die. But I don't know what you're getting so riled up about, takes Pa an hour sometimes."

"So, you . . . and him, huh?"

"Goodness no! We ain't no white trash. Him and Ma, of course. She always says *Hallelujah* when he finishes. Timed them once."

"Sorry, I thought . . ."

"I know what you thought. We're poor folks but we know right from wrong. That's what Pa always says."

"Well, this isn't helping. How do I get out of here?"

"You're leaving? We just got here."

"Can't do what I came to do, so no sense hanging around."

"Well, golly. I thought maybe we could . . . never mind. You just keep going right and you'll either come out on the beach or the road."

He took two steps, and then turned around. "Give me the beers and that pie. I ought to get something for my money."

"Oh, you got plenty, Skeeter, a good look and a feel. Just don't be thinking I'll drop my drawers for you every payday! Next time you best come courtin'." She handed him the two bottles of Wagner's and the pie.

"That'll be the day." He took a bite of the pie, and then another. "You really made this?"

"Sure enough. Guess you like it."

"Passable. Now get dressed, I'm leaving."

"Hey, Skeeter. There's still time to make the picture show in Tavernier, there's a second showing. Don't ya wanna go with me? We could mess around. Maybe it'll get bigger."

"Fuck, what did I get myself into? Remember what I said!" He stomped off.

"*Hey, Skeeter!* We're having a picnic Monday. You'd be welcome to come if you change your clothes and watch your mouth. Pa's roasting a pig!"

"Fuck it!" He kept walking.

* * *

Bernice Mae watched him vanish into the trees. "Not very gentlemanly, least he coulda said I was pretty. Well, I sure think so. The boys always steal looks at me when we go swimming. What do you think?"

Rosey and Snowy looked up and blinked in unison. "Little me? Oh, dahling! You're too, too kind." Bernice Mae stood sideways to them, with her cheek resting on her left shoulder, eyes seductively half-closed, left knee bent, arms outstretched to her sides, fingers spread. A mosquito took a liking to her wrist. She slapped it hard.

"Still don't know what the big fuss is all about . . . sniffing and licking my privates! Men are just like dogs. Kinda nice when he picked me up and kissed me though, got all tingly like. He sure is strong!" After putting her dress back on she considered the cash and wondered how she would explain it. "Maybe I'll just ask Cathy to keep it for me, like a bank. Ma and Pa never ask where she gets her money."

Bernice Mae collected her stuff and took a short cut down to the road, the deer following. It was dark when she reached it. "If I come home early Ma will pester me with questions. I'm not as good a fibber as Cathy. Ma might just catch on. Now, I do want to see that movie. If I can hitch a ride maybe I'll get there in time for the cartoons." After a few minutes she saw car lights approaching from Islamorada. "Headed in the right direction, guess I'll give it a try."

When the car got close, she stepped right up to the road and held out her thumb. It slowed and stopped. Inside was a young white couple. The woman in the passenger seat smiled at her. Her dark hair was short and curly. She was gorgeous, could have been a motion picture star. "Hi, honey! Where're you headed?" the lady asked.

"Tavernier, ma'am, trying to get to the Keys Theater."

The man laughed. "You think we should take her, ma'am?"

The woman punched him in the arm. "I'll 'ma'am' you!"

"Ow! Come on Roz, just kidding." He rubbed his arm.

She turned back to Bernice Mae. "Honey, climb on in. That's where we're headed. Oh, look! Aw, such cute little things!"

"Just my pets, Rose Red and Snow White. Like in the fairy tale, you know?"

"Yes, honey, sure do. They coming, too?"

"Oh, no! Y'all run on home now, ya hear? And mind crossing the road!" The deer trotted off. Bernice Mae made herself comfortable in the back seat. "Sure do appreciate the lift, sir."

This time the woman laughed and the driver made a face. "I'm Rosalind and this old coot here is George, my fiancé."

George started the car.

"Say . . . *Rosalind,* I have some fried conch sandwiches and Nehis in my basket. It should go good with the show, if'n you and George get hungry."

"Now that's a first for a hitchhiker. Thanks! I think we'd like that. Ever tried conch before, Roz?"

"I have. I'd love some. That's very sweet, honey."

George looked back over his shoulder at Bernice Mae. He had a receding hairline but couldn't have been more than 20. "I thought I'd seen you before. You work at the little store by the train depot, one of the Russell girls?"

"Yep, there're my sisters Catherine Elizabeth, Sarah Ellen, Henrietta, and Doloria. Then there're my cousins Irene, Rose Mary, Alberta Tay, Lorraine, Phyllis, Florine, and Cayrie. And then there's me, Bernice Mae. I'm the only one with a job this summer."

"Pleased to meet you, Bernice Mae."

"Charmed, I'm sure."

"George can't shake, so I will." Rosalind reached over her seat back and shook Bernice Mae's hand. She nodded at the basket; the blanket was half out. "Coming from a picnic, honey?"

"Yeah, but things didn't turn out like I thought . . . so, left-overs."

"Happens sometimes." Rosalind gave the girl's hand a squeeze.

George spoke up. "There's a big fella on the road up ahead, looks to be bumming a ride. What do you think, girls?"

Bernice Mae leaned out her window for a better view. "Keep driving."

"Better do what she says, Georgie."

"Yes'm, uh . . . *dear*." George drove by without slowing. "Did you see the look that son of a gun gave me?"

"Serves him right!" Bernice Mae smirked.

"Was he the one who stood you up?" Rosalind asked.

"In a manner of speaking. So, y'all getting hitched, huh? Set a date?"

"It's kinda complicated, honey. Soon, we hope."

"But y'all not waiting, I mean you step out together and all that, don't ya?"

"Yes . . . er, no honey, we're not 'waiting'."

"Good! By my way of thinking there just ain't all that much time to waste."

"Hah! We picked up a little philosopher, eh, Roz?"

"Just don't know what tomorrow will bring. Could rain or something, never know," said Bernice Mae, setting her chin on the seat back.

"Oh, little lady, you have at least twenty thousand tomorrows to look forward to." George gave her a wink over his right shoulder.

"What's that . . . sixty years or something? Sure don't cotton to waiting no sixty years!"

"Don't think that's very likely, honey. Say, you're invited when we tie the knot. It will be in Key West. That's where I'm from."

"Gee! Thank you kindly. Never been to Key West before."

"Well, we'll just have to show you around. Won't we Georgie?"

"You bet!"

"There's so much to see. And the movie theater is only a short stroll from the house. You'll stay with us, our first house guest."

"Golly! Sure hope things get uncomplicated."

"Oh, Bernice Mae you have no idea how much we want that, too!" George laughed.

"Honey, just thinking, I'm taking the train back to Key West tomorrow morning, would you like to come along with me? It'll be fun. We can go shopping in town."

"Tomorrow? Well . . . that's very nice of you and all, but I already said I'd work all day at the store, and I have chores at home, and Ma and Pa, they might think running off to Key West with a strange lady, a beautiful one mind you, is a bridge too far, and we're having a big picnic Monday and I'm a pretty good baker so I'll be in the kitchen mostly . . . and, and . . . you see there's someone down there this weekend I might not want to see, and it could be sorta embarrassing if'n we met up."

"I understand, Bernice Mae, honey lamb. Just a thought."

"Uh, Roz, we have a date Saturday night, remember?"

"Well, if'n y'all be back on Matecumbe Monday and get tired of doing all your fiancé stuff come on by the house, the big one on the beach. There'll be conch fritters, key lime pie, roast hog, and more Russells than you can shake a stick at. You'd fit right in."

"I really don't want to be a wet blanket, but Monday's already a full card for Roz and me, with all the holiday stuff going on in Key West. Tell you what, I'm around all the time, I can drop by the store next week and we could set a date for when Roz visits again for all that exhausting 'fiancé stuff'. Sound good?"

"If'n the sun comes up and the creek don't rise. Look, there's the movie house!" Bernice Mae pointed.

"Can you see what's playing, Georgie?"

"*China Seas* with Jean Harlow and Clark Gable. Good, haven't seen it."

"Oh, I love Clark!" Rosalind clapped her hands.

"Me, too! And Jean has so much fun messing with him."

"Oh, they're just acting, Bernice Mae," said George.

"Sure like Mr. Gable to act on me that way."

"Why, Bernice Mae!" exclaimed Rosalind.

Chapter 6

Friday, August 30, 1935 – Introductions

The Casa Marina stood alone on the ocean side of town. Taxis and limousines filled its driveway. A ritzy crowd waited in the porte-cochère for their rides. Fred carried a small bouquet of flowers he'd bought on the way from a kid outside a restaurant. Dressed in a pair of worn dark trousers, brown jacket, white shirt and grey bow tie, he looked decent enough, but no one would mistake him for a million-dollar trouper.

Fred figured she'd be late. At about half past nine he saw her stroll out the door onto the hotel veranda. Cindy was dressed in a knee-length, low cut, yellow frock that showed off her figure even better than the dress she had worn that morning. A blue sash wrapped around her waist. Slung over her shoulder was the same small purse, looking like an old Army cartridge box. The kid with the flapper cut was with her, dressed totally different in a slinky, high collar, long sleeve, midnight black number that shimmered when she moved. Her face had been pale, now she glowed red. They had an escort, tall, about Fred's height, dark, broad shouldered, Latin looking, wearing a Panama fedora. He had a small black mustache and pomaded hair, like some movie star. Under a white jacket his shirt top was open, a gold chain glittered, the suave type the girls seemed to go for, gambler, maybe a gangster, fucking dago. He wondered if he could play the guitar. By habit he sized him up and thought he could take him.

Fred marched resolutely up to the veranda. Cindy spotted him as he reached the first step. "Oh, you're here!" She turned to her companions, "See what I mean?"

The other girl kissed Cindy's cheek. "Remember what I told you, *Schätzchen.*"

The Latin looked at Fred, up and down, then tipped his hat and winked at Cindy. He gingerly took his girl's arm and escorted her towards the parked cars along the driveway.

Cindy waited for him to come to her. When she noticed the flowers, she laughed. Her tan was deeper now and her nose looked overdone. She took his hand. On impulse he kissed her cheeks, *à la française*. They were hot. He inhaled her fragrance. She smelled of the beach with a dash of Noxzema.

"Perhaps we should introduce ourselves. I'm Fred Dunn, currently employed at VWP Camp One. I have no prospects."

"Oh, I think you do."

"Yeah, a fifty million to one shot at President."

"Better'n mine. I'm Cindy Rattigan. Cornell Class of '36. Rah, rah, sis boom bah!"

"Sorry, Rattigan?"

"That's my name, ask me again and I'll tell you the same. So, what's VWP?"

"Veterans Work Program. That's the second name, the first was Vets Rehabilitation Program, like we were a bunch of sorry bums, which we are. You don't mind taking a walk with a bum, Miss Rattigan?"

"Delighted to, Mr. Dunn."

"No kidding?"

"No kidding!"

"Now that's just peachy."

He took her bare arm still warm from the afternoon sun and escorted her down the veranda steps, past the cars in the driveway, and right on to the sidewalk. They stopped a short distance further on, between the streetlights, along the iron fence bordering a park. A cat sauntered by. Palm fronds littered the pavement.

"Well?" She looked up at him. Fred leaned forward and softly brushed her lips with his, circling round her mouth. He traced the soft curves of her breasts with his fingers and then caressed her back, feeling no clasps or straps. She wrapped her arms around his neck, and thrust her taut body tight against his, radiating heat. She kissed him with an abandon and ferocity that first shocked and then totally consumed him. Her left leg climbed up his thigh. The flowers fell to the ground unnoticed.

The moment was broken by the headlights of a passing car and a blast of its horn. "Get a room!" Loud laughter pealed from the open windows as it sped by.

"Fred, I need it, bad."

He looked at her with wonder. His lips were bruised by her kiss, and the sweet taste of her mouth was on his tongue. "I know a place. It's on Division Street near St. Mary's, that's a bit of a hike from here, about 20 minutes. I could get a cab . . .?"

"Nah, let's walk."

He held his arm around her waist and they crossed the street. Although he was several inches taller, he managed to match his pace with hers so there was no break between them as they walked along.

"Those two back there, Dixie Dugan and Rico, for a moment I thought they were coming with us."

"Ha, ha. Their names are Ella and Emilio, she's my dearest friend and he's my brother."

"He doesn't mind?"

"What?"

"You know, you going out with a bum."

"Of course not, we're adults."

The yards and gardens along Reynolds Street were lush with tropical growth. A rash of purple bougainvillea blossoms protruded between the slats of a whitewashed picket fence. Cindy paused to pluck one and place it behind her ear. She asked, "So, how'd ya wind up down here anyway, building that darn bridge?"

"Well, pretty much like the other fellas. Last winter the word was that General Hines had jobs for vets down South. All you had to do was show up in Washington with your discharge papers. Figured it would be a nice vacation. There's St. Mary's." Fred pointed up the street.

"The Star of the Sea. I know the priest, Bill Reagan."

"First name basis?"

"Yeah, I'm a heathen so we're informal."

"And how did that happen?"

"Well, my dad took me to a service there a couple of years ago, he's a sometimes Catholic, you see. Sang some hymns. Bill noticed my voice and after the service asked me if I'd like to join the choir."

"And did you?"

"No, we were leaving for Havana the next day. But I have an open invitation."

They crossed Division Street at the church. Half way down the block was a big three-story Bahamian style house with a wide porch surrounded by a picket fence. A red neon sign glowed in the front window, *Rooms*. They could hear it faintly buzzing like a drowsy hive in the heavy, fragrant air. They entered.

Inside was a smoky, softly lit room with several overstuffed sofas and loveseats fitted with white antimacassars. Couples were seated about sipping drinks, the men in jackets and ties, the girls, a regular League of Nations, in lounging robes. One couple was headed up an ornate staircase. On a couch along one wall sat four girls smoking cigarettes, drinking from small glasses, legs bare to the thigh and beyond. One, a China doll, winked at Fred and then said something to the others, a red head, a blonde, and a fuzzy wuzzy cutie. They all giggled. Near the garden doors a Cuban quartet on upright piano, guitar, conga drums and maracas played *Amor Sincero*.

A formidable Creole lady resplendent in a Chinese silk dressing gown was seated at a mahogany table near the entrance. A large leather-bound ledger was open before her and a telephone on her right.

"Frédéric, ça va ?"

"Très bien, merci, Madame Joséphine. We'd like a room."

"Une chambre pour la nuit ?"

"Oui, s'il vous plaît."

"Très, très joli."

"Merci, Madame," replied Cindy with a little curtsey.

Joséphine smiled. *"Très intelligent aussi ! Frédéric, avec une fille comme ça je te donne le nombre dix, d'accord ?"* She reached behind the table and took a key from a rack.

"Très bon." He placed a fiver on the table.

Joséphine's smiled and pushed it back. *"Non, non, Frédéric, un cadeau."* She pressed the key into his palm, with both hands.

"Merci beaucoup!"

Ascending the stairs Cindy squeezed Fred's arm and whispered, "You took me to a *whorehouse*?"

"Best in the town. They always have clean sheets."

Fred unlocked the door of number ten, reached in and turned on the light. "Come on in, Joséphine's finest."

"Okie Dokie." Cindy stepped into the center of the large room and spun around. "Very nice! And a bathroom. How modern."

A wide canopied bed dominated the room. There were table lamps and a dresser. Beside the bed and running its length was a large framed wall mirror. The French windows opened onto a narrow balcony overlooking an inner courtyard garden. A red upholstered love seat and table were placed in the center. The floors were hardwood with several pastel-colored cotton carpets scattered about. Picasso prints decorated the rose-pink walls. Two champagne glasses sat on the table beside an ice bucket with a bottle of Veuve Clicquot. Probably cost more than a month's pay, Fred thought. On a platter under a glass dome was a stack of cocktail sandwiches. He marveled at Joséphine's generosity. Above Cindy a ceiling fan hung still. Fred stood in the door and admired her.

"Close the door, Fred."

"OK." He turned, shut and locked it.

"Now just stand right there and close your eyes."

"Fine, but no monkey business! I'm a sensitive guy."

He peeked slit-eyed as she tossed her purse and sash onto the bed, and undid a button or two. Her dress slipped to the floor in one smooth flow. All she had on were a silk chemise and heels. For a moment she reached between her legs. "Open."

Fred blinked and laughed.

The chemise went next. Then she kicked off her shoes sending them across the floor. It was hot in the room and her body glistened with perspiration. Vivid tan lines traced a two-piece swimsuit. His eyes were drawn to her razor cut patch and the purple blossom planted there. Reaching up she pulled the fan chain. On her toes with her arm stretched high she was a sculpture beyond mortal skill, a goddess demanding worship. It would take him years to explore that body, but he might have only one night. He couldn't believe his luck. Was this some dream? His cock swelled. He felt dizzy. The blades began to revolve, quicker and quicker. Cindy shivered for an instant and then luxuriated in the cool breeze, twirling about. Her nipples stiffened. "Jeez that feels good. Ya gonna join me, Fred?"

He was swaying and steadied himself by leaning against the wall. She turned beneath the fan, then stopped. "You OK, Fred?" She turned again.

"Just looking."

"Want me to bend over, squat, spread my legs? Splits? I can do a cartwheel!" And she did, brushing against the table. The glasses clinked.

"Is any of this working? Getting hard? Need to play with yourself? Want me to?"

"Walk slowly across the room."

"OK, whatever twists your knob. I didn't count on you being just a looker."

"Shut up and walk." She did, back and forth.

"Want me to dance, too? I can kick over my head."

"In front of me, left kick, right kick."

On the right kick he grabbed her ankle. Startled, she hopped on her left foot to keep balance. "How does that flower stay in there?"

"I'm clenching."

He slid his free hand up her leg and plucked it.

"Uh . . . there! Diddle me. I took you for a hands-on guy."

"Sing something." He let her leg go.

"What?"

"Anything, you told me you could sing . . . *On the Good Ship Lollipop*."

"Sure, bright eyes. But I need to concentrate on something. Come on, drop your pants and show me what ya got."

He didn't last long.

Afterwards they cuddled. The inexpressible delight of holding this woman tight against his naked body made him giddy. He licked and tasted her. She was musky in the right places with a hint of salt all over. There was something, though, that irked.

"Should have told ya, I have a rubber."

"Just one?"

"Five pack."

"My! But I'd rather not have Mr. Goodyear between you and me. I take good care of myself. Are you hungry? Let's eat those sandwiches."

"Yeah, I'm starving." He got up and went for the platter.

"And I need some bubbly. Join me?"

"I quit, sober for 25 days."

"Champagne doesn't count. Kids drink it on special occasions. Isn't this special?"

They cleaned the plater and emptied the bottle. Cindy snuggled close. "Tell me about your first time, Fred."

"Really? That's kind of a personal question," he answered.

"Oh, come on. I'll tell you mine. Nothing bad, was it?"

"Well, sorta. She gave me a garland of roses that took a few days to blossom. That's what we called it during the war, doesn't sound so bad that way. The corpsman felt it was worth a day of light duty."

Cindy pulled away. "You got the clap? Jeez. You're OK now, right?"

"Oh, they did a good job, hurt like hell though. I think the treatment was so rough to discourage us from trying again."

"And were you?" Cindy asked.

"What?"

"Discouraged, of course."

"Oh, no. The French troops got issued rubbers. We traded cigarettes for them. OK, so when was your first time?"

"Tonight . . . ," she laughed. "I'm lying. But it should have been. That was better'n most."

"Well thanks, I guess. So, how about college, then. I never had the pleasure. So, when do you go back to school?"

"September 16th. Fall registration is the following Monday. My senior year and all, it's a big deal."

"What are you studying?"

"I'm in Arts and Sciences, history, government, economics, languages. I want to be a journalist, a foreign correspondent. I'll do my graduate work at Columbia, that's just a few blocks from home. And the way the world's going there'll be plenty to write about."

"A regular Dorothy Thompson."

"You know about Dorothy Thompson?"

"Don't look so surprised. Matecumbe ain't Timbuktu, ya know. We get the news. Every morning the train drops off the papers. And we get radio from Miami."

"It's just that I didn't expect . . ."

". . . that us bums think about anything besides the next drink? Even when I was drinking, I read a lot."

"No, it's not that. I just didn't expect to travel 1500 miles and meet *you* by chance. It's just funny."

"More like lucky. So, on the school paper?"

"Oh, sure, and cover women's news? The boys at the Daily Sun don't believe girls can write anything serious. Actually, I've submitted a few articles under my boyfriend's name. The pricks printed them!"

"Boyfriend? Serious?"

"Oh, Fred! You're jealous and we only just met. He's a freshman from Jersey, wears a beany. How serious is that?"

"Sorry, none of my business, again. What do you do for fun?"

"Forensics . . . you know debating? I'm in the women's club. Yeah, just girls. We get to go on a lotta road trips for matches with other schools. The girls are smart and funny and we get to skip classes."

"I can see the fun in that. But why Cornell? Why not a women's college with a newspaper you could write for in your own name?"

"My parents met there. I'm a legacy! My father was Commandant of the Cadet Corps. All the underclassmen have to play soldier, Land Grant stuff. He saw to it they didn't get hurt. My mother was a coed. He took her to the Military Hop once and here I am."

"They must be very proud you're graduating."

"My mother passed on when I was four."

"You poor kid, that's rough."

"It happened very fast. They wouldn't let me into her room. We had our Halloween decorations up."

She sighed and snuggled deeper into his embrace. "I remember her lavender perfume, her beautiful long blonde hair, her voice. She was always singing. Oh, how I loved her voice! I cried a lot. I still do at night. I remember riding on the train bringing her body back to her family home in Ithaca for the funeral. I didn't understand why I couldn't be in the baggage car with her coffin. I knew she was alone and cold. I remember staring out the window for hours. At every station there were big stacks of long wood boxes on the platforms. I asked my grand mom what they were. 'People just need a lot of those these days,' she said; 'some are filled, others waiting to be filled.' Years later I realized they were coffins for the influenza dead."

"When they buried her, everyone dropped a handful of dirt onto her coffin. I found a smooth round stone and warmed it against my tummy. When it was my turn, I threw the stone in. It made a loud thump and people glared at me. The stone didn't bounce off, it sat right on top. I cried, 'Mommy, please don't be cold!'" Fred felt her breathing stumble and heard her sniffling. "I guess that's the real reason I go to college there, to be near her. God, I never told anyone that before. Squeeze me hard!" Cindy sobbed.

"Daddy felt that a little girl without a mother must be loved twice as much by her father. When he returned from Germany, he left the Army and made a point of being with me every day, took me on his business trips to Europe. He also wanted me to be tough, because the odds were now twice as great I'd become an orphan. From early on he'd take me to a camp in the Adirondacks. We'd hunt and fish and sleep out under the stars. About ten years ago we began coming to Key West regularly. He had work in Cuba and we'd always stop here for a few days. I love the ocean."

"That was way more than I expected, Cindy. Thank you." He kissed her.

"I'm over it. Kiss me again." He did. "Tell me about your family."

"Hmm, not much to tell, they're all dead so far as I know."

"Fred,'" she hugged him, "that can't be true."

"My big brother, Steve, got himself killed in the war. Ma and Pa died a few years later. I suppose I have a cousin somewhere, don't know for sure."

They made love again and slept.

* * *

Cindy woke to his cries. "Fred, what is it?!" The only answer was the frantic keening of a wounded animal. Frightened, she grabbed his shoulders and shook. She couldn't wake him. He pulled abruptly loose and sat up in bed. His eyes open and staring at some horror she could not imagine. "Fred, honey, remember this morning? It was sunny and warm and I loved you so much. And we shared your drink and it was so cold and good."

She kissed his cheek and stroked his brow. He howled and swung his arms wildly, knocking her to the floor. She stood up and stared at him in disbelief. He was thrashing about the bed as if trying to fend off a pack of rats. She remembered the ice bucket. She grabbed it off the table and emptied it on his head.

"No, no!" he shouted, grabbing Cindy around the neck. He was strangling her, his eyes wide and bulging. His hands cut stone; she couldn't break the grip. He had her on the floor. She reached desperately under the bed. *Where is my purse?* Her right hand felt the empty champagne bottle. She swung it with all her strength against his head. The bottle shattered. He fell back and landed hard, blood dripping from his face. The crying stopped.

"Fred, are you awake?" He didn't move.

"Oh shit, I killed him." She knelt, pressed her fingers against his neck feeling for a pulse and found one. She lifted an eyelid. There was movement. "Fred, wake up!" She slapped him.

He groaned and shook his head. "Did Joe Louis just KO me?"

"I'd have noticed that. It was a bottle. I'll get you a drink." She looked around and found a cup. She filled it from the bathroom faucet. He took it from her hands and emptied it in a gulp.

"Did it break?"

"Yeah, so watch your step. Here's a towel. Wipe your nose."

He looked up, rubbed his eyes and looked again. "Oh my god, you're glorious!"

Cindy cocked her hip to one side, rested her hand on it and leaned against the bed post. "OK, back in bed. You owe me one, if you think you're up to it."

Slowly standing, he swayed then sat down heavily on the bed. "It's wet."

"And it's going to get wetter." She pushed him onto his back and straddled him. "I'll leave the light on so you can watch."

This time she started slow and deliberate. She didn't want Fred to come too soon. There was something divinely dirty about it, knowing she was being watched, studied, and appreciated, in a brothel! The darkening bruise on Fred's bloodied face excited her. Leaning forward she gave him a long, deep kiss, their tongues grappling. She could taste his blood and smeared it over her cheeks and breasts. She had never felt so aroused. Minutes before he was killing her, now they were fucking. It was primal. He panted, grimaced, eyes squeezed shut. She glanced over at the mirror. Was that her? A stranger's face looked back, raw, savage, more beautiful than any woman she had ever seen. It was the final nudge off the cliff. Rocking wildly, she began to climax in wave after crashing wave. Fred wailed, arched his back and thrust his hips upward lifting her high off the bed. He shuddered. She felt him fill her completely. They convulsed and collapsed.

Fred gave her a kiss and fell back on the bed. He was exhausted and drunk with her, falling quickly asleep. She watched him for a long time. He twitched, grumbled, mumbled, snored, drooled, burped, farted.

But I can only see his beauty. She searched for a word. *Adoration, like nothing I've ever felt before! Je t'adore, Frédéric. So, is this true love or mere infatuation? Well either way I'll never see him again after Sunday. And with any luck he'll do something to make me hate him. No regrets. Wait, he did already try to murder me!*

Cindy turned and admired herself in the wall mirror. *Damn, I look good.* Reclining, she arched a leg to improve the pose. She placed a hand on Fred's sweaty chest and smiled back at her reflection with insolent triumph.

Chapter 7

Friday, August 30, 1935 – Date Night

Emilio got behind the wheel of his car and smiled. "Ah! Essence of linseed with a hint of lime. Too much sun today?"

"Can't you see? I look like a lobster. Cindy warned me not to go swimming until after three. But I couldn't wait. She called the hotel doctor to come see me. He said I had sun poisoning and to stay out of the sun for a week or I'd be in the hospital, and gave me this oil to put on, carron oil."

"You should have listened to Cindy. Tourists get burned all the time their first day at the beach. The sun's much stronger down here than up north."

"Oh, I got sunburned in Germany. But it took all day. My mother was always nagging me to cover up."

"You should listen to your mother."

"Yes, dear, I promise."

They drove to a little café by the harbor and took a table on the deck over the water. There were fish swimming beneath the boards, big ones. He helped with the menu which was all in Spanish. Ella chose the pescado del dia, fresh dolphin with a shrimp creole sauce. It was wonderful, not too spicy. Emilio ordered a plate of ropa vieja and a bottle of Hatuey. For dessert she got a torta de limon, he had a flan de coco. They finished with sweet Cuban coffee.

"So, what is it you do?" Ella asked.

"Work for change."

"Shine shoes?"

He laughed. "That's Cindy's joke. She told me you worked for the Party, I'm a freelancer."

"Who's paying you now?"

"We don't discuss that."

"If I weren't on vacation, I'd get it out of you."

"Don't strain yourself. I'll tell you all you need to know."

"So that's how you play it. *Vous êtes un ami de l'A-B-C ?*"

"*El A B C es la esperanza de Cuba. ¡Todos unidos bajo la bandera del A B C !* " He raised his fist. So, you've read Les Misérables. But those French students throwing away their lives on the barricade was a stupid waste. There are more effective ways to fight tyranny."

"Well, that's good to know. I'm just glad you're not working this weekend. When she picked up that bum, I thought I'd be the third wheel. Isn't that what they say?"

"Yes, exactly. Your English is excellent."

"Papi . . . father insisted I study English. He says the future will be either American or Russian and English is easier to learn."

"True. But you can't go around saying that in Germany."

"Just between him and me . . . and now you."

"In Cuba, too, you must watch what you say. Batista runs a police state, as bad as Machado's. The Americans are fine with that as long as it's good for business."

"American imperialism. But America sure impressed me the moment I stepped off the ship in New York. Actually, that took a while. The Immigration man thought I might be a white slave, brought here for immoral purposes. There I was dressed like an ingénue in school girl braids, acting like I had no idea what he was talking about. He had me wait on board until Mr. Rattigan arrived to claim me, after showing proper identification, of course. I was a little drunk by then, the nice steward kept bringing me drinks."

"Fine introduction to America."

"Why yes, it was actually. He – the Immigration man – was a gentleman, he explained it was all for my own protection. There were criminals who worked the terminals looking for innocents like me, fresh off the boat, and snatch them right off the street. He advised Mr. Rattigan to keep a close eye on me as I was so obviously vulnerable to enticement. I tried hard not to laugh. My father had to pay the Nazis a big bribe to get me out of Germany. I couldn't wait to get aboard the SS Manhattan. I traveled first class! Everyone was so kind to me. And when Mr. Rattigan offered his arm and escorted me off the boat and into a big limousine on 12th Avenue, I felt like a princess."

"You've probably seen the best of America, living with Cindy. Wealth and privilege go a long way."

"Listen to you! The Depression doesn't appear to have crimped your style any."

"I believe in social justice, but I'm not a damn fool about it."

"And the workers and peasants? Do they live as well?"

"It's no problem with them. I've fought and gone to prison. *Los guajiros* expect a man to enjoy himself, especially with a beautiful woman. It is the simplest yet most sublime of pleasures."

"Used that line before?"

"Never! You just inspire me. So why Cornell? Bet you could have got into any college."

"Not without Mr. Rattigan's help. I have a police record, you know. Besides, Cindy thought it a grand idea. We'd have lots of fun."

"Have you?"

"Oh, yes. I'm on the debate club with Cindy and made lots of friends in the Young Communist League on campus. Oh, Abby asked me to give you something, you know, your father's housekeeper?"

"We're old friends. What was it she wanted you to give me?"

She leaned close and kissed him on the lips.

"Uh . . . oh, that was nice of her."

"You're blushing! So, anything serious?"

"I've known Abby since the war."

"How old was she?"

"Oh, a teenager, a couple of years older than me."

"I see . . . "

"She was working for the Rattigans, even then, as a maid."

"And where were you?"

"Santiago . . . Cuba, with my grandparents. You see after my mom died - I was just a baby - my father arranged with them to raise me. The agreement was that I would have their name, Ruz."

"Did he ever visit?"

"Every year or so. In 1916 he brought his new wife with him, Emmeline. She was much younger. A beauty."

"I know, I've seen her pictures. Cindy looks just like her."

"Well, in October 1918 they closed the schools in Santiago because of the flu, and I thought it the perfect opportunity to visit New York and see Emmeline. Pop was in France. Maybe I'd get a kiss. I had a bad crush on her. It was so stupid of me, my own stepmother!"

"It happens."

"I caught the flu somewhere during the trip to New York. I was delirious for a week or more. When I woke the house was empty except for Abby. She told me that Emmeline had caught the flu and died. I killed her."

"No! You can't believe that! So many died, you couldn't be responsible."

"You're being rational. I only know she's dead because I wanted a kiss. Damn right I killed her! But little Abby cared for me. Kept me alive, fed me, bathed me, shaved me, cut my finger nails, changed the sheets, risking her own life. I don't suppose she told you this, but her husband was also in France. The telegram from the War Department arrived the day before, on Armistice Day. She showed me. We both cried together. And then . . . Abby should tell you the rest."

"Dear, dear Abby! You made love, didn't you?"

"My first time."

She kissed him again. "That one was from me."

He smiled. "Thanks, that helped. Did you know I went to Cornell, too? Pop said he'd fix it. But I got in on my own. And there's a Cuban connection. Garcia Menocal is a graduate, class of 1888. He was President from 1913 to 1921."

"Really? You'd think the school would advertise that. What became of him?"

"Well, he led the revolt against Machado in '31, was jailed, exiled, returned last year, and plans to run for President again in December."

"So, if he wins maybe he'll appoint a fellow alum to some office?"

"I did a job for him once."

"What was it?"

"Take a shipment of arms and ammunition from New York to Gibara, and get it to *los insurrectos* in the mountains."

"That sounds risky. So, what happened with your revolution?"

"Started just fine. Then the planes began strafing us. Then the Army and Navy showed up. Trapped us in a train tunnel for two days."

"Did you escape?"

"Spent a week hiding in the swamps. Some Rural Guards found me. Thought I could bluff my way out, but they saw I was wounded and handed me over to the *porra*."

"Please?"

"Club, the kind they beat you with, slang for the secret police."

"How long did the . . . porra hold you?"

"112 days."

"My God! How did you survive?"

"Thought it would help if I just admitted the obvious, that I was an American gunrunner. A bad idea. The porra thought they could get a lot of money for me. It took my partners some time to get the cash together. The porra got impatient, thought if they treated me badly enough, they'd get the money sooner, so they took disgusting pictures and sent them demanding more money. Eventually they got paid and put me on a boat to the States."

"What did they do to you?" she whispered.

"Ella, I've said too much, already." Emilio clutched his fists on the table, so tightly they trembled. She placed her hands over his. For a moment he flinched then looked into her eyes, and relaxed.

"Dear, we have a lot in common."

"You got me talking about myself. I never do that."

"It helps to talk; you should try it more. So, can you go back to Cuba now?"

"Yes, but I'm careful. The police have me on their watch list."

* * *

They strolled hand in hand to the Habana-Madrid Club on Front and Duval. The place was on the seedy side but the liveliness of the crowd and the music more than made up for it. Hector Barroso's Spotlight Band was playing Rumba Tambah. The large dance floor was crowded with Cubans, locals, tourists, shady ladies, sailors, marines, soldiers, Negroes, some older rowdies Ella took to be veterans from the camps. She could act a role in such surroundings, but Emilio gave Ella the confidence to be herself. It was unfamiliar and delightful. In America no one chased her. The looks she got here were curious or friendly or, perhaps most appreciated, indifferent. Nobody thought they had a right to bother her. This is what freedom means.

Emilio raised her to a new level. With him it was OK to be noticed. She could be loud and carry on. And if a stranger got too close, one look from Emilio sent him packing. And how he could dance! It didn't matter if she didn't know the steps. He led her surely and happily around the floor, trading jokes and looks. Ella watched and learned from the other girls, letting the rhythms guide her. It was exhilarating. She thrust her hips against his, barely a millimeter of fabric separated them. He laughed. Cindy had been right, she really liked him.

They'd been at the club for two hours when the manager sought Emilio out. He was wanted on the phone. Emilio parked Ella with some friends and went to take the call. When he returned a few minutes later he'd become very serious.

"I'm terribly sorry, Ella, something's come up and needs my attention. Will you forgive me if I take you back to the hotel?" Seeing her crestfallen expression, he got down on one knee, took both her hands in his, kissed them, and then looked up at her with a sad puppy dog look. She could not resist, laughed, pulled him to his feet and kissed him. The crowd cheered. They must have thought he'd proposed.

"Take a rain check?"

"Sure, but next time you're coming home with me."

Now Emilio grinned. "Cindy told me to take good care of you, you think she'd mind?"

"I think that's exactly what she had in mind."

At the hotel Emilio stopped the car at the entrance, came around and opened the door for her. "Hasta mañana."

"Breakfast?"

"Promise." He gave her a quick peck on the forehead. She watched a him drive off.

* * *

Ella sat alone in her hotel room wearing only a man's white shirt. A damp linen mask covered her sunburned face. On the dressing table the parts were laid out neatly. She slipped a cotton swab into the eyelet of the rod, dabbed it with solvent, and ran it down the barrel. It came out clean. She did it again with a dry swab. Satisfied, she rubbed a light coat of oil on all the metal surfaces. Then she replaced the recoil spring over the barrel, narrow end first. Holding the receiver in her right hand she replaced the slide, and with her index finger repositioned the trigger guard. She pulled the slide back partially and then allowed it to snap forward. It moved with silky precision. She pushed a full 6 round magazine into the grip until it clicked, pulled the slide fully back and released it. With the safety catch off and hammer cocked she raised the gun and lined up the sights with her reflection in a floor mirror across the room. She spread her legs and aimed. Her finger teased the trigger with a butterfly's touch. *"Paff!"* she breathed. She brought the gun down and caressed the cool, slick barrel with her inner thighs. Her breathing quickened, coming in little gasps, her body shuddered. She leaned back, went rigid and exhaled. Relaxing, she raised the pistol to her mouth and kissed the muzzle. Then with safety on, she removed the magazine and ejected the cartridge.

It was a 9mm Walther Polizeipistole Kriminal or PPK. Last summer Cindy had gone to a Berlin women's clinic and then with her father to Zella-Mehlis to pick up a pair of PPKs he had ordered. Cindy asked him to buy one more. That was when they decided to get Ella out. They were too late.

Ella hid the pistol under her pillow and started reading a magazine. She nodded off part way through a story. The old dream returned.

I am naked. The men walk me down a brightly lit hallway. Their steps echo loudly off the white tiled walls and stone floor. My bare feet are cold. The air smells of disinfectant. There is no turning, no slowing. They take me to the end where two black doors wait. Signs above the doors read Leben on the left and Tod on the right. I have no choice. I reach for the handle. A bell is ringing . . .

Chapter 8

Saturday, August 31, 1935 – Sunrise

Ella awoke to a ringing. A pair of moths circled the bedside light. Unsteadily she walked across the room to the telephone. "Yes?"

"¡Buenos días mi amor! Get dressed and downstairs. I'm in the lobby."

"Emilio? What time is it?"

"6:30, sunrise."

"What's happening?"

"Breakfast. Remember? We have a date."

"OK," she yawned, "I'm coming."

She glanced at her reflection in the mirror. The burns were livid. It stung when she splashed cold water on her face. Stiffly, she drew on her yellow beach pajamas.

* * *

Emilio was leaning against the counter chatting with the night clerk when Ella appeared. "You look great, come on."

"Where're we going?" She handed her room key to the clerk.

"A fisherman's breakfast. There's a place by the harbor where all the pelicans hang out."

"Will I fit in like this?" Ella spread her arms.

"One look at you and they'll all fly home and change."

"Yeah, sure. So, what do fishermen have for breakfast?"

"Whatever fish they just caught, usually snapper, with a heap of fries, coleslaw, two eggs over easy and a bowl of Cuban coffee."

"Sounds good. I'm hungry."

They got in the car and started driving.

"Cindy didn't come back last night."

"I know."

"Is that why you left the dance?"

"It was nothing, she's fine."

"I worry. This vet she picked up; his kind can be trouble."

"Maybe. We'll see what she thinks. We're going on a boat trip today. I think you'll enjoy it."

"Fort Jefferson? The guidebook says it's a wonderful excursion."

"Not there. After we eat, I'll take you back to the hotel to change and pack something for overnight."

"Oh, come on, just tell me!"

"Havana."

". . . why?"

"It'll be fun and I have some business there."

"There might be a problem, and not just you. I hear they don't like Communists visiting. Last ones who tried were arrested and deported."

"Yeah, some workers' delegation from New York, Batista knew they were coming, was ready for them. We'll be there and gone before anyone gets curious. Just act like a tourist."

"I will. I'm never going to prison again."

* * *

Fred sat up in bed and rubbed his eyes. "I had my dream again last night. Hadn't happened in weeks. Thought I was finished. Idiot! I didn't hurt you, did I?"

"Have you looked in the mirror?"

He glanced up and examined his face. "Well, when I get back to camp, they'll have something to say. . . I guess I deserved it."

"Yes, you did. You scared me. I couldn't wake you up."

"At Walter Reed the headshrinker just wanted me to talk about the event, every detail, over and over. He thought I'd be cured if I got it off my chest. But the night terrors came back right after they discharged me. Turned to booze, took the edge off. I quit that 26 days ago . . . until last night. Sorry for scaring you. By rights it should have gone without a hitch. After all, you're my payoff."

"I'm your what?"

"You know, when you win a bet, you get a payoff."

"How's that? I'm the prize in some game? This is funny, right?"

"Not so much for the other guy. You see he's dead, got killed doing something I bet he couldn't. So, I tried it and lived. So, he owes me."

"Ah, Fred, that's crazy talk. The papers say you vets are all psychos. I thought they were exaggerating."

"Well, everyone's a little crazy by someone's thinking. I bet there's something crazy about you, kiddo."

"No more bets! You got too rough with me. If I'd found my gun, you'd be dead."

"In the Army you always know where you leave your weapon."

"Well, sorry I fucked up."

"I understand, you're a civilian."

"Lucky for you." She began to disentangle herself from Fred.

"Just a minute, I don't want you to get too far behind in the count." He put his head between her thighs. "Now try not to move."

"That tickles . . . uh . . . jeepers!" She gasped. "How do you know that?"

"Marie was a good teacher."

"Thank her for me. Right now, we have things to do, people to meet, places to go. I'm taking a shower. I've got you all over me."

"I'll see if I can rustle up something from the kitchen."

A half hour later Fred returned with a large platter of ham and eggs, *tartine de confiture*, strong coffee, and fresh squeezed orange juice. A single yellow orchid from the garden lay across the plate. Cindy was clean and dressed, brushing her hair. The blue scarf she'd worn as a sash was now wrapped around her neck.

He placed the platter on the table and watched her simple, graceful motions, the gentle bounce of her hair after each pass with the brush, the peace and beauty of it all. He had forgotten, it had been too long. Life with men was hard-edged, gritty, and violent. He wondered if he could go back to it. When he got close, he caught a hint of her Chanel. He kissed her bare shoulder and lingered, his lips gliding over the tiny hairs. He began nibbling. She pressed her head against Fred's and caressed his cheek . . . for a moment.

"Whoa there, ya big lug! We have to get moving. Plenty of hot water, Freddie. Oh, look what you brought! That's so sweet."

With two bobby pins she fixed the orchid in her hair. "What do you think?"

"Gorgeous, kiddo. Help yourself. I ate plenty in the kitchen." Fred went to the bathroom and closed the door.

* * *

Cindy noticed where he had tossed his jacket the night before. She lifted it off the floor and shook the wrinkles out. Some things fell from the inside pocket. She picked them up, a worn Army certificate, a snuff box, a laundry receipt and an envelope roughly torn open. There was a letter stuffed inside, she considered reading it, but then Fred began loudly singing. She recognized the tune, *It's a Long Way to Tipperary*:

That's the wrong way to tickle Marie,

That's the wrong way to kiss:

Don't you know that over here, lad,

They like it better like this.

Hooray pour la France! Farewell, Angleterre!

We didn't know the way to tickle Marie,

But now we've learned how.

She smiled. "Marie, huh?" Cindy returned the articles to the inside pocket, folded the jacket neatly and draped it over a chair back. Her purse had ended up under the bed. She checked that the pistol was still there, then took out a two-dollar bill and left it on the table near the door with an apologetic note for the maid.

Cindy stepped out into the hallway. Between rooms 10 and 12 was an unmarked door. She tried the handle. It was unlocked. She slipped inside. There was a heavy black curtain behind the door, and enough space to close it and open the curtain. Beyond was a small dark room. She turned on the light. There were several chairs and tables with filled ashtrays and empty glasses. The carpet was stained. There were towels on a rack. All the chairs faced a wide, curtained window. She opened the curtain. On the other side of the glass was the bed in room 10.

Chapter 9

Saturday, August 31, 1935 – Outbound

"The hotel is back there." Fred indicated a direction they were not walking. "So, where're we headed, Cindy?"

"You need a haircut. There's a barber shop up ahead. I don't want to look like I'm slumming."

"Next you'll be insisting I buy a suit."

"Not necessary."

They entered the shop and found the barber sitting in one of the chairs, reading a magazine. When he noticed Cindy, he jumped up, smiled and gave her a nod. "Good morning, miss!"

"My man here," she tapped Fred's shoulder, "needs a classy look, shorten the sides and back, not too high, not too tight, no sideburns, part on the left, long enough on top to reach his nose when combed forward, a dab of Dapper Dan, you know, like Gable."

The barber laughed. "And you, sir?"

"What she said."

"Excellent choice, sir."

The barber brushed off the chair, ushered Fred to his seat, and got to work. 20 minutes later, he spun the chair around. "Voila!"

Cindy appraised the result, nodded. "That'll do."

"Hey, give me a mirror, my neck feels drafty." The barber did so and Fred checked out his new style. "Looks swell, thanks!" He made a point of leaving a large tip.

Cindy took his arm. "Next stop, the San Carlos. I want to be there when the *consulado* opens. We're going to get you a *tarjeta*, a tourist visa"

Fred stopped. "Cindy, what's this all about?"

"We're going to Havana. Ever been there? We'll have a ball. Come on."

"Cindy, I can't afford a trip like that and I have to be back in camp Monday."

"This is Emilio's treat. He owes me. We'll be back tomorrow. You'll have fun and in Cuba I'm not as inhibited."

"Well, then, lead on señorita."

The consular office had just opened when they arrived. There was already a short line. From the secretary's desk Cindy picked up a blank tarjeta de turista, a clip board and a pencil. They sat down on a bench to fill out the form.

"Name, Fred Dunn. Is that one n or two?"

"Two."

"Nationality, USA. Address?"

"Put Washington, D.C., that's where I signed up."

"Sex?"

"Anytime."

"Date of birth? Ella and I were guessing about that."

"March 12, 1900. Did you guess right?"

"Closer than Ella. So, you were 17 when you enlisted?"

"Still in high school, just two months from graduation."

"Did you get your diploma?"

"When I did come limping back two years later, wearing my uniform and my medals, the principal said I'd have to make up the senior year. Told him to fuck off."

"That argument rarely works. Blue eyes. Height and weight?"

"Six one and 185. I've put on 30 pounds since coming here. That's what 3 squares a day can do for you. You're not writing."

"Oh, I'm just curious."

Cindy looked over the form and then handed it to Fred with her pen. "Sign here on the bottom where I made an X, and here, too."

"I'm not enlisting in the Cuban Army, am I?"

"Silly, why would I want that? We're pals now, aren't we?" She gave his thigh a squeeze

"Wouldn't exactly call us pals. I kinda think of you as my girl, now." Fred signed the application and Cindy handed it to the secretary.

"Fred, this weekend I'll be your girl, no promises after that." She kissed him on his good cheek. "Now I gotta make a call." The secretary let her use the wall telephone. Cindy spoke for a few minutes. She hung up and returned to Fred. "I called Emilio. He and Ella are gonna pick us up in his car. I don't wanna march across town in this dress. I got all sweaty coming here."

"Mr. Dunn?" said the vice consul, a thin man with a stiff collar and pince-nez spectacles.

Fred stood up and walked over to his desk. "That's me."

"Two dollars US, please." Fred handed him the cash. The consul stamped the visa and gave it to Fred. "Enjoy your visit to Cuba."

They waited at the curb for a few minutes before a shiny, bright yellow Chevrolet sedan pulled up. Ella was in the front passenger seat and eyed Fred coolly. "Get in a fight?"

Cindy cracked, "You should see the other guy."

Fred smiled. "No harm done, just clumsy."

Emilio leaned across Ella. "Should have kept your guard up, buddy. Nice look, Cindy."

"Thank you," she touched the orchid. "A breakfast gift from Fred."

Cindy and Fred got in the back seat. She held his hand as they accelerated down Duval. When the car turned right on Southard Street Fred asked, "Not going to the hotel?"

"No. Ella collected my stuff so we can go right to the boat."

They'd gone just three blocks when they reached the open gate of the former Navy base. Emilio parked the car at one of the piers jutting out from the quay. "Here we are."

A motor yacht was moored beside the pier, gleaming in the morning sun. Fred paced its length, from stem to stern, about 80 feet. The cabin was white, topped by a flying bridge and an inverted skiff. The decks were teak, the hull mahogany, and the brass buffed to brilliance. The bow was boldly raked and the transom sharply cut. A large American flag hung from a staff above the stern. Below it in gold script was emblazoned *Esmeralda, Key West*.

Cindy ran up to Emilio. "Your letter didn't do her justice!"

"She's the former Sea Hawk. In '32 the Coast Guard caught her smuggling 400 cases of Bacardi from Havana," Emilio explained. "They painted her grey, added some armor plate, installed radio gear and machine guns, and commissioned her as the CG-968. Faster than anything the Coast Guard had, they used her as an 'X' boat. She'd sneak up on the rummies, then run them down. Last year she was put up for auction. Got her for a song, $502. Had her overhauled: new engines, galley, head, cabin, fittings, everything. Picked her up in June, better than new."

A graying Negro was neatly coiling lines on board. He stopped and waved his straw hat, *"¡Hola!"*

Emilio waved back. "Eduardo is my first mate, cook and the best lenguado fisherman north of Jamaica."

Eduardo laughed, stepped ashore and shook their hands. "Just call me Eddie." Ella took her camera out and snapped his picture, then the boat, the harbor and everything else.

Fred pointed fore and aft. "Impressive. Those gun pintle mounts?"

"Yeah, on hinges, I kept those. Never know, might be useful one day."

"Pirates?"

"Still happens, you know. Bought the two Lewis guns the Guard had on her."

"That legal?"

"Four hundred dollars in registration fees. They're stowed in the bow locker with ammo."

"I qualified on a Brit Lewis during the last war."

"Good to know. That's some shiner. Sucker punch?"

"Don't remember much, kinda drunk. We have an ex-prize fighter in camp, Jimmie Conway, welterweight. He taught me a few moves. Didn't help, though."

"Conway? Sounds familiar."

"He went the distance with Jack Britton in 1920, lost on points."

"Say, we'll have to do some sparring. I boxed in college." Emilio checked his wristwatch. "Well let's get going."

Fred handed over the girls' overnight bags to Eddie, then grabbed hold of the cabin railing and jumped onto the cockpit deck. He turned and held out his hand to help Cindy. Ella was in smart khaki slacks, a long-sleeved striped pullover, white socks and sandals. She wore a red silk foulard over her hair. Emilio lifted her aboard.

A large hatch was open on the after deck and Fred could see two young men working below. They stopped when Emilio approached, exchanged words, nodded and began cleaning up. Fred wandered over and peered inside.

Emilio gestured to the men below. "Enrique and Fernando, they're brothers. Full time job keeping those beasts running."

Fred counted the cylinders and whistled. "V-12 Packards?"

"Three of them, aluminum block, rated at 1200 horses. We can do 40 plus knots loaded."

"So that's what, two hours to Havana?"

"Flat out; running her easy takes about three hours. I have to check below before we cast off." Emilio went into the cabin and Cindy followed, leaving Fred with Ella. She sat on a bench and studied him while he inspected the controls.

"How did you get hit?"

Fred turned. "I was sleeping, having a bad dream. When I woke up, I was sitting on the floor with my nose bleeding and head ringing. Cindy said she slugged me with a bottle, said I deserved it."

"Did you hurt her?"

"You'll have to ask her. I can only remember the fun we had." He smiled. Ella was not amused.

"Cindy is my angel. I would die for her," Fred said.

"I will kill for her."

"You want me to leave?"

"Ella! Are you bothering Fred?" scolded Cindy coming up from the cabin with Emilio. "Of course, he's staying. We have a date in Havana."

"Look, I'm just a buck-a-day quarry coolie. Everything about this gig is way out of my league, you especially. I should leave before I screw up again."

"Don't be an ass, Fred. The weekend's not over, there's still more to that payoff."

"Payoff?" Emilio asked.

"Yeah, Fred thinks he won me in a bet."

"Unlikely. You're no prize out of a Cracker Jack box. What did he ante up?"

Cindy smiled. "His life. Says he made a bet with a dead man."

"Interesting. Just how did that go, buddy?" asked Emilio.

"Jumped the track in front of a train. He died, I lived. Seemed reasonable to expect something big in return."

"Suppose there's some logic in that. I'll level with you Fred. There's some business I have in Havana. Things could get a little rough. Everyone on this trip has to pull their weight. I need to know if I can count on you."

Fred turned to Cindy. "You knew about this?"

"Sure, Emilio wanted someone to do a little play acting. I figured you'd be a natural. But you can still bail if you want. I'd be heartbroken if you did, though." Cindy frowned adorably.

Fred shrugged. "Well, if you put it that way, I guess I could handle the job, whatever it is."

"Great." Emilio removed his black captain's hat and handed it to Cindy. "Just a little test. You told me you could box. Give me your best shot, bare knuckle, right on the chin."

"Sure about that, pal? I pack a pretty mean wallop."

"He wants you to hit him, Freddie, so hit him."

Emilio shuffled his feet and threw a couple of tight punches in the air. "Show me what you got, champ."

"You asked for it!" Fred swung with a right hook.

Emilio dodged, but not enough. Fred hit him hard, just above the jaw. Emilio landed on his back. He sat up and shook his head. "Whew, you really have a punch, didn't see it coming." Emilio extended his hand.

Fred took it and pulled him up.

Cindy hugged Fred. "That's the first time I've ever seen Emilio get decked!"

"He does this a lot, does he? Must scramble his brains."

Cindy laughed. "Usually he defends himself."

"So, I passed the test?"

"Yeah, Dempsey, you're in."

"Need some ice for that cheek, jefe?" asked Eddie.

"Never mind the cheek, put the ice in some rum." Emilio took the conn on the port side. "Stand by to cast off!" The brothers jumped onto the pier and loosened the bow and stern lines. Emilio cracked the throttle on the center engine, switched on the fuel pump, advanced the mixture control to full rich to purge the fuel lines of vapor, and then retarded it to idle cutoff. He turned the starter key. There was a deep rumbling, followed by an eruption of blue exhaust smoke from beneath the transom. He advanced the mixture until it was running smoothly. Eddie returned from the cabin with a tumbler. Emilio took it and swallowed half. He checked the manifold pressure and tachometer. Satisfied he shouted, "Cast off!"

Enrique and Fernando tossed the lines onto the boat and leaped aboard. Using gaffs, they pushed the boat away from the pier. Emilio eased the center throttle forward and Esmeralda came to life. Emilio lit a big Romeo y Julieta and alternated puffs with sips of rum.

Cindy took Fred's hand. "I'm going to change. Come with me and I'll show you around the cabin." He nodded. They walked past Emilio and Ella, and down the steps.

"Hah! Those two are like minks. Look on the right," Emilio pointed with the cigar. "That cabin cruiser with the black hull. It's Hemingway's boat, the Pilar, a Wheeler from Brooklyn. Surprised he's not taking her out today. Care for a drink?"

"Kind of early for me."

"Eddie can mix you something sweet. And it will get you in a Havana mood."

"Well, OK."

"Eddie!" Emilio yelled and the mate poked his head out of the cabin. "Make the lady a Daiquiri, one to one, por favor." Eddie nodded. "Oh, that scarf won't protect your face at sea. There's a pile of proper fisherman hats like Eddie wears on the shelf above the galley. He'll help you find one that fits."

Ella went below and returned happily a few minutes later in a wide brim straw hat and carrying a cocktail glass. She took a sip. "Gee, this is good! Like the hat?" She spun around.

"It's you. Now see those buoys, painted red and green? The channel runs between them. When you enter a harbor, returning, the rule is to keep the red buoys on the right and green on the left, and when departing, like were doing, do the opposite, keep the green buoys on the right and red on the left. Just remember red, right, return.

"OK, I guess . . . What's that steamer docked over there? The one-stacker."

"The SS Cuba, tourist boat. She's sailing for Havana today, too."

"We could have taken it . . . her?"

"Too late, she doesn't arrive until six and I have an appointment this afternoon."

"Show me how to drive Esmeralda."

"Just how old are you, kid?"

"18 . . . on Thursday."

"Close enough. When we clear the channel, I'll show you how to steer."

Ella took another sip, and leaned back against the ladder to the flying bridge.

"You really should put some ice on that cheek. Does it hurt?"

"Kind of numb."

"Fred said he had a bad dream. Veterans can explode some times. I think he hurt Cindy. You still want him around?"

"She does. Best part, he won't be missed."

". . . What?"

"Those bums go AWOL from the camps all the time, particularly over pay day weekends. When he doesn't show up for roll-call Tuesday, nobody will think a thing of it."

"He's not coming back?"

"Fred knows the deal. Don't you get it? He's the fall guy."

"That's Fred's job?"

"Only if things go bad. Otherwise, it's easy peasy. Just be a first-time tourist in Havana. That's what he is, right?"

"Me, too. So, what's my job?"

"Look pretty. Now come over here. You take the wheel."

Chapter 10

Saturday, August 31, 1935 – Havana

Cindy led Fred through the main cabin with its compact galley, retractable table and bench seats. Eddie was frying some fresh caught yellow-fin with garlic and onion on a gas stove. The aroma filled the cabin. On the bulkhead a flag was hung. It had 8 vertical red stripes and a blue eagle on a white field. "Coast Guard?" Fred asked.

"Emilio says he found it in a locker cleaning out the boat. Bit of history."

Moving forward she opened a door and entered a twin berth stateroom. Just inside on the deck was a large white duffle bag marked with blue letters, USCG. Fred picked it up to make room and noticed the heavy duck canvas was vulcanized. The opening was sealed with a rubber gasket between brass rings held tight with three wing nuts. A hefty steel shackle was strapped with triple stitching to one end.

Cindy closed and locked the door behind them. There was an open hatch in the ceiling allowing in some humid air. She turned to face him and started to quickly undress. "I can't wait 'till tonight. That fight got me all hot and bothered."

She removed the scarf. The bruises on her throat were vivid. The hand marks were clear. "You know I like it a little rough, but not this rough."

"Jeez, I did that? Sorry, I should have warned you. If Dixie knew she'd kill me. She said as much before you showed up. Does she carry a gun, too?"

"Just like mine. But she carries hers in a thigh holster. Not likely she'll misplace it."

"I'll just keep that in mind."

She unpinned the orchid from her hair and placed it on a shelf.

* * *

Ella was at the wheel; her third Daiquiri secure in a brass cup holder screwed to the console. Each time they hit a wave the spray swept over the cabin and splashed against the cockpit windshield. Some made it inside and everyone was getting wet. Eddie and the brothers were hanging on to the railings with one hand and holding a fish sandwich with the other. Wedged between the benches was a bucket filled with ice and bottles of Wagner beer. Cindy grabbed Fred's arm and pointed up to the flying bridge. When they got to the top they leaned into the spray, laughing and shouting.

Ella ran full throttle for about ten minutes before Emilio had her ease back. "Look out there," he pointed with his hand, "where the water gets darker. That's the Gulf Stream. It runs from west to east. When we get into it, we'll be pushed east so watch the compass and keep a steady course, 188 degrees."

"Can we go faster?"

"A little. Move the throttles forward a third."

The engines rumbled in response and the boat kicked forward. Ella threw back her head and yelled, *Ji-hah!*

Fred and Cindy climbed down to the deck soaked and happy. Fred turned to Ella, "Good job, kiddo. You could sell rides on this boat."

After finishing his second beer Emilio told Ella to show Fred the ropes, Eddie would keep them both out of trouble. He went below to take a piss. Cindy followed and waited outside the head for him to come out.

"Was it you behind the mirror?"

"What mirror? What are you talking about, Cindy?"

"In the whorehouse."

"Cindy, you're on your own in New York. You do what you want with whomever you want, it's not my concern. But Key West is my town. What you do here is my concern, particularly when you go off with some beach bum you just met. I had Eddie tail you. He phoned me when he saw where that nut case took you. I told the madam to keep an eye on you."

"You were spying on me."

"If you hadn't clobbered him, Josephine would have stopped it. She knew I'd hold her responsible."

"So, you're saying that fat old bitch was watching me fuck Fred?"

"It's a bordello for Christ's sake, what did you expect? Did you wonder why she didn't charge for the room? She must have been calling her clients two minutes after you walked in the door. If I hadn't warned her, you think she would have stopped him? She'd have charged those perverts extra to see you get killed. She would have dumped your body in the Bay, or worse, sold it to a necrophile. I know that place."

"She made money off me. I'm a real whore."

"Only if you get paid."

"Not all whores get paid."

"Josephine told me Fred wasn't in on it."

"I never thought he was, the poor sap. I've got that man crazy for me. He's funny that way."

"Say, you're not falling for this bum, are you? Remember he's supposed to disappear when the job's done, so don't get attached. Look, I took him aboard on your say so; didn't seem to be a problem that he nearly killed you. I had another guy lined up for the job, offered him a grand, didn't tell him a thing more, except he might get killed, didn't say by who. He was standing by this morning if your boy didn't work out."

"You'll have to shave your mustache." Cindy touched his lips. She sat down on the bench seat beside the table. "I . . . I felt someone was watching. I thought maybe it was you. When I found the mirror window in the next room it excited me. That's sick."

"It's sick if you enjoy hurting someone. Get over it. This is dangerous stuff, you get distracted, you miss something and someone really gets hurt." He bent down, held her by the shoulders and kissed her on the lips. "Are you my girl?"

"Si, Emilio, si."

* * *

"Fred, if you want to make an impression in Havana you have to dress the part. Emilio's got something I think will fit you. You've got the same build. Wanna try it on?"

He had been running the boat for half an hour and was soaked with spray. "Well, I'd like something dry. OK." He waved to Ella and throttled down. She took the wheel.

Cindy led him below to the state room. Laid out on a chest were a crisp seersucker suit, white shirt, tie and bucks. A straw boater rested on top of the pile.

"Go ahead, put them on. I'm changing, too."

Fred stripped down to his skivvies and began dressing. "So, what's Rico wearing?"

"Emilio's wearing work clothes, he likes to blend in." In moments she had transformed from boyish to delicious, a pleated white knee length skirt, a very tight-fitting blue and white striped French sailor's shirt, a white aviator's scarf, and a round blue cap with a red pom-pom.

"Très nautique, eh?"

"You look like a sundae with a cherry on top. Can I have a bite?"

"Just a lick, don't want you to spoil your lunch. Let me straighten your tie . . . and the handkerchief just so. And the pocket watch. It's Emilio's so don't break it. You know how it goes on?" Fred nodded. "Now put on these sunglasses. There! Just like Gary Cooper . . . super-duper!"

He looked in a mirror and loosened his tie a tad. "That's the look. I'm on vacation, right?"

"We'll paint the town!"

* * *

Eddie was at the helm, running with the waves. Ella stood on the flying bridge with the binoculars. Emilio was beside her. "See it? That white speck on the horizon, *El faro*."

"What's that?"

"The Havana lighthouse on Morro Castle, El Morro. We're about 30 minutes out. At night you can see the light from 15 miles: two white flashes every 15 seconds."

Emilio looked down and noticed Fred, "I thought they'd fit. Justo como mi gemelo."

"Clothes make the man," Fred called up. "I haven't worn a suit in years. Look at Cindy!" She curtsied sweetly, winning smiles from all the men.

Ella handed the binoculars to Emilio, climbed down and turned to Cindy, "I'd better change, too. Emilio says it's my duty to be beautiful."

Emilio followed her down from the bridge. "I didn't mean it that way. It's just in Havana women dress rather more . . . flamboyantly."

Ella curtsied and touched her index finger to her chin. "Boop-boop-be-doop."

Emilio motioned everyone closer. "Here's the deal. Eddie will take the boat in and moor her. The port police will board us at some point and ask a few questions, purpose, length of stay, registration. They may make an inspection if something doesn't suit them, so keep them friendly. Fred, you're listed as owner. Eddie will help if the questions get tricky. Just play it natural."

"And where will you be?" Fred asked.

"Out of sight. I'm not exactly welcome here."

Fred nodded "Righto. So besides you, any other subject I should avoid?"

"That's about it. You don't know enough to cause trouble."

"I like it that way."

Cindy gave him a kiss. "You'll do great, Fred. You could just act seasick, that usually works."

The city was visible now, a jumble of white and pastel buildings stretching for miles along the shore. Waves smashed against the sea wall, sending spray high in the air. Eddie motioned to Emilio. They exchanged a few words. He raised the Cuban courtesy flag on the mast. Emilio turned to Fred and Ella. "Eddie wants to point out some sights."

Fred took in the scene. "Looks like a movie set."

Eddie brought the boat close to shore near a bluff. It was topped by an imposing multi-storied building with twin towers. At the foot of the bluff behind the seawall was a monument, two tall pillars crowned by a huge eagle. "That's the Maine Memorial, when we enter the harbor, I'll show you where she blew up."

Cindy pointed. "That's where we stayed last year, the big hotel on the hill, the National. They were patching bullet holes back then."

Ella took a picture. "Is that where we'll be staying tonight, Emilio?"

"Not this trip. Maybe we could go to the night club, though."

Eddie sped up and made a tight turn, throwing a sparkling arc into the sky. People on the seawall pointed. "They call that street along the ocean the Malecón. To us veterans it is La Avenida de Maceo."

"And why is that?"

"Just ahead there, do you see it?"

Fred squinted and then used the binoculars. "The man on the horse?"

"That man is my general, Antonio Maceo y Grajales, *el más valiente de todos*."

"You'll never see a statue like that anywhere in the States."

Fred looked again. "Must be a hundred statues like that in Washington alone, Emilio."

"How many of those men were black?"

"Looks bronze to me."

"Wasn't there slavery in Cuba?" Ella asked.

"My mother and father were slaves when I was born."

"What happened to you?"

"By law I became a *patroncinado*, which meant the slave master could use you without pay until your 18th birthday, and then only half the pay of a free man until you're 22. But when I was eleven the Spanish freed everyone, that was in 1886. It didn't change much for *los guajiros*, we still worked for the same *patrón*. In '95 I sharpened my machete. It was time to fight."

They were now opposite the statue. Eddie idled the engines and the boat slowly rolled in the swell. He stood to attention and saluted. Ella snapped a picture.

Cindy wiped something from her eyes. "Oh, my."

"So, your general, did he become President or something?"

"No señor Dunn. The Spanish ambushed us at San Pedro in '96. I ran. He died."

Cindy covered her mouth and exchanged looks with Emilio. The boat was close enough to shore to hear music playing.

Fred rubbed the back of his neck. "Pal, I know about that. If I hadn't sworn off, I'd say let's get drunk tonight." He snapped a salute.

"That's mighty white of you, Yank."

Emilio nodded toward the statue. "Funny thing, Fred, in Cuba a Negro soldier gets a monument, in the States he gets lynched."

"Yeah, after the war there were race riots all over the country. Colored vets were strung up still wearing their uniforms."

Ella frowned. "But why, Fred? They served their country!"

"Well kiddo, some folks felt the coloreds coming home needed a reminder how things stood, thought they were a mite too cocky, gotten used to killing white men and fucking white women. OK by me, the Krauts deserved it and the mamselles wanted it."

Eddie revved the engines and headed for El Morro. Atop the old fort was the *Estación Semafórico*. The harbor master was there, controlling the port's comings and goings. The channel was narrow and could accommodate only one large ship at a time. Eddie radioed for clearance.

As the boat turned into the channel Fred examined the fort with the binoculars. There were khaki clad soldiers in campaign hats lounging about. One waved to the boat. He waved back. Fred noticed three waist-high objects on the ramparts covered in tan canvas. "MG's," he pointed. "Browning M1917s, I'd say. We used canvas cases like those in the trenches. A Browning could cut us in half at this range, reckon it's about 250 yards." A soldier studied them through a pair of large pedestal-mounted binoculars.

After passing El Morro another fortress appeared. Eddie pointed, "On the left that big fort is La Cabaña, Batista uses it for executions. On the other side of the channel, you can see the Presidential Palace. And that dome farther back is the capitol building. They say it's a copy of the one in Washington. I don't know, never been there."

Fred nodded. "Yeah, there's a definite resemblance."

A motor launch approached from the inner harbor. The words on its hull read Policía Portuaria. "Good, it's the harbor police, not the Nacionales. Give the officer this." Emilio handed Fred a thick envelope. "You're the owner now, I'm going below."

Eddie slowed Esmeralda and had the brothers stand ready with lines. The police boat circled once and then came alongside. White uniformed sailors took the thrown lines and made them fast. A well-fed police officer smiled and waved, "Permission to come aboard!" He was staring at Cindy, reclining on the bench seat. Fred, a half-empty cocktail glass in one hand, offered the other to the officer and helped him cross over.

"Buenas tardes señor. ¿Cómo está?"

"Muy bien gracias. ¿Y usted?" They shook hands.

"Yo también, gracias."

"¿Usted habla español, señor?"

"Muy poco. We're just here for the night. First time in Havana. I've heard there's a lot to see."

Ella sat down close beside Cindy, touching her shoulder. Removing her hat, she casually shook her hair into place. She had changed into a low-cut lace blouse. A shy smile parted her lips. "I am sure your visit will be most enjoyable, especially in the company of such beautiful young ladies!"

"My nieces."

"No me cabía ninguna duda, señor, sus sobrinas. But first a small formality. May I see your vessel's registration?"

"Eddie! Ship's papers, please."

The officer examined the documents. "Everything in order, Señor Dunn. Enjoy your stay!" For an awkward minute he stood there smiling. Fred noticed Cindy gesturing to him. He reached in his jacket pocket for the envelope and handed it to the officer who quickly looked inside. His smile broadened. From his pocket he produced a small ledger and made some notations inside. "Sign here, Señor Dunn, por favor." He tore out a form and handed it to Fred. "Your mooring permit." Before leaving he bowed to each of the girls, took their hands and kissed them.

"That went well," observed Cindy.

"Didn't even ask for my tarjeta. More interested in you and Ella."

"Well, better put my jersey back on. I can feel the sun prickle already." Ella went below.

Eddie started up the boat. "We'll dock near San Francisco Terminal so you and the ladies can go ashore. Fernando will help you with the bags. We'll moor out in the harbor."

Ella took the binoculars and scanned the ships in the harbor. "Looking for something, kiddo?"

"Swastikas."

Chapter 11

Saturday, August 31, 1935 – Bank Job

"Watch it, Pedro!"

"Perdón, señor," replied the mustachioed *porteador*, his eyes masked by the lowered brim of his straw hat. The angry tourist glared at him, then with his lady friend on his arm, strode away. The porteador stooped and collected the spilled fruit from the crate he was carrying. Wearing stained pants, open shirt, and huaraches, his face smeared with engine oil and partially concealed by the hat, he was unremarkable. He made his way around the busy stalls of the *mercado* in the Plaza de San Francisco stopping at the ornate fountain. There he soaked his bandana in water and tied it loosely around his neck. The hotel was only three blocks away but with all his twists and turns it took 15 minutes to reach it.

At the hotel's rear service entrance, the door was propped open. No one questioned him when he placed the crate beside others on the kitchen floor. The corridor leading into the hotel was empty. No one saw him when he entered the stairwell. On the 5th floor landing he paused. When the hallway was clear he found a room with a small scrap of paper wedged in the door on the hinged side, a foot from the floor. It was unlocked. The key was under the bed. On top, neatly arranged was a set of clean clothes. A pocket watch sat atop a straw boater. It was just after one o'clock. He wound the stem and holding the watch to his ear listened to the ticking. A large, double-handled, gladstone bag was sitting on the bench beside the bathroom door.

Emilio stripped and wiped down with a wet towel. He scrubbed the grease from his face, shaved off the mustache and combed back his slicked hair. In a few minutes he was dressed in a seersucker suit. He put on a black necktie, white bucks, and adjusted the rake of his boater.

The watch went into his vest pocket, the silver chain through the third button hole from the bottom, stylishly slacked. Emilio looked in the mirror, the bruise on his left cheek had blossomed into angry black and blue. He grimaced as he rubbed it. Next the sunglasses, they gave just the right touch. The gladstone contained three clay bricks and an envelope. Inside he found the bank documents, Fred's tourist visa and Army discharge certificate. Returning them to the envelope he placed it in his inner jacket pocket. He checked the watch again. There was an hour and a half till closing. Hefting the gladstone, he entered the hallway, and locked the door behind him.

Emilio took the open cage elevator down to the lobby, and left his key with the desk clerk. On the counter top were a few remaining copies of Saturday's English language Havana Post. He picked one up. There was a report that the secret police had captured a spy in the city working for Communist terrorists in Mexico. Other arrests were expected. The weather forecast was 86° and very humid. He walked up to the doorman. "Get me a cab, Pedro!" he drawled. One appeared almost immediately. Emilio sauntered toward the cab waiting at the curb, a dented black Model B Ford.

"¿Adónde va, señor?" asked the hack.

"El Banco Americano." He climbed into the back seat, placing the gladstone beside him. The driver looked around with raised eyebrows and shrugged his shoulders.

"¿Cuál?"

Emilio made a writing motion with his hand. The driver nodded and handed him a pencil. He wrote 310 Aguiar in the margin of the newspaper's front page and held it up.

The driver smiled, *"Ah, El Chase. ¡Por supuesto, señor!"*

"There's a dollar tip if you get me there in ten minutes." He folded the paper and stuffed it in his jacket pocket.

"¡Muchas gracias, señor!"

Traffic was the standard Havana chaos. It took half an hour to drive the few blocks to the bank. Calle Aguiar was only an alley by New York standards, two cars could sideswipe themselves trying to pass. It ran north and south. Tall buildings on either side ensured direct sunlight intruded only at midday. Now it was in afternoon shadow.

Arrows on the walls of buildings at intersections marked Aguiar as a one-way street, an ordinance, like parking limits, universally ignored. The hack worked his way around a caravan of pushcarts piled high with the pale carcasses of freshly slaughtered hogs. Emilio noticed two not-so-secret police agents in a black sedan blocking half the street partway to the corner of Aguiar and Presidente Zayas. A pair of uniformed guards stood at Number 310, two steps up from the narrow sidewalk. He paid the cabby, left a 50-cent tip and strode to the bank entrance in his best gangling Yankee style.

"Good afternoon, sir," greeted the guard as he opened the glass door. Inside a bank dick eyed him and nodded.

The interior of Chase's shrine to American capitalism was designed to awe a client with the power and glory of the Yankee dollar: gleaming marble floors, soaring sky-lighted ceilings, extravagant tropical plants in huge ceramic pots. Behind polished mahogany counters fitted with gleaming brass bars were the sober faces of male tellers in immaculate white suits. And finally, the centerpiece, the enormous circular vault door, all shiny chromium steel and complex radial locking mechanisms, left open during bank hours.

He expected some trouble from the staff, but his English was better than the teller's and the manager responsible for the safe deposit boxes was congenial.

"Not much activity on that box. Seems you're the first since, let's see, in over two years. I was here when the General last visited, just a teller then, mind you. Very impressive man, had that military bearing. Is he still . . . fit?"

"Actually, I never met him. This was all arranged through an intermediary. I'm sure you understand. Here are the documents."

"Goes without saying. So, updated Appointment of Deputy, Lessee's signature guarantee by the New York office, letter of introduction by the assistant vice-president for foreign affairs. Everything appears to be in order. You have some personal identification?"

"I took the precaution of obtaining a tarjeta de tourista. Did I say that right?" The manager nodded. "Also, I always travel with my discharge papers. A little tattered now."

"Ah, a veteran. I served a stint before landing this job, peacetime, you know. Let's see . . . Purple Heart, DSC, Verdun, St. Mihiel, Meuse-Argonne Campaign . . . my! Please, let me shake your hand again, Mr. Dunn. Thank you for your service. You're planning to stay on in Cuba for a time?"

"Like to, my first visit. The weather is not nearly as bad as summer in New York. It can be quite insufferable this time of year. But my client insists I return tomorrow."

"Certainly, I just need your signature here."

He took the form and removed his sunglasses. He scanned through the signatures on the entry record. "My client is quite particular. He insists I obtain a copy."

"Well, we have a radio facsimile machine. I could send the copy directly to the Home Office in New York."

"My client wishes a hard copy with original signatures and a bank certification of authenticity."

"Somewhat unusual but I'm sure we can accommodate your client's request. I'll transfer the heading information on to a blank form, sign as the Bank representative, then you sign both forms. Then I will affix the Bank's seal. Satisfactory?"

"That would please my client. I apologize for the extra effort."

"No effort at all, we aim to satisfy."

When the manager finished, Emilio signed both forms. "Oh, that's quite a shiner, didn't happen in Havana, did it?"

"No, actually, on the boat coming over. Went over a wave, lost my sea legs and fell on the deck."

"You might want to visit the pharmacy across the street. They could fix you up with a poultice."

"Nah, got to get right back to the hotel. Big night planned, starting early."

"Here's your form. Now if you would accompany me to the vault, Mr. Dunn."

He felt a moment's alarm when the key he'd brought failed to open the lock, but on the second try it clicked. The manager had no trouble with his key. Inside the safe was a large metal box. It was heavy. The manager helped place it on a wheeled cart and push it into the client's private room. Emilio locked the door and glanced around for mirrors and peep holes. Finding none he raised the lid of the box and caught an autumnal whiff of freshly fallen leaves. For a moment he paused in wonder and then began counting.

* * *

Back at his desk the manager was on the phone. "Yes, he's here now . . . some American, Fred Dunn, fancy lawyer type, war veteran. Came by boat, bruised his face in a fall . . . No, he didn't say. All his papers are in order . . . Yes, he's carrying a large gladstone bag . . . I'll call when he leaves. Good bye, sir."

* * *

Ten minutes later Emilio exited the client's room, pushing the cart with one hand and carrying the gladstone in the other. He released the cart and waved at the manager seated as at his desk.

"Everything in order, Mr. Dunn?"

"Very much so."

"Excellent! I just need to replace the box, and you'll be on your way."

The manager took the cart and wheeled it into the vault. When he lifted the box, it slipped from his grip. "Heavier than before," he laughed. He tried again, this time successfully. Emilio smiled. They locked the box with their keys.

"Well, then, good day, sir." The manager held out his hand. They shook.

"Pleasure doing business with you. I'll tell the boys in New York how helpful you've been."

"Very kind of you, sir!"

He walked calmly out of the vault. It was almost 3 PM and the bank lobby was empty. Emilio waved to the teller whose window was still open and exited the bank. Instinctively he checked the calle for anything out of place. Despite the afternoon shadows he put on his sunglasses. A troupe of Afro-Cuban street dancers in gaudy costumes was hurrying along. They were laughing and when one of them began a rhythm on the bongos he was carrying they all started singing a raunchy rumba tune. A couple of ragged newsboys carrying large canvas bags filled with the afternoon editions shared a stubby cigar. One of the pushcarts loaded with pork was parked beside a delivery truck across the narrow calle opposite the bank entrance. There were no cabs in sight. Emilio followed the dancers toward Parque Cervantes two blocks north.

One of the performers, a young barefoot mulata wearing a red headscarf, off the shoulder blouse and bright orange skirt lagged behind her friends. When he came up to her, she smiled and spun around. The hem of her dress lifted up, revealing ripe coffee-colored thighs and a hint of luxurious black bush. He smiled back. She laughed and ran after the others.

He had reached the street corner and was about to disappear behind the Basque Bar when the street behind him lit up like a photo flash. His oddly elongated shadow appeared sharply defined on the pavement before him. The concussion struck an instant later. He hit the street hard and rolled over twice. The scene seemed to skip a few frames. His head ached and ears rang. The sunglasses went missing. The boater spun across the street, bounced over the curb and came to a halt against a wall. A hog's head landed with a wet splat on the cobblestones beside him, its dead eyes open and staring. He looked back down the street through a cloud of smoke and yellow dust. It reeked of nitro and shit. Shredded newsprint fluttered down. The cart and its cargo had disappeared. The delivery truck was in pieces and burning fiercely. The bank's windows were shattered, the door blown in. The guards had vanished. A dozen bodies were scattered about the calle in varying degrees of gory dismemberment. A woman — who once may have been pretty — stood silently screaming in her torn red dress. One arm hung by a slender tendon from her shoulder. The police car was on its side. A hand reached through the broken windshield. For a second, he considered running back to finish off the agent who may have seen him. But as his hearing returned sirens wailed and he knew the street would soon be filled with police and firemen.

 Emilio stood up and winced as his arm took the weight of the gladstone he was still grasping. Feeling under his sleeve he found where a large nail was sticking out of his skin below the elbow. He shifted the bag to his left hand and retrieved his boater. He placed the newspaper over his bloodied right sleeve. Up the street the mulata, apparently unhurt, stood staring at him, eyes wide. She may have said something. He waved her away. The sunglasses lay in the street. Scratched but unbroken, he put them back on. He reached into his vest pocket and felt the smooth watch surface, the crystal was intact. Pulling it out he checked that the second hand was moving, the dial read 3:05. He wound the stem. Turning right he headed quickly up Zayas.

He stopped at a hole-in-the-wall tasca, bought a drink, went back to the dank wash room, and latched the door. He hung his jacket on a hook and tore his shirt sleeve back. He drank half the glass. He tried to work the nail loose with his free hand but he couldn't get a tight enough grip. It kept slipping through his bloody fingers. Leaning over the sink he bit down hard on the protruding end of the nail and sharply jerked his head back. The nail had nicked the bone. A piece of flesh came loose. He spat the nail into an overflowing trash basket. Before the pain had a chance to dull, he poured the rest of the rum into the wound. He closed his eyes and took a deep breath. Blood was dripping into the sink. With his left hand he shook the newspaper open, and held a few pages tight against the wound while he counted slowly to 120. When the burning finally faded, he threw away the bloodied section, replaced it with the remaining clean pages, and tied them over the wound with his handkerchief, tightening the knot with his teeth. He ran some water into the sink to wash away his blood and draped the jacket over his wounded arm.

Emilio continued on a block and hailed a cab that took him back to the hotel. He stopped at the counter. "Room 511, please. Any messages for me?"

"No, Mr. Dunn. Here's your key."

"Thanks. Can I use the desk phone?"

"Certainly, sir."

Emilio placed a call to the Weather Bureau office in Key West. It went through quickly. He asked for the latest report. "Sir, this just came in over the wire from Jacksonville: Weather Bureau Advisory 3:30 p.m., Tropical disturbance of small diameter, central near Long Island, Bahamas, apparently moving west northwestward, attended by fresh (19-24 mph sustained) to strong (25-31 mph sustained) shifting winds and squalls possibly gale force (39-46 mph sustained) near center. Caution advised Bahama Islands and ships in that vicinity. Sounds like the second storm of the season and it's headed our way, sir." He thanked the agent and hung up. "Paper and envelope, please," he requested of the clerk. After quickly writing a note he sealed it in the envelope and addressed it: Motor yacht Esmeralda, Key West, Sierra Maestra moorage. He gave it to the clerk, along with a five-dollar bill. "This must be delivered immediately. *Comprende?*"

"*¡Si, si señor! Inmediato.*"

Next, he placed a second call to a number in Atlanta. He had to wait a few minutes for it to connect. He cursed silently. Finally, the other party answered, "Hello, how can I help you?"

"*Cuba libre.*"

"Is that all, sir?"

"Yes."

"Very good sir, goodbye."

Emilio took the elevator to the fifth floor and entered his room. He placed the gladstone on the bed, stripped off his clothes and the makeshift bandage. Standing under the warm shower, he watched drops of blood spiral down the drain. He dried off and wrapped his arm tightly in a piece of cloth torn from his shirt sleeve. It made him feel queasy. He started vomiting just as he collapsed before the WC. Everything came up, and then the dry heaves. Exhausted, his head bowed over the bowl, he reached blindly for the chain and yanked. Slowly he stood up and leaning on the sink looked in the bathroom mirror. His face was ashen, blood trickled from his right ear. He filled the sink and plunged his head into it. Slowly the nausea receded. He took a long drink of water from the iced pitcher on the side table. He put his old porteador clothes back on, mussed his hair, grabbed the gladstone with his left hand and tried the connecting door. It was unlocked, he entered.

"Emilio!" exclaimed Ella. She was wearing a red Cornell T-shirt and white shorts, sitting in a wicker chair by an open window, trim legs stretched out on an ottoman. An electric table fan blew in her face, rustling her hair. A copy of the Havana Post lay in her lap. "We were expecting you an hour ago."

"Things took longer than I had planned, Ella. Where are the *visónes*?"

"Oh, you're terrible. They're next door. Cindy said we had to stay inside until you got back. She's been messing around with Fred. I was really feeling like the third wheel. Just been sitting here reading. Heard an explosion and called the front desk. The clerk said something about a bomb in the financial district. Anything to do with you?"

"Not responsible. I'm sorry but we have to leave, now."

"Scheisse. You're not in any danger, are you?"

"Just a precaution, but I'll feel a lot better back in Key West."

"You shaved your mustache. I liked it."

"Really? Well, some people know me here. Better if they don't find out I'm in town."

"Not much of a disguise."

"Just a piece. The whole is convincing."

"So, what's in the bag?"

"Nothing to concern you." He turned and walked across the room to the other connecting door, and knocked. "Cindy, are you decent?"

"Who's asking?" she replied from the other side.

"Me."

"OK, me. Just a sec." When the door opened, Cindy stood there in a white hotel bath towel wrapped around like a sarong. "You want an empanada? I had room service send up a platter."

"No, not now. We have to get back to Key West tonight. There's a bad storm headed this way and I'll need all day Sunday to get the boat ready. Let's get packing."

"Fuck! We were supposed to go dancing tonight."

"Fred, if anyone asks, you took a cab to Chase Bank this afternoon."

"Didn't rob it, did I?"

"All perfectly legit."

"Peachy."

"Cindy, you're gonna wear that poor boy out." Emilio raised the gladstone and gave it a shake. Cindy beamed and kissed him on the lips. Emilio smiled, then removed an envelope from his pocket and passed it to Cindy. "Thank Fred for me."

Ella felt a twinge inside. She brushed it off and considered the gladstone. Emilio had lifted it with some effort. A red drop glistened on his earlobe.

Chapter 12

Saturday, August 31, 1935 – On the Run

"Taxi, señor?"

Wearing his borrowed suit, Fred carried the gladstone bag. Cindy fidgeted in a clingy, low- cut, mango colored, knee-length dress, tussled blonde hair adrift over her tanned face. Ella wore a white ankle-length pleated skirt and a baggy French sailor shirt. Wisps of raven hair strayed beneath the rim of her sun hat. Behind the trio waited Emilio, cap pulled low, a large suit case in each hand.

"No thanks. It's not far, we'll walk," Fred answered the doorman.

A man leaning against a light pole across the street lowered his newspaper and studied Fred and his pretty companions. For an instant his eyes locked with Ella's. He smiled. She smiled back, and then demurely looked away. He entered a nearby tienda.

Fred set a leisurely pace, pausing frequently to ogle the señoritas. Cindy acted annoyed. Ella laughed.

Twenty minutes later the little procession turned the corner onto Avenida del Puerto. Esmeralda was visible, gently rocking against the quay, not 50 yards away. A police siren wailed. A ripple seemed to pass through the mass of harbor workers, peddlers, shoppers and idlers crowding the street. It abruptly parted and three serious looking men appeared. The one leading was heavy set, in a well-tailored white linen suit and a Panama, the others wore rumpled dark suits and fedoras, carrying Thompson submachine guns. They stepped directly in Fred's path. He didn't hesitate but moseyed right up to the man in white, stopping with their noses only inches apart, some of which were vertical.

"Well?" he inquired of the shorter man, who retreated a step and produced a badge from his inner jacket pocket.

"Buenos días, Señor Dunn. I am Major Antonio Menendez, Chief Inspector, Havana Police." He saluted. "There was an unfortunate incident this afternoon and I have a few questions for you."

"Know my name, huh? Shouldn't be surprised. But we're in a hurry and I can't have the ladies just standing here in the street getting stared at. Comprende, Tony?"

"We can do it here or at police headquarters, Señor Dunn."

Fred shrugged. "Ask away, but make it short."

"No longer than necessary, señor. You have just arrived in our beautiful city, why are you departing so soon?"

"You see that boat over there?" Fred pointed. "Her name's Esmeralda. She's worth more to me than all of Bacardi's rum. The U. S. Weather Bureau just issued a storm warning. I take these things seriously and I won't rest easy until she's secured in a good American harbor. Is that reason enough?"

"A most excellent reason, Señor Dunn. I, too, own a boat, in Cojimar. I shall be taking similar measures. Sadly, though, there is the unfortunate incident I spoke of, there were injuries. A taxi took you to the Chase Bank on Calle Aguiar this afternoon. What was the nature of your business?"

"Banking. And no, I didn't see anything suspicious. Oh, there were some Army planes flying around. Not another revolution, is it? Seems you folks have a lot of them down here."

"You are critical of our government?"

"You're fishing, Tony. No nibbles here."

"On Saturdays the bank closes at noon, yet it was open today until 3 o'clock. For you?"

"Me? Hardly. On a Saturday I'd have thought they would stay open late to accommodate us tourists planning a night on the town. Why don't you ask the manager?"

"Unfortunately, he is unable to answer any questions."

"Did he leave town, too?"

"No, he's in the hospital. You saw or heard anything unusual at the bank?"

"It's all unusual to me, first time in Havana."

"You saw the explosion?"

"Explosion? Is that what you've been pussy footing all around? Didn't see a thing. Heard something mighty loud, though. Thought maybe folks were starting the celebrations early. They do that in the States too, before Independence Day."

"No, Señor Dunn. We have every reason to suspect it was a Communist terror attack."

"There are so many cops hereabouts I'd have thought you'd be able to prevent unfortunate incidents."

"Fred, honey, can we go now? It's hot out here." Cindy made a face and grasped his hand, the one gripping the gladstone's handles.

"Just a minute, sugar. We're guests in Cuba and have to respect the police." From the corner of his eye Fred saw Emilio steal off with the two suitcases. "I'll have to mention to Ambassador Caffery how polite Major Antonio Menendez has been, considering the circumstances. He could have brought me in for questioning. Are we finished now?"

"Just one thing more, Señor Dunn, I must look in your bag. A very handsome gladstone, is it not?"

"You have a warrant?"

"That is not necessary in Cuba, Señor Dunn. The Police have absolute authority."

"How convenient." Fred looked around. The crowd was giving them a wide berth. Menendez's men were pointing their Tommie guns at him. Ella had shifted to one side, right hand against her thigh. She was studying the major with predatory intensity. Fred removed his sunglasses and rubbed his nose. "Then we have a problem."

"For Pete's sake, Fred, just show him the fucking bag!" Cindy slid her hand from Fred's onto the gladstone's buckle, loosened the strap and pulled hard. The contents spilled out. Three bottles of founder's reserve shattered on the pavement. A fourth survived, its fall cushioned by some empanadas and several sets of women's underwear, remarkable for their brevity and festive colors. And lying amidst the broken glass and spilt rum was an unusual object not unlike a large toothbrush, but with rubber knobs in place of bristles. Major Menendez's men started laughing. They leered at Cindy.

"What y'all gawkin' at? Just my French novelties!"

Menendez squinted, his lips quivered, finally he allowed a small snigger. "My apologies Señor Dunn for any misunderstanding. Perhaps you will stay longer next time. You and your lovely nieces are free to go." He saluted and together with his men, turned and left.

Fred glared at Cindy, "Dammit! Do you realize how much those bottles cost?"

"Wasn't your money. Want the empanadas?"

"Not now."

Two lanky strays had begun sniffing around the mess. "This one's still good."

"No thank you."

Cindy put the unbroken bottle, underwear and tickler back in the bag, re-buckled it, and passed it to Fred.

He adjusted his glasses. "Vamoose, chicas!"

They quickly walked to the yacht. Eddie helped them aboard. Enrique and Fernando, stood ready at the bow and stern lines.

Once on deck Cindy jumped up on Fred, wrapped her legs around his waist, and kissed him a dozen times. "Oh . . . my . . . God! You were wonderful!"

"I've handled cops before. Depends on how you're dressed and I was feeling mighty swell. No difference down here. I was more worried about what Ella might do."

"Gestapo are the same everywhere, however they're dressed," Ella observed grimly.

"He let you go," Emilio called up from the open engine hatch.

"You should have heard Fred! He does 'Yankee tourist' so well."

"Well, we're in for it." Emilio started the engines, and when satisfied with their response ordered the crew to cast off.

"Menendez knows me. I had to disappear."

"Figured as much, Emilio. You don't seem very happy we got away."

"I wasn't expecting it. Menendez still could change his mind. And now I can't just disappear."

* * *

Esmeralda motored up the channel at low wake. Cindy reclined on the foredeck, sipping a cocktail and waving at appreciative *pescadores*. Ella climbed up beside Fred on the flying bridge. "You know Emilio played you, don't you? Another minute and he would have left us behind. We would have taken the clipper back to Key West tomorrow."

"Too bad, I ain't never flown before."

"I meant Cindy and me. They would have arrested you. You know what they do to prisoners at La Cabaña?" She nodded towards the massive stone fortress overlooking the channel.

"Shoot 'em? Cindy told me this gig is only for the weekend. Most men don't get even an hour of this much fun their whole lives. Can hardly begrudge a few scrapes along the way." He rubbed his bruised cheek.

Ella shook her head. "If you survived, you'd never forget."

"Plenty about the war I've tried hard to forget, but keep getting reminded of."

"My father was in the war. You both may have been trying to kill each other."

"Officer?"

"Hauptmann . . . Captain."

"Pretty sure I never shot any officers. Not on purpose, anyway."

"So, what did you do?"

"Killed some Krauts I guess, somebody told me. That's the part I forget. In the hospital they tried to get me to remember, just made me sick. Only thing I'm sure of, getting blown up . . . So, what happened to you? Something must've."

She hesitated before replying. "You will never forget, he promised me, and I haven't, not a second of it. I was 15."

"Better not go there, Dixie. Stuff like that will tie you in knots."

"Dixie?"

"You never read the funnies? You look just like her, you know, Dixie Dugan."

"Never seen it. What's so special about her?"

"Well, she's a showgirl, pretty hot stuff, used to have your haircut. And she doesn't let anybody fuck with her, so to speak."

"I guess that's some kind of compliment."

"I sure meant it that way."

"So, this cartoon character bobs her hair?"

"Oh, until last year. They changed it, I guess, to keep Dixie up to date. Flappers are old hat, you know."

"You're saying I'm not chic? Mr. Julian said I'd be chic with all my clothes off."

"And a sight to see. So, was he the one?"

"Now that's funny. He's my hairdresser back in New York."

"I'm no judge of haircuts. I just know what I like and you look great."

"That's better. So, you and Cindy, how do you expect that will go? She really loves you, you know."

"Life is a tragedy; it always ends badly. If you're lucky you'll find someone to love. Luckier still if she loves you back, and you're really lucky if you get to spend some time together, even just a weekend, but it always ends badly."

"Well, you've done pretty well this weekend."

"So far."

* * *

El Morro loomed above them to starboard. "We clear that," Emilio called, "and I'll open her up."

Ahead, a handsome two-masted schooner, half again as large as Esmeralda, slowly entered the channel, close hauled. Flying from the foremast was a blue British ensign with a crown and the letters RBYC. Cindy blew a kiss to the fashionable assemblage seated around the deckhouse. Several men stood up and waved back. One toasted her with his drink. An elegantly attired lady started filming with a hand-held camera.

Ella noticed a commotion atop El Morro at the harbor master's office. A man was raising a black and yellow flag. Another was aiming a signal lamp in their direction, flashing repeatedly: dot-dash-dot-dot. A klaxon blew.

"Emilio! What's that all about? You think they're signaling us?"

He looked up and then back down the channel to the harbor. A police boat was moving out at speed. He edged Esmeralda towards the approaching yacht, now only 20 yards ahead to port.

Fred leaned around the cockpit. "Hey! Those boy scouts up on the castle are taking the wraps off their Brownings. What's up?"

"They won't shoot if they might hit those Brits. It'll buy us a few seconds. Everyone, take cover and hang on!"

Fred jumped onto the foredeck and lay atop Cindy. Ella dropped into the cockpit and crouched against the bulkhead, face down, hands over her head. Eddie and the brothers knelt and braced themselves.

Esmeralda zigged sharply across the bow of the schooner which heeled hard to port, then zagged down the schooner's starboard rail, brushing by the red channel buoy on his port side. The British skipper shook his fist. As Esmeralda cleared the schooner's stern Emilio shoved the throttles all the way forward. The deck tilted sharply back and the boat bolted. An enormous rooster tail shot up in Esmeralda's wake, drenching the schooner and its passengers. The roar of the three Packard engines drowned out their cries.

"Get down!" Emilio shouted.

The first burst was wide. The gunner was spraying and praying. Some rounds must have hit the schooner. Esmeralda would be in range of El Morro's guns for several minutes. The soldiers would get the range soon enough. Emilio maneuvered violently to throw them off. *Damn, my head aches!* A second gun opened up. This gunner knew what he was doing. He fired continuously and walked the line of bullet splashes across Esmeralda's path. For a few seconds she was bracketed. A score of rounds splintered the after deck. The boat bobbed and weaved, bounding over the crests, and slamming down in the troughs. A third gun began firing.

Fred shouted, "Go right! The lighthouse will mask their fire!" Emilio spun the wheel hard over. The next burst passed just over Fred's head, the tracer rounds leaving tight corkscrew trails. Esmeralda barely cleared the rocks at the base of the fortress.

"OK, we're clear!" Emilio turned north but didn't slow. The police boat fell astern. Ella looked up, "Anyone hurt? Fred, Cindy?"

"Just fine. So, we're home free, Cap'n?" Fred asked.

"Afraid not. We're out of MG range but that just got their blood up. We're not finished with them."

Fred shrugged. "Seen worse."

"*¡Jefe, humo!*" Eddie shouted.

Emilio cut the engines. Acrid, blue smoke rose from the split decking. The brothers grabbed fire extinguishers and Eddie forced open the engine compartment hatch with a gaff. Smoke and flames leapt out. They emptied the extinguishers into the fire and jumped down into the opening. They quickly had it under control. Eddie climbed out covered in soot, his clothes burned in places. "A bullet must have hit the fuel line. I patched that but the water pumps aren't working and there's gas everywhere. Looks like the oil pump is damaged, too."

Emilio looked back towards Havana. The patrol boat was closing fast. "We have to reach the 12-mile limit before they catch us. I'll try running slow on one motor, just enough to keep them out of range." Eddie grunted and went below. Emilio started the center engine. It coughed and sputtered before catching. "I'll run it until it overheats then switch. We've got about 10 miles to go."

Esmeralda began making headway. "Fred, I need you to mount the Lewis guns. We may have to shoot our way out of this. Girls, keep watch with the binoculars. Shout if you see a boat or a plane." He swayed, then vomited over the side.

Cindy gripped his arm. "Emilio, what is it?! Are you hurt? You look terrible."

"Just an upset stomach." He took the wheel again.

"You seasick, buddy? Your nose is bleeding."

"Bumped it on the deck, Fred."

"Thought they were finished with us. What changed?"

"Menendez must have figured it out. What did you tell him?"

"What you said. Went to the bank and saw nothing unusual."

"There was someone who saw me when the bomb went off. I forgot, should have warned you. She must have told the police. Now Menendez thinks you lied to him. He hates that."

"If it's me he wants why not just stop? I'll go quietly."

"Too late for that. The girl in the street and the bank clerk, if he's still alive, were close enough to know it wasn't you. Menendez will make you talk."

Fred smiled. "I can keep my mouth shut."

"Not in La Cabaña, buddy. No one can."

"I won't be taken, I'll die first," Ella vowed.

"I understand. Fred, there's a Coast Guard uniform below. Cindy will show you. It's tailored for me so it'll fit you. Then bring up the guns, boat number placards and the Coast Guard ensign."

"Aye, aye Cap'n!" Fred and Cindy went below.

"Ella, stay near me if I start to fade again."

"The bomb . . .?"

"Dynamite, maybe 100 sticks. Bowled me over like a tenpin, hit my head hard on the street. Thought the nail in my arm was the worst of it."

"This isn't turning out like you expected."

"No kidding."

"You're risking all our lives. Is it worth it?"

"We've lucked out so far. Exciting, isn't it?"

She sighed. "You and Fred are more alike than just looks." She picked up the binoculars and looked astern. "There's another boat passing El Morro, throwing up a lot of spray . . . turning towards us."

"They saw the smoke."

Fred and Cindy appeared. He was dressed in a blue uniform and had a Lewis in each hand. She carried two ammunition boxes and the folded ensign under her arm. She placed these on the deck and went back for the placards.

"Say, that cop boat is getting close." Fred mounted a gun on the aft pintle and locked in a 47- round pan magazine. "I can take it out at 300 yards."

"We can't shoot back, Fred, we're still in Cuban waters."

"Mind if I check out my weapon? A burst to the side? Might make them think twice about coming closer."

"Good idea."

Fred fired twenty rounds making an arc of bullet splashes visible for a mile. The police boat slowed.

"Nice shooting. I think our amigos got the message. But I need to open it up a bit." Emilio started the starboard motor and ran the two together at half speed for two minutes then shut down the center motor.

Eddie climbed part way up from the engine compartment. "Jefe, stop for five minutes and we'll have the pumps working. Then you can run all three." He dropped below without waiting for a response.

Emilio turned off the engine. "We're dead in the water. This is gonna be close."

"How much further?" Fred asked.

"If Eddie makes good, maybe 20 minutes. There's no buoy out there. You can estimate it by how much of El Morro you can see, about one third. If we get close, we can brazen it out. They don't want to start a war."

After Fred left to mount the bow gun, Ella asked, "How are you doing?"

"Bad. Your training's going to pay off. There's another uniform in the cabin. It's the smallest. With your hair under your cap, you'll look regulation."

"What about Eddie? Shouldn't he drive?

"I need Eddie on the other Lewis."

"Enrique and Fernando?"

"I don't want them to get too involved."

"What? We're all in this."

"They signed on as mechanics, not accomplices. Besides I know I can trust you. Now hurry."

The five minutes stretched to eight, then ten, the police boats gaining steadily. Fred had come aft and was keeping the nearest in the Lewis gun's sights.

"Start 'em!" Eddie shouted from below. Emilio ran the engines at half throttle. Esmeralda surged ahead at 25 knots. The police boats couldn't keep up and fell behind. He sent Eddie below to change into a uniform and tell the brothers to stay out of sight. "Ella, take the wheel." He sank down onto the cockpit bench. Cindy sat beside him.

"What's really wrong, Emilio?" She leaned close.

He kissed her. "It's just been a long day and we're not home yet."

"Well, you'd better get us home or Daddy will kill us both."

"Then I guess I should come up with something. Fred! Can you be an officer?"

Fred looked at the chevrons on his sleeve. "Hell, no! I work for a living."

"Petty officer, OK? Those crossed anchors mean you're a boatswain's mate."

"Bosun, huh? Do I get a pipe?"

"Not this trip. Cindy, climb up on the flying bridge with the binoculars and see what's in front of us."

She wasn't there a minute before shouting, "Emilio! There's a big steamer ahead, one stacker, coming this way."

He looked over the side. "That's the SS Cuba from Key West, right on schedule. Fred, fix the short placards to the bow and the long one on the transom, there're brackets they slide into, with a latch. Don't drop them over the side. Then raise the ensign. Ella, run up along her left side. We'll pass port to port. When we get close give the horn one short blast. We want Esmeralda to disappear."

* * *

The SS Cuba sounded its horn in response to the newly re-christened CG-968. Waving passengers jammed the railings. Eddie and

Fred in their Coast Guard uniforms saluted smartly. A search of the horizon revealed no other vessels. They should make U.S. waters in two hours. They relaxed.

* * *

Cindy spotted it first, a speck against the afternoon cumulus clouds. She was on the flying bridge lounging in Fred's arms. "Is that a bird?"

"What? Where?"

She stood up and brought the binoculars to her eyes. "Airplane. You know planes?"

"Let me see." He took the binoculars. "Um, biplane, headed this way . . . something underwing. Four of them. Hey Cap'n, we got a bomber after us!"

"Back in uniform, positions everyone!" The brothers secured a tarpaulin over the damaged engine hatch and went below with Cindy. Emilio crouched low in the cabin door. Ella hid the cocktail glasses, straightened her cap and placed both hands on the wheel. Eddie and Fred manned the Lewis guns.

It was clearly visible now, flying low and slow. The plane was unmistakable. The white star in a red triangle in a blue circle was the insignia of the Cuban Army Air Corps. Blue, white, red and yellow stripes adorned the wings and tail surfaces. The engine cowling was red and the wheel spats yellow. A large black 21 was painted on the silver fuselage.

Emilio shouted, "Look smart there!"

The plane appeared to hover, barely 20 feet above the water, the pilot closely examining the boat and its crew. He passed directly overhead and drifted along both sides, the noise from the big radial engine deafening. Ella was astonished; she had never been this close to a plane. *How can it just hang up there?*

Fred caught the pilot's eye and delivered a snappy salute. Eddie on the bow gun grinned and waved his cap. The pilot smiled and saluted back. He banked left, turned west and climbed. At about two thousand feet he rolled into a near vertical dive and released all his bombs. They dropped in a steep arc. Four splashes spanned the boat's wake, a hundred yards astern. An instant later four geysers erupted. The explosions lifted the boat almost out of the water. The pilot swooped back toward them, inverted. Passing directly over the Esmeralda, barely clearing the boat's radio aerial, he delivered an upside-down salute. Laughing, he rolled over and climbed into a ¾ inside loop. He did a half roll, dropping low again and then climbed into a second ¾ inside loop, another half roll, and leveled off just above the water. A wing waggle and he headed back to Cuba.

Fred laughed. "He made a figure 8! If that don't beat all get out."

"Who was that?!" exclaimed Ella.

"*El Americano loco,* Batista's Yankee pilot," Eddie answered.

Emilio watched the plane fly off. "He knew. All that showboating was just to let us know he knew."

"Then why'd he let us go?" asked Fred.

"Guess we passed muster, looked friendly enough and passably Coast Guard. And I don't think he was up to bombing a boat flying the Stars and Stripes."

"Oh!" Ella touched her mouth. "You think he noticed my lipstick?"

Chapter 13

Montreal - July 11, 1935

A man was waiting in the lobby of the Mount Royal. He introduced himself and escorted Daniel Rattigan to a modest suite on the third floor. He was frisked before entering. General Gerardo Machado was seated on a sofa, and a younger man stood beside him.

"Daniel!" The General remained seated and offered his hand. Daniel came over to him and shook it. "Please excuse me for not rising, my health has not been what is used to be. And I've been as you American's say, on the run, for two years."

"Perfectly understandable, General. Nothing serious, I hope?"

"No, no, just a cold." Machado nodded towards the other man. "I'm sure you remember my son-in-law, José Obregón."

"Of course, José." They shook hands. "After you resigned from Chase in '31, we could find no one qualified to replace you, so we terminated the position. I understand you've been traveling with the General?"

"Yes, Colonel Rattigan, I assist El Presidente with his legal and financial interests."

"Please take a seat. Would you like a drink? I brought my own liquor."

"One of your Daiquiris, General. You do have ice here?" Daniel smiled as he took his seat.

"Certainly, my friend. José, please?" Obregón made three, placed the serving tray with the glasses on the coffee table, and seated himself on the sofa beside Machado. "Cheers!" The men took a sip.

"Delicious, José, you have the gift."

"Muchas gracias, mi amigo."

"Any news from our friends in Havana?" Daniel asked

Machado handed Daniel a telegram from a file folder on the table. "I received this on September 25, last year." It read: MUCHAS BOMBAS EN SU DIA PUNTO HACIENDO VOTOS MUERTE INMEDIATA FELICIDAD CUBA ABC. "You understand?"

"Many bombs on your birthday. Making death wishes, instant happiness Cuba, ABC. Nothing since?"

"And I received one just like it in '33, I'm expecting another. My birthday is September 28th, the third anniversary of my dear friend's murder. You remember that day, Daniel, when those *hijos de puta* gunned down Vázquez?"

"Of course, I knew him well. Whoever sent that is probably dead by now. Batista is no friend of the *Abecedarios*."

"It is to be hoped. Still, I must take precautions and personal security is costly. Even more so are my legal expenses, fighting extradition cases wherever I travel. I risk arrest if I visit my family in New York and providing for them in Bermuda and France has stretched my finances. I hope one day to settle in Miami. With sufficient funds I may realize my wish. Here is where you may help me."

"Of course, sir. I will do whatever is in reason."

"I have a safe deposit box registered under my name in the Havana branch. For obvious reasons neither I nor my people can travel there, especially José who knows the bank so well. Would Chase, in consideration of our relationship, business and personal, arrange for the contents to be delivered to me? Of course, there would be generous compensation for your services. Confidentiality is essential."

Daniel took another sip of his drink and considered the General's request. He had anticipated something like this and came prepared. From his briefcase he removed a delegation of authority form. "General, do you trust me?"

The General swallowed his drink. "I wouldn't have asked you if I didn't. You are the only Yanqui I do trust."

"Understand that I cannot do this myself. The Ministry of Justice named me in the public works bonds imbroglio. The secret police know you are a client and watch the bank, and likely have an inside man. They would notice if I showed up and emptied a box you own. I'd need a contingent of Marines and a gunboat to get the contents out of the country. Ambassador Caffery would never agree to that, nor the Board. Which means I must use someone the police don't know and who I trust implicitly. I need the total amount and denominations."

Machado took a cigarette paper from a box on the table, and wrote some figures on it. He folded it in half and handed it to Daniel.

Daniel opened it and calculated for a few moments. "About 11 pounds. Good, one man can handle that easily enough. But it will be a great temptation for him to simply disappear with it. He will need a substantial share and other enticements to stay loyal. Also, the support team must be generously compensated. Bribes will be necessary, and then there's my own compensation to consider." He returned the paper to Machado.

"Ten percent?"

"Half."

José, touched Machado's arm. El Presidente brushed it away.

"Steep my friend. But as we say, *media rodaja de pan es mejor que nada*." Machado added tobacco to the paper, deftly rolled it into a cigarette, licked the adhesive edge, pressed it firmly together, and put it to his lips. Obregón leaned over and lit it.

"Then please sign the delegation of authority form and give me the key."

Machado took the form, and signed it. From his pocket he took a small envelope and handed it to Daniel. The envelope was marked with the box number. Daniel checked inside for the key and nodded.

"This may take a month or more to arrange, my friend. I'll give you a call to set up the delivery. I don't have to remind you that any leaks could get people killed. Not a word must leave this room. Agreed?"

"Estoy de acuerdo, mi amigo."

"And you, José?"

"Of course, Colonel Rattigan, as El Presidente wishes."

José escorted Daniel to the door and whispered to him, "The old man trusts you, I don't."

"But he trusts me more than you. Good day, José."

* * *

On the train back to New York Daniel mulled the matter over. His concept was to have the Havana branch stay open late for a few hours on a Saturday with minimal staffing. The courier had to be unknown and disappear completely after the operation, unpleasant but necessary. Daniel had no need to know the details. The fewer people who did, the better.

Chapter 14

Saturday, August 31, 1935 – The Law of Storms

Two men stood on the quay under a lamp pole, one a Coast Guard officer and the other in a business suit. They watched a motor yacht slowly cross the dark basin. The officer pointed, "That's her." As the boat drew up, he caught the bow line tossed by a deckhand and secured it. "Permission to come aboard," he called.

The skipper answered, "Granted. What's up, officer?"

"Lieutenant Cavendish, Key West Station." He jumped deftly onto the deck and shook hands. "Is there a Frederick Dunn with you?"

"He's my charter."

"You're Mr. Emilio Ruz, the owner of the Esmeralda?" Cavendish asked.

"That's me."

"You went over to Havana today?"

"Yes, sir."

"Mind if I come aboard, too? Guy Reeve, U.S. Marshal for the Southern District of Florida."

"Certainly, sir. You want Dunn, too?"

Reeve clambered on-board. "Just a few words."

Fred appeared from the cabin, dressed for a night on the town, Cindy and Ella on either arm. Emilio glanced over. "Well, here he is. Mr. Dunn, these gentlemen want to talk to you."

Fred considered. "So, the Coast Guard and . . .?"

"Guy Reeve, U.S. Marshal for the Southern District of . . ."

"Florida? Right? Good, so am I under arrest for something?"

"No, no, just a few questions. Mr. Dunn, could I have your address and occupation?" Reeve took out a notepad and pencil.

"Sure thing, I'm from Washington DC, work for the U.S. Government, the Federal Emergency Relief Administration to be precise, deputy to Mr. Harry Hopkins. I'm visiting the veterans' camps down here. It's sort of sensitive so I'd appreciate you not mentioning it to the Florida folks. So, what's this about?"

"Two hours ago, we received a phone call from the Cuban Ministry of Justice demanding your arrest pursuant to a charge of terrorism. They're sending over some officials tomorrow. Don't worry Mr. Dunn, America doesn't extradite its citizens. We're meeting at the U.S. Courthouse on Simonton, should you care to attend. You're under no obligation to do so."

"I'll pass. So, terrorism, huh? I told everything to that cop in Havana, Melendez, I think his name was, said I was free to go."

"Yeah, Antonio Menendez, I've dealt with him before. Usually it concerns smuggling guns, rum, or Chinamen. First time a bombing has come up."

"Oh, is that what this is about? Guy, I had nothing to do with that."

"Noted. Do you have an address here in Key West where I can reach you? I'm sure you will be interested in how the meeting goes."

Fred glanced at Cindy, she nodded. "The Casa Marina," he replied.

"Fine, and how long will you be staying?"

"Monday. Have to be back to work on Tuesday. I wasn't sent here for a vacation."

"Too bad, Key West is a great town. I also need the particulars of everyone else on board."

"Let me get the crew list," replied Emilio going below.

"I'm Cindy Rattigan, New York, college student. Freddie and I are friends."

"I'm Ella Kaufmann, from New York, a student and I'm a friend, too."

"Kaufmann? Spell that with two n's?

"Yes, sir."

"Foreign?"

"Yes, sir, German, I have a student visa."

"Both of you also staying at the Casa Marina?"

"Yes, sir. Sharing a room. Will this get in the papers?" Ella asked.

"I'm not making any statements to the press, Miss Kaufmann. But there's always a reporter around the Courthouse. No doubt it'll be in the Havana papers tomorrow. Heard some people got killed."

"How terrible!"

Emilio returned and handed Reeve the list. "Here you go."

Reeve glanced briefly through it. "Good, that's all for now. Thank you very much for your cooperation. Good evening, Mr. Dunn, Captain, ladies." He tipped his fedora to Cindy and Ella, climbed back on the pier, and left.

Cavendish stayed behind. "Captain Ruz, we also received a call from Havana, Commodore Butterfield of the Royal Bermuda Yacht Club, no less. He was entering the channel when an American power boat, the Esmeralda, imperiled his schooner. His was the stand-on vessel under sail but had to maneuver to avoid a collision. Know anything about that?"

"We did cross another vessel, but at the time we were under machine gun fire from El Morro." Emilio pointed to the bullet holes and burns on the deck. "Don't suppose the Commodore mentioned that little detail."

"Fair enough, trigger-happy crowd down there. We also received a radio message from the SS Cuba this afternoon about the sighting of a Coast Guard cutter heading north, the CG-968. We had no vessels in the area at the time and the CG-968 was decommissioned a year ago. Ring any bells?"

"Damn civilians must've got it wrong, probably some Cuban boat."

"Maybe, but we also got a call from Captain Povey of the Cuban Army Air Corps. Says he spotted the CG-968 about 40 miles south of here. Did a fly by. Funny thing, he said the helmsman was a cute kid."

Emilio grinned. "Hah! Nobody on my crew." Enrique and Fernando laughed.

"Yeah. Say, mind if I look around? Esmeralda reminds me a lot of the X-boat I served on during Prohibition, the CG-968, coincidentally."

"No problem, take your time. You'll find two Lewis guns in the forward locker. They're legal. I have all the paperwork."

"Expecting trouble, Captain Ruz?"

"Pirates."

"Any chance we can get in some marlin fishing tomorrow, Cap'n?" asked Fred.

"Sorry, Mr. Dunn, I'll need all Sunday to repair and secure the boat for the storm. I'll give you a refund of course."

"Don't bother. You'll need the money for the repairs."

"Thanks, that's mighty white of you, Mr. Dunn."

Cavendish looked up from the helm. "The Weather Bureau thinks the storm might pass through the Strait between here and Havana. That would put us in the right front quadrant. You'd be wise to take every precaution."

"Right front quadrant? What's that about, Lieutenant?"

"The Law of Storms, Mr. Dunn."

"And do storms obey the law?"

"Generally. You see a tropical storm in the Northern Hemisphere rotates around its center in a counter-clockwise direction. The winds to the right of the direction of travel are more severe because the storm's movement augments the force of the wind, and the storm wave is high because the winds are stronger and blow more or less directly toward the shore. These conditions are greatest in the right front quadrant. The opposite is the case on the left side."

"Interesting. Sort of like a right hook punch, leaning in. So how accurate is the Weather Bureau?"

"Only as good as the accuracy and number of the ship reports, air pressure, wind speed and direction. The Bureau plots them on a big map as they are received by radio. Then the forecasters try to determine the storm's position, direction, strength and speed. They do their best but there's a lot of room for error, and they can be off by a hundred miles. So, the Coast Guard always errs on the side of caution, and if the storm misses it's just good luck."

"So, when do we start heading for the hills? And I've noticed there're not too many here in the Keys."

"The Weather Bureau will send advisories over the radio and the newspapers will print them. Or in Key West you can just look over at the Weather Bureau office on Front Street. Also, any light house. They'll fly one flag for a storm and two for a hurricane warning, one above the other. The flags are red with a black square centered. One flag means prepare your plan, the second means execute it. If you haven't done the first, you'll be too late for the second. You may have only a couple of hours."

"Good to know. Thanks for the explanation, Lieutenant."

"You're welcome. More people should show an interest, could save some lives." Cavendish turned to Emilio. "We may have to close the port Monday."

"We'd better get a move on then. Hey, Eddie, launch the skiff!" Emilio shouted.

"OK, jefe," Eddie replied.

"Say, captain, OK if I lend your boy a hand?"

"Eddie's my first mate. Ask him."

"Roger that." Cavendish went forward where Eddie had started unlashing the boat.

"Fred, why all the questions? Emilio could have told you that."

"Well, Cindy, impressing someone isn't just sharp clothes and bluster, works best when you acknowledge their smarts. And it was interesting, wasn't it?"

"Yeah, sure. Right front up my ass. And why impress him?"

"Always useful to have someone with authority in your corner."

"Ah Fred, now I'm impressed. Why don't you take the girls out to dinner? Celebrate, you all did great today. Here're the car keys. Cindy has plenty of dough. We've got a couple hours work here tonight."

"Just my thinking," Fred replied.

"Emilio, shouldn't you see a doctor?" asked Ella.

"Oh, I'm much better. Just need a good night's sleep."

"Hope so. I'll stay with you anyway."

"Want me to take your bag back to the hotel, Ella?"

"No thanks. You want yours?"

"Yes." Both girls went below.

"Fred, careful who you meet in town."

"Why's that, Cap'n?"

"It's likely the Cubans made some more calls to Key West."

"I can handle myself."

The girls quickly returned with the gladstone bag, both grasping a handle. Fred lifted it with a grunt and swung it onto the pier. Cindy helped herself off the boat. "What's in this thing?" he asked her.

Cindy leaned close. "The rum, along with what Eddie picked up, didn't want that handsome sailor to find it. He's snooping."

Fred glanced down at Ella standing on the deck. "Is she telling the truth?"

"Mostly."

Fred laughed. "Well, take care of yourself, Dixie."

Ella watched them walk to the Chevy, then turned to Emilio. "Something I can do?"

"Dixie?"

"Oh, Fred gives nicknames to everyone, says I look like some comic strip character. He calls you Rico."

"Could do worse. Ever swab a deck . . . Dixie?"

"I think I can handle that, Rico."

* * *

About 8:00 PM Cavendish stepped onto the pier. He faced about and saluted. "You run a smart ship, Captain."

"Thanks, Lieutenant."

Grinning at Ella, Cavendish tipped his cap, "And Miss Kaufmann, you make a very smart helmsman." She laughed as he swaggered off.

"It'll be all over town by tomorrow."

"What?"

"He knows, just like that crazy pilot and maybe that marshal, you know, me and the guys, and Esmeralda playing Coast Guard."

"Yeah, guess so."

Emilio told Eddie to bring up some gear. He returned with the canvas sea bag stenciled "USCG" and a tool box, and lowered both into the skiff to Emilio.

Ella asked, "Need any help? I'm pretty handy."

"Just patching some bullet holes. Can you tie a cleat hitch?"

"Of course, I was in the *Wandervogel*."

"The what?"

"Wandering Bird, it was like the Girl Scouts. Our flock leader was Frau Fischer. She lived in German Samoa on a copra plantation before the war, and was an expert in all matters nautical and tropical. I learned a lot of useful stuff."

"OK, then." Emilio tossed a line up from the skiff. "Tie this to the cleat on the bow. Then you can make us some coffee."

"Aye, aye, Captain."

* * *

Ella had a pot brewing in the galley about a half hour later when Emilio appeared. "Oh, you made some coffee. That was thoughtful."

"Uh . . . just following orders."

"What? Oh, sorry, forgot. I sent the brothers home. They can finish on the motors tomorrow."

"Eddie?"

"He lives on board, likes to keep an eye on things."

"What about you?"

"Staying here tonight. Have you seen the state room?" He started to walk toward the door, swayed and stumbled. Ella caught him.

"Let me help you. Lean on me." Together they made it into the state room. Emilio collapsed onto the bed. "This isn't good, Emilio. You're going to the doctor in the morning . . . Emilio?"

He lay there, face down. Her gentle shaking did not rouse him. She rolled him over onto his back. His mouth was slack on one side, drooling. "Emilio! Wake up!" He did not respond. She pinched his cheek. Nothing. "Eddie!" She ran up on deck. "Emilio needs help!"

Eddie was tying the skiff to a stern cleat. "What's wrong?"

"He's out cold, just fell into bed and won't say or do anything."

"Long day, must be bushed."

"No, it's not that. He hurt his head when that bomb went off today."

"Let me see." They both went below to the state room. Eddie checked Emilio's pulse, lifted his eyelids, and listened to his breathing. "You're right. I'll call an ambulance. There's a phone booth down the quay." He closed the door behind him.

She knelt beside the bed holding Emilio's hand, stroking his brow. "Please, please come back to us. Cindy will be very cross if you don't." She began crying. *"Verdammt! Ich kann jetzt nicht schwach sein!"*

She heard footfalls on the deck. Eddie's back, thank God. More steps and voices. The medics here already? "Eddie . . .?" She hesitated. Was that Spanish she heard? She got up, reached under her skirt and felt the holster strapped to her right thigh. The voices were getting louder; Eddie's was not one of them. They were in the cabin. Ella drew her pistol and moved to the hinge side of the state room door. She reached for the lock but the handle just then started to turn. She pressed herself back against the bulkhead. The door slowly swung in. Two men entered, in dark suits and hats. They paused when they saw Emilio. One approached the bed with a revolver in his hand. Ella brought her pistol up.

Above on deck two shots sounded. The man nearest the bed turned and saw Ella. She fired first hitting him in the chest. He dropped his gun, and fell to his knees. Ella threw herself against the door slamming it shut, fired at the other man, and missed. He got off one shot that hit the door. Ella fired twice more. The bullets struck him in the left arm and hip. He grunted, lurched about and fired again. But Ella dived to the deck and his shot went wide. She fired, hitting his forehead. Blood spurted from the wound. He fell on top of the first man who jerked and moaned.

The door burst open. Ella rolled over and took aim. It was Eddie holding a .45 caliber automatic. He glanced around the state room and checked the two intruders. One was dead, the other not quite. He took the wounded man's head in his hands and gave it a sharp twist. The man's eyes bulged. There was a loud snap.

"Emilio?" Eddie asked.

"They didn't touch him."

"He told me you could handle yourself." Eddie helped her up off the deck. "I wounded one porrista but he got away. I'll get rid of these two. The ambulance is on the way. You know what to do."

Ella nodded. "What did they want?"

"He didn't tell me, just another Havana run. You know how Emilio is, 'need to know' only. Señorita Cindy knows. Must be something to do with the bank that got bombed. He was acting very cagey back in Havana."

"I'll help with the bodies."

"No, Señorita Ella, you'll get blood on yourself. They can't see that. The police will be checking about the gunfire."

Eddie pocketed the loose guns, grabbed both bodies by their collars and dragged them up onto the afterdeck. He lifted them over the transom and dropped them into the skiff. Ella wondered what their names were, if anyone would miss them.

"*Buena suerte*," Emilio called as he rowed off.

Ella noticed a trail of blood. She ran back to the galley, put on an apron, grabbed some towels and mopped up across the cabin, up the stairs and on the deck. She dumped the bloody rags and apron into the fish well. Hearing the ambulance siren, she went back to the state room. She grabbed two blankets and spread them on the deck to conceal the blood stains, then hurried topside to meet the medics.

* * *

The hospital on Emma Street was only a few blocks away. Ella rode in the ambulance with Emilio. A lady doctor was waiting at the emergency entrance. She quickly checked Emilio's vital signs.

"How long has he been this way, miss?"

"He's been out about an hour. But he'd been acting odd since this afternoon, told me he'd fallen in the street and bumped his head. Said he felt sick and his head hurt."

"This bruise on his face?"

"He was sparring this morning with some guy and got hit. Knocked him down. Seemed OK afterwards, though."

"I'm going to X-ray his skull, should know something then." She waved to a pair of orderlies who transferred Emilio to a gurney and rushed him inside. "I'm Doctor Henderson." She held out her hand to Ella. They shook. "Names, please?"

"He's Emilio Ruz. I'm Ella Kaufmann. We just met yesterday."

"I see. His occupation?"

"He's a charter boat captain."

"Does he have any family in town?"

"He has a sister here. I came down with her for the holiday. Is there a phone I can use?"

"Yes, I'll show you."

They went inside the hospital where a nurse sat at a desk.

"Nurse Swanson, this young lady needs to make a phone call. Now Miss Kaufmann, I have to go attend to my patient. I'll let you know my diagnosis as soon as I have something." She leaned close and whispered, "There's blood on your leg."

"Thank you, Ma'am."

"I prefer Doctor." She turned and strode down the corridor.

Ella picked up the phone. "Sorry, I don't know the number. The Casa Marina?"

"That's 308, dearie."

"Thank you." She dialed. When the night clerk answered she asked for her room. After a minute he told her there was no answer and asked if she'd like to leave a message.

"Yes, please. It's for Miss Cindy Rattigan in room 206. Call the hospital . . ." she glanced at the nurse.

"The Marine Hospital."

"Yes, Cindy, please call the Marine Hospital immediately. From Ella. Thank you." She hung up.

"Nurse, is there a powder room I could use?"

"Yes, dearie, just up the hallway and on your right."

A short time later as Ella returned to the waiting room two policemen came through the front door. One spoke to Nurse Swanson, "We're investigating reports of a shooting down at the submarine basin.

Heard an ambulance just picked someone up there. Did it come back here?"

Ella retreated to the waiting area and took a seat. She picked up a magazine and started reading.

"A man was brought in a while ago, comatose. He's in X-ray now. Don't have any details."

"Was he shot?"

"The doctor didn't mention it."

"How about the drivers, are they around?"

"They're out on another call."

The other policeman nudged the first. "Joe, it was probably just some kids with firecrackers, let's go."

"OK. Nurse, have the doctor give the station a ring when he's free."

"Will do, and he's a she."

"Yeah, thanks." The policemen headed for the door.

"Night, boys."

Ella looked up and mouthed, *Thank you*. Nurse Swanson winked back.

An hour passed and Cindy had not called. Doctor Henderson returned with a clipboard in one hand. "Miss Kaufmann, please come with me."

"Is Emilio all right?"

"He's resting. I'll take you to him."

They entered a ward with several empty beds and one screened off. Behind the screen Emilio lay neatly tucked in. A bandage was around his right arm. A nurse was shaving his scalp. Ella winced at the sight. Doctor Henderson clipped an X-ray onto a light box attached to the wall. She switched it on. "This is Mr. Ruz's skull. This large bright area is a blood clot. You can see a small fracture here. The clot is being pinched between the bone and the tissue encasing the brain. The medical term is intracranial extradural hematoma. It's getting larger as arterial blood leaks into it. It's compressing Mr. Ruz's brain. Left untreated this will kill him. The only treatment is to open the skull, drain off the blood and cauterize the artery. We are fortunate to have a surgeon on call who is familiar with the procedure. He will be here in an hour. I will assist. We are prepping Mr. Ruz now. This is a very risky procedure with such a large clot. There may have already been irreversible brain damage. We will do everything possible to save him. Have you contacted his sister?"

"No . . . I can't . . . *Lieber Gott im Himmel!*" She shook and wept. The doctor helped her into a chair.

"In emergency cases it is not necessary to obtain consent. But his family should be prepared."

"I called our hotel, Cindy's not there. I don't know where she is. I'll call again." She began to stand up, but sank back, bent over.

"Does he have any other family, mother, father, other siblings?"

"His father lives in New York, his mom died when he was a baby. I think he has some people in Cuba. I don't know."

The doctor pulled up another chair and sat down beside Ella. She took her hands. "Miss Kaufmann . . . Ella dear, believe me, we will do everything for your friend. It would help if I knew exactly what happened to him. You said he fell in the street. Where, when?"

"I wasn't there. He told me it was this afternoon around three, in Havana, there was an explosion, a bomb, dynamite, terrorists, hit his head in the street, a nail in his arm. But he laughed and joked, he got us back to Key West. It was on the way back, he started to feel sick, vomited, headachy, he couldn't stand for long, had to sit. Then tonight he asked me to make coffee, but then forgot he did, then he collapsed. We just met yesterday, you see, Cindy wanted me to meet him, he had this trip to Havana planned, it was supposed to be fun, a lark. Then everything went bad. He's a dear, dear man, I like him very much. I'm so afraid what this will do to Cindy, she so adores him. And I can't find her!"

"How old are you, Ella?"

"Seventeen."

"Where are your parents?"

"Germany, I'm from Germany. I go to college with Cindy."

"What college, Ella?"

"Cornell in New York."

"Do you like it there?"

"Oh, very much. The campus is beautiful and the professors and students are so nice. Cindy got me into the debate club. I just want to go back there." She started crying again.

"Sorry, I was trying to cheer you up a little and just made you sadder."

Ella gave her a weepy smile. "I know. I do appreciate it, really."

"Doctor Wilson was chief surgeon at an Army hospital in France during the War. He treated many brain trauma cases like Mr. Ruz's. There's not a better man who could operate tonight. This will take several hours. Why don't you go back to your hotel and wait for Cindy? I'll call when we know the outcome. I'll get you a cab, OK?"

"No thank you. I need to stay. I can't leave him alone."

"He won't be. He'll be attended at all times."

"No, that's not it. I'm the closest thing to family he's got. He must be with someone who knows . . . loves him. That's important, don't you see?"

"All right, you can stay with him. But you'll have to wait outside the operating room."

"Thank you."

"That blood on your leg," Doctor Henderson gestured, "I see you cleaned it up. Your period?"

"No, it wasn't my blood."

Chapter 15

August 31, 1935 – Southernmost Charm

They stopped under the hotel's porte-cochère. Fred unloaded Cindy's bag, and tossed the keys to the valet. "Boy, we're going out again in an hour. There's a dollar in it if you clean off the bird shit."

The colored valet grinned back. "Sure thing, boss."

At the reception desk the clerk was busy with another couple. "Two nights in the wedding suite, I am sure you will be satisfied with the accommodations. Please sign here, sir."

Cindy nudged Fred in the ribs. "Newlyweds," she snickered, rolling her eyes. The young woman before them turned and smiled.

"Congratulations!" Fred offered his hand.

"Why, thank you!" They shook.

"I'm Fred and this is Cindy."

"I'm Gayle . . . Mrs. Ray Sheldon that is!" She giggled and blushed.

The man turned and put his arm around Gayle's waist. "Hi, I'm Mr. Sheldon, Ray that is. Not quite newlyweds, Labor Day is our one-week anniversary."

"How romantic! Hear that, Freddie?" She punched his ribs.

"Ouch! Take it easy, champ." Fred rubbed his side. "Pleased to meet you, Ray." They shook hands. "Say . . . it's late and after checking in we were going out to eat. If you don't have any other plans, would you like to join us?"

"Well, thanks. We were looking for a restaurant driving through town. You know one open at this hour?"

Cindy chimed in. "Delmonico's nice, open late and the food is good."

"Sounds swell. Gayle?" Ray asked.

"Oh, I'd love that! I do need to freshen up first. We were on the ferry all day, seems like. Left Matecumbe at two and just now getting here."

"I always take the train. Arrived yesterday in time for a swim and got too much sun."

"Well then, meet down here in about an hour?" Fred suggested.

"Will that be OK, honey?" asked Ray.

"Perfect, and thank you for the invitation."

Cindy watched the Sheldons start up the staircase. "Nice couple. You were mighty sociable there, Freddie. Something I don't know?"

"I know him, doesn't know me, though. Give me some of your cash. It would look funny if you paid at the restaurant."

"You realize this is just play acting, don't ya? Don't get used to it."

"Emilio said to be careful. Our Cuban friends might be watching."

"Did he, really? That's not like him. Must be starting to trust you." She took his hand.

"Why not? You do." Fred winked.

"So, check in already. I'm getting randy again. Newlyweds!"

When Cindy asked the clerk for her room key, he handed it to her with a telegram. She quickly read it, then waited for Fred to check in. The clerk called the porter for her bag. He took it up the stairs to her room. Cindy and Fred followed a few steps behind.

"Nothing serious I hope."

"Just my father asking if I'm having fun."

"Are you?"

"Let's see, I've been strangled, shot at, and bombed. This weekend's going about how I expected." She kissed him.

They came to Cindy's room. She unlocked it and the porter placed the bag inside. He hesitated a moment. Fred handed him a fiver. The porter's eyes went wide, "Gee, thank you sir, thank you!" Fred pressed his index finger to his lips, and winked. The porter nodded and closed the door as he left.

"Does your pop know about me?" Fred asked.

"Of course not! No need to know. He's flying down here Monday. You'll be long gone by then, the ferry sails at 8 AM. I'll drive you."

"I was kinda thinking of going AWOL."

"Just the weekend, Freddie, that was the deal, three nights. Then you turn back into a pumpkin. Emilio won't mind if you keep the clothes. Now shut up and make love, stupid."

* * *

An hour later the two couples drove into town. Fred parked on Caroline Street and then they walked to Delmonico's at 218 Duval. On the way Gayle stopped at a news stand and bought some post cards. Ray picked up a copy of the Key West Citizen.

Above Delmonico's side door a sign hung, COLORED. A line of well-dressed Negro men and women waited. Fred, Cindy and the Sheldons entered through the front door marked, WHITE. The dining room was crowded but Fred placed a Lincoln in receptive hands and a table was quickly found. A radio show played over loud speakers, the musical stylings of Ray Noble and his Orchestra broadcast live from the fabulous Rainbow Room high atop New York's Rockefeller Center, what passed for the "live entertainment" advertised outside. After ordering drinks, they studied the menu.

"So, what's good here Cindy?" asked Ray.

"The turtle steaks, arroz con pollo, fresh caught fish, and of course Delmonico steaks," she replied.

"Don't let the price bother you, sport. This one's on me. Consider it a wedding gift."

"Gee, thank you! Isn't that nice Ray?"

"Thanks, but I can't accept. We just met, and you gave us a ride. Wouldn't be right. I'll pay."

"Now I couldn't allow that. I invited you, so you're my guests. Well, how about I pay for the drinks and pick up the tip?"

"Just the drinks, I'll give the tip."

"I don't drink. So, I'll leave the tip, it'll be bigger," Fred replied.

"Only if I pay for breakfast."

"Dunno, we're late risers."

"We have the honeymoon suite! I don't think you'll beat us down stairs."

"Oh, Ray!" Gayle giggled.

"Peachy. Nine thirty, then?"

"OK, pal."

"Enough already. Men! Always trying to impress with the size of their wallets. Well, I'm starved. We were on a boat most of the day, too."

"Deep sea fishing?" Ray asked.

"Oh, no. Round trip to Havana," Cindy answered.

"Havana! How magical! I've always wanted to go. Can we, Ray, please?"

"Not this time, honey," Ray took Gayle's hand. "Maybe I can swing it this fall. So, just a day trip, huh? Why'd you come back so soon?"

"Ha!" Fred guffawed. "People keep asking that. Haven't you heard? There's a storm a brewin'. The skipper heard about it in Havana and said we had to get home quick and batten down the hatches. He didn't want to get caught in Cuba, rough crowd down there."

"Charter?" asked Ray.

"Yeah, motor yacht."

"Must have cost a pretty penny."

"Nothing I can't afford."

Cindy kicked Fred under the table.

Ray looked at the paper he'd bought, "Here it is on the front page: Storm reported to eastward of Bahama Islands. If disturbance continues on its present course, it will go south of Florida mainland. That means the Keys might get hit."

"Yeah, Coast Guard guy said it could hit Key West hard on Monday, seems we're on the bad side. Didn't know storms had sides, good or bad. Sure spoiled our holiday weekend. We had big plans for Havana tonight. And the skipper won't even take us out fishing tomorrow."

"Ray honey, does that mean we'll have to go back?"

"Well, not before morning, anyway. I'll give the weather bureau a call when we get back to the hotel."

"So, Ray, you work around here?" Fred asked.

"On Matecumbe, veterans camp superintendent."

Cindy looked up from the menu. "Read about those places. Pretty sketchy bunch from what I hear, shell shocked, whiskey shocked, depression shocked psychopaths."

"It's true, they're terrible! Ray doesn't let me anywhere near them. We live in the Hotel Matecumbe miles from the camps. Drove here so we wouldn't have to sit next to them on the train. Ray says the railway should make them ride in a separate car, like coloreds."

"So where would they stick Negro vets? In a box car?" Cindy smiled sweetly.

"Not my problem. My camps are white-only."

Fred rearranged his silver ware. "Those vets, bad lot, eh, Ray?"

"Shiftless lowlifes. Hardly get any work out of them. Pay them a dollar a day and they buy ten beers, money that should be sent home to their families. I have a clerk who volunteered to manage the vet trust fund, saves their money for them at a bank in Homestead. You've met him, Gayle, Poock, Canadian guy. I've checked his books, keeps them like some Jew banker, and you know what? Barely 150 men have signed up with him. 150 out of near 700! Well, the free-loading will be over soon. Camps shut down in November."

"Where will they go?" Cindy asked.

"Well, the few who can and want to work will get jobs in the CCC, the others a one-way ticket home, if they even have one."

Fred looked up from his menu. "Do you have any prospects?"

"Probably another state job. Know some folks. What's your business, if you don't mind me asking?"

"Import, export."

"Must pay well."

The sound of raucous laughter came through the wall.

"The coloreds seem to be enjoying themselves." Cindy smiled.

Ray sneered. "They shouldn't allow blacks in a restaurant for whites."

"There's a divider, 'separate but equal'. It's the law, you know."

"Not separate enough and too equal by half."

Cindy leaned back in her seat and glared at Ray. "Must be tough going through life hating all those people."

"Cindy, be nice. She's a New Yorker," Fred explained helpfully.

"New York City? Gosh."

"New York's alright for a visit . . ." began Ray.

". . . but I wouldn't want to live there!" Fred laughed.

Cindy sat up straight. "Well, I don't know about that. There's Ray Noble for sure, Broadway, Wall Street, night clubs, the Empire State Building, Mayor LaGuardia, the Yankees, Giants and Dodgers! We've got Irish, Chinese, Italians, Russians, Poles, Germans and a whole bunch of Jews. Nazis and Reds scuffling in the streets, cops beating them with clubs, movie stars, gangsters and millionaires. And, you'll like this Ray, you can go uptown where Harlem sits, puttin' on the Ritz. More uppity Negroes than you can shake a noose at."

"Cocky, huh? That's what happens when you let them forget their place. The problem with you Yankees is you don't know your darkies."

"And how many do you . . ."

"Here come our drinks!" interrupted Fred,

"Cindy, would I be too nosy if I asked about how you two met?"

Cindy smiled at Gayle. "Well, now, it was love at first sight, swept me right off my feet." She kissed Fred's cheek. "He knows how to treat a lady. How about Ray, does he keep you happy?

"Cindy, isn't this powder room talk? You're embarrassing us men folk."

"Well, I'd like to hear what Gayle thinks. Do I make you happy?"

"Oh, Ray, now you're making me blush. I've never been happier."

He squeezed her hand.

Gayle smiled back at Cindy. "How long have you and Fred been married?"

"Infatuated, yes, blissfully, crazily infatuated. But married? Not ready for that gig, sister. I'm free, white and 21, at least until my birthday. Now Freddie and me, it's only a weekend fling. We met yesterday, all very physical, sex, you know. Kind of a test drive for laughs and giggles, with no intent to buy."

Gayle stared, open-mouthed.

"Nothing against marriage, honey. It's all right for a girl to marry a model husband, but she should be sure he's a working model."

"That's my girl!" Fred gave Cindy a hug. "So, Ray, what happens if that storm hits?"

"Well, if it becomes a hurricane, we evacuate. The camps sit on the beach, not safe at all. We'll bring all those jokers back to the mainland. Pity the town where they end up. We have an agreement with the railway, $335 for a special train."

"But Ray, we wouldn't have to go on the train with all those awful men, would we?"

"Oh no, dear, one of my staff will drive you. I'll have to take the train to see the vets all make it. Glad it's not my decision. Hate to have it come out of my pay for guessing wrong!"

"Really, they'd do that? People say it's best to err on the side of caution."

"Well, Cindy, those people don't have to meet production goals. You won't get any work done and waste a lot of money trying to be too safe. You can't shut everything down and then have nothing happen. They'd say you're a bad manager, irresponsible, overreacting."

"So how much warning do you think you'll get?" asked Fred.

"Well, the paper says it's like 500 miles away, and the center moves at about 10 miles per hour; that's 50 hours, so it would be Monday at the earliest before we felt it. And most hurricanes stay out to sea. Not a problem. I've been through plenty of storms. Just need to watch your barometer. The faster it drops the closer it is."

Gayle sighed. "Can we talk about something besides the weather?"

"Politics, religion?" Cindy grinned.

Fred glanced at the ceiling. "Better not."

"So, what do you do, Miss Cindy?" Ray asked, "I mean before you met Fred, that is."

"Little me? I'm a college girl. It's back to school in two weeks."

"Oh, my. I barely finished high school."

"Nothing wrong with that, sister. Be proud! I'm just lucky my dad could afford it. Most of the girls are only there to find a rich husband. I'm looking for a profession."

"And what might that be, young lady? Seems you already have one."

"We live in interesting times, Ray. I want to write about them. That's something else a woman can do and get paid for."

"Here comes the food, and about time!" Fred exclaimed.

They were all hungry and said little as they dived in. The music stopped. *"We interrupt this broadcast to bring you a special advisory direct from the Weather Bureau Office in Jacksonville, Florida . . . Saturday August 31, 1935, 9:30 p.m. The tropical disturbance is central tonight near or over the northern end of Long Island Bahamas moving rather slowly west-northwestward attended by strong shifting winds and squalls over a considerable area and probably gale force near center. Indications center will reach vicinity of Andros Island early Sunday. Northeast Storm Warnings ordered Fort Pierce to Miami, Florida. We now return to our scheduled broadcast."*

Gayle looked at Ray. "Fort Pierce to Miami? Does that mean Matecumbe, too?"

"Yes, honey, everything from Miami to Key West. But not a hurricane, nothing to be concerned about. But I think I'd better not wait to make that call. After dinner, we'll get a cab back to the hotel, Fred."

"Wouldn't think of it, we'll take my car."

* * *

On the drive back to the hotel, Gayle and Cindy sat in the back seat ranking their favorite movie stars, the men up front talking baseball. When they arrived, Fred stopped in the driveway, and everyone got out.

"Thanks for the wonderful evening," Gayle gushed, giving Fred and Cindy big hugs.

Ray shook Fred's hand. "If the weather forecast improves, maybe we'll find something to do together. We're planning on staying until Monday."

"Sounds good, there's a lot to do in this town," Fred replied.

Ray tipped his hat to Cindy. She turned away. He shrugged and left with Gayle. Cindy returned to the car and sat in the driver's seat. Fred got in beside her.

"I was thinking about Emilio. We should check with him before going back to the hotel. He was pretty sick on the boat."

"Just seasick, besides Dixie's there to nurse him. She's sweet on him." Fred grinned.

"Oh, yeah! But I won't be comfortable until I see how Emilio is doing."

"OK, then."

Chapter 16

August 31 - September 1, 1935 – Late Night

The basin was quiet except for the lap of water against the quay wall. The pier was empty. "Hey! Emilio, Ella . . . Eddie, anyone home?" Cindy called. There was no answer. She jumped aboard; Fred close behind. Seeing nobody topside they went below and Cindy turned on the electric lights. They searched the cabin. In the galley a coffee pot sat on the burner. She touched it and then lifted the lid. "Cold coffee. Want some?"

"No thanks," Fred replied. He opened the door to the stateroom and entered. Cindy followed. "Look different?" he asked.

"Bunk's messed up, blankets on the floor and . . . what's this?" Cindy touched a hole on the door. She stuck her little finger in it. "It goes right through." She shut the door and then looked through the hole. On the far cabin bulkhead, directly opposite was a small patch of splintered wood. She opened the door, walked over and examined the spot. "Another hole, Fred and there's something inside." She found a filleting knife in the galley and poked the tip in the hole. "I think I can work it out. Here it comes. Take a look, Fred." She handed him a slug.

He rolled it between his fingers and held it up to the light. ".38. Anyone pack a revolver you know of?"

"Emilio and Eddie carry .45's."

"Ella?"

"She has a 9mm, just like mine," Cindy answered.

Fred nodded and went back to the cabin. He lifted a blanket from off the deck. "Look here, blood underneath."

"Shit! We thought the Cubans would have followed us, not gone for the boat. So where is everybody? I can't believe they could have been taken."

"Not with all that firepower, maybe they went somewhere safer. Something else missing . . . that Coast Guard bag."

"Is it important?"

"Don't know."

"Why don't you check the storage lockers? I'll look around topside again."

Starting at the stern, Cindy moved deliberately along the transom, gunwales and side rails, running her hand across the surfaces. Under the bow line where it was tied to a cleat, she felt something odd. She looked closer. It was a length of fishing line knotted tight. It was no ordinary line. Emilio used 36-thread for marlin and this felt the same. Barely visible in the dim light the other end disappeared into the water. She pulled and could move it slightly from side to side but not upward. Trying again with both hands she could raise it only an inch or so. The line began to cut into her fingers and she let go.

"Find anything?" called Fred from the cockpit.

"Nothing."

"Well, the two Lewis guns are still in their cases. Need cleaning."

Cindy climbed back onto the pier and turned to Fred. "Someone might be hurt. Let's go check at the hospital."

* * *

"We're looking for someone who might have been injured tonight."

"We always get a bunch on Saturdays. Got a name, dearie?" asked the nurse.

"Well, there's a Mr. Ruz."

"Just a sec." The nurse checked a register. "Yes, Emilio Ruz was admitted. You know him?"

Cindy grabbed Fred's hand and squeezed hard. "He's my brother. Can I see him?"

"He's in surgery now. A girl came in with him. She's waiting outside the operating room. I'll take you to her, she'll explain."

They found Ella dozing on a bench. Cindy gently shook her shoulder. "Hey, wake up. It's me."

Ella opened her eyes and started. "Oh, Cindy! I called the hotel but you weren't there." She stood up and asked the nurse, "Is the operation still going on?"

"I'll check," the nurse entered the operating room. She returned a minute later. "Another hour the doctor said. It's going well."

Cindy and Ella sat down together and hugged. "We just came from the boat, found a bullet hole and blood on the floor. Tell us what happened. Was it the Cubans?" Cindy asked.

"I think so, but they didn't hurt Emilio. Eddie and I took care of them. It was that explosion in Havana, it injured Emilio's brain. There's a blood clot. The doctors are fixing it."

"Eddie wasn't on the boat, Dixie. Do you know where he went?" asked Fred.

"No idea, wherever he dumps bodies I guess."

Fred leaned close to the girls. "Jeez, this is getting deep and I seem to be the only one without a gun. Maybe we should just get out of town now and keep driving."

"I'm not leaving Emilio. Why don't you go get a bite? Fred will drive you, Ella. Then back to the hotel to sleep. I'll leave a message with the desk clerk if anything changes."

"I know an all-night burger stand."

Ella took Cindy's hand. "The police were here a few hours ago, there was a report about a shooting at the basin. They asked if the ambulance had brought anyone in from there. The nurse didn't tell them anything. But they might come back. You can trust the lady doctor. She's all business but nice. Just be sure to call her Doctor Henderson." She kissed Cindy's cheek and left with Fred.

* * *

Cindy sat staring at the operating room door for what seemed like hours. It entered her dreams. *Out walks Emilio, all hale and hearty, cracking jokes, a small white Band-Aid on his forehead. He pinches the nurse's butt, or was it the nice lady doctor's? He dances a few steps and came to her. They kiss. Someone is speaking.* When she opened her eyes a woman in a stained white gown stood before her. "Miss Rattigan? I . . . Miss Rattigan, are you awake?"

Cindy shook her head. "Where is Emilio? I was just . . . Sorry I must have fallen asleep. What time is it?"

"Five-thirty in the morning. Come with me and you can see your brother."

"Is he alright . . . Doctor . . . Henderson?"

"He's stable, but there were complications during the operation. When he wakes up, we'll be able to perform some tests and determine if there is any lasting impairment. There was another condition I thought it best not to discuss with Miss Kaufmann, seeing as she just met your brother."

"Yes, what?"

Henderson sat down beside Cindy. "I'll be clinical, he underwent a radical orchiectomy. It was done violently, maybe three or four years ago, perhaps by an animal, like a large dog. It's a miracle he didn't bleed out."

"Radical what? Just tell me!"

"He was castrated."

* * *

The night clerk gave Fred his key and handed Ella a telegram. "This came in for you late last night, miss."

She opened the envelope and made a face. Fred noticed something was up. "Everything OK, Dixie?"

"Nothing important. I need to get some sleep." Ella took her room key from the clerk.

They climbed the stairs and walked to her room. He stopped Ella from entering after she unlocked the door. "I'll go in first."

Ella waited in the hall while Fred searched inside. "All clear. We have to be extra careful, now that the Cubans have been bloodied."

Fred picked up Cindy's bag and set it on her bed. "Let's see if anything is missing." He released the straps and spread the bag open. "More rum. Take a look, all there? You saw Cindy pack it."

"Well, we bought 12 in Havana, broke 3 in the street, so there should be 9."

Fred counted. "Eight. Check the closet and drawers for anything out of place."

"Wait, there're some men's clothes. How thoughtful of Cindy. She wants you to look the part even in Key West." She handed them to Fred.

"She picked me back in Islamorada because I was Emilio's size, right?"

"I didn't catch on until I met him, but she also liked that you weren't drunk and she thought you were kinda sweet . . . for a vet."

"Thanks, she told me I could keep what I'm wearing. So, our visitors liberated a bottle of rum. What were they really looking for, Dixie? It's about time you came clean."

"Eddie said Cindy knows. What I know is that bag was empty on the way to Havana. When Emilio returned from the bank it was heavy. He was disguised as you when the bomb exploded."

"So that's why Menendez wanted to see inside, must be money and a lot."

"I think whatever it was, it's still on the boat, but I'm really too tired to care now."

"OK, we'll check later. So, sleep tight, and don't let the bed bugs bite."

"What?"

"You know . . . oh, never mind, just an expression. This is a very clean hotel." He kissed her on the cheek and left.

Ella shook her head and locked the door. She sat on the edge of her bed and read the telegram again:

ELLA
WILL ARRIVE KEY WEST MONDAY MORNING STOP CAN NOT WAIT TO SEE YOU RENARD

Chapter 17

Manhattan Weekend

Saturday, June 15, 1935 — They got off the Lehigh Valley train at Pennsylvania Station and took a cab to the apartment at 815 Park Avenue. There were three letters waiting for Ella in the pewter dish beside the door. The ones from her boyfriend and parents she read quickly. The third was addressed to "Miss Ella Kaufmann. C/O Mr. Rattigan," but it bore no return address and was postmarked from the Bronx. She told Cindy she needed to freshen up, it had been a long, hot day on the train from Ithaca, and took the letters into her room.

Held before the bare bulb of the lamp on the side table the mystery envelope was opaque, nothing visible inside. There was no sign of staining, wrinkling or tearing. The handwritten address was unmarred. With a letter opener she sliced across the top, careful not to damage the contents. She removed a folded sheet. Holding it close to the lamp she examined the edges. There, across the open edge she found a single strand of fine white hair. The seal was intact. She unfolded the sheet and read,

Dear Ella,
Welcome back! Do you remember the diner at 9th and 57th? Coffee and cake.
C. H. F.

There was a diner at 9th Avenue and 57th Street but the rendezvous would be at another address. The alphabetical sequence of the initials could raise or lower the numbers. A middle initial gave a sign change or multiple, or at times something even simpler. It wasn't precise, what with Manhattan's complex street grid and multitude of eateries it wasn't intended to be. Her tourist map was already starting to split at the folds, time for a new one. Ella tried a couple of code variations with no matches, then an obvious one. *Kaffee und kuchen* meant Sunday at 3. What did he want this time? It was summer break.

* * *

Sunday, June 16, 1935 — Ella didn't get in until 3 a.m. from her date. Waking around ten, she opened the small gift box on the bedside table. Inside was a gold necklace. It gleamed in the sunlight. She removed her chemise and sat before the dressing table mirror, fastening the necklace so the pendent lay between her breasts. It burned into her skin. Ella took it off and replaced it with the hamsa.

Abby prepared a light brunch for Ella. Cindy was out on some errand. Daniel had gone to the office. Ella skimmed through the Herald Tribune for any news about home and found a report on the marvelous new Autobahnen. It was Father's Day, had Cindy remembered? Perhaps they would all go out tonight.

Abby sat down beside her with a cup of mocha java. "I heard you come in last night. You know Ella, if you ever need someone to talk to about . . . you know, private matters, I'm here and can keep a secret."

"I'm a big girl. I know how to take care of myself."

"Just the same, accidents happen, particularly in this town. I've been around the block a few times. I know a thing or two . . . or three. Guys will say anything to get what they want, until they knock you up and then nothing. There're a lotta bums like that. Listen Ella, if you ever need help, I've been there."

"Just because I wear my hair like a school girl, I'm no ingénue. At least I know enough not to use Pepsi-Cola or Lysol, for goodness sake! You wouldn't believe what the girls at college do."

"Uh . . ."

"Abby, I'm sorry. I appreciate the offer. We're friends, right?"

"Oh, sure. It's just . . . so what do German girls use?"

* * *

About one o'clock Ella left the apartment. She looked chic in a white silk blouse, sleek khaki slacks, black patent leather belt, sandals, and sunglasses, hair coiled around her head in a milkmaid braid, partly concealed under a wide brimmed Panama. Her lips were crimsoned, and a glint of gold shown at her collar.

She took the Lexington Avenue Line down to Grand Central, then crosstown to Times Square. She circled the block twice, stopping at the Walgreen Drugstore, sipped a chocolate soda very carefully, and then doubled back to 2nd Avenue and the uptown El. She found a seat beside an open window and enjoyed the breeze. Along the way she exchanged looks with second floor apartment dwellers, many relaxing on their fire escapes.

She got off one stop past and strolled the six blocks back to East 86th, pausing frequently to window shop. Yorkville appeared so different in daytime. If not Munich then Stuttgart, she thought. So clean! Sidewalks and stoops washed, glass polished, even the gutters were swept. But the flower boxes! They were in nearly every window, geraniums and nasturtiums in bloom. She smiled thinking of the pride Mutti had in her flowers.

She arrived early. Just up the street a small crowd had gathered around a delicatessen entrance. Workmen were preparing to replace the storefront window. The people were staring at a Star of David and some words crudely scratched in the glass: Das ist ein Jude! An older couple stood back a little way, his arm tight around her waist. She was crying. A detective was taking their statements. Ella continued down the street, stopped before a closed store front and regarded her reflection in the glass. She put on the other necklace. The gold pendant glittered boldly. A slight adjustment of her blouse, a little more décolletage, just so.

At precisely three o'clock she stood outside the Café Hindenburg at 220 East 86th Street. A notice was pasted to the door: Der Hitlergruß, bitte! Inside, the café's walls were decorated with tourist posters of the Rhine, the Alps, the Brandenburg Gate, ample Bürgermeisters with raised steins, clean limbed Nordic youth in lederhosen and dirndls, the recumbent Graf Zeppelin lazing above Lady Liberty, and glamorous, impossibly slender ocean liners.

Centered high on the wall behind the bar, the Stars and Stripes hung from a short staff. It was flanked by two other flags mounted flat: the red, white and black German Imperial Tricolor and the Nazi Party Swastika. Below this patriotic display were two large framed photographs. There was the old Generalfeldmarschall himself in full regalia, still draped in black crepe. Beside it was one of the Führer, in heroic pose, wreathed in fresh flowers.

On a small stage near the bar three musicians performed on accordion, tuba and clarinet. The song they played was new to Ella. It was catchy and, on the chorus, everyone joined in: *In München steht ein Hofbräuhaus: Eins, zwei, g'suffa!*

The café was filled with happy couples, entire families, grandparents to babies, all very *gemutlich*. Several merchant marine sailors had pushed two tables together in the center of the room. They were enjoying themselves hugely, downing drafts in time with the song. Their apparent leader wore a steward's uniform. He was the only mildly sober one. The sailors noticed her too and were interested, ogling her and exchanging ribald comments.

In a booth facing the door, a pudgy, balding man wearing round tortoise-shell glasses stood up. In a dark wool suit, vest, wing collar and silk necktie, he motioned to the bench seat opposite his. "My, you are looking fit! Please take a seat." His eyes fixed on her necklace. He smiled. "Excellent! Where did you . . .?"

"It's a gift, Iggy. You're not the only Nazi I know. I thought it would fit in here." She sat.

"Yes, indeed. You're a very good fit. The *käsekuchen* here is also very good. May I order you some?"

"No, thank you. Just tea, please."

"A small bite, then. You could change your mind. They make it different." He neatly sliced off a piece from the untouched side and using a clean fork held it out to her. "Go on, it's really delicious." She leaned forward and took it off the fork with her teeth.

Geshmeckt?"

"A bit too rich."

"Perhaps something else? Oh, I am sorry for disturbing your vacation but you have an urgent assignment."

"I have a job."

"You're not doing it now. Besides you are uniquely qualified for this one. Shouldn't take you long, just a change of accessories my little chameleon."

"What is it?"

"That's better. What would you like, then?"

"The apple pie and tea."

"Waitress! Could you please bring an apple pie and tea for the young lady? With a scoop of vanilla ice cream."

"You can have the ice cream."

"We can share if you like. What you will do is give me a name. Simple, yes? He's a seaman on the SS Manhattan. He's been smuggling seditious rubbish into Hamburg."

"I made the crossing on the Manhattan last year."

"I know. It may help. He's a Red, *natürlich*."

"How long do I have?"

"She sails on the 19th from Pier 61 on West 20th Street."

"That's Wednesday. It arrives when?"

"The 27th, there's a bonus for early delivery."

"Expenses?"

He removed an envelope from the inside pocket of his jacket and slid it across the table to her. "That should cover everything, plus cab fare." She slipped it into her purse.

"What will they do with him?"

"Ella! What happens to Communists in the Reich?"

"But he's an American, right?"

"They will not protest too much."

Her order arrived. She nibbled on the pie. "You're right, of course. They value good relations with the New Germany. What's some radical?"

"Precisely! *Morgen die ganze Welt.*" He reached across and took a spoonful of ice cream. "And perhaps a different coiffure for this assignment? You do have a certain look."

She removed her hat. "More or less Aryan? Should I go blonde?"

"Oh, no! Keep it dark. It becomes you. Can you imagine Him blonde? Hah!"

"And the drop?"

"We needn't be so melodramatic." He passed her a matchbook from the café. "Call this number, Regent 4-9258. Ask for Mr. Irwin Jones."

"Is that all?"

"This assignment may require some intimacy . . . I am a doctor of women's medicine, you may recall."

"So?"

"If you should find yourself in need of any feminine hygiene services, I would be pleased to provide them, gratis."

"I'm sure you would. But you see, I have no need. I must be going."

"So soon? I thought we could chat a while about college life. How are things with your *jüdischer Physiker*?"

"It's all in my report."

"I read it. Quite comprehensive I believe, but don't understand a word of it. Perhaps your information was not garnered solely from his classroom lectures? And unmarried, I understand."

"I have to get back to the apartment, I cannot stay, I must be going." She stood.

"Well, then." He got up reluctantly, took her hand and kissed it. "À bientôt ma chérie."

She straightened, raised her right arm stiffly and angled above eye level, hand extended. "Heil Hitler!" She spoke perhaps too loudly. Heads turned. There were smiles and nods.

Iggy snapped to attention, clicking his heels, "Sieg Heil, Fraulein!"

As Ella strode by, the sailors came unsteadily to their feet and saluted her with their own sloppy Heils! She didn't stop or turn but marched to the door, back straight, shoulders back, eyes front, chin up, her right arm raised, bent back at the elbow, palm up and level over the shoulder. The recognition was immediate and for a moment everyone stared in disbelief. Her imitation of the Führer came dangerously close to mockery, but then the laughter began, timidly at first as if seeking affirmation then erupting across the café. Even the sailors joined in. It died out, however, when the steward began to sing in a strong clear baritone, *"Die Fahne hoch! Die Reihen fest geschlossen! SA marschiert mit ruhig festem Schritt!"* The musicians picked up the tune. There was no hesitation this time, even those who didn't know the words joined in with whatever sounded close. They sang nearly through the second verse before the sailors began reaching for their seidels.

* * *

Doctor Ignatz Griebl, former president of the Friends of the New Germany, removed his glasses and cleaned the lenses with a handkerchief. He shook his head. *Just a year in the States. A pretty girl can get away with a lot. There is no doubt she'll deliver that name on time. Imagine if I were her target! Is there a secret I would not betray?*

Glancing at his pocket watch he grunted, 40 minutes until his next agent arrived. He wound the stem. *Willy is such a bore.* He pulled the dish of apple pie to his side of the table.

* * *

Walking back up East 86th Ella paused to remove her necklace. In Times Square she bought copies of the Daily Worker, and the Sunday Post to wrap the Worker in. One more stop before returning to the apartment. It was on 5th Avenue. She hailed a taxi.

The cab stopped outside Mr. Julian's Salon. She paused for a moment on the sidewalk and fingered her hair. Finally, she sighed and walked inside. It was crowded. Several ladies were having their hair done by girls in white smocks. A slender, pomaded man with a William Powell mustache, wearing a white dinner jacket, black flamenco trousers, a pink carnation and lavender ascot was acting out some story. "So, he runs home, goes right to the bedroom, throws open the door, takes one look inside and says, Oh, you nasty man! Hyuck, hyuck, hyuck!" Everyone laughed hilariously except Ella. He noticed and studied her with the shrewd gaze of a casting director. "Should I tell it again?" he inquired pleasantly.

Ella smiled shyly. "I'm so sorry I missed it."

He nodded. "Remove your hat, my dear." She did so. He circled Ella like some feral cat, and then stood still for a moment, regarding her with his chin between thumb and forefinger. "Very. . . quaint. So how may I help you?"

"I'd like my hair cut like Lulu."

He frowned, "Lulu?"

Ella looked around. On the wall was a collection of celebrity photographs. She pointed to one.

"Ah, the Louise! It's been years. May I?" Ella nodded. He unpinned her braids; they uncoiled down to her waist. He felt her hair, and considered. Suddenly he clapped his hands. Startled, everyone in the salon looked up. "Yes," he exclaimed, "Mr. Julian will do this! Himself!"

He seated Ella in the one vacant chair, in the center of the salon. "You've made a very smart choice, young lady." Mr. Julian spoke in a voice loud enough for all to hear. Everyone was very attentive. He began combing out her hair. "To be truly chic a woman must have a chic hairstyle, so even totally nude she will still be chic. *N'est-ce pas*?" He gave a knowing wink. His audience tittered. "Most American bobs lack refinement," he explained making his first cut. One of Ella's long tresses fell to the floor. A matron festooned with curlers brought her hand to her mouth and gasped, "Dear me!"

"In the hands of a lesser coiffeur a vulgar, heavy look results, like a steel helmet! Boyish yet ineffably feminine is the goal, neither Buster Brown nor Jeanne d'Arc. The true artiste must work a cinematic collaboration: Moore in front, Negri on the sides, Vidor in the back." He trimmed her bangs to a line above her eyebrows, shaped the sides in points at the cheekbones, cut it short in back and trimmed the neckline into a delicate fringe. It was marvelous. Mr. Julian kissed her cheek when he finished and presented her, "The Louise Brooks!" The clients and staff applauded. He bowed. She curtsied. "And mademoiselle, please, no hat for the season. It would be *un grand dommage* to conceal such artistry." Before permitting her to leave he extracted a promise to return every two weeks for a trim. "It won't be just you traipsing around Manhattan, but also the reputation of Mr. Julian! That will be six dollars with the 15% discount."

When Ella returned to the apartment, Cindy was in the parlor reading a magazine. "I have a little surprise."

Cindy looked up, her eyes went wide, and screamed, "Oh my God!"

"Watch this!" Ella spun around quicky. Her hair flew all over. But the instant she stopped every strand fell back perfectly in place.

Cindy took both her hands and gushed. "Gosh, you're beautiful!"

Ella tilted her head and winked, "Boop-boop-be-doop!"
* * *

Daniel Rattigan's gaze kept returning to Ella during dinner. Finally, he laughed. "I considered asking Louise to join us tonight . . ." He let it hang there for a moment. Abby, Ella and Cindy giggled. "I'm sure she would have been flattered. When I see her again, I'll ask where she gets her hair done. Ella, do you think that would be too personal a question?"

"Of course not, ladies ask each other that all the time. It's taken as a compliment. Now if a handsome gentleman asks, she'll likely swoon."

"Swoon, is it? Well, I'll just have to give it a go then. But what will your parents say? They sent me a school girl in braids and now you're a flapper."

"Mother will love it, she's a big fan of Miss Brooks. Father . . . I don't know. He still thinks of me as his little girl."

Daniel smiled. "Oh, he'll come around. I know him pretty well." He took a drink of wine, emptying his glass. He poured himself another and cleared his throat. "Did your father ever tell you how we met?"

"No, not much . . . during the war, wasn't it? He never talks about the war."

"Neither do you, Daddy."

"Things happened that I'd rather not remember." He turned to Ella, "Imagine your father feels the same. The day we met, November 11th, he saved a life, an American's life. I thanked him."

Abby's eyes glistened. "Tell me."

He took Abby's hand and squeezed it. "It was the day I received the telegram about Emmeline. It broke me. What monstrous joke would take her life and leave me untouched at the front where millions died? I had the crazy idea that somehow my death would reset the account, and bring my darling back. I resolved to die somehow that morning. Jack, my Sergeant Major, had read the telegram. He knew what I was thinking. Jack reminded me that I still had my son and daughter, and that I could not make them orphans. He said when a mother passes, the father must love his children twice as much. It was my duty to live for them. I owe Jack my life."

The girls sat very still.

"But men did die that day, all my boys. None of them should have died. It was just a raid, reconnoiter the German positions opposite us, and quickly return to our lines. But a raid is still war, men die. I sent 20 brave young Americans across the river, and 12 were killed before the ceasefire at 11 o'clock. I went to every one of them, knelt and begged their forgiveness. And the other 8 were all wounded. One had made it all the way into the German trenches. He was bleeding badly, his leg broken but he still took out a machine gun nest, single-handed. Then he passed out. The Germans were about to bayonet him when their captain arrived. He stopped them."

"I went to the sector where it happened. An officer was talking with his soldiers. It seemed outlandish that they were standing atop the parapet in full view. Two hours before they all would have been shot dead standing like that. I shouted and waved my arms at the officer. He came over and saluted. He said he'd already told everything to the American captain. His English was better than my German. Yes, I replied, but why did you do it?"

"He told me the American was deaf, hadn't heard the cease fire whistles, that too many men had already died and this one was just a boy. 'My orders were to observe the ceasefire, regardless,' he said. Josef was happy the war was over, so now he could see his wife and baby daughter. He had missed your first birthday, Ella. I told him about you, Cindy. He said our daughters must meet and become best friends. We shook on it. He asked about my wife. I just stood there. He put his hand on my shoulder and said quietly, I understand, Kamerade."

Now everyone was crying. Abby held Daniel's hand, Cindy got up and hugged him. Ella sobbed, "Papi never told me!"

Daniel dried his eyes with a napkin. "I think we should raise a glass to a mensch this Father's Day, Josef Kaufmann."

They all stood and drank a toast.

"And what became of the soldier?" Abby asked.

"He came home."

Chapter 18

Monday, June 17, 1935 – On the Job

Today she took the most direct route, the Interborough express to 14th Street, not caring if anyone followed. It was where they'd expect her to go. A short walk and she was at the Headquarters of the Communist Party of the United States. Next store was a smoky canteen, crowded at a quarter to eight with white-collar Reds steeling themselves for a long day of agitational propaganda. She unfastened the top three buttons of her blouse and with Saturday's Daily Worker tucked under her arm stepped inside. She bought a cup of coffee and a doughnut.

On the wall hung a huge portrait of Comrade Stalin, regarding the vanguard of the proletariat with a Mona Lisa smile. She found an empty chair at a table where two men sat, mid-twenties she guessed. One was white, the other Negro. The ash tray between them was filled. They were debating some fine point of dialectical materialism.

"Louis in 6, by a knock-out."

"I think it will go the distance. Primo has the reach."

"Bet Braddock could take them both."

"Is this seat taken?"

The men looked up, and did a double take. Ella couldn't help but laugh. "No, no," they spoke together. "Please!" They both scrambled to their feet.

"Well, thank you and good morning!" She sat with a little twist of her hips and a low dip. Her skirt rode up over her knees. After removing her hat, she casually shook her newly bobbed hair into place. It had become a habit after less than a day. "Comrade Ella Kaufmann."

The white apparatchik spoke, "I'm Comrade Bill Tyler and this is Comrade George Simmons."

She offered her hand, smiling as each man shook it.

"Bill always thinks he has to introduce me. You're new here, I'd have remembered. Is that today's Worker?"

"No, I bought it yesterday. It's why I'm here. There's a story that bothered me." She opened the paper to page 2. "Here it is: *Terror in Nazi Germany, Literature Floods Saar . . . Karl Molter. . . was seized circulating Communist pamphlets and was immediately sentenced to three years' hard labor by the People's Court.* I was arrested for the same thing in '33."

"KPD?

"Young Communist League. I got out last year."

"So, what brings you here?"

"I can help, George. I know the craft. And I can write. I know the Party line. I need a cigarette." She opened a pack of Lucky Strikes from her purse. Two lit matches immediately appeared.

"Hold those closer." With her left she grasped their hands, moving them together. With her right holding the cigarette she lit it from both matches, inhaled, looked up and puffed out a ring. It was all elegantly done. The two men exchanged amused glances.

"What have you been doing since leaving Germany? In college?" George asked.

"Yes, and I'm legal. I've got my visa."

"What school?"

"My sponsor decided for me, but I found out the very first day it couldn't have been a better choice."

"Really? You're gonna make us guess?"

"It's easy."

"Smith, Vassar, Bryn Mawr, Radcliffe, Barnard, Wellesley . . .?"

"Nope."

"Not Mount Holyoke?"

"No. I'll give you a hint: coed."

"Cornell?"

"Go Big Red!"

They laughed.

"And not just that. They cancelled classes for the anti-war strike in April and they even have a chapter of the Young Communist League!"

"And a good football team," Bill added.

"Well, we didn't do so well last season, 2 and 5. They say it's time for Coach Dobie to retire. Even lost to Columbia."

"I went to that game. Did you come down for it?"

"Wanted to. American football is so exciting: the rallies, the parties, cheer leaders, marching bands, and the boys in those uniforms. Rah! Rah! Sis boom bah! But I had to study that weekend."

"You're becoming a real American girl."

"You think so? There's so much to learn."

"They say the best way to learn about America is to have an American steady."

"Funny, in Germany they say the best way to learn French is to have a French lover. N'est-ce pas? Oh, I do have a boyfriend here. Don't look so disappointed, Bill."

"Just a thought."

"Cornell's integrated, too, I hear."

"Well, George, about that, there's no obvious quota on Jews. But you'd be hard pressed to find any Negro students. There is one girl I know. No sorority would pledge her. None at all on the faculty."

"That will change in Soviet America."

"So, Ella, just what did you for the Party?" asked Bill.

"What do kids do? Posters, running messages. Is this part of the interview? Never been interrogated over coffee and donuts before. Surely somewhere in this building there's someone who does vetting. I just want to fight the Nazis. I still have family and kameraden in Germany."

"Actually, Ella, George is your man.

"And if you check out, I know a job you'd like."

"What is it, 9 hours later in Moscow? Call Records Central now, give them my Party number, and you'll have your confirmation."

George took out a pencil and small notebook.

"Here? The Gestapo . . ."

"They're idiots but know enough not to come snooping around here, they'd get their necks broken. They don't stray far from Pier 86 and Yorkville, boozing and bullying. We do get G-men nosing around sometimes." Bill stood up and peered about the crowded room. "None today, though. Can't miss 'em. They all wear the same suit."

George glanced at his wristwatch. "Eight. Would you like to come to my office? I'll make the call. They're some forms to fill out."

"If Bill comes, too."

"Well, of course! I wouldn't miss it."

They took an open cage elevator to the third floor. In the corridor a sign read, Keep the Place Clean, Maintain Proletarian Order in Your Center! In a dim corner she noticed a young couple seated on a packing crate holding hands. The boy's shirt was open. George unlocked the office door and ushered his companions in. He followed, locked it and pulled down the shades.

* * *

It was 11:30 when Ella found room 330. She made sure her necklace was visible and opened the door. "Hello! Is Comrade Rachel Untermeyer here?"

Several people were busy in the office, running a mimeograph machine, typing, bundling leaflets. On the wall was a collection of editorial cartoons and Soviet posters. One was new, the figures of Stalin and People's Commissar of Defense Voroshilov towering above the Kremlin at this year's May Day parade: *Long live the worker's and peasant's Red Army, the true guard of Soviet frontiers!* A middle-aged woman with frizzy brown hair looked up from a cluttered desk and took Ella in. "Let me guess, George sent you."

"Why, yes, he asked me to give this note to Comrade Rachel Untermeyer in Propaganda."

"Well, give it here, girl. I'm Rachel."

"Pleased to meet you. I'm Comrade Ella Kaufmann." She handed Rachel the note.

"Charmed. Take a seat." She read it quickly then peered over the top of her half frames. She studied Ella. "German, huh? George is not easily impressed. Well, college girl, do you have any special aptitude for agitprop?"

"I know what sells in Germany, and I can write, edit, print and distribute. Men take all my hand outs."

"That I believe. Nice cut."

"Oh, you're just being kind. It's not too short?"

"It's perfect. I could never do that with my hair." Rachel squinted at the charm Ella was idly fingering. "Shalom aleikhem."

"Aleikhem shalom. My mother is the real Jew in the family, my father and I are the social realists."

"Can I see it?"

"Sure." Ella removed the necklace and handed it to Rachel.

"The Arabs call it the Hand of Fatima, the Prophet's daughter. For Jews it's the Hand of Miriam. I went to Palestine once with a delegation of Zionists, saw one like this. It's supposed to give divine protection. But I suppose you know all that." She gave it back. "Says here you were arrested once. How did that go?"

"They hurt me, said it was a lesson I would never forget and let me go. My parents got me to the States as soon as they could."

"Did those bastards . . .?"

"Please, Rachel, I don't want to go back there." Her eyes began to tear. She took a breath and dabbed at her eyes with an embroidered handkerchief. "I can help."

"OK, honey. It just so happens you can. Can you start now?" Ella beamed and nodded. "We have some material going out this week. My German editor didn't show up today, I was about to look for someone else when you walked in. Go through the proofs and find the typos." She handed Ella a bulky manila folder and a red pencil. "This needs to be ready for the printer tomorrow morning. There's an empty desk by the window."

"I'll finish before I leave. And . . . and thank you, Rachel."

Ella went to the desk, sat and allowed herself a moment to lean back and relax before getting to work. Across the room, directly opposite her desk a large cartoon was tacked to the wall. It was a rat with a swastika on its back crawling down a mooring line from the SS Bremen. She smiled.

Chapter 19

Wednesday, June 19, 1935 - A Walk in the Park

Standing beside the doorman was a stranger, a cigarette dangling from his lips, high-cheek- boned, oval face, medium height, slender, in a natty 3-piece grey wool suit and fedora. They were chatting amiably. Ella considered crossing the street and circling the block, but the doorman had already noticed and was gesturing. The stranger looked up, flicked the butt onto the sidewalk, crushed it with a twist of his polished wingtips, and started walking quickly towards her. She looked straight ahead and continued on to the door. When he got near, she angled to the right. He took a step to his left, blocking her.

"Guten Tag Fräulein. Ein Wort, bitte sehr?" He tipped his hat.

"Und wer sind Sie?" She reached into her purse.

"Entschuldigen Sie mich." He took a step back. "Please, I mean no harm. Special Agent Edward Renard, Federal Bureau of Investigation, United States Department of Justice, at your service." Reaching into his jacket pocket he produced a brass badge. It was pinned to his wallet.

Slowly she removed her hand from the purse. "A G-man, huh? Like Jimmy Cagney?"

"I don't sing or tap dance, but yes, I'm a G-man. May we talk someplace, the park perhaps? I have just a few questions."

"All right, lead on, though I can't imagine what the FBI wants with little me. Shouldn't you be chasing kidnappers and bank robbers?" They crossed Park Avenue and headed west on 75th Street.

"Not all the time. Just working through my case files, your name came up."

"Was there a photograph?"

"From your passport, not too helpful. Had to ask the doorman to point you out."

"Never liked that picture."

"If you're fishing for a compliment, I'll bite. You're much prettier in person. Great hair."

"Why, thank you!" She passed her fingers through her lustrous black bob. "Now about you, your accent, it's . . . unusual."

"I was born in Kobryn, heard of it? Used to be Russian, Polish now, maybe German tomorrow."

"Something else there, British?"

"Good ear. I studied in London."

"My English teacher at the Gymnasium was British."

"Yes, I can hear it."

They continued across 5th Avenue, turned right and strolled to the park entrance on East 76th Street. Renard paused and pointed at the opening in the low stone wall bordering the sidewalk. "Notice the name of this gate?"

"Where?"

"It's on the wall, see, Children's Gate."

"I'm not a child."

"Didn't mean to imply anything. I thought you'd think it charming. Most people do."

"There was nothing charming about my last interrogation."

"If that was what this is, I'd be taking you downtown. Figured we'd keep this friendly. And if I can work a walk in the park with an attractive young lady into my day, that's a plus."

"Then you should do it right." She offered her arm, he took it.

A short distance inside Central Park they found an empty bench overlooking the Conservatory Pond. They watched the toy boats sailing as laughing kids chased them around the shore.

Renard took out a cigarette pack. "Smoke?"

"Yes, thank you."

He handed her a cigarette and lit it with a shiny Zippo, then lit one for himself. "Nice necklace. Don't see many like that."

She rubbed the gold hamsa pendant between her fingers. "Birthday present, reminds me of home."

"Good memories?"

"Before Hitler."

They smoked together for a while and watched the passersby.

Renard gazed at two children playing tag on the other side of the pond. Without turning he spoke. "You've been spending a lot of time at Communist Party Headquarters. Yes, we have men there, recording comings and goings. When someone new shows up we try to identify them. No secret that, the Reds watch us, too. When you first appeared Monday morning it didn't seem important. There are walk-ins all the time. But you stayed until 10 p.m. and then you came back yesterday for another long day. Reported for work again this morning, but left at 9:35 a.m. We lost you in Times Square. That got my attention. You're no amateur. A records check showed you're here on a student visa. And yours required a waiver. You were arrested when you were 15 . . . for prostitution."

"Charges were dropped."

"State Department policy is to treat any derogatory information as credible. Also, your rap sheet was stamped with a J and KPD, which would be enough for the consul to deny a visa outright. The appeal was interesting reading: a personal acceptance letter from the Cornell registrar, glowing recommendations from your teachers, and a pledge from your sponsor, Mr. Daniel Rattigan, to act in loco parentis. We're familiar with him, quite the traveler. You're spending the summer at his apartment so he should be aware of your activities. Right? . . . Didn't think so. The waiver was conditioned on his guarantee of your good behavior. The visa can be revoked for any number of reasons, definitely for radical or subversive activities." He took a bag of roasted peanuts from his pocket and offered her some. "So, Comrade Ella Kaufmann, what are you doing for the Reds?"

A gray squirrel ran under a pram pushed by a uniformed nurse whose attention was focused on the handsome young man walking beside her. It stopped before the bench, sat up and caught Ella's eye. She selected a nut from the bag and tossed it to him. "Here I am in the park, feeding a squirrel. You know, the last time someone asked me that I was a scared kid squatting in my own blood and vomit."

"We do things differently. There's no sawdust on our floors."

"I thought the third degree was the rule here."

"Most people want to tell the truth. I try to make it easy for them. Another nut?"

"No thanks." She removed a leaflet from her purse. "Here."

He began reading, taking his time. "You wrote this?"

Ella nodded. "Started editing someone else's draft, thought I could do better and just rewrote it."

"Excellent German, grammar, spelling, logical development of the argument. Not your typical Red rant."

She looked at him sharply and raised an eyebrow.

"I also went to school in Berlin. Mind if I keep it?"

"No, you can have it, there are hundreds of others."

"Have they gone out yet?"

"No, but they needed them fast."

"For distribution in Germany? The SS Manhattan is sailing today for Hamburg."

"Maybe not, there's a strike."

"What about?"

"Maritime law requires a continuous watch. Can't do that with just two radio telegraphists. And they want a raise, an eight-hour day, and a union shop. You don't need to be a Communist to appreciate that."

"Fair enough. You heard that at Party headquarters?"

"No, the ISU, the International Seaman's Union."

"This morning?"

She nodded.

"No surprise, they're all Party members. The courier is taking a big risk, you know. If caught he'll do hard time. And this leaflet could create problems here, for you."

"Anti-Nazi propaganda is a problem only for the Nazis."

"Don't be naïve. This calls for the violent overthrow of a friendly capitalist government. In translation it could as easily be about America as Germany. Foreigners have no free speech rights. You could be deported just for parting your hair on the left."

"It's the Nazis threatening world peace. The Soviet Union is the only country trying to stop them. You know that."

"I was with the American Relief Administration in Russia during the famine, tens of thousands died, the result of Bolshevik policies."

Ella bridled. "Civil war, imperialist intervention, capitalist-inspired wrecking added to the ruin the World War inflicted on a backward economy forced the Soviet Government to build from the ground up. Little wonder there were disruptions in food distribution!"

"That sounds like Comrade Browder talking, but I was there. I saw the starvation, the typhus, the terror. I saw cannibalism . . . cannibalism! All for a crackpot political theory."

"It was war. Now there's peace and Comrade Stalin has proven Communism works for the people."

"You should go there and see the workers' paradise for yourself."

"And how is capitalism doing in America? Millions of workers jobless, homeless, and hungry, farmers driven from their land, while the bourgeoisie take vacations and complain about their taxes."

"You won't get any argument on that. Times are tough."

"For the proletariat. So, are you going to deport me?"

"The Department of Labor handles deportations. But it's up to you. Cooperation is the ticket. The Bureau can cover for you."

"What do I have to do . . . sleep with you?"

Renard frowned. "Is that what you think this is about? I know the sex trade and you're not the type, just a nice little Jewish girl. And I'm not that kind of guy. We're meeting this way to protect your identity. If the Reds suspect you're working for the Bureau it won't go well for you."

"Sorry. I can't forget what the Gestapo did to me. I'm in America and people have been nice to me, but when a policeman questions me, I'm back in Tübingen." Ella gripped the bench hard and stared at the ground.

Renard raised his right arm as if to place it over her shoulder, but quickly lowered it. "You don't have to explain. We'll protect you. What we want is a source on the inside. Just keep doing what you're doing. But when you hear of something big coming, let me know."

She looked up. "Like what?"

"Oh, bombing a bank, sabotaging an airship, inciting a riot, that sort of thing. You're a good girl, you don't want innocent people getting hurt."

"Anarchist provocations. The Party doesn't do things like that, only propaganda and peaceful demonstrations. It's the police who turn them violent."

"In that case just tell me whatever the Party is planning and I'll decide if it's significant."

"I go back to college in September."

"Plenty of Reds at Cornell. You could still be useful. We'll talk about it then."

"So, how do I contact you? You have a business card?"

"Now wouldn't that be awkward if someone found it? Just call the Bureau, Rector 2-3520. Ask for Special Agent Renard. Memorize the number or just use the phone book. Otherwise, I'll find you. Abraham Lincoln . . . heard of him?"

"Of course, he freed the slaves."

"Yeah, that one. He had a saying; You can't fool all of the people all of the time.

"Your point?"

"You're a smart girl, think about it. We'll keep in touch, then." Renard stood up. "It looks like rain. You should get home. Oh, one more thing kid, in New York you must be 21 to be licensed to carry a handgun, and you're what now, 17? That could get you deported, too. *Auf Wiedersehen, Kameradin.*" He raised his right fist. *"Solidarität!"*

She lamely returned the salute. *"Solidarität, Kamerad."*

Renard started walking casually south around the pond. Ella watched until he was out of sight. She exited at the Children's Gate, and headed uptown on 5th Avenue to 79th Street. There was a public telephone booth on the corner. She dropped a nickel in the slot and dialed Regent 4-9258, drumming her fingers on the shelf while the call went through. "Café Hindenburg? . . . Mr. Irwin Jones, please . . . tell Iggy I have the name."

Chapter 20

Friday, July 26, 1935, The Bremen

"We're in the parlor, Ella."

Cindy sat with her father and Abby around the coffee table drinking their after-dinner cocktails. When Ella entered, they smiled. She wore tan jodhpurs, black riding boots, and a tweed jacket over a frilly white blouse.

"Drink?" Daniel asked.

"Bitte."

"Like a Manhattan?"

"The El and Rikers Island, too," Abby sang and held out her empty glass for a freshening.

"Cindy says you're going out together." Daniel stirred the whiskey, vermouth and bitters in ice and strained the mix into glasses. "Planning a trot around Central Park?"

"We're handing out pamphlets at a Union rally on the West Side, figured I should be ready for anything."

"And for which union would that be, the Soviet?" He added cherries and handed Ella and Abby their drinks.

Ella took a sip. "Umm, good. No, it's the International Seamen's Union, the ISU."

"Bunch of Reds from what I hear."

Cindy sighed. "Oh, Daddy. They're not plotting a revolution, just protesting the Nazis."

"You have one of those pamphlets?" he asked.

"Got one in my purse; just a sec . . . here!" Cindy handed her father a copy.

He took a look at the cover. "Welcome to the New Germany! This is anti-Nazi propaganda?"

"Irony, Daddy. Open it."

Inside was a drawing of a leering SA storm trooper bayonetting a woman clutching her baby. Facing it was a picture of a concentration camp. Behind the barbed wire 3 skeletal bodies were hanging from a gallows. Above the gate a sign read *Arbeit Macht Frei*.

"Strong stuff, should get their attention. Be careful who you hand these to. Could start a fight, plenty of Hitlerites on the waterfront," he warned.

"Oh, we have others." Cindy handed her father another pamphlet.

"Same cover, but inside . . . Hah! Rhine maidens, beer and swastikas, they can't object to that. Just don't mix them up."

"We know what we're doing, Nazi in the right pocket, anti-Nazi in the left," Ella explained, patting her jacket.

"You're going to Pier 86, right? That's where the Bremen is berthed. She's sailing tonight."

Ella nodded.

He swirled his Manhattan. "It's about the flag, right?"

"It's an incitement to violence. Why doesn't the mayor do something?" Cindy asked.

He finished his cocktail. "La Guardia's already in a tiff with the local Nazis over a German masseur's business license. Telling Hitler what flag he can fly on his ships is way beyond the Mayor's bailiwick."

"Then it's up to the people."

"Seems so, Ella. It's also against standard maritime practice. The shipping line's flag goes on the bow. The national flag goes on the stern. But Hitler decreed Germany has two coequal flags. So, he flaunts the swastika on the bow over 12th Avenue and relegates the old tricolor to the stern over the Hudson. Story goes he designed the flag himself. You know what would really yank his chain? If somebody tore it down. He'd start chewing the carpet or something. Seriously, if your rally turns sour don't hang around. I'd rather not have to bail you out tonight." Daniel wagged a finger.

"Yes, Daddy."

"Ella?"

"Yes, Colonel Rattigan, sir." Ella saluted.

"Good. And leave your pistols at home. Now I have to get ready for my night out."

"With Brooksie?" asked Cindy.

He shrugged. "After her show at the Plaza. She was too busy to return my calls for a week, now she misses me."

"Do you miss her, Daddy?"

"Terribly."

Cindy laughed. "A girl doesn't like to be taken for granted, I think she was just reminding you. Should be a good date."

"I'll iron you an extra handkerchief, Dan. Ya never know, might get lucky. You kids need some help with the pamphlets?"

"Sure, if you don't mind consorting with a bunch of Reds."

"Depends what their drinking, and I like sailors. Guess I better change. The idea is to look posh but practical, right?" Abby asked Cindy.

"Don't we always? That navy jacket is perfect on you. I'm wearing my trench."

Daniel placed a hand on Abby's shoulder. "Mind you watch out for our girls."

"Sure, I'll have them back by dawn."

* * *

12th Avenue was jammed for blocks with lines of taxicabs and chauffeured limousines dropping off passengers and their well-wishers. Three fashionably dressed ladies crossed arm in arm at West 46th Street. They stopped in front of the Bremen's bow. Centered in the spotlights, sixty feet above the street, was the swastika flag. A contingent from the ISU chanted, *Let Simpson Go!*

Ella opened her purse. "Here're your dimes for the visitor pass."

Cindy waived the coin away. "No thanks, I'll pay my own way."

"Big spender!" Abby held out her hand. "I'll take mine, good for a cup of mocha java."

"Oh, look. The marchers are here!" Ella exclaimed.

Hundreds of people approached from downtown, overflowing the side walk and spilling into the avenue. In the vanguard flew a dozen American and Soviet flags. A chorus followed, men and women, black and white. The strains of their anthem soared above the street noise:

So, comrades, come listen,
For the struggle carries on,
The Internationale unites the world in song.
So, comrades, come rally,
And the last fight let us face,
The Internationale unites the human race . . .

Abby turned to Ella, "I'll credit you Reds for one thing, catchy tune."

Many of the demonstrators carried placards: Nazism Breeds War, Free Ernst Thaelmann, Free Lawrence Simpson, Down with Anti-Semitism, Unite Against War and Fascism.

Ella pointed, "Abby, that's what we're protesting."

"Thaelmann's that German Red, right?" Abby asked.

"Party chairman, he's been tortured for two years in a Nazi prison."

Abby pointed at another placard. "Who's Simpson?"

"Larry's in the same prison. He's an American sailor, ISU member. Last month the Gestapo nabbed him off the SS Manhattan, an American ship, even before it docked at Hamburg. Claimed he was carrying anti-Hitler propaganda."

"Larry? You know him, too?" Cindy gave Ella an arch look.

"Just another District assignment," Ella replied.

"Yeah, for sure, Ella."

"He got arrested for carrying leaflets? Uh, that's what we're doing."

Cindy leaned close to Abby. "One more thing, we're going to pull a stunt on board. Things could get rough. So, if you want to bow out . . ."

"Not on your life! I'm in this all the way. Besides I promised Dan, I'd see you both home safe."

"We need to look like Friends of the New Germany." On the sidewalk vendors were selling souvenirs. Ella bought a large Hitler button. "This will match your jacket, Abby."

Cindy picked out a small Vaterland flag pin with a picture of a German schloss. "Castle Frankenstein, anyone? Ella, aren't you getting something?"

Ella unfastened the top three buttons of her blouse, revealing a necklace and pendant. Resting above her breasts a half-dollar sized golden swastika gleamed. She started walking. Cindy and Abby exchanged glances and then followed Ella into the Hapag-Lloyd terminal.

Over the gate a large sign read: Boarding 7:30 p.m., Closing 9:30 p.m., Sailing 12:30 a.m. The terminal clock showed 8:35. A stream of people passed through to the forward gangway. Police officers patrolled the pier as the ship's purser checked tickets on the passenger manifest and sold visitor passes. A dozen brawny young men got into line behind Ella and her friends. She made eye contact with one, a particularly handsome, well-dressed fellow. Ella winked, he winked back, both deadpan.

After boarding the ship Abby gravitated to the bar in the first-class ballroom and the threesome sampled the wares. They began distributing their pamphlets, selectively. The American passengers and visitors were handed the anti-Nazi versions. Ella drew attention with her sleekly bobbed black hair and revealing décolletage. Men gawked unabashedly, her swastika pendant their presumed political focus. When one came up and tried some tired pick-up line, she'd hand him a Nazi version, saying in her posh accent, "Oh, I do so love what Mr. Hitler has done for Germany, positively ripping!"

A ship's officer appeared, clicked his heels together and bowed to Ella. He came to attention, and smiled. *"Guten Abend junge Dame. Darf ich mich vorstellen? Ich bin Erster Offizier Heinrich Lorenz, zu ihren Diensten."*

Ella stared blankly for a moment before responding. "Please? I have no idea what you just said."

"My sincerest apologies, I assumed that you must be German what with your patriotic choice of jewelry. If you permit, I'll try again in English. Good evening young lady. May I introduce myself? I am First Officer Heinrich Lorenz, at your service."

"Charmed, I'm sure," Ella extended her hand. Lorenz bowed and kissed it.

"I noticed you distributing some literature to our passengers. May I take a look?" asked Lorenz.

"Oh, it's just a little thing I saw at a travel agency. I liked it so much I took all they had." Ella removed a copy from her right pocket and handed it to Lorenz. "The Jews and Communists spread those terrible lies about Mr. Hitler, such utter tosh! I thought I'd do my bit to spread the truth."

Lorenz looked through the brochure. "Excellent! The Line should stock copies. May I keep this one, Miss . . .?"

"Wannop, Valentine Wannop. And yes, you're welcome to keep it." Ella glanced up at the wall clock. "Oh dear, it's past nine already! I did so want to view the city from the ship's balcony. Could you please direct me there?"

"I'd be honored to escort you there myself, Miss Wannop," Lorenz replied.

Ella clapped her hands. "Oh, thank you so veddy, veddy much. Such an evening! Just let me find my friends."

Abby and Cindy were watching nearby with increasing concern. Ella motioned them over. "Mr. First Officer, sir, allow me to introduce Carol and Ginger."

"The pleasure is mine, and just call me Heiko." Lorenz, bowed to each.

"Charmed," said Cindy.

"Enchanted," said Abby.

"Now if you ladies will accompany me." Lorenz offered his arm to Ella.

She accepted, chuckling, "Righto Heiko!" The little group climbed the grand staircase. A corridor led to a window overlooking the bow.

"Oh, Mr. Heiko, is that the flag out there?" Ella ran up to the window "The Swastika over New York! What a majestic sight! Can we get closer, please?"

"Certainly." Lorenz opened the door and ushered the trio through. "We're standing on the promenade deck. It's permitted to go as far as the railing. That will give you an excellent view of the flag against the Manhattan skyline. Below us is the forecastle or as the English say, fo'c's'le. The flag is on the jackstaff on that platform at the very tip of the bow. This is as close as passengers . . . or visitors are permitted."

Lorenz cleared a path through a large crowd of on-lookers. He made room along the railing. On the forecastle several crewmen worked amid coiled lines and anchor chains wound around enormous windlasses. Floodlights made the scene as bright as day.

Ella clapped her hands. "Oh my! I should have brought my camera!"

Lorenz checked his wrist watch. "Ladies, I suggest you cover your ears."

Cindy and Abby did as advised. Ella buttoned up her blouse. At the tick of 9:30 on the minute hands of the Bremen's synchronized clocks, the ship's steam whistle blew a loud blast. Loudspeakers announced: *All ashore that's going ashore. Visitors must now proceed to the nearest gangway and disembark.* The man Ella had recognized and three others began pushing and shoving their way toward the stairs leading down to the forecastle.

"Those boys are going the wrong direction. Please excuse me, ladies." Lorenz hurried off.

Cindy opened her trench coat. A roll of cloth was tightly wrapped around her waist. She removed it and unrolled a banner. Ella and Cindy tied it to the outside of the railing with lengths of string stitched into the fabric. Then each pulled handcuffs from their pockets and locked their left hands to the railing. The banner read, *Kush meyn tukhes, Adolf!*

Abby bent over the railing. "I can't read upside down, what's it say?"

Cindy laughed. "You couldn't read it right side up. It's in Yiddish, *Kiss my ass, Adolf!*"

"He can read Yiddish?"

"Doubt it. Pity his translator."

Lorenz stopped an ISU man descending the port side stairs. Ella shouted, "Heil, Heiko!" Lorenz glanced up at her. In her right hand dangled the Nazi necklace. Rearing back, she pitched it over the railing into the river. Then with her arm straight out, palm up, she raised her middle finger. Before Lorenz could react, the ISU man clobbered him with one punch. The loudspeakers blared, *Alle Männer jetzt zum Bug!*

Abby wrapped her arms around Ella and Cindy, "Golly, you weren't just whistling Dixie. I guess we're in for it now."

Cindy raised her fist and began chanting, "Let Simpson Go, Let Simpson Go!" Her strong, soprano voice cut through the shouts and cries. Ella and Abby joined in.

On the forecastle a wild mêlée raged between the crew and the ISU men fighting their way toward the bow. More German sailors arrived. Police rushed forward. Ella watched her friend break free from two sailors and leap over a sea breaker. He sprinted to the short ladder of the jackstaff platform. Climbing to the top, he reached up and yanked on the flag. It tore but stayed attached to the halyard. With his switchblade he cut the rope, and hurled the flag off the side. It fluttered down, to float on the filthy river water. The marchers on the street below roared their approval. The girls cheered.

Now the ISU men fought to escape. But the crew quickly overwhelmed them. They were knocked down, kicked and pummeled. One was lifted up onto the railing. The police intervened just in time. Two gunshots rang out followed by a scream.

With the deck finally under control Lorenz noticed the banner. He ordered his men to take it down. They ripped the banner to shreds and then turned on the women. Ella and Cindy defended themselves with their free hands. Abby laid into the Germans, kicking and clawing. The police stepped in to break it up.

"You ladies, OK?" a big cop inquired.

"What kept ya'? We almost got raped!" Abby asserted.

"But no harm done," Cindy emphasized.

"Many thanks, Mr. Officer, sir," Ella added.

"Well now, let's just get you ladies down to the pier before any more ruckus . . . what's this, handcuffs? Did those Nazi sons of bitches — pardon my French — do this?"

Ella explained, "No Mr. Officer, sir, they wanted to throw us overboard. The handcuffs seemed a good idea at the time. But the keys got lost in all the scuffling."

"I'll try my keys. Lots of these cuffs are keyed the same," the cop said hopefully. After several unsuccessful attempts he called to his partner, "O'Shaughnessy, go find me a bolt cutter. Must be one on this goddamn boat!"

"Well now, ladies, I need some information for my report. Names please?" the officer requested, opening his notepad.

Ella spoke, "Mr. Officer, sir, could you please not take our names? You see our parents didn't know we were coming here tonight, and well, we'd be in big trouble if they found out we almost got killed or worse. I was so frightened!" She began to weep.

The cop gave her his handkerchief, a clean one. "There, there now, little lady, that won't be necessary."

Ella dabbed at her eyes. "So very kind of you, sir."

Lorenz approached. "Officer, I have some information of interest."

* * *

In the dingy holding cell of the West 47th Street Police Station three wayward women waited to be questioned.

"Well Ginger, here's another nice mess you've gotten me into!" Abby chided.

Cindy snickered. "Aw, come on! You haven't had this much fun since the night they repealed Prohibition. And I'm Carol, you're Ginger, obviously!"

"Just get it straight, you two, we're Catholics lawfully protesting Hitler's oppression of the Church. The cops are mostly Irish, I've noticed."

"Oh, Val, lighten up. I think we did very well tonight," Cindy/Carol remarked.

"Valentine . . . One-up!" a policeman shouted into the cell.

Ella stood, winked at her friends and followed the policeman down the hallway. He stopped in front of the interrogation room and opened the door. She entered and took a seat across the table from a grey-suited man.

"I was beginning to wonder if you'd show."

"Smoke?" he offered.

"Rather!" she accepted.

He lit two cigarettes between his lips and handed her one. "Valentine Wannop, where did that one come from?"

Ella blew a smoke ring. "Character from a novel I read, something of a Girl Guide. So veddy British, what?"

"Well, Valentine, I spoke with First Officer Lorenz after the riot, he admitted you fooled him. Thinks you're some radical socialist from jolly old England."

Ella frowned. "We'd have gone scot-free if he hadn't denounced us."

"He's Abwehr, Military Intelligence, took it personally."

"So tetchy. Nazis can't take a joke." She ran a hand back through her hair.

"I'll bear that in mind. By the way, none of this would have happened if Captain Ziegenbein had taken our advice to stop visitors from boarding. He wouldn't hear of it. Seems the Line makes good money catering Bon Voyage parties. But thanks to your tip the police were ready." He took a deep drag. "And the Bremen sailed on schedule . . . with a new flag in place. Apparently, they keep several on-hand. Incidentally that Alien Squad detective who got clobbered is a Jew. Your comrades had anything to do with that?"

"Can't always tell who's a Jew. We're sneaky like that. Think we'll make the front pages tomorrow?" she asked.

"Plenty of reporters on-hand, should."

"Think it'll play well in Moscow?" she pressed.

"Oh, I'm sure they'll eat it up."

"Aw, you're just saying that." Ella leaned forward and softly placed her hand over his.

"No, really . . . Hey, don't try that shtick on me!" He pulled his hand away.

Ella sat up straight. "Sorry, force of habit. Look, we're very tired and just want to go home. Can you arrange something?"

"Lorenz must be past Montauk Point Light by now. He won't be back to testify. You're all free to go."

"And Bill Bailey?" she asked.

"They'll keep him and his friends in jail overnight, then in the morning take them to court for a bail hearing."

"Will they get off?" Ella flicked some ashes on the floor.

"They're charged with unlawful assembly and felonious assault. The judge might buy a provocation defense. After all, the swastika is a gangster sign, like the Black Hand or Skull and Cross-bones."

Ella crushed her cigarette in the ashtray, an old tuna can. "The Party has good lawyers, I'll go watch." She got up and raised her fist. "Toodle-oo."

"Solidarität, Kameradin," replied Special Agent Edward Renard.

Chapter 21

September 1, 1935 – One Day More

"Ma'am, can I see Cap'n Ruz? Heard tell he came here last night wid his brains all scrambled up."

The nurse looked up from the magazine she was reading. "And who are you?"

"Eddie, ma'am," careful not to look her in the eyes. "I works on Cap'n Ruz's boat. I needs to know what he wants me to do wid it, what wid the storm coming, and all."

"Sit in there, I'll check if he's receiving any visitors," said the nurse indicating the Colored Waiting Room.

"Yes'm."

A few minutes later, Cindy came running, with the nurse following. "Eddie! We were so worried about you." She gave him a hug and took his hand. "Come with me."

"I'll have one of the orderlies stay with you, miss."

"Why?"

"Hospital policy, miss."

Cindy stopped and turned to face the nurse. "Eddie is family. I don't need any fucking orderly to chaperone me!"

"Why, I never!"

"Come on, Eddie." Cindy led him into Emilio's room, and shut the door behind them.

"Señorita Cindy, there's a way to handle these folks and playing Stepin Fetchit works for me. It only causes trouble if you act up."

"Yeah. She would have peed her knickers if I kissed you . . . Hey, don't back up, I know my place. I've had a long night. So, what did you do with the bodies?"

"No need to know. How is el jefe doing?"

"He's been out of surgery for nearly two hours. He's breathing. That's all I know. Doctor Henderson said we'd just have to wait until he wakes up before they'll know anything definite. She saved his life. She told me something else, too."

"What?"

She took a breath. "Emilio was . . . castrated. Did you know?"

Eddie, blinked. "He made me promise never to tell anyone."

"Who or what did it?"

"The porra held him for four months after Gibara, we had to come up with a ransom to get him out. They keep *un imbécil* in La Cabaña, *un enano loco. Un monstruo.* They use it on the hard cases. They chained Emilio naked to a wall and unleashed the monster. It chewed Emilio's *cojones* off. They sent us a picture."

Cindy sat speechless, her eyes wide, staring at Eddie and then she retched on the floor. Eddie supported her. When she stopped vomiting, he wiped her face with a damp towel and mopped up the mess. Cindy wept. He held her.

The door opened. "And how is our . . ." began Doctor Henderson. "Oh, I'm sorry, should have knocked first." She stepped inside and quickly closed the door behind her. "Nurse Collins mentioned a Negro gentleman was visiting. Well, not her words exactly. So, how is Emilio doing this morning, Miss Rattigan?"

Cindy dried her eyes with a handkerchief. "No change, Doctor. This is Eddie, he's first mate on Emilio's boat."

"Pleased to meet you, Eddie," Henderson held out her hand. They shook.

"Likewise, Doctor Henderson. Señorita Cindy told me you saved his life."

"I merely assisted Doctor Wilson, he's the specialist. But Mr. Ruz is not out of the woods yet. Excuse me while I examine him."

She efficiently checked Emilio's vital signs and recorded them on his chart.

"Any improvement?" asked Cindy.

"He's stable, but I want another X-ray to evaluate the clot, and consult with Doctor Wilson. This will take a few hours. Why don't you go eat and get some rest? I'll call you when we're finished. Still at the Casa Marina?"

"Yes, Doctor . . . You know, we only just met, but you're already a dear friend. May I call you by your first name?" Cindy asked.

"Why . . . yes, Cindy. I'm Emma, like the street, but my mother named me for the novel."

"Loved that book."

Before leaving, Cindy kissed Emilio on the cheek. She marched past Nurse Collins without a glance, hand in hand with Eddie.

Outside, he smiled, "Congratulations, no scenes."

"Yeah, it was an effort. Let's walk to the boat, I want to check out something." When they reached the quay, she told Eddie to go on, she had a phone call to make.

* * *

Fred woke just before eight. He lay there and listened to the rumble of surf on the beach, the cries of seabirds, the morning stirrings of the hotel. He inhaled the salty sea air from the open windows and watched palm frond shadows flicker across the floor and walls. He reached across the double bed. No warm body rested beside him, eager for his embrace.

He got up, shit, showered and shaved, dressed, and called the desk to be connected to Ella. "Howdy do Dixie, hope I didn't wake you. Any word from Cindy?"

"She called this morning. Emilio's out of surgery and resting. Eddie showed up. She wants to meet us at the boat."

"Wonder what his story is. Well, would you like to join me for breakfast on the terrace? You must be famished. We'll have company."

"Who?"

"The Sheldons, a couple we met last night. We went out to dinner together."

"OK, but then we have to go see Cindy."

On the way to the terrace Fred stopped at the desk. "Any messages for Room 216?"

"Yes, sir," The clerk handed Fred a folded slip. He read it quickly.

Ella appeared. Fred took her arm and escorted her to an empty table.

"Seems the Sheldons checked out. They took the morning ferry back to Matecumbe."

"Why was that?"

"Says he was needed at the vet camp . . . Ray is the superintendent. Must be important, since they only checked in last night. Just as well, I think I told him I'd pay."

Ella was famished. She finished off two omelets, several strips of bacon, three slices of buttered toast with half a jar of apricot marmalade, washed down with a large orange juice and two cups of coffee.

"Golly, Dixie, you can't eat like that. It's your duty to be beautiful."

"Ate a big one yesterday morning, too. A 'fisherman's breakfast', Emilio called it. And I don't feel very beautiful today. Look at my nose, it's peeling!"

"Aw, that'll grow back. Go brush your teeth. There's a piece of bacon stuck in there. I'll get the car and meet you in the drive way."

Fred waited in the Chevy, watching guests come and go under the porte-cochère. He noticed one man who appeared to be loitering near the door. Finally, Ella arrived wearing a yellow scarf over her head under a wide brim Panama, oversized sunglasses, white pleated ankle length skirt, boat shoes, knee socks, and a long sleeved, buttoned up blouse. Fred honked and she jogged over. He got out, came around and opened the car door for her. Before she entered, he whispered, "That guy by the entrance, seen him before?" She nodded and took her seat. When Fred turned to look the man was gone. He started the car and began driving.

"Didn't you notice? He was on the terrace, a few tables away sipping coffee and reading Saturday's Miami Herald. Handsome, about thirty, six foot, 180 pounds, muscular, blue eyes, expensive white linen suit with a black pocket square, saddle shoes, dark hair slicked down, starting to bald, small cut on his left cheek, maybe from shaving, gold wristwatch, chain-smoker, shoulder holster bulge under his jacket. I caught his eye, he smiled, one gold tooth, left upper incisor. Don't think he's Cuban, maybe Italian."

"Get his name and phone number, too?"

"No, I looked hideous."

"Well, guess he has your number. The longer we stay here the more attention we're getting. Cindy wants me gone tomorrow. You two better take the afternoon train."

"Cindy will never leave Emilio. And that telegram I got last night was from my handler. He's flying down here tomorrow. He wants to see me, and find out what's going on. He'll want to talk with all of us."

Fred braked the Chevy hard and pulled over. The car behind honked, the driver shouted "ass- hole" as he passed.

"Handler? Just who are you, Dixie?"

"I've been doing some work for the Party this summer, the Feds found out and now I'm doing some work for the FBI so they won't deport me. Only I didn't tell them that I was leaving the country. Just for the afternoon. But there was that bombing and the nice marshal man asked you about it, and the Cubans are coming over today to get you arrested because they think you're the bomber, and he must have cabled Washington with all our names because you told him you worked for the Government, and now the FBI is involved and of course Mr. Hoover would send my handler down to investigate. Kind of obvious."

"That's a lot to swallow, and I do so work for the Government. Does Cindy know this?"

"Well, not the FBI part, anyway. No need to know."

"So, why tell me?"

"You're supposed to disappear, remember? You're the patsy, but you're enjoying this game way too much, the play acting, the money, clothes, the sex. Emilio set you up to take the fall, he didn't plan on you sticking around."

"Yeah, I gathered that. But now I want to hear what Cindy says. We have a deal." Fred started the car.

* * *

Cindy walked out on the pier. All three men were busy with the engines. Eddie wiped his hands with a rag, "Got a lead on that pump. You should rest in the state room."

"OK, Ella and Fred are coming over later," she said.

"Say hello for me."

The stateroom was a mess. Cindy cleaned the blood stains with a sponge and bleach, mopped the floor, and wedged a cork into the bullet hole in the door. She lay down for ten minutes, but couldn't sleep and went topside. She noticed a twin-engine monoplane approaching from over the ocean. It appeared to be headed straight for her. When it reached the basin, it dipped low and circled around, the motors very loud. She could see people inside. Cindy waved, and the plane waggled its wings. It was in Cuban Airlines livery. After a second pass the plane resumed its flight heading east over the city, in the direction of Meacham Field.

A car honked on the quay. She met Fred and Ella on the pier. "We have to talk," Cindy told them. She led them into the stateroom and closed the door. "Emilio had a plan for all this, but didn't leave me a copy. I've had to piece it together. Emilio disguised himself as you, Fred, bluffed his way into the bank vault and got access to a safe deposit box. He robbed its owner, not the bank."

"Wait, why did the bank think it was OK for me to open the box?" Fred interrupted.

"Because I had a delegation of authority form, signed by the owner, but with the delegate's name left blank. You signed it at the Consulado yesterday. I slipped it in with the tourist application. Emilio practiced forging your signature. The bank was fooled. So, he emptied the box into his bag and started back to the hotel. That's when the bomb went off. He hit the street hard, that's what caused his brain clot. Those Cubans who attacked Ella and Eddie last night were waiting for us. There are others. They will try again, tonight. Eddie came up with a plan to take the money to Miami unseen. I have to stay here with Emilio, and Eddie is married to Esmeralda."

"Are you saying Fred and I take it to Miami?" asked Ella.

"No one else I'd trust," Cindy replied.

"So, when will this all happen?"

"Tonight."

Fred leaned forward. "Just how much money are we talking about?"

"Don't know. We'll count it tonight on the boat before you go."

Fred snapped his fingers. "The Coast Guard Bag! Emilio put the swag in the bag and hid it over the side."

"Right," Cindy said. "One other thing." She stood, picked up the tackle box, and dropped in Fred's lap.

"Careful there Cindy Lou, I damage easily."

"Just open it, Fred."

"Alright . . . why looky here! Emilio's .45, right?"

"Yes, he won't be needing it for a while. There's a loaded magazine in it and there are two more, if things get sticky."

"Gee, Cindy, I don't know what to say."

"It's not for keeps, you lug, return it before you turn back into a pumpkin. Now I have to get back to the hospital and see how Emilio's tests went. Ella, can you come by and spell me around two? I think I can last that long. I'll call you at the hotel if anything changes."

"Cindy, I have some news. I'm having a visitor tomorrow. He'll know something's up if I don't show."

"Who are you expecting?"

"A guy I met in New York. He's a . . . G-man."

"Oh, come on Ella, I don't feel like joking."

"No Cindy, it's true. I couldn't openly work for the Party without the FBI finding out. We sort of have an arrangement. I tell them things and they don't deport me. He knows I'm involved somehow in all this Havana business."

"And the Bremen business . . . is that how we got off so easily?"

"Worked out, didn't it?"

"Why are you smiling, Fred? Did you know about this G-man?"

"Dixie told me driving over here. Nearly got rear-ended. Oh, and there's some guy watching us at the hotel. Dixie knows quite a bit about him."

"Jeez."

"You and Emilio have not exactly been very open with us, either."

"No need to know, Ella. Might work out better if you stiff the Fed. At least until Fred gets clear of this Cuban rap, then there'll be no case to investigate. Give me a ride back to the Hospital, will ya, Ella?"

"Can you drive a car, Dixie?" asked Fred.

"Hah, Papi taught me how to drive his Model B Ford when I was 12."

"OK, I'll just sit in the backseat and shut up."

* * *

At the hospital Cindy, Ella and Fred went directly to Emilio's room. He wasn't there. They rushed into the hallway and found a nurse. "Where is the patient in room 3, Mr. Ruz?" Cindy demanded.

"I think he's in X-ray. I'll go see," the nurse answered.

A minute later Dr. Henderson appeared.

"Emma, how is he?" Cindy asked nervously.

"Dr. Wilson is examining the X-rays, now." Emma led them inside. "Ella, dear, you're looking better. Maybe some Noxzema on that nose? I don't recognize you, sir."

Cindy answered quickly. "Oh, he's my friend, Fred."

"Well, Fred, pleased to meet, you."

"My pleasure." They shook hands.

"Emilio's still stable but unresponsive to stimuli. After a serious brain injury, patients may remain comatose for quite some time, perhaps weeks. We've placed a feeding tube. You should consider transferring him to a hospital more convenient for you. Our facilities are limited and we are not equipped for long term care."

"My father is coming tomorrow from New York. He'll want to take Emilio back with him."

"I'll be available to discuss the case with him. OK?"

"Yes, Emma, I was just praying you'd see some improvement."

"We can't rush things. The body heals at its own pace. The good thing is that his vital signs are strong. We must be patient. I'll keep you informed of any changes. Good day." Emma left.

"Why don't you go back to the hotel, have lunch and freshen up. I'll stay."

"You're right, I'm fading. Come on Fred and stop mooning over Emma. Just remember I'm your girl until tomorrow."

"Sorry, just thinking about her bedside manner."

"Oh, please!"

* * *

Cindy asked for her room key from the desk clerk. He handed it to her and then noticed Fred. "Mr. Dunn, sir, I have an urgent message for you."

Fred took it, read it, asked for his key and turned to Cindy, motioning her to follow. He stopped in the alcove below the staircase.

"What is it, Fred?"

"You know the U.S. Marshal who met the boat yesterday, Guy? He wants to see me, as soon as possible, like now."

"Should go then. At the Courthouse? Better leave the gun with me."

"I should change first, always a good idea to dress smarter than the guy who thinks he has something on you. I'll take you to your room first."

"I know the way, Fred."

"And so do the mugs who rifled our rooms last night. Better if I check first."

They walked up the stairs to Cindy's room. "Wait here." He drew the pistol and unlocked the door. He entered quietly and searched the room, closets and bath. Satisfied, he called to Cindy, "Safe to come in."

She lay down on the bed. "Freddie. I missed you this morning something awful. Make me happy."

* * *

Fred parked the Chevy near the Courthouse. The windows were shuttered, sandbags stacked neatly around the front steps and a wood ramp placed to assist visitors. He nearly bumped into a policeman coming out the door. "Sorry, Sheriff." He stepped aside to let the man pass.

"No, excuse me, sir! I'm in a hurry." Sheriff Thompson took two steps, then turned to face Fred. "Have we met?"

"Don't recall, I'm just visiting. Think the town is ready for that storm?"

"Well, we haven't had a bad one down here since 1919. I'm making the rounds to remind folks to take proper precautions. Just had a talk with the Feds inside. Asked them to open the building to folks we have to evacuate from their homes. The Courthouse is new, you know, finished in '32, built with storms in mind. They said they'd take my request under consideration. Mealy-mouthed motherfuckers. Well good day, sir."

"You too, good luck Sheriff." Fred tipped his boater.

Fred entered the building and stopped at the reception desk. "Good day, Miss," he removed his hat, "Fred Dunn. I have an appointment with the U.S. Marshal, Mr. Reeve."

"Lovely day, Mr. Dunn. His office is upstairs and to the right, at the end of the hall. I believe he is waiting for you."

"Thank you, Miss." Fred stood there gazing at her.

"Is anything wrong Mr. Dunn? You're staring at me."

"Oh, my apologies, I was struck by your hair, how it catches the light, the color, the style … sorry, I'm running on like an idiot." He glanced at a wall clock. "And I'm running late. Good day Miss." He smiled and then walked quickly to the staircase. As he reached the first step, he turned and looked back at the receptionist. She was watching him. He waved back and then bounded up the stairs, taking two at a time.

* * *

"Welcome Mr. Dunn, glad you could make it, please take a seat. I asked Lieutenant Cavendish to be here, busy as he is today." Reeve sat at a large conference table, across from Fred and Cavendish. A colored girl sat at the head of the table. "And Miss Hammond is my stenographer."

"Pleased to meet you. Sorry for the delay, Guy, but I ran into Sheriff Thompson at the door, and then spoke briefly with the receptionist, I just had to linger a bit."

"Yes, Miss McCord frequently has that effect on visitors. What did Thompson have to say?"

"He was in a hurry getting folks to take this storm seriously, said he wanted the Courthouse to accept evacuees. He didn't appear satisfied with the response. It looks to me like you're expecting an invasion."

Cavendish nodded. "Yeah, one from the ocean. The water could get several feet deep in the streets. Entire city blocks could be flooded. If it gets that bad people will die."

"Guy, are you prepared to take in folks if things get that bad?" asked Fred.

"Judge Ritter has scheduled a meeting with all the office managers on that very question. Do you know Thompson? I took it you were new around here."

"Long enough to recognize him. I guess he just wanted some friendly ear to confide in, must be under a lot of pressure."

"What did he say, precisely?"

"Off the record?"

"Yes, strictly off the record." Reeve glanced at Miss Hammond. She put down her pencil.

"Well, you understand he was not referring to anyone in particular, rather a general impression of the management. Miss Hammond, I'd advise you to cover your ears."

"Mr. Dunn, there's nothing I haven't heard or can't spell."

"Well then, he said, mealy-mouthed mother-fuckers."

She giggled. Cavendish guffawed and even Reeve cracked a smile.

"I'll just have to pass that bon mot on to Judge Ritter. Now, let's get down to business. I see you did not bring your attorney."

"Hard to find one on a Sunday, Guy."

"Of course. We could postpone this interview until later in the week, but that would delay proceedings, and I understand you wish to leave tomorrow. This meeting is simply to obtain sworn testimony of what you told me last night and your initial response to the accusations presented by the Cuban delegation. You would then be free to go on your own recognizance. Is that agreeable?"

"Certainly, the sooner the better."

"Fine then. Raise your right hand. Do you swear to tell the truth, the whole truth and nothing but the truth, so help you God?"

"Yes sir, I do."

"Miss Hammond will record my questions and your answers."

Fred smiled at her, "Miss Hammond." She glanced up at him for an instant, then looked down, pencil poised above her steno pad.

"State your full name, age, occupation and home address."

"Frederick Edward Dunn, 35. Deputy Assistant Administrator for the Veterans Work Program, Federal Emergency Relief Administration. I'm frequently on the road, so it's best to use my office address, in care of FERA, Walker-Johnson Building, 1734 New York Avenue NW, Washington, D. C."

"OK, Mr. Dunn, I met with the Cuban delegation this morning, they insisted you be detained and the United States Government conduct an inquiry into the bombing yesterday of the Chase National Bank branch in Havana, and if the evidence of your involvement warrants, prosecute you for murder in accordance with US/Cuban treaty provisions."

"So, what was their evidence?"

"They produced several witness depositions placing you at or near the bank at the time of the bombing. That you fled the scene. That you then attempted to flee Havana by speed boat. That you refused to stop the boat when required to do so, and exchanged gun fire with Cuban patrol boats, endangering Cuban naval personnel. That the bombing killed 12 men, women and children, wounding 20 more."

"It's a frame up, Guy. Like I said, I was at the bank yesterday afternoon, but left before the bombing and returned to my hotel. I did hear an explosion but was not near when it happened. We heard a storm might pass through the Florida Straits, Sunday or Monday. Ruz decided we'd better return to Key West immediately. We checked out of the hotel and walked to the quay. That's when Menendez appeared with his little friends. After an amusing conversation he permitted us to depart. When we came abreast of El Morro the Cubans started shooting. Ruz reacted instinctively to get beyond the range of their machine guns. Despite his best efforts, the boat was badly damaged. We managed to limp back to Key West. Cuban gun boats pursued us for a time. We never returned fire. One of the crew did fire once but only as a warning shot. And the guns are legal. I believe the Lieutenant can attest to that."

"That part is true, Marshal Reeve, the paperwork is in order."

"Now, I take no responsibility for what Ruz did. True, I chartered the boat but Ruz is the owner. And at sea the skipper is in charge. Saying that, I have no problem with his actions and would have done exactly the same if our roles had been reversed and I knew anything about boats. Perhaps you should ask Admiral Buttercup to testify."

"That's *Commodore Butterfield*. I did try to contact him this morning but he had already sailed for Kingston. He heard the advisory, too."

"It may be argued, Mr. Dunn, that flight refutes a claim of innocence."

"Lieutenant Cavendish would also attest that they are a trigger-happy crowd down there. Those soldiers had their blood up. I believe his actions were justified under the circumstances. And I am very grateful to Mr. Ruz."

"Is he around? I intend to depose Mr. Ruz and the other crew members, as well as the two young ladies."

"I'm sure they would cooperate, but I'd rather the girls not get involved. They don't deserve to be dragged through this. You understand, of course."

"Of course, Mr. Dunn, but the decision is not mine. The U.S. Attorney must make that determination. Herbert Phillips is a gentleman of the Old South and would certainly be sympathetic to your request, but he's also a tough criminal prosecutor. He may wish to have them questioned, perhaps informally. Let's leave it at that. Now I believe Lieutenant Cavendish has some questions. Lieutenant?"

"Yes, the Cubans brought along some photographs obtained from the passengers of the SS Cuba. I understand they induced cooperation by offering free processing and a complimentary roll of film." He slipped them over to Fred. "These pictures were taken yesterday afternoon as the purported CG-968 passed the Cuba. They've been enlarged to show details. You'll notice that the bow gunner is a colored man, bearing a striking resemblance to Eddie, the first mate on the Esmeralda, and the stern gunner looks a lot like you, Mr. Dunn. Both are wearing Coast Guard uniforms. The stern gunner has a Boatswain Mate's uniform. Unfortunately, there are no clear pictures of the helmsman. The canopy over the cockpit blocked the view."

"Excuse me, but what is this evidence of? Even if this guy is me, and I'm not admitting he is, what laws have been broken?" asked Fred. "I don't believe wearing a sailor suit is a crime."

"If someone impersonated a boatswain's mate in Key West it would attract the attention of the Shore Patrol. Could get you locked up overnight and referred to the civil police to verify your identity. They could charge you with any number of misdemeanors."

"In Key West, exactly. Just where did these boats meet?"

"About 20 miles north of Havana."

"International waters. I believe we can disregard this crime, then."

"Not just you and Eddie were disguised, but the Esmeralda herself was marked as a Coast Guard patrol boat, the CG-968. That could be argued as evidence of intent to commit piracy, in that outfitting a private ship to commit hostilities against U.S. citizens or their property is a federal crime."

"Now, I'm no lawyer but that seems a bit of a stretch. Mr. Ruz just wanted to get us safely back to Key West. And it was a good thing he did disguise his boat, if that's what he did, otherwise that fool pilot would have sunk us."

"Captain Povey?" Cavendish asked.

"Never met him, but the crew said he was *el loco Americano*. Put on a show for us."

"Yeah, that's him. He flew the delegation over here this morning. Said he came right over the submarine basin to point out your boat to his passengers."

"He's here?"

"Likely left by now."

"Too bad, I'd have liked a word with him. Say, Guy, could I see those witness statements?"

"Here, there are translations attached."

Fred, read through them for a few minutes. "The one by the gypsy girl, says she saw an American carrying a bag get knocked over by the explosion . . . took him awhile to pick himself up, seemed hurt, waved her away and then limped around the corner. The Cubans claim that was me. Now, do I look hurt?" Fred spread his arms wide.

"Well, Mr. Dunn, you do have a rather ugly bruise on your face. Wouldn't you agree, Lieutenant Cavendish? Miss Hammond? Let the record show they both nodded."

"Oh, you mean this?" Fred touched his left cheek. "That's from Friday night, got into a brawl and got clobbered with a champagne bottle."

"I'd think a beer bottle would be more plausible on a Friday night in Key West," said Cavendish.

"It was an empty champagne bottle, Lieutenant!"

"Just possible. Well, that's all I have, Marshal Reeve."

"Then unless you have any questions, Mr. Dunn, these proceedings are concluded."

"None, Guy."

"Miss Hammond will type the transcript for your signature. Shouldn't take long, Miss Hammond is very proficient." She stood, smiling, gathered her materials and left the room.

"Mr. Dunn, there is one more thing. The Department of Justice is sending down a Federal Bureau of Investigation special agent tomorrow to question you and the others. He's due to arrive around ten. I'll take your word that you will stay in town until he completes his interview. Should be finished in time for you to make the afternoon train. U.S. Attorney Phillips will review the interviews and our recommendations. You needn't stick around here for that. Just keep us aware of your whereabouts. Would you care for a drink while we wait for Miss Hammond?"

"Do you have a Coke?"

* * *

Standing on the Court House steps Fred took a deep breath. On the other side of the street a man was smiling at him, the sun caught a golden glint in his mouth. Fred crossed the street and walked up to him. "So, what's the deal, pal?"

"Mr. Dunn, can we talk? It concerns a matter of mutual interest."

"Alright, there's a joint near here."

"Lead on Macduff. Lovely day we're having."

They walked a block without saying a word. On the corner was The Happy Days Club. It had a beer garden open to the street. "We'll sit here," Fred said, pointing to a table. Fred took the seat facing the street. A waiter appeared.

"What's yer poison, gents?" he asked.

The man with the golden tooth replied, "a Cuban coffee."

"Sure, Mack. And you, buddy?"

"An orange Nehi."

The waiter frowned, "I'll have to check the cellar for that." He hurried off.

"OK, your dice, Goldy."

"Tony, if you please. I represent a client who is familiar with your activities in Havana yesterday. He is prepared to offer his protection in return for an item of no use to you."

"And why would this item be of no use to me, Tony?"

"Because you are in no position to benefit from it. Accept the offer and you and your friends will be protected from both the Cubans and the Feds."

"The Feds have nothing on me and I can handle the Cubans."

"I beg to differ, Fred. The U.S. Attorney may yet acquire incriminating evidence and the Cubans, as you know, will try again, better prepared this time. What you may not realize is that both Batista and Machado desire the aforementioned item. And both have their people in town. And neither respects U.S. law. You are well out of your depth. And of course, there are Miss Rattigan and Miss Kaufmann to consider. This is your way out. And if you accept my client's offer now, he is prepared to pay you a substantial finder's fee."

"Who do you work for?"

"Someone with a very long reach."

"This requires serious consideration. Does the offer extend to tomorrow?"

"I read the weather bureau advisories, too, Fred. We might not be here tomorrow. Midnight tonight or I will be compelled to take other measures."

The waiter returned with the drinks and a bowl of pretzels. "Sorry Mac, no orange, only peach."

"Peachy . . . no, Stoopnocracy is peachy."

"Correct, Fred, Stoopnocracy is peachy. Here's my number." Tony wrote it on a paper napkin and passed it to Fred. "If I don't hear from you, I'll come see you . . . wherever you are."

Fred downed his Nehi, burped, stood up, and placed a dollar bill on the table. "I'll get back to you."

Tony nodded and sipped his coffee.

* * *

Fred walked back to the Chevy by a roundabout route, pausing occasionally to glance behind him. When he got back to the car, he noticed something was lying over the steering wheel. Looking through the driver's side window he saw it was a newspaper. Large black letters were written over the front page, spelling "BOOM!" Fred pondered the implications, then unlocked the door, and sat behind the wheel. He removed the paper. It was Saturday's Miami Herald. He turned the key.

* * *

Emma and two orderlies entered the room. Ella was seated beside Emilio's bed holding his hand. She looked up.

"Ella, we are going to bathe Emilio. I think it would be better if you leave while we do this. I'm afraid you might find it disturbing. It shouldn't take long."

"I . . . you're right. I'll comeback when you've finished." Ella left the hospital and walked to the Weather Station next store. She read the latest advisory. It was still rather noncommittal. The only thing for certain was the time of today's sunset. There was a newsstand nearby. She bought a copy of Saturday's New York Times and found a shady bench to sit and read. A front-page article described the tragic death of Queen Astrid of Belgium in a car crash. The King had not yet told their three young children. She wept.

A car honked. She lowered the paper and saw Fred drive by. He parked across from the hospital and walked over to her. He carried a paper bag with dark grease stains, and a soda bottle. "Hi Dixie, thought you might be hungry." He sat beside her and placed the bag and bottle between them. "Burger, fries and a Pepsi, dig in." She lay the Times on the bench and wiped her eyes.

"Is Emilio OK?"

"They're giving him a bath; Emma kicked me out. She's acting like my mother. Thinks I'll be corrupted by the sight of a naked man. But I was ready for a break anyway. So why aren't you with Cindy?"

"I think I bought us some time. Your nice marshal man wanted to see me at the Courthouse to discuss what the Cubans had on me. He also wants me to stay in Key West tomorrow to talk with your G-man friend."

"He questioned you at the Courthouse? That wasn't wise, you should have put him off and left town tonight with me. He wouldn't start looking until tomorrow afternoon, if he even works on holidays."

"I didn't tell him anything he didn't already know."

"Doesn't matter, he had the time to question you at his leisure on his turf. If he's any good he must have learned a lot about you. Enough to poke holes in your story."

"You gonna eat that?"

Ella took a big bite from the burger and chewed for a while. "Can you open this?" she asked Fred, handing him the bottle.

"Never without my church key." Fred popped the top and gave the fizzing Pepsi back to Ella.

She took a swallow.

"So, guess who was waiting for me when I left the Courthouse? Your admirer from breakfast, Goldy. Call's himself Tony, sounded like some mobster. Wanted to impress me with what he knows, more than the Feds, but not everything. Didn't say a word about Emilio, thinks I'm the mastermind. He made me an offer. If I give him the 'item', his boss will give us protection and a finder's fee. He mentioned you and Cindy by name. He expects an answer by midnight. I put him off. I think I could take him, mano a mano, but a gun fight would be a toss-up. And he might have some heavies with him, said he'd come for me wherever I was. I hear you have some experience with this kind of stuff, what do you think?"

"Fred, you just can't keep your mouth shut. Finish the burger and let me think." She slowly sipped the Pepsi. Fred munched and read the paper.

"Fred, give me the car key. You go a few blocks and grab a cab back to the hotel, wake up Cindy and take her to the hospital. She needs to stay with Emilio. Keep her company. This will take a while. Wait for my call."

Chapter 22

Sunday, September 1, 1935 - The Ballad of Goldy and Dixie

Ella returned to the hospital and used the ladies' room to wash her face, check her teeth, freshen her makeup, comb her hair, undo the top three buttons of her blouse, tie the yellow scarf loosely around her neck, and ensure that her hamsa pendent was discretely visible. She wore the sunglasses and the brim of her Panama upturned on the left. She kept the newspaper.

Passing the nurse receptionist, Ella received a warm smile. Ella smiled back. A squad of Marines climbing the hospital steps stopped, grinned and whistled as she descended. She gave them the cold shoulder. Ella wondered if she were overdoing it, and nixed the idea of buying a lollypop to suck on from a street vendor. She drove the Chevy in a loop around town, Emma Street to Southard to Simonton past the Courthouse to Front, stopping a few times to window shop and buy a couple of post cards. Near the harbor she found a shady outdoor café where she could park. She took a small table and ordered an espresso and pastry. Then she opened the Times and began reading again.

It didn't take as long as expected, and she was only half way through a review of Garbo in *Anna Karenina.*

"Ist dieser Platz frei, junge Dame?" a man asked. Ella lowered the paper.

"Excuse me?"

"Oh, I'm sorry. May I sit here?"

"Why here? There are plenty of empty tables."

"Well, I noticed you at breakfast this morning at the Casa Marina and . . . you looked rather lonely sitting here all by yourself."

"I want to be alone."

"Sorry to intrude."

"Smile."

"Uh, sure if you wish." And he grinned ear to ear.

"OK, now I recognize you, that gold tooth. Rather ostentatious don't you think?"

"Got my real tooth knocked out. Not good for my line of work, looking like some gap-toothed yokel. May I sit?"

"If that's the only thing you want."

He sat down. "My intentions are entirely honorable. May I introduce myself? Tony Conte."

"Show me your hands, Tony."

"I just washed them." Tony held them out.

"That's in your favor, but I'm looking for wedding bands, or any tan marks showing one has recently been removed."

"Do I pass?"

"Probationally. My name is Ella . . . Kaufmann. But you probably know that." She extended her right hand.

Tony kissed it. "And the other?"

She held up her left hand, turning it around to show both sides. "No rings. Says nothing though. I dislike them, get in the way when I'm playing."

"And what games do you like to play, Ella?"

"Well, this one is becoming tiresome. What do you really want?"

"I'm a private investigator. I know you traveled to Havana yesterday, and would like to hear what happened."

"Oh . . . My . . . God! The jig is up. The cat's out of the bag now. Please, please don't throw me in the briar patch, Br'er Fox! I'll do anything, absolutely anything!" She seemed about to cry, slowly smiled and then laughed out loud. "You should have seen your face! Go ahead, order something."

"OK, you got me. Are the espressos any good here?"

"Not so bad."

Tony whistled to the waiter. "Double espresso, please."

"Sure thing, pal."

She removed her hat, shook her head vigorously, and checked in her compact mirror that everything was to Mr. Julian's standard. "You see Tony, about yesterday, my friend Cindy took me along on this overnighter to Havana, so she and her sugar daddy could casino hop and rumba till the cows come home at the Tropicana. I felt like a third wheel, but Fred is fun and easy with his dough. Anyway, after going to the bank to cash a check to gamble away, he got all antsy and said we had to get back to Key West because of some hurricane coming. Then it got interesting, this Cuban cop stopped us, all in white, I thought he was gonna shoot us or sell ice cream, then Cindy started acting like the dizzy blonde she is, but in spades, got him laughing and he let us go. Then when we were on the boat and on our way home, they did start shooting. If it weren't so scary it would have been funny. But we made it, and now I'm bored. Tell me about yourself, Tony."

"I met Fred earlier today; told him I knew that his bank visit involved more than check cashing. He clammed up. I told him . . ."

"Oh please, Tony, I've had it with Fred, he's so full of himself, out to impress everyone. You're Italian, right? I guessed it this morning. I'm usually right about these things. What town do the Contes come from?"

"Well, my father left Bozen in 1902, Bolzano since the war, found a nice girl from Palermo, and a year later I showed up in New York."

"They must be good-looking."

He smiled, "And why's that?"

She tapped his chest with her fist. "Tony, don't play dumb with me, I'm only talking to you because you're cute. Bet I'm not the only girl who thinks so." She unwrapped her scarf, folded it neatly and placed it in her lap. Her pendent caught the light.

"Yes, my mother is *bellissima* and my father *molto bello*, in the Tyrolian way. Now tell me about that gold charm of yours."

"This little thing?" She plucked the hamsa from between her breasts and held it up beside her ruby lips. "It's a gift from my mother and she is very beautiful, Tony."

"I can't tell whether your eyes are violet or blue."

"That's because you're too far away."

The waiter returned with the espresso. "Here ya go, buddy."

* * *

Ella and Tony lay side by side in her bed. She touched her body somewhere and he'd kiss it. Then it was his turn. This couldn't go on for long and soon they made love again. It wasn't as gentle this time. He groaned, she moaned. They wrestled, rolled into different positions, testing their endurance and imagination. It was an adventurous trip and when they arrived, they covered each other's mouths to stifle the screams. Afterwards they laughed and cuddled, sweaty bodies slipping through embraces.

Ella lay atop Tony, their toes tangling, her head on his chest. She glanced at the clock. "Honey, ya wanna go see the sunset? It's at 6:46 tonight, we've got plenty of time to make it. It's a big deal in Key West. Who knows, it might be our last chance for a long time. I'll bring my camera. We can get a bite . . ." she nibbled his nipple, ". . . and then go back to bed."

He glanced at the other bed, "And your roommate?"

"I'll tie a ribbon on the doorknob, she'll get the message. Besides she'll want to sleep with Fred tonight . . . you won't bother them, will you?"

"Here in the Hotel?"

"Just down the hall, room 216."

"Why not? You can be my hostage."

"And tie me up! . . . Tony, we're leaving Friday, will I see you again?"

"I have some business to finish, then I have to get back to New York."

"New York City? That's where we're going! Two weeks there, then back to college."

"What college is that?"

"Cornell, ya know, upstate."

"I have business in Saratoga Springs, maybe . . ."

"That's kinda far, how bad do you want to see me again?"

"This much." He rolled Ella over and began covering her with kisses from nose to toes. Ella by turns gasped, tittered, and trembled.

"Jeez, Tony, can you get some time off from your job? Think your boss will understand?"

"He's planning a big acquisition. After the dust settles, I think he'll agree."

"Is he a good man?"

"Wife, two sons, he's pretty ordinary. He does like the horses, though. And …" he reached up and fiddled with her necklace, ". . . he's a Jew."

She laughed, reached down and fiddled with his cock, "And you're not! I have to go to the bathroom, you know, girl stuff, just take a sec."

* * *

They parked on the quay. She took Tony's hand and they walked together to the pier where Esmeralda was moored. "Let's go to the end, there's a bench. Best view in town."

Eddie glanced up when they passed. "Hi, Eddie! We're gonna watch the sunset. Look how pretty the sky is!"

"Sí, señorita Ella, muy bonito."

Tony turned to Eddie and tapped the brim of his fedora. "Friend of yours?" he asked Ella.

"Oh, yeah, we'd all be in some Cuban prison but for him. Quite a guy."

"Any idea why they wanted you so much?"

"Not me, just Fred, but since we were together, they'd have taken us all in for questioning. And I don't go to jail, ever."

"Hah, I've been more times than I can remember. Cops worked me over some but I always got off."

"You weren't a 15-year-old Jewish girl. I will never forget."

Tony stopped and turned to face her, holding both her arms. She leaned her head against his shoulder. "Damn them, damn them!" she wept.

He kissed her. "Come let's sit. Yes, the sky is very pretty." They sat on the bench at the end of the pier, Ella to his right, his arm around her. There was a clear view over the mole out to sea.

"Sorry, Tony, I never break like that, thanks for being here for me." She adjusted the shutter speed and aperture on her camera and began taken shots of the golden clouds above the setting sun. "I'll get these developed Tuesday. You can take one home with you, so you'll remember."

"Smart girl, just sky, no people, no questions. But I'll remember the photographer." He kissed her again. "Kinda quiet out here, just some hammering from the town."

"Yeah, this afternoon you couldn't hear yourself think, everyone getting ready . . . Tony, should Fred worry about you? I mean I don't really care that much, he's a gambler, he'd bet his life on any crazy thing, but Cindy . . . I think she's in love, sorta. Usually she loves and leaves them, no regrets, but with this one, I just don't know. Is what you want so important?"

"What he wants isn't his. I made him a decent offer. He should take it. Ordinarily I don't leave loose ends, but for you, I'll make an exception."

"Really? I noticed your shoulder holster back at the hotel." She reached under his jacket with her right hand and tickled his armpit.

"Hey, Ella, I don't know you that well! In my business a gun is a necessity."

"Sorry." Ella withdrew her hand. "Fred gave me this silly nickname, Dixie Dugan, like in the funny papers."

"Yeah, Dixie Dugan, that's good. But you're better looking. The mugs I work with all have some moniker. There's Dutch, Lucky, Bugsy, the Accountant."

"Oh, a guessing game! Let's see . . . Schultz, Luciano, Siegel, and . . . Lansky, he's your boss, right?"

"Read the papers a lot."

"Why sure, it's important to know who runs the rackets in town. And Lansky has a reputation for busting Nazi heads in Yorkville. I like that. So, what's his interest in Havana?"

"Oh, Batista is a business associate, but you probably know that, too."

"Gambling, horses, prostitution . . . banking?"

"Smart girl."

So, what's your nickname? Goldy?"

"Why, yes. How'd ya guess?" They laughed.

"Look, it's setting! An omega sunset! That's good luck, you know." She took another picture.

They watched the last sliver of brilliance vanish into the sea.

"Nice, show's over. Where do you want to eat? They have pizza in this town?" He made to stand up.

"Settle down, Goldy, the best part is yet to come. The clouds get lit from below the horizon. The colors are gorgeous. Just sit back with me and enjoy, Goldy and Dixie." She took two more pictures. "Well, too dark now." She placed her camera on the decking beneath the bench. They snuggled deep into the twilight. "Look! The crescent moon!"

"Where?"

"Just to the left and a little above where the sun set. Beautiful, huh?"

"Sure thing, Dixie." They kissed.

There was a roar and series of loud backfires as Eddie tested the engines. Tony turned left and looked over his shoulder. With her right hand, Ella reached under her skirt and drew the PPK from her thigh holster. "Eddie can really fuck up a moment." She slipped the pistol under Tony's jacket and fired three times into his heart. He slumped towards her. She pushed the body off, and propped it against the back rest and bench arm. She wiped the muzzle on Tony's shirt and returned the pistol to its holster.

"You OK, Ella?" asked Eddie, from behind.

"A shame really, we hit it off." She went through Tony's pockets and took his keys, wallet, gun, and watch. Eddie handed her a sack to put them in. She retrieved her camera and stood. "I'm going to freshen up and then pick up Fred and Cindy. Just one thing more." She kissed Tony, and tasted blood.

"It should take me about an hour. It will be dark enough then." Eddie lowered the body into the skiff tied to the pier. He climbed aboard and covered Goldy with a tarp.

Chapter 23

Sunday, September 1, 1935 - The Night Before

They sat around the afterdeck, each with a pistol in one hand and a drink in the other. A kerosene lantern suspended from the flying bridge ladder was the only illumination. Fred checked his watch, it was 9:30 p.m. "OK, Dixie, I told Cindy about Tony, so dish."

"His name is Tony Conte, works for Meyer Lansky, the New York mobster with dealings in Miami and Havana. Friends with Batista. You were right, Fred. He didn't mention Emilio once. I think he's sincere about letting you walk if you cooperate, and killing you if you don't. But he won't bother us tonight. I persuaded him." Ella replied.

"Ella, what did you do?" asked Cindy.

"What I do very well, thank you."

Something bumped against the the boat. Fred jumped.

"It's me," came Eddie's voice. "Fred, you want to give me a hand?"

"Sure," Fred got up and looked over the side.

"There're a pair of heavy leather work gloves and a knife on the rack in the cabin. Bing them to the bow. I'll meet you there in the skiff."

A few minutes later Fred stood at the bow.

"You ever land a marlin?" Eddie asked from below.

"Nope, never had the pleasure."

"See this line I'm holding? The end is fastened to the bow cleat. Find it?"

Fred felt around. "Got it."

"We're going to lift the bag out of the water and get it into the skiff. You lift from the boat, and I'll lift from the skiff. It has about 30 lbs. of weights attached. Brace yourself. Here we go."

They pulled the line up about a foot, wrapped the loose line around their hands and lifted again. Fred felt the line cut into his glove. "I can see the bag under the water. Two more lifts should do it"

"OK, Eddie," replied Fred, "this marlin is a fighter. Let's go."

They grunted and pulled twice more. "Hey, I can see it now, just breaking the surface."

"One more should do it, then I will have to let go to swing it into the skiff. You can hold it up by yourself?"

"Just a dumb fish." Fred spread his legs and grabbed the line with both hands. "Go."

There was a splash as the bag rose above the surface. Eddie let go of the line, grabbed the bag by its strap, and pulled it over the skiff's side. "OK, Fred, let the line slide back down."

Fred shuffled his feet to stay balanced. Eddie called up, "Steady now . . . good, let the line go."

There was a wet thump in the bottom of the skiff. Fred uncoiled the slack line from his hand and worked his stiff fingers. With the knife he cut the line from the cleat and tossed it into the skiff.

Eddie looked up, "Meet me at the transom."

Fred climbed around to the afterdeck where the girls were seated. They looked up. "So, what did you catch?" Cindy asked.

"A whopper, Eddie is bringing it around."

They could hear Eddie's oar strokes, then a bump against the transom. "Fred," spoke Eddie softly, "move the lantern onto the pier." Fred did so, and returned to take the bag Eddie handed him. Eddie climbed aboard. "Now you folks go to the cabin and start counting. I'll stand watch. Look lively there!"

"Yes, sir!" Fred replied, "Come on, girls."

In the cabin, Fred closed the curtains and Ella lit a lantern and placed it on the floor. They knelt around the bag. Fred wiped it dry with a towel and unscrewed the clamps. "Well here goes." He pulled the bag open. "Voila!"

"Expecting a rabbit to jump out?" Cindy asked. She reached a hand inside. "Well, it feels dry. Ella, I'll hand them to you. Please lay them on the floor in groups of ten." She handed the first to Ella. It was a neat stack of bills, bound together with a paper strap.

"What denomination? I can't see clearly from here."

Ella held it close to the lantern. "Hundreds . . . no, they're thousands! I'll count them."

"Holy Grover Cleveland, Dixie, we're in the money!"

After a minute she finished. "One hundred."

"Now that we've established that little fact, let's see how many stacks we have." Cindy resumed passing them to Ella. When they finished there were five piles of ten stacks each, five thousand bills, five million dollars altogether.

Cindy picked up a stack and examined it closely. "Daddy let me hold one of these at the Bank once." She looked closely at the strap and read aloud, "Federal Reserve Bank of Atlanta, Sep 14 30, initialed RJR." She checked stacks from the other piles, "They're all marked the same." She slid a bill out of a stack, held it against the lamp, sniffed and bent it. "It's crisp and smells like fallen leaves, uncirculated. Daddy told me about an emergency shipment of cash to Cuba in 1930, to keep the banks open, $40,000,000 he said. Looks like Machado skimmed a bit off the top."

"So, it was Machado's box Emilio rifled. Looks like Daddy was in cahoots with Emilio on this heist. And if Lansky, Machado and Batista don't get the loot, the Feds will impound it."

"Well, that's the problem, Fred. Nobody is going to break a $1000 bill except a bank. And any large denomination bill is checked by the teller to see if it is counterfeit, and then to see if the serial number is on a Federal Reserve watch list. These aren't counterfeit. Daddy taught me how to tell the difference. And they wouldn't be on any stolen list. Machado's finance minister would have had all of them properly accounted for. They would be recorded as transferred to a Cuban bank. And if they start showing up five years later in America, the Secret Service will be interested. Machado must have planned to deposit it all in some foreign bank where they care less about provenance. But he got chased out of Cuba before he could visit the Havana branch. During Prohibition the rumrunners used Canadian and British banks to launder cash. The closest one is Nassau."

"So, that's where we're going?" Fred asked.

"Got a better idea?"

"Nope, sounds like you know your way around banks. So, whose account will this be in?"

"If we had made a clean getaway from Havana, Emilio would have gone directly to Bimini, then on to Nassau Sunday and deposit at Barclays on Monday morning. Not a holiday there."

"Is it a joint account?"

"Of course, I helped him set it up. Here's the account information." Cindy handed an envelope to Ella. "Afterwards you can relax in Nassau until I arrive and make arrangements."

"And Daddy?"

"You have no need to know. Fred, you'll get your cut." Cindy repacked the bag. "OK, seal her up."

"You missed one," Fred said pointing at a stack she'd left on the floor.

"A hundred grand for Eddie, anyone object?"

Ella shook her head. "Not me."

"He's earned it. But what can he do with it here? Just the one bank and it would look suspicious, ya know. A black man with that kinda money, they'll think he stole it."

"Silly, he has an off-shore account, too."

"Should've known."

"How much cash do you have left, Fred?"

"About fifty bucks."

"Here take another two hundred, that should be enough for both of you to get to Nassau and be comfortable. OK, so Eddie will row the skiff around to the inner harbor and meet you at the pier at the end of Grinnell Street at eleven thirty. Drop me off at the hospital."

Ella spoke. "We don't know how many are watching the boat right now. If we all get in the car it will make it easy for them to follow. We need to divert them. I had an extra car key made this afternoon. Cindy, take a large bag with my stuff and whatever else you need to fill it. You and Fred park near the Weather Station on Front Street, leave my things in the car and then walk back to the hospital with the bag. Fred, stay there an hour, kiss Cindy and the bag goodbye, then walk to the Habana-Madrid Club. I'll meet you there in the car, and we'll drive to the pier. Simple?"

Fred smiled. "I'm a little confused, so they'll be flummoxed."

"Good." Ella went topside and told Eddie, "Five million. Cindy set aside a hundred-thousand for you. How do you want to work the transfer?"

"There's a grey duffle in the galley. Put the Coast Guard bag inside. Have the others come up, you follow and place the duffle under the bench seat. Stay out of sight."

When Cindy and Fred appeared, Eddie whispered to them. "There are groups of soldiers and sailors walking on the quay. There's one coming now, wait until they get near the pier then head for the Chevy, casually. Fred, you take Cindy's bag." Eddie stood and extinguished the lantern on the pier and placed it on the deck.

Several soldiers approached, horsing around and joking, returning from town on their way to Fort Taylor. "Now." Fred helped Cindy onto the pier, kissed her and strolled to the car. Passing the soldiers, he greeted them loudly, "Had a good time, boys? Better hurry, Top is waiting to kiss you nighty night!"

"Weekend pass, buddy, we're going back to the barracks for reinforcements," one of them replied. "And Top is not my type!"

"You sure look like mine, soldier boy," Cindy laughed.

"Hey, you promised to be my girl tonight!" Fred spun her around, dropped the bag, leaned her back in his arms and kissed her con brio.

The soldiers hooted. "That's the way to treat her! Oooo la la!"

Fred hustled a grinning Cindy into the Chevy, honked the horn and waved to the troops.

Meanwhile, Eddie had boarded the skiff, moved it to Esmeralda's starboard side, away from the pier. Ella dropped him the bag. He rowed off. She locked the cabin door and set the alarm Eddie had installed. If the door were forced the alarm would start the horn blowing. It should attract attention.

Ella waited 15 minutes and then left the boat. She saw a man on the left side of Southard strolling along casually, just abreast of the gatehouse. He took another step, then turned to his left and paused to examine a garden bordering the sidewalk. Ella looked right and then crossed the street. She expected him to wait until she had lost sight of him, but this guy was eager and moved a moment too soon. It was just a glimpse from the corner of her eye. He was dressed like a harbor worker or fisherman, a long-sleeved shirt and dungarees, boots, a blue Yankees baseball cap pulled low in front. She'd seen many like him all day around the basin and harbor. He was taller than most and strongly built.

Ella continued up Thomas and turned right on Fleming. Again, she looked left and right, he was still dogging her. She increased her pace, not like she was afraid of what was behind, but eager for what lay ahead. She went two blocks and then turned onto Duval at La Concha Hotel. Half a block away Ella saw what she was looking for, a crowd of men loitering outside a bar. She stopped in front of a storefront window and made a show of rouging her lips and fussing with her hair. She saw the guy reflected in the window, standing across the street smoking a cigarette.

Ella sashayed up to the men, catching a few looks. There was a Marine smiling at her. She recognized him, one from the squad she'd ignored at the hospital that afternoon. "Hey, got a light?" she asked him, holding a cigarette.

"Sure." He lit a match, and cupped his hand as she inhaled. "Thanks, Marine. Got a name?"

"Jack, miss."

"And I'm Dixie, Sergeant."

"Oh, I'm just a Lance Corporal, Miss Dixie, see on my sleeve, one stripe up, crossed rifles in the center. A Sergeant has three stripes up, crossed rifles in the center."

"You look like a good kid, Jack, I bet you'll make Sergeant in no time." She punched his insignia and grinned. Then she looked behind her. The guy was leaning against a lamp post, cigarette in hand. She turned angrily, crossed the street, stopping a car on the way, marched right up to him and shouted, "You fucking bastard, stop following me. I said no, and meant it!" Then she hawked back and spit in his face.

"Little cunt!" He slapped Ella hard with the back of his hand. She stumbled, tripped over the curb, hit the pavement, and screamed bloody murder. Jack and his pals came running and the fight was on. Someone helped her up, she thanked him and moved quickly away from all the commotion. She turned left on Eaton and dashed the two blocks to Front Street. She found the Chevy, caught her breath and drove to the Habana-Madrid Club by way of a few extra turns.

* * *

Cindy sat beside Emilio, holding his hand. Fred stood at the foot of the bed, he glanced at his watch. "I'll have to leave soon, Cindy. Don't suppose I'll be seeing you again. Just want you to know it's been a hell of a ride."

"We have a date in Nassau, remember, silly?"

"Too many ifs along that route, kiddo. Gotta feeling this run of luck won't last that long. Besides, I turn back into a pumpkin at midnight, and you're not the kind that's satisfied with pumpkins."

"Wait for me. I'll come, maybe for Halloween."

"Ha, ha. What makes you think I won't take it all and run?"

"Because you're not a thief and besides, you'd blow it all in a year, left to yourself. Together we could do some good with it."

"With just a bit we could live well in the West Indies or Tahiti."

"Not before I graduate, Freddie. I didn't go to college for three years just to shack up with some beach bum."

"Dunno, kinda of like the idea of you in cut-offs and a T-shirt selling mangoes in the market place."

"A sarong is more my style. But I told you Friday that I'm going to be a foreign correspondent."

"Then I'll follow you in the press."

Cindy stood and came to him. They kissed. "Fred . . . it's not midnight yet." She began unbuckling his belt. He stopped her and leaned the chair up against the door knob.

* * *

Standing in front of the Weather Station Fred checked his watch – 11:15 p.m. Several people were reading the bulletin board lit by an overhead bulb. He joined them.

Advisory 9:30 p.m.: Tropical disturbance central about two hundred sixty miles east of Havana, Cuba moving slowly westward attended by shifting gales and probably winds hurricane force small area near center. Caution advised vessels Florida Straits next thirty-six hours. Northeast storm warnings displayed south of Miami to Ft. Myers, Fla.

He remembered what Lieutenant Cavendish had told him about the law of storms. Maybe we all should leave Key West tonight. He walked up Front Street and noticed the Chevy was gone. Well Dixie is on schedule, must have had it easy.

* * *

Eddie pulled away from Esmeralda with long, powerful strokes, quickly crossing the basin and clearing the mole. The sea was calm, hardly a ripple. Looking south west he could see Sand Key Light on the horizon some eight miles away, it's beam sweeping over the ocean. Displayed vertically above the light were two red lanterns, the storm warning. The sky was clear and with no moon the stars were brilliant. If need be, he could have easily navigated by them alone. There was no need, however, the city lights were sufficient, just keep them to starboard and he'd soon find the harbor entrance. But not so close that he could be seen from shore, staying about 200 yards out from the waterfront.

Eddie heard the faint sound of a motor. He stopped rowing and listened, trying to determine its direction. The sound grew louder. He searched about him for the luminescence of a boat's wake. Towards the city there appeared a glimmer in the water. He began rowing again, carefully dipping and lifting the oars lest his strokes create their own glow. Wisteria Key was barely a quarter mile north west, he could just make out its dark wooded shore. He heard another motor to his left. Looking, he saw a glowing wake paralleling his own course. The sounds from both motors were clear now. He abandoned any hope of concealment and began rowing with all his strength, each stroke striking sparks from the sea. Behind him a man shouted through a megaphone: Coast Guard, heave to! Stop or we'll shoot! A search light suddenly turned on, its beam illuminating the water to port. Eddie, kept rowing, Wisteria's low shoreline was just ahead. Several loud splashes came from the boat to port, its motor revved, pulling away quickly. There was a crunching sound, then silence. The boat behind audibly slowed, it's light scanning the shoreline. Eddie made one more powerful stroke and boated the oars. The skiff drifted a moment, then low hanging tree branches scraped along the hull, bringing it to halt. He pulled the skiff in under the branches and lay down flat on his back. Looking up he could see the search light playing through the trees above him. Abruptly the beam swung out of sight. A short distance away the man on the megaphone shouted again: Everyone stand up, hands raised above your heads! This is a customs and immigration check!

Another man spoke up. "We're just fishing for squid! Can't a man make an honest living anymore?"

There was the sound of Guardsmen jumping aboard the grounded boat.

"So where are your passengers? Saw some splashes back there. If you drowned any Chinamen that's murder," shouted the Guardsman.

"Don't know what you're talking about, never had any chinks on my boat."

"Hey, Chief, look what I found below, stinks down there," another Guardsman said.

"Do you read Chinese, skipper? No? It's an address in Miami. That's evidence enough for me. You and your crew are under arrest and your boat impounded."

"I want a lawyer!"

"I'm sure you do, but tonight you're spending in jail. And tomorrow we'll be back searching for bodies."

Eddie listened for the patrol boat to take the smuggler in tow. There was the sound of axes chopping tree limbs, and men grunting as they shoved the smuggler off the muddy bottom with poles. Finally, the patrol boat motor started up and began moving away. Eddie took a deep breath and sat up in the skiff. The boat lights dwindled crossing the channel toward Key West. He took an oar and started pushing the skiff out of the tangle of tree limbs.

A hand suddenly grasped the side of the skiff. It took Eddie a only a moment to decide whether to split open the skull of the hand's owner or haul the poor slob aboard. When the Guard found the body in the morning, they'd think the smugglers did it, and they'd be 90% right. If he stopped to help the guy, he'd be late for the rendezvous, and he was already running behind. If Ella had to wait for him, she'd be in danger. But above all he was bound by the Law of the Sea, to never abandon a soul in peril.

Eddie lay the oar down and took the man's hand in his. With his other hand Eddie reached over the side grasping the swimmer under the arm and lifted him aboard. He lay gasping for breath in the skiff.

"Any others?" Eddie asked.

The man mumbled something Eddie couldn't understand and then clearly, "No." He gagged and started coughing up water.

"Hang in there, buddy, I'll get you ashore." Eddie pushed the skiff clear of the tree branches and quickly beached it nearby. "Let me help you up, buddy." With Eddie's assistance the man stood and wobbled. "Hey, put your arm over my shoulder. Not far to walk." Together they stumbled up to the tree line where Eddie lowered him onto the sand. The man mumbled something else, in Chinese, Eddie guessed. "¿Hablas español?"

"Muy poco." The man held up his hand, thumb and index finger barely touching.

"Speak English?"

"Yes, pretty well."

"OK. We're on Wisteria Key. Those lights out there are in Key West. Guess that's where those smugglers were taking you when the Coast Guard caught them. In the morning the Guard will be back to look for you and your friends."

"How . . . how far is Key West?"

"About half a mile."

"Don't think about swimming that, the tide is turning and will carry you out, and anyway you don't look like you're in any condition to try."

"Can you take me?"

"Sorry buddy, no can do. The Coast Guard is on alert now. If they spot me with you, they'll assume I'm a smuggler, too. They'd deport you and would detain me unless they believe I was only playing life guard. And I have a date tonight. Understand? Look, buddy, here's five dollars. Tomorrow is a big holiday, Labor Day. There will be lots of people partying here, fishing and swimming. I'm sure you could find someone willing to take you across the channel. I'll get you something to drink."

Eddie walked back to the skiff and found a bottle of beer. He returned, bent down and handed it to the man. He grabbed Eddie's hand and yanked it down. Off balance Eddie fell down onto the beach. The man rolled on top of Eddie and thrust a knife into his side. Eddie wrenched free his hand still holding the bottle. He smashed it against the man's head, and thrust the bottle's jagged edged neck into the man's throat and twisted. Blood spurted, drenching Eddie. He pushed the man off him. He gurgled for a few seconds, his blood soaking into the sand. Eddie stood and checked his wound, it bled freely. An open switch blade lay on the ground.

"¡Idiota, idiota! Sólo quería el barco."

Eddie dragged the body by its feet back to the skiff. He checked the man's pockets and took back his fiver. With some cord he bound his kerchief tightly over his wound. He wrapped the body in a section of fish net, securing it with more cord and heaved it into the skiff. He knelt at the water's edge washing as much of the blood off him as possible. Then Eddie secured the weights from the Coast Guard bag to either end of the netting and launched the skiff with a grunt. He rowed slowly and painfully into mid channel and boated the oars. He drew his 6-inch blade fishing knife and plunged it to the hilt into the dead man's belly. Then he rolled the body over the side. The splashing water ignited. The body glowed. He watched the luminescence diminish and vanish as the man sank into the depths.

* * *

Fred waited outside the club, smoking and watching the crowd ebb and flow. The air was still and very humid. The cigarette smoke hung around him. Most of the vets had taken the afternoon train back to camp. He wondered who would take the morning ferry. There would be no way of avoiding them, he'd have to come up with some story to explain the car and Dixie. Sure, he'd hit the jack pot, but that wouldn't satisfy their curiosity, they'd want the details.

"Why, howdy Freddie! What have you been up to? Just check out them fancy duds, hardly recognized you."

"Howdy yourself, hombre. Why are you still around? Thought for sure you'd take the train."

"Got lucky in a crap game and clean forgot the time. Won so much thought I'd stick around and lose it all before heading back. Still got my return ticket. So . . . what's with the new look? Like some city slicker."

"Well, Chucky, it's sorta like this, my uncle died and left me enough to retire. Just stopping in Matecumbe long enough to hand in my resignation, don't want any bad press following me."

"Freddie, that's just about the mostest lame ass fib I've ever heard tell." There was a car honk. They both turned to look. Ella was parked across the street in the Chevy, waving. She honked again. "Better get shakin' Freddie ol' pal, looks your little filly is hot to trot." He laughed and punched Fred's shoulder.

"Good luck, buddy." Fred shook his hand. "And don't get wet." He crossed the street and got in the Chevy. Ella waved back at Chuck and blew him a kiss.

He watched the car drive off. "Shit, and I thought I was lucky!"
* * *

"What happened to you?" Fred asked as Ella headed across town. "Run into a wall?"

"Oh, does it show?" She glanced in the rear-view mirror. "Scheisse, it didn't feel that bad when he hit me. I was acting mostly to make it seem worse than it was."

"Is it worth asking, Dixie, or don't I have a need to know?"

"We're in this together now, Fred, so it doesn't much matter anymore. I was followed after leaving the boat. The only way to lose the guy tailing me was to get him into a fight. So, after flirting with a handsome Marine I provoked the guy into smacking me. He was big. I rolled on the street hollering, quite a performance I should say. Not just my Marine but the whole squad came to my rescue. I sneaked away unnoticed, during the brawl."

"Took one for the team, Dixie, I'm mighty impressed."

"Thanks Fred." She squeezed his hand.

Ella parked on Grinnell about a block from the pier. "Slide over Fred, be ready to go as soon as I get back." He nodded. She opened the door and walked briskly to the harbor. It was quiet, few people around. When she reached the pier, her footsteps resounded on the boards. Four fishing boats were moored there, two on either side. Between the two right side boats a shadow moved. She approached slowly and stopped between the pilings where the boats were tied. A duffle bag appeared from the shadows and slid onto the deck. Without a word spoken, Ella took the bag by its carrying strap and returned to the idling Chevy. She placed the bag on the rear seat floor and sat up front beside Fred. "Let's go."

They left town taking the Over-Sea Highway to Stockton Island and then the long causeway to Boca Chica Key parallel to the rail way. There was little traffic. Ella kept watch behind. The few headlights following them would soon turn off onto side roads. Fred switched on the radio and tuned to a station with Bing Crosby crooning, Where the Blue of the Night Meets the Gold of the Day.

"Oh, please, Fred! That will put me to sleep in another minute. Find some swing or jazz!"

"But I like Bing . . . well, OK." He resumed tuning and stopped on CMBG Havana, coming through clearly with a live performance direct from Casino de la Playa. A catchy rumba was playing.

"Now that I could dance to." Ella laughed and started rocking in her seat to the rhythm.

"But I don't know the words, Dixie."

"Doesn't matter. Shut up and drive."

There came along a stretch of highway over open water, then some towns on small keys. After an hour or so they arrived on Big Pine Key. "Watch for a left turn up ahead, Ella, it goes to the ferry landing." There was no traffic, all the homes and businesses they passed were boarded up.

"No Name Key, what does that mean? Is that the turn?" Ella pointed.

"Yeah, no one could be bothered with naming it. Don't know why, they named every other goddamn thing in Florida."

Fred turned and drove another four and a half miles over dark roads. The headlights lit up a sign for the ferry and another beside it reading No Name Lodge with an arrow pointing right. Several small cabins stood on either side of a building marked Office. In the window flickered a neon sign, Vacancy. The only car was an old Ford parked near the Office.

"We're in luck. Wait in the car and keep your head down." Ella nodded. Fred parked and walked to the Office. Through the window he saw a grey-haired woman seated at the front desk, staring at the opposite wall. He knocked, she turned to the window and waved him in. "Good evening, Ma'am, I'd like a cabin for what's left of the night."

"You know the ferry's not running, don't you?"

"Ah . . . no, hadn't heard. What happened?"

"Some mechanical problem they say. Might fix it tomorrow or might not. What with that storm coming my bet is not. Still, want the cabin? Everyone else turned around and went back to town when I told 'em. There's a hotel in Big Pine."

"Honestly, I can't drive another mile. I'll just take my chances in the morning. How much?"

She glanced briefly over his shoulder and smiled. "Two fifty, cash, if you please, and sign here."

"OK . . . there. Here you go, keep the change" he handed her a five. She looked twice, held it up to the desk light, and put it away. "Any place nearby for breakfast?"

"You can eat here, it's included. Nothing fancy, boiled fish and grits, or whatever Hettie can whip up. At seven."

"Never pass up home cooking, I'll be there. Thank you."

"Here's your key, Cabin 6, the last one on the left. Indoor plumbing, hot water, radio, double bed, clean sheets, and towels. The bridal suite."

Fred heard a tap, turned and glanced at the window. Ella was looking in. She grinned and waved.

"Thank you kindly, uh . . . we thank you a whole lot. Mind if I ask, are you riding it out here?"

"This is my home, nowhere else to go. Hettie's from Marathon, no way to get there with the ferry down. She should have left yesterday. Glad she stayed though, can't run this place by myself."

Ella opened the door and stepped inside. "Hi, I'm Dixie."

"Name's Sarah, Missy."

"Great! Come on Freddie."

"Well, good night then, ma'am."

"Good night to you and . . . enjoy yourselves."

* * *

Ella dropped her bag on the floor and surveyed the cabin, checking the bath and lifting the bedspread. "Looks clean, smells fresh, I'm taking a shower, it's been a long day."

"Don't use all the hot water."

"There's a hose outside . . . just kidding, I'll leave some." She closed the bathroom door behind her.

Fred stepped outside for a look. He'd parked the car behind the cabin so it couldn't be seen from the road and went around checking the locks. All secure. He was about to go back inside when he noticed several pairs of little reflections, about waist high, near a patch of woods. They blinked. He drew his pistol and slowly approached. He heard the shower running. The bathroom window suddenly opened, lighting the area. A pack of tiny deer looked back at him. "Hi there, fellas," Fred murmured. He took a cautious step forward. The deer all turned their heads right and dashed into the woods. He returned to the cabin. Inside he closed the curtains, locked the door with the bolt latch, and leaned the backrest of a chair under the door knob. The duffle bag he flattened and hid behind the sofa against the wall. From the closet he took an extra blanket and pillow and made himself a bed on the sofa. He placed the pistol under the pillow, took off his shoes, lay down, and drifted off.

* * *

"Fred! Wake up, take a shower, and brush your teeth. I left plenty of hot water and a spare tooth brush for you." She felt his chin and cheeks. "Better shave, too."

"Is it dawn already?"

"No, it's one in the morning. You need to clean up before coming to bed."

"Dixie, I was having such a nice dream. Just let me sleep. Plenty of time to wash up before breakfast. We're having fish and grits, specialty of the house." He looked up at her. She was wrapped in a white towel, her face scrubbed, her hair damp and clinging. She looked very stern.

"Don't be a putz, Freddie. It's Monday, so you're not Cindy's anymore. Clean up and come to bed with me."

"Uh . . . with you?"

She looked around. "Anyone else here? Of course, me. You know you want to. This could be our only chance. I'm not wasting it."

"And how do you know I want to?"

"I've known that since Friday morning. A lady simply knows when a gentleman wants to. Am I wrong?"

"Well, I did briefly consider the possibility, but Cindy hasn't given me a moment's rest since we met. Given the possibility then, just how old are you, Dixie? They got a law here in Florida."

"Eighteen on Thursday. Emilio said that was close enough."

"So, you slept with him?"

"How could I? He's impotent."

"I . . . didn't know that."

"Cindy tells me everything, not you apparently."

"Did she tell you about Friday night?"

"Of course." She lifted the towel, revealing a holstered pistol strapped to her thigh. "You see? I can't misplace my PPK. So, you'd better behave."

"OK, but why do you want to?"

"A gentleman doesn't ask a lady such questions. He's grateful, that's all. But seeing as we're friends now, I'll tell you. I hate sleeping alone and Cindy says you're a hoot in bed."

"She recommended me? I feel so . . . used."

"Don't we all."

"OK, you have this pretty well covered." He stood up, yawned and stretched. "Give me a few minutes." He walked to the bathroom.

"My! Such enthusiasm, makes a girl feel so sexy. Leave me the .45, I'll clean it. It'll keep me in the mood."

"Uh, not sure how that works, but here it is." He took the pistol from under the pillow and handed it to her. "Haven't shot it any, should be pretty clean."

"Whatever. Hurry now, haven't got all night. And don't jerk off in there."

Fred nodded and removed his clothes, and started to fold them neatly. "Oh, come on! I don't need any more teasing." Ella grabbed the pile and tossed it on the floor.

"Gee, I have nothing fresh to wear tomorrow and I have some business on Matecumbe. I have to look sharp."

"Oh, so that's your big concern with me all ready to go. *Scheisse!* I'll fold them, you wash up!"

"Thanks, Dixie." Fred shut the bathroom door behind him.

Ella collected his clothes, laid them on the bed and checked the pockets. Along with his wallet, and some loose change were two envelopes. One contained his discharge papers and tarjeta de turista. The other envelope was addressed to Frederick Dunn, C/O Veterans Work Program, Islamorada, Florida, the corner with the return address ripped off. Inside was a crumpled letter, neatly typed. Without a moment's hesitation she began reading, she was a spy after all:

Chase National Bank 18 Pine Street
New York, New York, July 31, 1935

Dear Frederick,
I hope this letter finds you in good health. You are cordially invited to attend the 308th Infantry Regiment's 15th Annual Reunion, Monday, November 11, 1935. After marching in the Armistice Day Parade – those of us who are up to it – we'll gather at the National Guard Armory, 68 Lexington Avenue, for dinner, drinks, speeches, and most importantly, meeting our old pals again. All those traveling from out of

town will have their expenses covered by the Reunion Committee. We earnestly desire everyone who can possibly attend to join us in this commemoration of those who gave their last full measure of devotion in selfless service to a grateful nation. Please join us in raising a glass in their honor.

A personal note – Fred, I've had the deuce of a time tracking you down. It has been an objective of mine that all our surviving DSC recipients be recognized together. Finally, this May I learned that you were working in the Florida Keys for the Government. I mailed you a letter in June but it seems you never received it. Please send me a brief note that you will attend this year and stand with the Regiment once again, proudly saluting the Colors.

A very personal note – I've invited Hauptmann Josef Kaufmann to be my guest at the Reunion. You never met him but you may have heard that he was the German officer who stopped his men from bayonetting you that morning. We became close friends after the war and now I am sponsoring his daughter's university studies in America. I cannot imagine what your feelings will be when I present him to you. And his upon meeting you. I only know that I will be deeply moved.

God bless you Fred and please come!

Signed/Daniel C. Rattigan, Colonel, U.S. Army Reserve

Ella, sank down on the bed sobbing, and read the letter again. *Bastard! You knew all the time! What game are you playing? Papi, you never told me you're coming to America. Why would they let you come?* She wiped away her tears, replaced the letter in Fred's jacket pocket and finished folding his clothes. She forgot about cleaning the .45. Dropping her bath towel on the floor, she curled up naked in the bed and pulled the covers up to her chin. She would find out Fred's angle. She was just starting to doze when Fred appeared.

"Here I am, Dixie. Still want me?"

Ella smiled up at Fred and welcomed him with a raised coverlet. He held up a condom in its wrapper. "Do you want to do the honors?" he asked.

"Toss it. I'm protected."

"Cindy told me the same thing."

"Yes, she followed my advice. Climb in."

He slipped into bed beside her. His skin was cool, damp and smelling of soap. She pressed her warm body against his, her hands wandered across his back and down to his buttocks and between his legs, probing and squeezing. He sighed, and she kissed him, their mouths open, tongues swirling. "I want to get better acquainted, hold still." She twisted around and began sucking and licking. He reciprocated with a skill and persistence Cindy hadn't mentioned. She shivered with delight.

Ella rolled over on her stomach, face down. He knelt between her thighs, fondling her cheeks, covering them with kisses. His tongue explored the cleft between, searching out and probing the pleasure spots. She giggled and squirmed. He slid up her body, kissing her back and nuzzled her neck, hands gripping her shoulders. Slowly he entered from behind, with long, slow, powerful strokes. Goldy hadn't shown such control, he had come quickly. She assumed some of him was still alive, swimming around inside her. How funny she thought, Goldy and Freddie would finally slug it out in her own intimate venue. Who would win? Didn't matter which one, whoever made it through the gate would fall victim to Ernst Gräfenberg's clever little guardian, guaranteed. Never before had two men made love to her in the same day. Not calendrically but within a 24-hour period, to be precise. The thought heightened her excitement, she felt like *une poule de luxe*, selecting lovers in accordance with her exacting standards, willingly and joyfully, not in the sad, brutal way of a common whore.

Fred nailed her to the sheets, reaching a hand underneath her belly for finger work. She stiffened and trembled.

Reality set in, she'd never wake up in time for grits, whatever they were, unless she got a little sleep. "Faster, honey, faster!" He responded with a deep, leonine growl. One more thrust and he stopped, sighing.

She twisted her head around. "What about me?"

"Uh, sorry. I got a little carried away."

"Yeah."

"OK, I owe you one. Shouldn't take long, still hard."

He began again and it didn't take all that long. When she came it was like a thunder clap. He didn't withdraw, they stayed joined together. She chose not to squeeze him out. It was only hospitable that she allowed him to rest where he flopped. They were both exhausted. They spooned, until sleep came for both.

Chapter 24

Monday, Labor Day, September 2, 1935 – The Game is Afoot

Ella woke before dawn. She took care climbing out of bed, so as not to disturb Fred. He hadn't slept well. For a time, he shivered and moaned. She had held him tight until he relaxed and fell into a deep slumber. Outside it was twilight. She quickly dressed, removed the chair back from under the doorknob and stepped outside onto the wet grass. Looking up she was struck by the splendor of the multi-colored clouds. She walked down to the ferry landing and out onto the pier. Perched on a piling, a sullen gull gave her a dismissive glance and a raucous ululation. The vista across the bay was unbroken to the salmon tinted eastern horizon. A sudden gust rippled the water, chilling her. She sat down at the end of the pier, legs dangling over the edge, and watched the sunrise.

In the golden light, a flotilla of pelicans paddled close by, dipping their beaks in unison. The sun rose above the horizon, quickly becoming too bright to watch. She looked away. The afterimages remained, fading slowly. Something caught in her throat. "Dear, dear Emilio, you'll never see another sunrise." She wept.

Fred came up quietly and sat beside her, placing his hand on her bare knee. She turned her face from him and rubbed away the tears. "How'd you sleep?"

"Pretty good."

"You seemed restless."

"Happens. So, what ya thinking, Dixie?"

She gestured toward the landing. "Look, no ferry. What do we do now? Can't go back to Key West, kind of burned our bridges. They'll be looking for us."

"Speaking of bridges, look off to the right. See that big one? That's the steel truss bridge to Bahia Honda. You can follow the other bridges east for miles. They go all the way to Lower Matecumbe."

A dark cloud swept over, obscuring the sun.

"So, you're saying we could drive there, over the rails?"

"Seen it done back in April on the Long Key viaduct. A newsreel crew came down to film a publicity stunt for the 1935 Chevrolet Master. Its new independent front suspension, Knee Action, made it a smooth ride, or so they claimed. Emilio bought the same model. That's our car, Dixie!"

"You're crazy. How far is that?"

"About 43 miles, but not all of that's over the railroad bridges. 15 miles on the tracks from Big Pine to Key Vaca, then there's a road through Marathon to Grassy Key, about 13 miles, then back on the rails to Lower Matecumbe, another 15 miles. After that, it's 94 miles clear sailing to Miami over the highway."

"You have a map? I can hardly remember where Miami is."

"No problem, Dixie. We just follow the railway, only one way to go, no junctions."

"Just peachy, Fred, assuming we don't drive off the bridge, get blown away by the storm, or the car doesn't break down. And also, the matter of meeting the Miami train on the single track. Haven't considered that little detail, have you?"

"Your mood sure has changed, mi amiga." His hand slipped up her thigh and gently squeezed. "Look on this as an adventure!"

"Sure."

"Breakfast ready!" Sarah shouted out the back door of the Lodge.

Fred stood and gave Ella a hand up. "Come on, Dixie, don't want your grits to get cold."

"Can't have that, I guess."

As they walked along the pier dark spots began appearing on the boards. "It's raining, Fred." Lightning flashed and thunder boomed across the key. The wind bent the trees. The rain came down in buckets. "Run!"

Fred and Ella sprinted hand in hand to the Lodge door, laughing all the way. Inside they stood dripping and grinning at each other. "I'll get you some towels. Now that was a sight to see, made my day."

Ella wringed water from her hair. "Why do you say that, ma'am?"

"Here's a towel, Missy. It's just that you were like a couple of kids out on a lark, splashing in the rain, without a care in the world. Made me feel good just looking."

"Well, ma'am, it was sorta fun but now I have to change."

"Sarah, could we bother you for some more towels? We could have breakfast then go to our cabin to change when the rain lets up. Dixie likes her grits hot."

"No problem. You two just sit right here." Sarah placed towels on the chairs at the big kitchen table. "Hettie, please serve our guests."

The young colored woman nodded, "Yes'm." She placed table settings before Fred and Ella, and quickly returned with a platter of food and drinks.

"Thank you, Hettie," Ella lifted her fork, then stopped. "Aren't you and Sarah joining us?" Hettie hesitated.

Sarah nodded. "I'd enjoy that, Missy. What do you say, Hettie?"

"Uh, I . . ."

"Come on, Miss Hettie, I don't know when I'll have a breakfast as delicious as this again, and I always like to eat family style."

"Thank you, Mister. I'll just fix another platter."

"The big lug's name is Fred, and he calls me Dixie Dugan."

Hettie curtsied. "Fred, Dixie, I'll be right back." She chuckled and went back to the stove.

"Mind if I turn on the radio, Sarah? I'd like to hear the latest on the storm."

"Not at all, Fred. It's already tuned to Miami."

There was some local news, then the announcer said, "And now a repeat of this morning's Weather Service advisory: Bulletin September second, 3:30 a.m. Tropical disturbance still of small diameter but considerable intensity is moving slowly westward off the coast of north-central Cuba attended by shifting gales and probably winds near hurricane force over small area; will probably pass through Florida Straits Monday. Caution advised against high tides and gales Florida Keys and for ships in path. The next advisory is scheduled for 9:30 a.m. The Labor Day forecast for Miami is for cloudy skies and showers, with a high of 84 and low of 74 degrees. Stay tuned to your Wonderful Isle of Dreams WIOD Miami radio, for the latest news."

Fred turned the volume down. "Not much change since yesterday. We were in Key West. Folks down there thought the world was ending. Say, you have someone to board up the lodge? I'd offer myself but we're on kind of a tight schedule."

"Don't give it a thought. I have some of the local boys coming round this morning to tend to that. Not expecting much of a blow, the barometer's barely budged."

"Freddie come eat, your grits are getting cold. You were right, they're really good with syrup and bacon."

"Miss Dixie, what is Key West like? I've never been," asked Hettie.

She finished swallowing, and dabbed her mouth with a napkin. "I only spent two nights there, and on Friday afternoon I got this sunburn," she touched her nose, "ouch. But I did learn to rumba at the Habana-Madrid Club."

"Gosh!"

"Oh, it was magical! And I had such a handsome partner, a Cuban, he spun me, dipped me and showed me how to move my hips." Ella stood and demonstrated with a quick thrust. "Shocking, eh?" The wet skirt clung to her body.

Hettie clapped her hands and cheered. Sarah frowned. Fred laughed. He found a Havana station playing some frenetic Don Aspiazu rumba.

Ella held out her hand. "Come on Hettie, I'll teach you the steps. Just let go and move with the rhythm."

The two girls began dancing around the kitchen. "My, you're a quick learner!" Ella spun Hettie out and back. "Dip me!" The girls took turns.

Sarah and Fred applauded.

* * *

The three New Yorkers met in Miami that morning. They had flown down Sunday, planning to continue on to their destinations the next day. They arrived early at the Pan American Seaplane Terminal on Dinner Key for the 8:00 a.m. flight to Havana, with a stop in Key West. Their taxis had pulled in within moments of each other. They followed the Negro redcaps carrying their bags into the airy, Art Deco building, painted in Pan Am's blue-white motif. A frieze around the high walls depicted the history of aviation. The 12 signs of the Zodiac decorated the ceiling. They paused before a huge rotating globe, it's axis correctly angled northward at 23½ degrees, partially sunk in the passenger hall's gleaming obsidian tile floor. It showed Pan Am's world-wide routes. A yellow line stretched from Alameda, California across the Pacific to Manila with kinks at Hawaii, Midway, Wake, and Guam.

"Pan Am is planning to fly that route in November, on the China Clipper," mentioned the older man leaning on the railing. He was dressed in a white suit, bowtie, sky-blue Oxford shirt, straw boater and white bucks. "Pretty impressive, huh?"

"Looks a bit short of the mark," the younger man replied. His look was conservative, a well- tailored dark suit, vest, four-in-hand, white shirt, grey fedora, and black brogans.

"Marketing. They'll get to Hong Kong soon enough. Hi, I'm Daniel. And this is Abby."

"I'm Ed. Pleased to meet you."

"Likewise, I'm sure." Abby's auburn curls were cut in a stylish bob under a provocatively angled white sun hat, a sleeveless pastel summer dress in a floral design hemmed just below the knees, and lavender pumps. She removed her sunglasses revealing lustrous green eyes and penciled black eyebrows. She smiled.

They shook hands. "I noticed you two on the flight yesterday. Where are you headed, Havana or Key West?"

"Key West."

"Why, so am I."

At the check-in counter Ed stood aside and allowed Daniel and Abby to go first. Then they took the covered walkway to Pier One. Moored to the floating dock a twin-engine Consolidated Model 16 Commodore rocked gently in the calm waters of Biscayne Bay. They waited for boarding to commence.

"So, been to Key West before, Daniel?"

"Used to work in Havana, we always stopped in Key West, traveling there and back. Love the place."

"A first for me. This is a business trip, but if I have time, maybe you two could show me around?"

"I'm available, Eddie."

"Uh . . . Daniel?"

"Sure, have fun. I'm a bit old for bar crawling."

Abby laughed. "Eddie, we're not married, if that's what you're thinking, just housemates. We're staying at the Casa Marina . . . separate rooms. Gardner, Abigail Gardner."

"Well, Miss Gardner, my name's Renard, Edward Renard."

"It's Abby, Ed."

"Right, Abby."

"May I ask the nature of your business, Ed?" Daniel asked.

"Legal matters, sorry, I'm not at liberty to discuss them."

"Lawyer, eh? Understand. In my line we're always involved in some litigation. But this trip is for pleasure."

The boarding announcement came. Their upholstered seats were across the aisle from each other. They sipped on orange juice and vodka highballs as the clipper taxied out into the bay. A man in a blue Pan American uniform appeared from the cockpit.

"Good morning, folks! I'm Captain Addison Person." He spoke loudly over the engine noise. "Frank Barker, the First Officer is at the controls, and the capable Milton Baxter is our Air Steward today. During take-off and landing all passengers are requested to remain seated with their seat belts fastened. The weather is a little unsettled today and we might encounter some turbulence during the flight. If so, I may ask you to fasten your belts, but there's nothing to be concerned about. The Commodore is a very tough bird. This particular one has flown down to Rio several times. We're on schedule for a 9:10 arrival in Key West, and for those continuing onward, we'll be docked at the Arsenal in Havana by 10:15. Now relax and enjoy the flight. We at Pan American Airways thank you for choosing to fly with us today."

* * *

By the time Fred and Ella checked out of the No Name Lodge the squall had passed and the sun was shining again. They drove back along the road to Big Pine. He turned on the radio and found the Miami station: "And now the Dorsey Brothers Orchestra with Bob Crosby on vocals performing their delightful little chart topper from Golddiggers of 1935, Lullaby of Broadway! Hit it, boys . . ."

"Bob Crosby, is he . . .?"

"Bing's kid brother, you'll like him better, listen . . ."

. . . the marigolds who sing and dance, At Salvatore's and Andy's . . .

"Yeah, that's better. But I've only seen Broadway marigolds in a florist shop, didn't think they entertained. Never been to Salvatore's or Andy's."

"Not flowers, Dixie. You know, pansies, daffodils. Guys who like guys."

"Oh, that kind. They're funny."

The good people of Big Pine were busy boarding up their homes and businesses, but Fred did find an open service station. He had the tank filled, oil and tires checked. The railroad tracks ran through town and then arced southeast. A narrow dirt road ran parallel. Fred followed it to where the Spanish Harbor viaduct began. He drove onto the tracks and parked astride the left rail, facing the bridge. West Summerland Key was clearly visible across the water, little more than half a mile away.

"So, how is this supposed to work, just get up on the rails and go like a train?"

Fred, reached across Ella's lap and opened her door. "Come 'round to the front and I'll show ya."

They stood facing the car. "Can't drive on the rails themselves, not stable, you'd slip off and damage the tires against the hardware. And you can't drive between the rails either, the car's track overlaps the rail gauge. This is how they did it for the newsreel." Fred pointed, "Left tires on the ties outside of the left rail, right tires between the rails. Look here," Fred picked up a handful of gravel from the roadbed. "This is what you call ballast. It keeps the ties in place so the rails stay true and provides drainage. Now here it's almost level with the tops of the ties. That makes for a good ride. You can drive pretty fast. But in places, especially on the shoulder the ballast may have shifted down as much as six inches, with a one-foot gap between ties. That'll rattle your bones. And then the tires hit the next tie with a wallop. Have to slow way down or get a blowout. Just have to be careful you don't drift too far left. Over land that would mean the right tires rubbing up against the left rail, or on a bridge, driving clean off and into the water. Bit of a drop, don't want that, spoil your whole day."

"To be sure."

"Now on the bridges, look here." They walked up to the bridge abutment. "See, there's another set of rails between the ones the train rides on, guard rails they're called. They're supposed to keep the cars from derailing. If there is a derailment on a bridge the cars will go into the water and likely damage the bridge on the way down."

"Will they keep the Chevy on the bridge, Fred?"

"Wouldn't count on it. If we brush up against 'em, likely we'd damage the tires before going for a swim. Ya gotta just steer clear. Now, I have to tie the front doors open." Fred took a cord he'd bought at the Lodge shop, cut two sections off the coil, and used them to tie the front door handles to the rear door handles. "The Chevy has suicide doors, so when the front doors are open you can see the tires better."

Ella, got back in her seat and leaned to the right. "So, I warn you if it gets too close to the rail?"

"You nailed it, Dixie. And I can see the left tire from my side. And here's the other good part, if we do drive off the bridge, we can easily jump clear before the car hits the water."

"Suicide doors, yeah, that figures. Now, about the morning train."

"Oh, we've plenty of time to make Key Vaca before it shows up. We'll pull over while it passes and then on to Matecumbe by noon. Piece of cake. We'll have lunch at the hotel and then reach Miami for supper. Spend the night and fly to Nassau Tuesday morning, free and clear. Good plan, huh?"

"Sure Fred, what could possibly go wrong?" Ella stepped out, opened the rear door, and removed the duffle. She pulled the Coast Guard bag out and tossed the empty duffle back on the rear seat

"What are you doing?"

"What's it look like?" Ella wrapped the sea bag's strap around her left arm. "My life preserver." She took her seat.

"Yeah, don't wanna lose that . . . or you, either. Here we go." Fred started slowly. The ride was little different than the pot-holed dirt road. When they reached the bridge, it got bumpier. The ballast was lower than on land and the Chevy dropped a few inches each time it crossed from one tie to the next, and the front and rear tires hit the ties at different times. The suspension absorbed much of that, but the constant jouncing was tiring. He shifted into second and accelerated to twenty. Now the vertical drops were less but the impacts of the tires against the ties were worse. There were no curves on the viaduct, so he had only to steer straight. But he could feel the bumps through the steering wheel, more so as he went faster. At thirty it got harder to steer. He had to force the wheel back to center. The impacts came rapid fire. At forty his teeth rattled.

Ella looked ahead grimly, her eyes fixed on the right front tire, bouncing up and down in a blur. "My knee action is starting to ache. Slow down!"

"Almost across, Dixie."

When the car made it onto West Summerland Key Fred stopped, got out and inspected the tires for damage. "Looking good, so far."

Ella joined him and stretched her body. "Whew! How many more miles of that, did you say?"

"Look. The ballast is better maintained here. Should be smooth sailing to the next bridge. You wanna try?"

"Sure, I think I can handle it. Give you a rest."

"Righto." He placed the Coast Guard bag on the rear seat. "Won't need that here."

She started driving "I've been on rougher roads." Ibis, herons, gulls, terns, pelicans and frigates were everywhere, calling and swooping about, flying low. "They seem upset."

"Birds know when bad weather is getting close. There's an osprey," he pointed.

It started raining and gusting again. The massive steel trusses of the next bridge loomed before them. "Stop here. We should wait until the squall passes."

Ella brought the car to a halt and set the parking brake. "OK, Dixie you want to try this bridge?"

"It looks different."

"This bridge has steel deck plates, no space for rock fill and ballast to lay the tracks on. Instead, the ties are longer, closer spaced and held in place by those side timbers, bolster curbs they call 'em. They're bolted to the decking and keep the ties from shifting. So just keep the left tire between the curb and the left rails. The right tire stays between the guard rails. The smaller gaps between the ties should make the ride smoother. Ready?"

"No, you take it. I'll watch this one."

"As you like." Fred started across the bridge, slowly at first, but faster as the jouncing was much less. "Hey, this is good. Make up some time here. Look how high we are! Must be 30 feet."

"Yeah . . . high."

Ella took over driving when they reached Bahia Honda. Again, the ballast between the ties was low over stretches of track and the ride got rough. There were places, however, where it was possible to drive over open ground.

"Rest stop, Fred." She pulled over into a clearing on the ocean side. Waves were visible through the underbrush.

"Me, too. I'll go left, you go right."

"Whatever, I'm going down to the beach. I prefer a pee with a view."

"Suit yourself."

Ella came upon a narrow path leading to the ocean. The surf was higher than she remembered at Key West. A stiff breeze blew spindrift from the wave crests. The birds were here too, in abundance. Many hung suspended in the air above the waves, waiting for some hapless fish to rise near the surface, then they darted down for the kill. She found a large palm above the tide line and squatted beside it. Her gaze wandered up and down the deserted beach. Mobs of sandpipers kept pace with the water as it surged and receded. The sun had come out again, she squinted at the sand's brilliance. The ocean sparkled.

They returned to the car. Before Ella could turn the key, Fred asked, "Dixie, what happened between you and Goldy? Level with me."

"You have no need to know."

"Aren't we friends now? No secrets between friends."

"You asked me to take care of him. We made love. We watched the sunset from the pier. I shot him. Eddie took the body wherever he takes bodies. Isn't that what you wanted me to do?"

"I . . . supposed I should have understood what I was asking. I didn't think it through. He was a gangster, after all, would've killed us all without blinking an eye. Still, I didn't think you were that kind."

"What kind, Fred? A whore, a monster?"

"Oh, no! You're sweet. You're loyal. You're funny. You cry over some kids in Belgium who lost their momma. You danced with that little colored girl. You look chic in and out of sailor suit. You love Cindy. You defended Emilio. You remind me of Dixie Dugan. You're great in bed. It's just hard to think of you as a killer."

"But that's what I am."

Fred leaned over and kissed her. She kissed him back, hard.

* * *

There were three short bridges linking Bahia Honda, Ohio, Missouri and Little Duck keys. Ella took these confidently but came to a stop on the abutment of the next bridge. "Fred . . . I can't see to the other side. Just how long is this one?"

"About seven miles; it starts out concrete arch then changes to steel plates in the deeper water. The whole thing is called Knight's Key Bridge, that's where it ends or starts, dependin'. Look way out there, you can see the tender's house atop the Moser drawbridge. It looks to be swung open."

"How long will it take to drive across?"

"Reckon about half an hour, if the bridge tender cooperates."

"Anyplace to pull over, off the tracks?"

"Well at Pigeon Key, that's past the draw, there might be some room. If you're thinking about the train meeting us mid-way, no chance of that. It's not even scheduled to stop at Long Key Fishing Camp until 10:09, that's way before Marathon. And it usually runs late. I've taken it enough times to know. I reckon it's only a little past nine now. We'll probably meet it near Marathon."

"You drive, then."

They changed seats. Ella held the bag in her lap. Fred inserted the ignition key. She placed her hand on his. "Wait a minute. Have you thought of just disappearing with all of this?" she asked, patting the bag with her other hand.

"Of course, but I've never stolen anything from anyone, and it's too late to change my ways."

"The people who call you veterans psychopaths would think that's crazy."

"Do you?"

"Emilio stole it from Machado who embezzled it from the Cuban people, and it was originally a loan from wealthy American investors using their profits from exploited workers, so who would you be stealing it from?"

"I reckon from Cindy, she trusted us with it. And I owe her a lot."

"She gave you a good time for the weekend. In return you nearly got yourself killed. Eddie got a hundred thousand dollars for his efforts. You deserve as much."

"Figure I'll just have to wait until she gets to Nassau to find out."

"And if she gives you a hundred grand too, what will you do with it?"

"You've heard about the war bonus the Government owes us vets? Think I might divvy it up amongst the men."

"Really? And how far would that go?"

"Well, for just the 700 fellas in the Keys, about $140 each."

"Is that all they're owed? Doesn't sound like much."

"There's a formula based on the number of days served and whether state-side or overseas. Mr. Poock, who runs the trust fund, calculated my bonus including the interest payable in 1945, as $1369.45. He said the average is about $1,100."

"Then you'd be donating only about 10%."

"Yeah, think of it another way, it's more than four month's pay. Might get some families through the winter."

"You've given this some thought."

"Sure thing, ever since Eddie got his share. So, what about you?"

"Bribe the Nazis to get my parents out of Germany."

"They're in danger?"

"Of course, they're Jews!"

* * *

The concrete arches were rough going what with shifted ballast and foot wide gaps between ties. He stayed at about 15 mph, so as not to annoy Ella too much. And there was the weather. There were patches of clear sky with bright sunshine. Then a squall would appear from the northeast over the bay. Once they had to stop altogether, the tracks ahead disappearing in a torrent of rain, the car shaking in the gusts. The rain blew through the open doors soaking them. "Should have worn our swimsuits," Ella muttered. The squall lasted only a few minutes and then they started up again.

Soon they were riding over the close spaced ties of the steel plate sections again. The outer wood curb made it safer. He picked up the speed. The draw bridge loomed before them and Fred stopped the car a dozen feet from the gap. He honked the horn, then got out and walked in front of the car. "Hey, Mack! Can you close the bridge long enough for us to the drive across?"

The bridge tender peered out a window in the house above the pivot point, midway between the two truss spans. He considered the situation. "Buddy," he shouted, "this is railway property, you're trespassing. You'd best just back up where you came from."

Fred turned around to Ella and shrugged his shoulders.

"Tell him I'm pregnant."

"I thought you said you were protected."

"Really!"

He turned back to the tender. "Hey, pal, look! There ain't no boats coming through and you'll have to close it anyway when the train gets here, and besides the little lady has a baby coming . . . fast, so whaddaya say?"

Ella stuck her head out the door and waved. She looked anxious.

"Railway policy is to close the bridge only for trains and maintenance . . . less'n there's some emergency. You pull the reins back on that little nipper, ma'am, while I call this in."

Fred leaned back on the Chevy's hood. "Think we got this, Dixie."

"I'm hungry, Freddie, and thirsty, and hot, and wet, and tired, and . . . I have to go to the bathroom."

"He can't hear you."

"Doesn't matter. I live my parts."

The lights on the bridge began flashing, a horn blew, and the span began rotating. It took five minutes before the bridge locked into the closed position.

"Thanks!" Fred shouted.

The bridge tender, waved back, "Best wishes to the missus."

"OK, let's go." Fred started the car and began driving, beeping the horn twice when they made it across the draw bridge. The tender immediately began opening it again. They passed over Pigeon Key on the steel plate bridge. There was a passenger platform and a ramp leading down from the track level to the island where several buildings stood. All the storm shutters were in place.

"Hey Dixie, look out there to the right. See the light house? That's Sombrero Light and it's flying just the single flag, so they haven't called a hurricane yet. That's good."

"Yeah," Ella fiddled with the radio. "Can't find that Cuban station. What's this business of yours in Matecumbe anyway? Do we have to stop? I'd just as soon go on to Miami, find a nice hotel, take a shower and mess around."

"Thought we'd have lunch and pick up my stuff at the camp. Maybe say good bye to my pals. Jimmy, my boxer friend, works at the hospital. He should be around."

"Want me to scrunch down low in the car, or do you think I'm presentable enough to be introduced?"

"Hah, I think you'll do pretty much whatever you like. Just don't act pregnant, the boys might get the wrong idea."

"Don't worry, I'm over that. You know we're leaving a trail behind us for anybody to follow. They'll be on to us by tonight. We can't drop any crumbs after Matecumbe."

"We'll pull a disappearing act. Problem is this car. Emilio should have bought it in black. Maybe I can swap it for something less attention grabbing in camp. Don't expect he would mind."

When they reached Knight's Key, Fred pulled off the tracks onto a dirt road and stopped. He got out and untied the door handles. "We have this down pat now, don't need the extra visibility. People will notice." He got back in the car and tuned to the Miami station.

* * *

The Commodore flew low over Key West, swung south past Fort Taylor, and turned northeast into its final approach. Were it not for the spray outside the windows the passengers would not have noticed the transition from flying to floating. The plane taxied into the submarine basin and was quickly secured to the Pan Am dock. Captain Person entered the cabin smiling.

"Welcome to Key West! Please check for any personal belongings before debarking, and thank you again for flying with Pan American. Those continuing on to Havana please remain seated until our Key West travelers exit. We'll be departing in ten minutes."

He walked to the rear of the seaplane, looked out the window and opened the hatch, then ushered Edward, Daniel, Abby and a young couple off the plane. Stepping on to the dock he was met by the Pan Am agent.

"Hey, Addison."

"Yeah?"

"Got a call from George Brands in Miami. He wants you to see whatever you can of that hurricane. He thinks we may have to shut down operations this afternoon. The Bureau says it's off north central Cuba. Brands says you should see the cloud tops easily from 8,000 feet if they're right."

"Tell him we'll keep our eyes peeled." Person looked down the pier and watched his departing passengers walking to waiting taxis, trailed by redcaps with their baggage. Three people stood waiting to board. "Let's get our Havana folks settled and we're off."

* * *

They said their goodbyes and parted. Ed took a cab downtown. Daniel and Abby headed for the Casa Marina. When they checked in, the desk clerk handed Daniel a note, "For you, sir."

Daddy,
Please come to the Marine Hospital, Emilio was hurt in an accident. He's resting now.
Cindy

He handed the note to Abby. She read it and gasped.
"Can you have our bags brought to our rooms?" he asked the clerk.
"Certainly, Mr. Rattigan."
They rushed outside and took a waiting cab.

* * *

"Curious thing, Guy, I met Daniel Rattigan on the plane this morning." Renard leaned back in the chair across from Marshal Reeve's desk and waited for a response.

". . . oh, some relation to Dunn's little friend?"

"He's her father and the other girl's sponsor. He's also a vice president at Chase National Bank. He was in charge of the Havana branch before the revolution in '33, and was allegedly involved in a fraudulent loan to the Machado Government. Rather interesting that he shows up in Key West two days after the Havana branch gets bombed, and both his daughter and protégée are keeping company with the prime suspect."

"Yes, I see your point. I told Dunn to be available today for your interview. Is noon good for you?"

"Yes. I'd like to review the transcript from yesterday."

"Hear it is." Reeve passed Renard a file folder. "And the others?"

"Actually, I'd like to speak with the Kaufmann girl first, then Dunn, Miss Rattigan, and the captain, Mr. Ruz. Rattigan will likely come along.

It would be awkward if he sees that I'm involved with the investigation, he might think I was spying on him. So, please ask him to wait outside. I may have a few questions for him."

"Certainly, I'll just make a few phone calls."

* * *

Daniel and Abby jogged up the steps of the Marine Hospital. Abby made it to the top first and quick stepped to the reception nurse. "What room is Emilio Ruz in?"

"And what relation are you to the patient, Ma'am?"

"We're family," Daniel interjected.

"Specifically."

"I'm his father!"

"Just a moment sir . . . Mr. Ruz is in room 6 down this hall and to the left. You may go right in."

Abby rushed down the hallway, and entered the room. Cindy was sitting beside the bed. She looked up and smiled.

"Daddy didn't tell me you were coming, Abby. I'm so glad." She stood and hugged her.

Daniel appeared in the doorway. "Cindy, what's this all about?" He saw Emilio, hurried to his side and bent close. "My dear boy, what happened?"

Cindy placed a hand on his shoulder. "Daddy, Emilio fell in the street and hit his head. Saturday night he lost consciousness and Ella took him here. Doctor Henderson says he had a blood clot on his brain. They operated for hours to stop the bleeding. He's still in a coma. I'll have her come and explain everything." She left the room.

Abby came around to the other side of the bed. She leaned over him, turned her head, bringing her cheek against his nostrils, feeling his faint exhalations. She kissed him. Her eyes glistened.

"I don't understand any of this. Emilio doesn't stumble, he's a dancer for Christ's sake! He's always alert and cautious."

"Dan, Cindy isn't telling us everything and where is Ella?"

Cindy and Emma walked in. "This is Doctor Henderson. She admitted Emilio and has attended him ever since. She's wonderful. Emma this is my father Daniel Rattigan and Abby Gardner, she's family."

Emma shook hands with Daniel and Abby. "Please sit down, while I check Emilio's condition." She took his vital signs and made notations on his chart. Then she turned to face the others.

"I'll be blunt, Emilio appears to have irreversible brain damage, it is unlikely he'll ever regain consciousness. If he does, his functions will be impaired. We have done everything medically possible. He may live on as he is now indefinitely, with full time care. But he will remain very frail, and susceptible to infection. Mr. Rattigan, Cindy said you may wish to take him back to New York with you. I can help with the arrangements. I am very sorry."

Abby began sobbing. Daniel put his arm around her shoulders, but she shrugged him off. "I know what he needs, but I can't give it to him!" she cried. Cindy knelt beside Abby and embraced her.

"Thank you, Emma," Cindy stood.

"I'll be available if you have any questions." Emma left.

"Cindy, where did this happen?" asked Daniel.

"He took us to Havana Saturday morning. We were supposed to go clubbing and spend the night. That afternoon he went to the bank to cash a check. On the way back to our hotel there was an explosion that knocked him to the street. He picked himself up and took a cab. At the hotel he called the Weather Bureau. They gave him a storm warning so he decided to return to Key West immediately. We made it back in the evening. He was working on his boat getting ready for the storm when he passed out. Ella and Eddie were with him and got him to the hospital."

"Why Cuba?" Abby exclaimed. "It's dangerous for him there. I asked Ella to give him a kiss from me . . . where is she?"

"Somewhere safe. She found out yesterday some G-man was coming today to question her. She works for the FBI now, informing on the Party and wasn't supposed to leave the country without her handler's permission. She thought it best to get lost."

"She's a spy? Cindy, this just gets deeper. We met a guy on the plane this morning. Handsome, looks like a G-man, Edward Renard. Did Ella mention his name?"

"No, Abby, she's like Emilio, won't tell you anything unless you have a need to know. I don't press either of them."

"No idea what he was doing in Havana?" asked Daniel. "And going to my bank no less. If the police knew he was in Cuba they would have picked him up, he's on their black list."

"He knew the danger. He had an alias and disguised himself, shaved his mustache."

"He couldn't have used his name at the bank, Batista has his spies there. Whose name did Emilio use?"

"He told me he needed a patsy for some scheme of his. I picked up this bum in the Keys, the porra were supposed to go after him if anything went wrong. After I dressed him up, he was a dead ringer. Emilio said he looked like his twin."

Abby rolled her eyes. "Deeper and deeper, Cindy."

"And where is this bum?" asked Daniel.

"With Ella."

"Jesus Christ, Cindy, this is like playing 20 questions!" Abby shook her head.

"None of this was supposed to happen! The bum was meant to take the fall and we would have made a clean getaway. But he surprised Emilio and fooled the Cubans. They let us escape, but now they want him for the bombing. There are people here with guns looking for him."

"And I bet that's not the half of it. I'm going to make arrangements to move my boy to a real hospital. Explain it all to Abby, don't hold anything back. She has a need to know."

* * *

Ella drove past the shuttered ferry landing on Hog Key and continued on the road to Marathon. Fred spotted an open general store in town. "Pull over here, we can get a cold drink. Should be a rest room, too."

The store was near the train station. With their sodas, an orange Nehi and a Coke, they sat on the platform bench.

"Ya know, Dixie, the boys in the camps like to be at the Islamorada station when the train from Miami stops. Most of us came on that train, and we're curious if someone we know might shows up."

"Hey, Cindy and I got off Friday morning, did you forget? I saw just how curious you bums are when a lady appears."

"Well now, she'd have gotten the same reaction at any work camp in the world. Put a bunch of sex starved bums together and they'll act like idiots when a pretty girl walks by."

"Were you expecting Cindy to show up Friday?"

"What? How could I have known that?"

"You know Colonel Rattigan, don't you?"

"What's that got to do with anything? She didn't tell me her last name until we met again at the hotel. Even then I didn't know for certain. Could have been just a coincidence. Something like 3000 men were mustered out of the 165th, almost a certainty she's met a few besides me over the years. What are you getting at?"

"You know who my father is, right?"

"Just what you told me, some German officer."

"For God's sake Fred, he saved your life!"

"What should I thank Hauptman Kaufmann for, killing Steve and letting me live to remember? His face was shot off, I only knew it was him because of his gold tooth. I swore I'd kill the fuckin' Krauts that did it, see if anyone recognized them when I got through."

"No, no, no! Papi is a good man, you can't mean that! It . . . it was war."

Fred began trembling. "Oh, shit!" He stood, rushed to the edge of the platform, doubled over and retched. Ella hurried to his side and held his shoulders to keep him from keeling over the edge.

"Fred, I'm sorry. Can you walk back to bench?"

"Uh . . . where's my Coke?"

"On the bench, come on." They sat. "Here," she held the bottle to his lips, "drink." He emptied the bottle.

"How did you know?"

"It's in the letter you carry around with you. Didn't you read it?"

"No, I couldn't get past the first line."

"It was wrong to read your letter. I get it, you don't want any reminders. I should've kept it to myself."

"I've had that letter for a month, could never get past the first line without getting the shakes and heaves."

"Cindy's father wants you to come to the reunion."

"I gathered that much. But I know what would happen, a waking nightmare . . . I could do it again. I'd embarrass myself and ruin it for all the sane vets. Who let that psycho in? . . . You've been fun all weekend, Dixie. I know you're some kind of spy, but I'm not hiding anything. Can you be fun again?" He looked up at her, there were tears in his eyes.

"Wipe your chin." She handed him her kerchief.

"No thanks, I have mine." He got up, went to the "White" water fountain, wet the handkerchief and cleaned his face. "Better?" He returned and sat beside her.

"Yeah." She kissed him on the cheek.

For a few minutes they sat silently together, holding hands, then the Havana Special screeched to a stop in front of them. The conductor stepped off, two women followed him onto the platform, and some guy took a mail sack he was handed. "All aboard," shouted the conductor, looking up and down the length of the train. He blew his whistle and the train began moving.

"Now that was exciting! Let's get going. I'll drive." Ella drove onto Grassy Key. They listened to the radio.

We interrupt our scheduled programming to provide our listeners with the latest advisory from the U.S. Weather Service: 10 a.m. Tropical disturbance central about two hundred miles east of Havana, Cuba moving slowly westward attended by shifting gales and probably winds of hurricane force small area near center. Caution advised vessels Florida Straits next twenty-four to thirty-six hours. Northeast storm warnings displayed Miami to Ft. Myers, Florida." We now resume with the Press-Radio News . . .

"Does that mean we're in danger, Fred?"

"I'm like the Coast Guard. I'd say we'd better get to the mainland." They continued on to Grassy Key and the Long Key viaduct, Ella driving.

* * *

Captain Person sat in Pan American's Havana office on the phone with Miami. "George, I just made some quick calculations. We were 40 miles northeast of Havana when I made my observations. The hurricane was about 100 miles east of us and 50 miles or so north of Carahatas, near Salt Key, awesome thing to see. Figure it will cross the Keys somewhere . . . Yeah, I've seen the 10 a.m. advisory, it's way off, so what do you want me to do? . . . I can leave by eleven, we're refueling now . . . we have some cargo and a couple of passengers standing by, eager to get to the States . . . OK, no stop in Key West, should arrive in

Miami by one . . . Yeah, I'll pass my report on to the Cubans. We'll see ya soon and park the bird safe in the hangar."

* * *

After Long Key the tracks traversed more than a mile of fill before crossing the Channel 5 Viaduct, a concrete arch bridge, nearly a mile and three quarters long. They had become used to the staccato jostling of the car over the ties. Another squall had come up. Fred noticed another squall line approaching and took his right hand off the wheel to point. A loud bang startled both of them. The car wobbled and fish tailed. The left rear tire bounced over the bridge's edge. Ella clutched the bag tightly in her lap. Fred tapped the brakes and steered just enough to the left to swing the rear of the car back onto the bridge. They rumbled to a stop. It had started raining again.

He took a deep breath and looked over at Ella. "OK?"

"Just about shit my knickers. Yeah, I'm OK. You stay put. I'll check for damage." She walked around to the back. "The left rear tire is shredded. The rim is showing. Looks dented. No room to change it. Your ass will be hanging over the water. Can you drive the car so the left tires are inside the guard rail?"

"Yeah, tell me when there's enough clearance." He turned the wheel sharply right, shifted to first gear and pressed the gas pedal. The front left tire slowly climbed over the rail. The left rear wheel scrapped against the rail, sliding along.

"Give it some more gas."

The motor revved and with a screech the left wheel jumped the rail and landed on the inside ties. "Now once more to clear the guard rail. OK, stop! You've got it."

Fred set the parking brake and came around to Ella. "Sheez, what a mess." He turned and looked back down the tracks. Pieces of rubber littered the road bed. "See something." He jogged a short distance, found a loose spike and walked back with it. "Best I can figure the front tire must have dislodged this, and spun it around pointy end up for the rear tire to hit. Well, let's get to work." He removed the rear-mounted spare, opened the trunk, and took out tools. He tossed the spike in. "Souvenir."

While Fred worked, Ella looked around anxiously for somewhere to run to if the train from Miami appeared. There were only outriggers supporting telephone lines, just big enough to sit on while the train passed.

Fred noticed her looking. "Don't worry none, Dixie. The train would see us parked here a mile away. The engineer would stop and dress us down. Have us arrested, well, me anyway. I got sort of a bad reputation on this line."

He finished up and wiped his hands with a rag. "Have to have that looked at by a mechanic, likely some alignment damage. So, you wanna drive?"

"No, if this happens again, I'd likely go for a swim. You did well, I must admit."

But keeping the car going straight became very difficult. The rear suspension was bottoming out with each tie. Ella leaned into the dash board wide-eyed. A half mile on was another draw bridge. This was a single leaf bascule design with the 57-foot-long span lifted vertically. It was in the open position. A small boat passed underneath. The bridge tender sat in his small house on the eastern side. Fred stopped about a car length from the edge and honked the horn twice. Nothing happened. Ella took the duffle bag from the back seat, rolled it up into a ball, and placed it under her skirt against her tummy. She climbed out of the car, "I got this."

"Good luck. Just don't let the bag fall out."

"Hey, mister!" she shouted across the gap, "could you please close the bridge for us? We have to get to Matecumbe before the storm." She waited, with her left hand supporting the bulge in her skirt. She was about to shout again, when a man stepped out of the house.

"Hah! You two. I listened in on the call from Moser. Saw you make a stop back there. Problem?"

"Yeah, we blew a tire and damaged something. Almost scared the baby out of me."

"Wait until this next boat clears and I'll close the bridge for you."

"Thank you, mister. Surely do appreciate this. We've been driving since eight and I think something's rattled loose." Ella rubbed her bulging tummy and laughed.

"You just hold in there, little lady." The bridge tender went back into his house. The boat skipper must have gathered what was about. He waved up to Ella, and quickly steered through the passage. Immediately, the bridge horn blew, the lights flashed and the span lowered. Ella got back into the car and Fred started the motor. The bridge locked in place and the tender motioned them on. Ella leaned out the window and blew a big kiss the tender. "You stay safe now, ya' hear?"

He laughed and waved back, "Good luck!"

It was a short drive to Craigs Key and then to Lower Matecumbe where the highway resumed. Just a few folks looked up when they came off the tracks. "Whew! No more bridges?" Ella exclaimed.

"Don't think we could have gone much further, the car's about to fall apart. Think I can get it fixed up enough at Camp 1 to get to Miami."

"Yeah, show me off to your friends, Let's just get to Miami tonight."

They started up State Highway 4-A, driving slowly. The key was narrow here. The bay and the ocean were only a fair golf drive apart. Camp 5 on the eastern tip of Lower Matecumbe was looking ragged. Several of the tents were flapping in the wind. Ella continued driving across the Indian Key Fill, the water was near level with the roadway. The ocean foamed around the Alligator Reef Light. "Still just the one flag, Dixie."

* * *

"Capitán Povey, llamada para usted." The bartender handed Len the phone.

"*Povey aquí... Sí Comandante... Sí... El Observatorio Nacional de Cuba? Sí... Sí... por supuesto, Señor ahora... inmediatamente... claro... ¡Sí Comandante!*"

"*¿Qué pasó?*" asked the Air Corps lieutenant seated beside him in the Officers Club.

"Search mission. Seems some Pan Am pilot told the Observatory that the storm that's supposed to hit us is not where it's supposed to be. So, I'm going to find it. You're in charge 'til I get back."

"*¡Sí señor!*"

The 10 a.m. advisory had placed the storm about 20 miles north of Cayo Santa Maria, moving slowly west. If the Weather Bureau was right the storm could hit Havana tonight or tomorrow morning. Evacuations had already been ordered in the lowlands near Cardenas and Sagua la Grande.

At 11:30 a.m., Len climbed into the open cockpit of his Curtis Hawk, Number 21, and adjusted his Kollsman altimeter to the airfield's altitude above mean sea level, 98 feet, and barometric pressure reported from the tower, 29.95 inches of mercury. He took off, passed over the city, climbed to 7000 feet and then followed the coast line east. The barometer had dropped to 22.9 inches during the ascent. This was normal in a standard atmosphere, about one-inch difference per thousand feet. Every ten minutes he recorded the compass heading, air speed, indicated altitude, air pressure and coastal landmarks in his flight log. The Sperry artificial horizon would show if he were climbing or descending to maintain the indicated altitude. Any variation in air pressure would be attributable to the weather conditions.

The coast was clear for as far to the east as he could see, and at 7000 feet the horizon was over 100 miles away. But to the north it was cloudy and he banked his plane to investigate. Only a few minutes passed before he saw it. An inverted cone of swirling clouds towered high into the sky. He estimated the height at 12,000 feet. Approaching the outer edge of the cone he could feel strong cross winds. Going any closer and he'd be in the clouds, flying blind. Because he was in a low-pressure area the altimeter was dangerously unreliable. It might show 3000 feet while he was on the deck. And with little to no visibility he'd have no way of knowing how close the sea was. It was raining. Lightning flashed continuously. He flew as near as he dared around the western edge of the cone. Through breaks in the clouds, he could see the ocean. The waves broke against each other like they struck the sea wall along Havana's Malecón. Len flew north until he could see the sky clearing beyond the storm. He estimated he was near Cay Sal, 60 miles northwest of Carahatas, and 70 miles southeast of Long Key. That was far enough. He headed back to Columbia Airfield, outside Havana.

Colonel Batista would be pleased with his report. Wednesday's Day of the Constitutional Soldier and Sailor celebrations could proceed on schedule. Now if his pilots didn't crash and his solo aerobatics act thrilled the crowds, Len could get a few days leave. By Thursday his flying buddies would be back from the National Air Races in Cleveland with tales to tell. Miami was just 90 minutes away in Number 21. The hurricane would be long gone by then.

Chapter 25

Monday, September 2, 1935 – Hotel Matecumbe

"I'm so tired of the lunches they serve in this hotel."

"Well, Gayle, if that hurricane weren't headed this way, we'd have gone to a picnic today. We went by the Russell place this morning but they were busy preparing for the blow. Mr. Russell takes his barometer seriously. We did get a slice of key lime pie."

"Picnic? I love picnics!"

"They were supposed to roast a hog." George stood up and walked to the lobby window. "Looks like we have visitors."

"Good! It's so boring sitting around waiting for who knows what. Wish we could have stayed in Key West."

The hotel door opened, and a couple walked in. Rosalind turned to see. The man was tall, well-built and very handsome, a touch of grey in his well-groomed black hair, a bruise on his cheek. He looked like he'd spent the morning changing a tire in the rain. That just made him more interesting. George noticed the girl, a cute little number with a flapper bob, striped matelot T-shirt and knee length pleated skirt. She had a mischievous look. They headed for the hotel restaurant entrance.

Gayle did a double take. "Fred! What a surprise!" She noticed Ella. ". . . uh, Cindy?"

"Weekend's over. This is Dixie. She's my co-pilot now. Dixie, Mrs. Gayle Sheldon."

"Charmed."

"Why thank you, me too. Let me introduce you to my friends, George Pepper and Rosalind Palmer. George runs the food warehouse here and Rosalind is his fiancée. This is Fred Dunn and . . . Dixie. We met Saturday night and had dinner together . . . at least with Fred, Dixie is new."

Rosalind smiled. "So, I gather."

"Gayle, is Ray around?" asked Fred.

"Oh, sure, they're just playing cards. He said don't go far, we may have to evacuate."

"Where did you say Ray is?"

"Oh, the office upstairs, there's a crowd of them there, can't miss 'em."

Ella whispered in Fred's ear, "They know you here, careful you don't step on it."

"Trust me on this, Dixie. Shouldn't take me more than an hour."

"An hour, what do I do for an hour?"

"Just talk with the nice people." Fred turned and climbed the stairs.

Ella took a seat beside the others. "Mrs. Sheldon, Fred mentioned he had a breakfast date with you and Mr. Sheldon yesterday morning but that you had already left the hotel. What happened? Nothing serious, I hope."

"Oh, please, I'm just little ol' Gayle. Ray, my husband, Mr. Sheldon, was concerned about the weather and thought it best to take the ferry back here. Sorry about breakfast. I was kinda looking forward to it, better than here I imagine. And Cindy is so funny!"

"Yes, she is. But Cindy had to stay in Key West so Fred and I decided to just drive up here."

"Excuse me, Dixie, did you say you and Fred drove here? But the ferry didn't return yesterday. It's laid up with a broken propeller shaft. Roz and I came on the evening train. How did you manage driving here?" asked George.

"Well, you won't believe this, but Freddie had this crazy idea to drive on the railroad tracks! Said he saw it done in a newsreel. Ha! Thought we were gonna die. But after we survived the first bridge, I took the wheel and it wasn't so bad, kinda fun even. Wasn't all skittles and beer, though, had a blow out in a rain storm. Nearly went for a swim and something busted in the car. Didn't drive so well afterwards. And the drawbridge tender was going to make us back up all the way to Big Pine until I said I was pregnant. Now that worked like a charm and he spun that bridge right around and let us cross. I laughed so hard I nearly peed my knickers!"

Rosalind and George stared at Ella, glanced at each other, and then started laughing.

"Dixie, dear, you're not really . . . ya know . . . in a family way, are you?" Gayle asked.

"Oh, no. I was just joking." Ella stood and flattened her clothes over her tummy. "Does it look like it? I have been eating a lot."

Rosalind smiled. "Not at all, you're positively sylphic. Don't you think so, George?"

"Definitely like a sylph or maybe even a nymph."

"Thank you, I think."

"And your hair, it's . . ."

"Old hat? That's what Fred says, reminds him of some girl in the funny papers, Dixie Dugan, that's his nickname for me."

"Oh, Dixie Dugan! I've been reading her comic strip since I was a teen."

"You see, old hat. I don't care a whit, though, I like it," Ella thumped the table with her fist. "I got soaked this morning, and look at it now." She shook her head vigorously.

"Oh my, it fell back in place! It's a perfect cut, just like Dixie Dugan! Nothing moves when I shake my head, permanent wave you know. Except I get dizzy."

"I meant to say your hair is very chic," said Rosalind.

"Oh, you really think so? My hairdresser said he'd make me chic without a stitch."

"My, that was pretty bold!" said George.

"Not so much, you see he's a daffodil, but not on Broadway. I sort of promised him I'd be his walking advertisement, Mr. Julian, 452 Fifth Avenue."

"New York?"

"Certainly."

"Cindy's a New Yorker, too," said Gayle.

"May I ask your real name, Dixie? For when I visit Mr. Julian," said Rosalind.

"Oh, he doesn't know my name, real or otherwise. I'm just the girl who wanted the Louise Brooks cut. But it's really Ella, Ella Kaufmann, with two n's."

"And what do you do in New York, Ella Kaufmann with two n's?"

"Go to school, Mr. Pepper. I'm a coed. Cornell!"

* * *

Fred followed the cigarette smoke and conversation to an open door. Inside several men were sitting around a table intent on their cards. In the table's center sat a pile of pennies. Ray Sheldon was facing the door and looked up when Fred entered.

"Fred!" Ray said. "What in the world brings you here? Thought you and that little blonde spitfire of yours were staying in Key West." The other players turned in their seats for a look at the newcomer. Ray placed his cards face down, stood, came around the table and shook hands with Fred.

"Oh, just passing through, thought I'd stop in and say hello. Key West got a little too hot for me. Cindy had to stay behind. So, working on a federal holiday?"

"Probably over reacting, but thought it prudent to call in all the boys yesterday in case that hurricane turns and takes aim at us. Last I heard from the Weather Bureau there is no danger to the Keys. Come I'll show you on the map I'm keeping." Ray led Fred to his desk where a map of the Caribbean was laid out. "The 10 AM report has it 200 miles east of

Havana moving slowly westward. That's 170 miles from us. I marked it with my pencil, there, see. Even if it makes a bee-line for Matecumbe it won't get here much before midnight, likely later. The fastest these things can move is only 17 miles per hour. Couple of the boys thought we should have evacuated the camps yesterday. Well, I've been through every hurricane in Florida since 1925. Know them about as well as anybody. And this one will likely miss us altogether. Look, the barometer's 29.85, barely budged since yesterday."

"Well, that's encouraging, Ray. But the natives are acting like all Hell is coming down on them. Saw Sheriff Thompson in Key West yesterday afternoon, running around pounding on desks like bloody hell, trying to get folks to wake up and take precautions."

"You know Thompson?"

"Not well, mind you, but our paths have crossed a couple of times."

"Saw him yesterday, you say? How did you get here, fly?"

"That's kind of a long story, Ray. I . . ."

Another man entered the office. Fred recognized him immediately. "Mr. Poock, good day, sir."

"Mr. Dunn, how are you doing?"

"You two know each other?" asked Sheldon.

"We've had some business dealings. Would you excuse us while we talk?"

"Of course."

"My office?" Poock suggested.

"Lead on." They left the room.

Ray returned to his seat at the table and picked up his cards. "Who was that guy, Ray?" asked the man across the table.

"Thought I knew, now I'm not too sure."

* * *

Fred and Poock walked down the corridor to a small office. "Good lord, they're playing penny ante poker in there! It's like fiddling while

Rome burns. Excuse me, I'm a little over wrought. Please take a seat Mr. Dunn." Poock sat at his desk. "How may I help you?"

"I'd like to make a contribution to the Trust fund. I came into some money recently and like to put it to good use."

Poock looked in his ledger. "You opened an account Friday. You have a balance of $15. How much would you like to contribute?" He picked up his pen.

"$800,000, if you please."

"800 . . ." Poock put down his pen. "Is this some kind of joke, Mr. Dunn?"

"Deadly serious, sir. I figure that would be enough to pay all the vets their war bonuses. If any is left over, just split it among the men."

"A fine intention Mr. Dunn, but . . ."

"You don't believe me." From his jacket pockets Fred pulled eight stacks of bills and placed them on the desk. "Sorry, a little damp, but it's all there. Go ahead, count it."

Poock did so with a banker's skill. Then he pulled a bill from the middle of each stack and examined it under his desk lamp. He checked for ink smudges and serial number sequences. "Should I ask the provenance?"

"Gambled with my life and won the jackpot. Enough said? I imagine it will take you a few weeks to break it all down into individual cash payments. Should be a good farewell gift when they close the camps."

"Have you told anyone else about this?"

"Nope, our little secret. You're an honest man, Mr. Poock. Shake on it?"

He took Fred's hand in both of his. "I will do as you ask, the men will get their bonuses. You can count on it. But why not do it yourself?"

"I don't have the skills required, nor the time. Besides it's much better if it comes from the Trust. The men who saved will be expecting payouts when they leave. If anyone questions the amounts, and I don't think many will, just say you invested the funds in a beef steak mine and made a killing, enough to pay off in full even those who didn't save."

"And those who don't have Adjusted Compensation Accounts?"

Fred smiled, "I'll leave it to your discretion. One for All . . . All for One. I don't want any hard feelings."

"Understand."

"Good. I'm leaving today and not coming back, ever. What are your plans?"

"If Mr. Sheldon doesn't need me, I'm going home. You see, my family arrived Saturday. Hadn't seen them in 5 years. Got a place for them in Homestead."

"Kids?"

"A son and three daughters. Thomas, he's 18, then there's Patricia 15, Frances 13 and Selma, she's 9."

"Five years, that's a long time not to see your family. Kids change fast."

"I was worried they wouldn't recognize me when they got off the train. I wrote Edna, my wife, that I'd be the bloke with the Canadian flag. But we recognized each other right off, only Selma was a little bit puzzled."

"You're a veteran, right?"

"King and Country, volunteered in August 1914. The First Canadian Division."

"See much action?"

"We had our baptism of fire at Ypres in April 1915."

"That was a bad show, I heard."

"I thought things couldn't get any worse, then came the Somme."

"You're a citizen, now?"

"Naturalized in 1929. Good timing, eh?"

"Great. Mr. Poock, include yourself in the distribution. And you'll have expenses. You should do your banking in Nassau. I hear Barclays is a good choice. No questions asked. Take the family with you, it would make a nice vacation and time to get reacquainted."

"This isn't just impulse, is it? You've given it some thought."

"Oh, don't know about that, the money came in only yesterday. This just seemed the right thing to do, I don't need it, and there's no one else I'd trust it with. Goodbye, take care. Give Edna and the kids a big hug for me."

"God bless you Mr. Dunn . . . Fred."

* * *

Fred walked back to Sheldon's office. Ray was on the phone scribbling notes on a pad. The others were watching him. He hung up and went to the map, took out a ruler and made some pencil marks. "Boys, I'll read this to you, the latest advisory from the Weather Bureau: Hoist hurricane warnings 1:30 p.m. Key West District. Tropical disturbance central at noon about latitude twenty-three degrees and twenty minutes, north longitude eighty degrees fifteen minutes moving slowly westward. It will be attended by winds of hurricane force Florida Straits and winds of gale force Florida Keys south of Key Largo this afternoon and tonight. Now that's about 115 miles south of us, still at least ten hours away. Plenty of time to evacuate. What do you think Sheeran?"

"The way the barometers been dropping all day, comparing the readings in Key West and Miami, the wind and squalls we're getting, we're in the low pressure area. The storm's much closer than 115 miles, we don't have anything close to ten hours before it hits. You should have ordered the train yesterday so it would be sitting at Camp 3 now, ready to go."

"The train is ready, but in Miami. Should be here in three hours. Is that time enough?"

"Could be. If you're right about the train."

Sheldon picked up the phone, "Operator? Jacksonville, please, Mayflower Hotel, Mr. F. B. Ghent . . . Mr. Ghent, Sheldon here. The Weather Bureau just hoisted a hurricane warning for the Keys . . . barometer reads 29.68 and falling . . . yes, near Cuba, 140 miles east of Havana, 115 miles south of Matecumbe . . . three hours? Yes, standing by, I'll call . . . Fine, I'll be by the phone. Goodbye, sir."

He looked up. "Ghent's ordering the train, boys . . . Operator? Miami, East Coast Railway dispatcher, please . . . This is Ray W. Sheldon, in charge of the veterans here in Matecumbe, Mr. Gaddis, please . . . well when he gets back tell him we're expecting a storm and that he should be receiving an order very soon to send the relief train down here . . . 10 coaches, 3 baggage cars . . . well, as soon as St. Augustine calls . . . between 5:30 and 6? Gaddis told me yesterday it would only take three hours . . . as early as possible, then . . . OK, thank you Mr. Sheeley, goodbye, sir." He hung up the phone.

"Shit, he had no idea what I was talking about. Where's Hardaker? He's supposed to be here."

Sheeran stood. "Well, I'm leaving, have to get back to my men and tell them to git while the gittin' is good. They can drive themselves, being civilians and all."

Sheldon nodded. "Do what you think is best, Ed."

"Yeah, I just will." Sheeran left the office.

"Ah, Fred you came at an interesting time," said Sheldon.

"For sure. One thing Ray, didn't the Weather Bureau say to expect gales in the Keys this afternoon?" Fred said.

"Yes, I believe so."

"Well, I have some experience with the railroads and a gale will slow a train, you know poor visibility, debris on the tracks. And there's no way to reverse the engine between Homestead and Marathon, so one of the legs will have to be with the engine running backward. That slows a train a lot. And, I'm just guessing now, but the railway might just not have a train standing by, steam up, ready to go and this being a holiday and all, no crew either. That would cost them. Just seems to me three hours is a mite optimistic for an 80-mile run starting from scratch. Just saying."

"Well, Fred that time came from Mr. Gaddis, the FEC's District Superintendent, not me. So, I expect them to get it done, somehow."

"Ray, a Coast Guard officer once told me that when they raise the second flag it's time to skedaddle, not dilly dally."

"Well, there's really no alternative to the train, Fred. Can't very well drive those bums out in the stake bodies, even if I could find enough sober drivers. It would be a rag tag convoy stretching for miles, making stops at every bar along the route, and terrorizing towns from Tavernier to Hollywood. Can you imagine the publicity? Besides, we have the time to wait. My interest is in the location of the hurricane not where or when any storm warnings are ordered up. They're not altogether accurate in my experience."

"Sure glad the camps aren't my responsibility. I've got a car and plan to use it."

"Headed for Miami?"

"Somewhere with better weather."

"Say, you never told me how you got here."

"Well, no ferry this morning so I noticed this bridge, thought I'd give it a try."

All the men in the room stopped what they were doing and stared at Fred.

"That's not possible," Sheldon said.

One of the men spoke up, "Oh yeah, there was a film crew here this spring and some guy tried it. Drove from the ferry landing to Long Key and back. Seemed to work well enough. I saw the newsreel, Chevrolet Leader News, back in June, as I recall. It was playing with *The Bride of*

Frankenstein, scared the shit out of me. They had 20 pretty girls in swim suits hanging all over the car . . . that wasn't the scary part."

"On the bridge?"

"Oh, that part was in Miami Beach. Same car though."

"I stand corrected. Well, drive safely, Fred. The road is wet."

"See ya . . . good luck, Ray."

* * *

In the hallway Fred recognized the man approaching. Their eyes met. They stopped a few feet apart.

"Sir, I'm bad at names but I'm sure I've seen you before."

"Possible, I used to work here," said Fred.

"Camp 1, the quarry, right?"

"Nailed it, Fred Dunn." Fred held out his hand. They shook.

"Bill Hardaker. Visiting?"

"Nope, just some unfinished business. I quit Friday. Say, doesn't your family live around here?"

"Yeah, my wife and child. We have a cottage nearby. Why?"

"You should get them out, now. Sheldon's waiting for the train. It's a mistake. Good luck, Bill." Fred walked away and took the stairs down. Hardaker watched him go.

* * *

The lobby was empty. Fred went outside and followed the short path to the beach. The sun had come out, but a stiff wind blew across the key, kicking up the sand. It made a buzzing sound against his trouser legs. He looked out over the white caps at Alligator Reef Lighthouse. A huge wave smashed against the iron work. For a moment the lighthouse vanished in the surf. Only the two red and black flags were visible, one above the other.

"Here he is!" shouted George, "On the beach."

Fred turned and saw Ella running towards him. George and Rosalind stood watching with their arms around each other. Ella laughed and jumped the last step. Fred caught her. They kissed.

"You were upstairs so long we went for a walk."

"Dixie cup, good to see you, too. Let's go back to the hotel and I'll grab something to eat. Then we'd better get moving. There's a mechanic in camp I'll ask to check the suspension. See the lighthouse out there? Two flags flying."

Ella turned and called to the others, "Look! Two flags on the lighthouse, time to clear out!"

Rosalind squeezed George's hand and placed her head on his shoulder. "She's right. Can you ask Sheldon if you can leave?"

"Won't hurt to ask. He won't keep Gayle here, for sure. And I have you to keep safe."

"In sickness and health . . ."

". . . come hell or high water." They embraced and kissed.

"They're getting married," Ella told Fred as they came up to the couple.

"Don't stare Dixie, it's not polite."

Rosalind came up for air. "It's true, Fred. What about you two?"

"We have a special circumstance, it's day by day with us. Where is Mrs. Sheldon?"

"Oh, she had to report back to Ray, Mr. Sheldon that is. She dare not stray too far, too long."

"Rosalind, he cares about her," George said.

"Just remember, fella, no leash on me."

"George, I spoke with Sheldon about an hour ago. Ghent ordered the relief train. He expects it to reach Islamorada by five. Then it will have to back all the way down to Camp 3, switch the engine around and return, crossing Indian Key Fill twice. That's a hell of a risk. We're going to Miami. You and Rosalind are welcome to come with us."

"Yeah, we have plenty of room," said Ella.

Rosalind nodded. "I was thinking along the same lines. Georgie?"

"I can't just leave, that would be desertion, I'd lose my job. I'll go see if Sheldon needs me for something. Can you wait a few minutes, Fred?"

"We'll wait," Fred and Ella answered together.

They hurried up the path to the hotel. A gust of wind, a loud snap, and a large branch broke loose from a tree and crashed to the ground a few feet away. Fred gabbed Ella's hand. "Come on, run."

At the hotel George went upstairs, Fred entered the restaurant, Ella and Rosalind sat in the lobby, holding hands. "What's stopping you and George from getting married?"

"Ella, I'm already married, we have to wait for the divorce to go through. And Fred, what's the deal with you two? His reason didn't make any sense."

"The first time we spoke was Saturday and I wasn't very friendly. There are things I don't like about him but I'm no angel either. Now that I know him better it'll be tough to leave him."

"Ella, you only met him two days ago and already you're thinking of dumping him?"

"Neither of us are good with long-term relationships, and the time has just about run out on this one."

George returned. "Mr. Sheldon says he needs me to evacuate the veterans' wives. There are several here who need rides. He'll find a car for me to drive them to Hollywood. I don't know how long this will take. Roz, you should go now with Fred and Ella."

"Darling, I left Key West with you Sunday, mother warned me not to go. I'm not leaving you now. I'll just squeeze in with the wives."

"I knew you'd say that." George smiled.

Gayle appeared carrying a suitcase. "Hi! Oh, did you find Fred?"

"He's getting some sandwiches," said Ella. "Going somewhere?"

"Why yes. Mr. Sheldon wants me to meet him in Hollywood with his car. He's having one of the boys drive me. He's taking the train. It's not fit for a lady to travel on, he said."

"Our men are so galant," Ella said.

"Oh, yes! I'm his little princess, and he's my knight," Gayle beamed.

"Come down to earth, girl."

Rosalind gave Ella a look. "Good for you, Gayle."

Fred returned from the restaurant with a paper sack. "So, who's coming?"

"Just little me, Fred, dahling," said Ella. "Everyone else has a ride."

"Well, then, we'd better be off. It was nice meeting you folks." He shook hands with George and Gayle. Rosalind gave him a hug and kiss on the cheek.

Ella made her farewells. When she came to Rosalind they embraced and kissed.

"I wish you and George a happy life together. I . . . I think we could have been great friends." Ella turned quickly away.

Fred waved goodbye, put his arm around Ella, and they left the hotel.

Chapter 26

Monday, September 2, 1935 – Picnic

Lying in his cot with an erection, Skeeter thought about the girl. He missed her. He even dreamed about her, her voice, her smell, her taste, her touch, her body. He couldn't recall how long it'd been since he'd obsessed over a woman, had he ever? She was adorable, the way she screwed up her face and flashed those big fiery eyes when she got angry. She sassed him, he liked that. No fear, no qualms. And she wanted him! How was that even possible? He was some big, loud-mouthed jerk, a bully, who couldn't even get it up. Now, and this was the hardest thing to admit, he cared for someone. No, not just cared, he was in love. Fuck it! He didn't want this. He'd never needed any girl for more than one night before. Now he couldn't imagine living without her. Well, there was no getting around it, it would only gnaw and eat at him. He'd just have to play it through.

What was it she said? A picnic today? He got up, put on his work clothes and jogged over to the Hospital for his daily soak. The ward was empty. After bathing, he brushed his teeth, and shaved. Outside the hospital, Doctor Dan and his staff were loading patients into the two ambulances.

"Hey, Doc!" Skeeter waved and walked over. He held out his hand. "I want to thank you, your treatment cured me, especially the baths. Hard as a rock this morning."

Main took his hand and shook it. "Happy to hear it! See you've been following my advice, no drinking and no fighting. I still want you on light duty the rest of the week."

"Sure thing, Doc. Where're they headed?" Skeeter asked nodding toward the patients.

"Hollywood. Easier for them to use the ambulance than ride the train with the men."

"Train?"

"The relief train, to escape the hurricane. We're all going."

"Really? Not me, I've got an invite to a picnic on Matecumbe."

"The Russell's?"

"Yeah."

"Well, good luck with that Mr. Clemons. It's not a day for outdoor activities."

"Maybe, there'll be something to do inside."

Skeeter returned to his shack. He scraped the mud from his boots and dressed in the cleanest clothes he had. He caught a ride to Islamorada on the back of a camp truck. The store and post office were shuttered. Inside the train depot the waiting room was empty. The big regulator clock on the wall read 2:30 p.m. He asked the railway agent where the Russell girl lived.

"Well, I'm married to one of them. Which one you interested in?"

"Bernice Mae. I've got something to ask her father."

"Really? That girl's a real pistol. Well now, her pa's Henry Otis Russell. His is the big place about a quarter mile west of here on the ocean side, can't miss it, always a passel of kids running around. Then again, he may be working on his farm, preparing for the storm. That's near the boat landing on the bay side."

A twenty-minute walk took him to a large Bahamian style house, covered porch, louvered window awnings, and tin roof. The agent was right about the kids, Skeeter counted five of assorted sizes playing on the wide sandy beach below the house. It seemed especially wide today, even more so than at low tide. He looked for the pig roast, he was famished. But there wasn't a whiff of it. A woman sat rocking on the porch nursing a baby in her arms. Skeeter removed his hat. "Good afternoon, Ma'am, I'm looking for Mr. Henry Otis Russell."

She took him in with a glance, smiled and asked, "And who might you be, sir?"

"Dilbert Clemons, Ma'am. But most folks just call me Skeeter. I have a question to ask Mr. Henry."

There was a shout from inside the house. Bernice Mae burst through the door, stopped at the edge of the porch, open mouthed. She was barefoot, hair tousled, in tattered jeans and an oversized man's work shirt. She was beautiful.

The woman stood up, moved the baby to her left hip, and closed her blouse, all in a simple, graceful motion. "Mr. Clemons . . . Skeeter, I'm Ruby Elizabeth Russell. Henry's my husband and this girl a-gawkin' at you is my daughter, Bernice Mae. I think you've met. Henry's working t'other side of the tracks, but you can say anything to me you'd ask of him."

Another girl, Cathy, rushed onto the porch, a bit taller than Bernice Mae, wearing a dress and shoes, her blonde hair neatly combed. She saw Skeeter and tried hard to hold back a giggle.

Skeeter glanced over at Bernice Mae, winked, then walked up and shook Ruby's outstretched hand. The porch was two steps up so they were at about the same height. "Well, Ma'am, Bernice Mae invited me to your picnic today, if'n I cleaned up my act. I figure she's worth it. Thing is I would be most obliged if you would permit me to court your daughter . . . Bernice Mae, that is."

Cathy squealed. Bernice Mae placed her hands on her hips, and smiled smugly. Ruby glanced at her daughters then back at Skeeter. "Mighty civil of you to ask me, Mr. Clemons, but in the Russell family the women folk speak for themselves. Bernice Mae, dear, please answer the gentleman."

"That's a mighty tall order, Ma. Have to give it some thought, if'n Mr. Dilbert Clemons ain't in any particular kind of hurry."

"Uh . . . Miss Bernice Mae, I am in kind of a hurry. You see the camps are fix'n to close and I'll have to leave."

"So, you want me to just pack up and leave with you just because you lost your job? Well, that doesn't sound like you're all that serious. I'm sure a big, strong man like you can get a job hereabouts. Now my Pa is always looking for some help on the farm. You any good at plantin', prunin', pickin' and packin'?"

"Sounds easier than cuttin' coral."

"I don't know about that, but if you make a good impression Pa might let you stay at the house. Is that OK with you Ma?"

Ruby nodded.

"I'd be mighty obliged."

"And you should be. Now getting hitched is a mighty big step for a girl, takes a lotta thought and planning. So, I'm thinking a spring wedding, say March, not this March, mind you, but the next one, 1937, that is, before it gets too hot, and it's between hurricanes. Cancelling a picnic is one thing, a wedding is something else altogether. I'll be 16 then, like Ma was, and won't need a baby to convince the judge, not that I don't like babies, but Reverend Hager will be more comfortable with the situation, and it will give my friends Rosalind and George time to uncomplicate things and get married, 'cause they're getting exhausted from all their fiancée-ing, you know, and I'd like a passel of that fiancée-ing myself. Really."

Ruby looked at Bernice Mae and raised an eyebrow. She ignored her mother.

"And it will give Cathy more time to find her man, seeing as she's so much older than I am and by rights should get hitched first."

With that Cathy reared back and gave Bernice Mae a swift kick in the pants that sent her toppling down the steps and into Skeeter's arms. He laughed, she sniffed, "You took a bath! That's a step in the right direction."

"Yes'm."

"Well, Skeeter, is it a deal?" Bernice Mae asked.

"1937, jeez, that's long time."

"Come on, you'll like me better after I fill out."

". . . Do I have a choice?"

"No."

"It's a deal."

"Then seal it with a kiss." And they did.

Ruby put her free arm around Cathy. "Well, those two won't wait for the formalities." She looked up at the delicate white tufted clouds drifting by in the deep blue sky. They started far out on the Atlantic horizon and passed high overhead in serried ranks. But over the bay another dark squall line was scudding in from the northwest. Lightning flashed, followed by the low rumble of thunder. A gust of wind rustled the palm fronds. "Oh, Skeeter," Ruby said, "you're welcome to stay for dinner, Skeeter. Skeeter?"

A muddy Ford stake bed truck pulled up behind the house. The driver, a tall, grey haired, deeply tanned man wearing bib overalls, scraped his boots and entered through the back door. A few minutes later he stepped out on the porch. He saw Skeeter and Bernice Mae still entwined. "So, what did I miss?"

"Bernice Mae has a beau, Pa." Cathy answered. "He's staying for dinner, I think."

"Looks familiar. Well, if he's not too busy maybe he'd like to lend a hand. Still have to finish puttin' up the storm shutters."

Ruby smiled. "Give them a moment, Henry. His name is Dilbert Clemons, goes by Skeeter. He wanted permission to court Bernice Mae. She said yes."

"After she set the terms, Pa. Two years of fiancée-ing!"

"A patient man . . . I just checked the barometer, 29.42 inches and dropping. Cousin John heard that the readings in Miami and Key West were higher. Looks like we're in for it. Don't think we can ride this one out in the house. I have a feeling, Ruby."

"I'll get the children over to the packing house with the picnic things and pallets. I'm sure Skeeter will help you once Bernice Mae lets him go. He so wants to make a good impression."

Bernice Mae dropped to the ground, held Skeeter's hand and turned to her parents. "We'll put up the shutters, Pa. I know how and Skeeter's got the reach."

Skeeter nodded "Mr. Henry, I ain't got nowhere else to be today."

"You work at the quarry on Plantation Key, don't you?"

"Yes sir."

"Thought so. I've seen you work. They should have moved all you folks out yesterday. Those little shacks will get blown away like so many match boxes."

"We're supposed to go at 4:30. Captain told us to stay in camp and wait for the train. But Bernice Mae invited me down here. Thought that was a better idea."

"Hard to fault that thinking."

"I'd be mighty obliged if you'd accept my help, Mr. Henry."

"Henry suits me just fine." They shook, for a moment testing each other's grip, Henry let go first. "We do need a strong hand. And Skeeter, you take good care of my daughter, you hear?"

"Sure will, Henry. She means a lot . . . everything to me."

"In deep, huh?"

"Way over my head."

Bernice Mae looked up, raised her hand high and squinted.

Henry turned to his daughter, hugged and kissed her. "And you, darlin' angel, take good care of your man."

"Oh, Pa!"

"I married Ruby Elizabeth when she was 16, Skeeter, and never regretted it for a second. OK, we all got things to do, let's get crackin'."

Henry hurried down to the beach, snatched up the smallest child and ran back to the house with her squirming under his arm. The others raced after him up to the porch.

"That's Sarah, Henrietta, Charles and William," Bernice Mae told Skeeter. "Pa's carrying Doloria, Cathy's got Hilton and Ma has Carl, looks to be sleeping."

"Pleased to meet you, kids." The little ones laughed and ran by.

"Nice to meet you, Skeeter," Cathy said, just a hair too friendly for Bernice Mae's taste.

"Come on, the shed's over here." Bernice Mae grabbed Skeeter's hand. "There are shutters and boards for 25 windows and three doors. Pa put in hooks above the windows to hang the shutters, you can reach that high easy, right?"

"First floor easy, second floor I'll need a ladder."

"Got one. After they're hung then we have to nail them down so they won't bang around loose." She unlatched the shed door. It was dark inside and there were spiders.

Skeeter entered and looked at the neatly stacked shutters. He lifted one. It was heavy, sawed from one-inch-thick planks, looked to be 4 feet wide by 6 long. That old man was fixin' to do the job by himself with just a slip of a girl to help. They got to work.

Chapter 27

Monday, September 2, 1935 – Inquiries

Reeve showed his badge to the reception nurse. "Here to see Mr. and Miss Rattigan. I understand they're visiting Mr. Ruz, a patient here."

"Room 6, sir. Down the hallway and on the left."

Reeve knocked on the door.

"Come in."

Reeve entered followed by Renard. "Is that Mr. Ruz? Sorry, I'm U.S. Marshal Reeve and this is Special Agent Renard, Federal Bureau of Investigation."

"I believe we've met, Agent Renard," said Daniel.

Abby just then walked in carrying a tray of sandwiches and sodas. "Edward! What a surprise."

"Is it OK to talk here with Mr. Ruz . . . in his condition?" asked Reeve.

"He's in a coma," said Cindy.

Renard coughed politely. "I had intended to interview everyone, less Miss Gardner, at the Courthouse, separately with a stenographer present. I understand now why you were unable to appear. But as the matter has become rather urgent with the disappearance of Mr. Dunn and Miss Kaufmann, I can take your sworn statements later. Does anyone know where we can find them?"

Daniel looked at Cindy, then back to Renard. "Dunn?"

Reeve replied. "Frederick Dunn, he chartered Captain Ruz's boat Saturday to visit Havana. I met him when the boat returned Saturday evening. It was full of bullet holes. He said he worked for the Federal Emergency Relief Administration, inspecting the vet camps here in the Keys. Said he ran into some ruckus in Havana and a Cuban delegation arrived yesterday with some serious accusations against him, murder and terrorism. I deposed him Sunday, he denied everything and assured me he'd be available today to speak with Special Agent Renard. He didn't show."

"Frederick Dunn? I know a Fred Dunn from the war, he was in my battalion. I heard he was working in the Keys for FERA, I wrote him two letters. He never responded."

"So, you don't know what he was doing in Havana?" asked Renard.

"Not a clue."

"Miss Rattigan, you said Dunn was a friend of yours when we spoke Saturday. Can you offer any explanation?" Reeve asked.

"Well," Cindy began, glancing at her father, "we met Friday. Seemed a nice guy, invited me and Ella, Miss Kaufmann, to come along on his charter to Havana. I had no idea Daddy knew him."

"Any idea where he is now?" asked Renard.

"Well, we had dinner together Saturday night with some friends, then we visited the hospital to check on Mr. Ruz, who had been injured in a fall. Sunday, he told me he had an appointment with you at the Courthouse. Afterwards we visited the hospital again. He left early and I haven't seen or heard from him since. Sorry I can't help you more."

"And Miss Kaufmann?"

"Oh, we're best friends. I think she may have gotten involved with Mr. Dunn, if you know what I mean. I guess she's shacked up with him somewhere."

"Any idea where?"

"Well, Ed, Key West is not New York, but there are still plenty of places to hide out."

"And why do you think he may be hiding out?"

"Let's see, accused of murder, wanted for questioning by the Feds, you don't have to be guilty to make yourself scarce."

"Miss Rattigan, in Dunn's sworn testimony he mentioned that he was stopped by the Cuban police while walking to his boat, Saturday. Can you confirm this?"

"Yeah, sure, they were very intimidating. But Fred talked them down, he was terrific. The top cop said we were free to go, all very jolly."

"Did anything unusual happen on the trip back to Key West?"

"Well, Fred and Mr. Ruz told Guy and that nice Coast Guard Lieutenant all about it Saturday. The Cubans tried to kill us."

"That's true, Edward," said Reeve.

"Any idea why the Cubans changed their attitude?"

"Beats me."

"And Mr. Ruz, will he be able to make a statement?" asked Renard.

"You'll have to ask Dr. Henderson that, Special Agent Renard, but she didn't give us much hope that he'd ever recover," Daniel said.

"I'm sorry to hear that, Mr. Rattigan. I can tell he's very important to you."

"He's my son, damn you!"

* * *

The two men sat on a bench in the shade of the hospital grounds. Renard rubbed his chin between his fingers. "When I met Rattigan on the plane this morning, he gave no indication that his son was injured or that he even had one. He was quite cheerful. And the son of a wealthy New York banker is a charter boat captain? Odd profession for a child he clearly loves. And his daughter gets picked up by this Dunn character, who he knows from the war and has been trying to contact. And this guy just happens to charter her brother's boat to Havana on the same day her father's bank gets bombed. And her brother didn't seem to care that his sister was Dunn's holiday honey, and we can't ask him about any of this stuff because he's in a coma maybe caused by the same bomb. And his protégée, Kaufmann, has run off with Dunn."

"All this makes sense, Guy, if Rattigan is pulling the strings. Last week the Cubans started proceedings against the directors of Chase National Bank in New York on fraud charges in connection with loans to Machado. Rattigan is the Bank's vice president for foreign operations, and before the 1933 revolt he lived in Cuba and was cozy with the Machado government. He arranged the disputed loans. And this week Senators Nye and Wheeler met with President Mendieta about delinquent interest payments owed to American investors on those same loans. Do you see it, Guy? This was all Rattigan's scheme to smuggle Machado's loot out of Havana. Ruz posed as Dunn at the bank so Dunn would take the fall if things turned sour, which they did with the terrorist bombing. Bad timing there. Ruz getting hurt was not considered. So now Dunn is running things and Cindy is covering for him."

"Could be Ruz was disguised as Dunn, so Dunn would take the rap. But why would a big shot Government man risk his job and reputation? How big a cut would make it worthwhile?"

"Maybe Dunn isn't who we think he is."

* * *

A black Ford roadster, its top down, parked in front of the No Name Lodge. Several men boarding up the cabins paused to watch. Two men in suits and fedoras stepped out of the car and walked to the office door.

"Hey Mack, is the manager around?" one of the men asked a worker.

"Yeah, she's in the kitchen fixing lunch."

"Through here?"

"Yeah, the dining room is on the right."

"Thanks, Mack."

He flipped a quarter to the worker who grabbed it deftly. "Thanks mister."

They entered, closing the door behind them. The shorter man nodded to the taller who quickly stepped to the reception desk and started looking through the guest register. The other continued into the empty dining room, found the kitchen door and knocked. "Hello! Is the manager there?"

"Yes, come on in."

The man swung the door open, stepped inside and removed his hat. "Sorry to disturb you ma'am. I'm with the U.S. Marshal Service in Key West," he quickly flashed his open wallet at Sarah. "We're trying to locate a Mr. Fred Dunn and his companion, Miss Ella Kaufmann. It's a matter of some importance. They may be in danger. By any chance have they passed this way?"

At the mention of Fred, the Hettie looked up and smiled broadly. At "danger" the smile disappeared and she shrank. Sara revealed no emotion. "What kind of danger?"

"I can't say much as this is an ongoing investigation. I can say that a friend of theirs was assaulted last night. The injuries are serious. Any information you could share may be of assistance."

Hettie pulled on Sarah's apron. After a moment Sarah spoke. "Yes, a Mr. Dunn came through here last night. He was with a girl. Told them the ferry was down, but they chose to stay anyway. They left early this morning. I guess they went back to Key West."

"Do you recall what they were driving?"

"A yellow sedan, sir," Hettie offered.

"Make?"

"A yellow Chevy, 1935, sir, and the girl's name was Dixie Dugan."

He laughed. "Dixie Dugan, eh? Well, is there any way besides the ferry to get to the mainland from here, ma'am?"

"Speed boat, seaplane, but with the storm warnings up I don't think that's very likely."

"The bridge?"

"You must be new around here, fella. It's a railroad bridge. Nobody's tried to drive on it since '27, and that was a publicity stunt."

"So, it is possible."

"I suppose so, but like I said, nobody's tried it since. Must be a reason for that. Likely get themselves killed."

"Well, thank you ma'am, miss. You've been very helpful. Goodbye."

The two men got back into the roadster. "What did ya find, Al?"

"Bingo, Fred Dunn signed in just after midnight. Checked out at 8:15. What did the manager say?"

"The girl was with him, using a joke alias, 'Dixie Dugan'. They're driving a brand new, yellow Chevy."

"That should be easy to spot. Did she say where they went from here?"

"She thinks Key West. But I think they just might have taken the railroad bridge. That's chancy, but they knew going back was riskier. Drive to that town we passed through and find a phone. I'll call Lansky. Maybe there's time to grab them before they reach Miami. Shouldn't be hard, there's only the one road."

"Think we should follow them?"

"Are you crazy?"

Chapter 28

March 8, 1919, Walter Reed General Hospital, Washington, D.C. – The Last Raid

"Private Dunn, today I'd like you to start with the day before, and just describe the events as they happened, all right?"

"Sunday?"

"Yes, that's right."

"Yes, sir. Well, we were all quite happy there was no attack order for Monday. The 77th was to hold the Meuse line, and watch Sedan get plastered. We could see shells exploding on the chateau. The French division on our left flank claimed the honor of taking the city, and they were welcome to it. The Boche had left a lot of stuff behind which the boys made use of, furnishing our dugouts and rifle pits. The river was only about 50 yards wide. A good man might chuck a grenade across. No one tried though, Boche snipers were hiding in the trees. We endeavored to stay out of their sights. Occasionally their artillery sent a round in our direction, just to let us know they were still in the war."

"Did you get a hot meal that day?"

"No, the field kitchens were stalled on the road someplace, just hardtack and bully beef for us. There was a can of ersatz coffee the Krauts had forgotten, which we brewed up. Smelled like burnt wool, didn't taste any better. One of the boys found some beer in the little town behind our position. That was much appreciated."

"How long had you been up front by this time, November 10th?"

"Well, let's see, since 18 August . . . 84 days, more or less"

"So, this was time for a little rest."

"Yeah, very little. Sarge woke what was left of us around midnight to prepare for a raid in the morning. Battalion wanted to know what was going on t'other side of the river, take a prisoner or two, and roust out the snipers. No boats of course. The plan was to send a couple of strong swimmers across first with ropes they'd tie to trees on the right bank. The other ends would be secured on the left bank and the rest of the platoon would pull themselves across. Only 50 yards, right? In the dark and fog. No problem, Sir!"

"You were already pretty tired, so this put you on edge, made you a little anxious?"

"Pissed, more like it. The Germans weren't sticking around. They'd likely be gone in the morning. None of us was keen on a cold bath and spending the day in a wet uniform, assuming we didn't get shot or drowned. And we heard the rumors, the war would end any day now."

"Do you remember who was on the raid?"

"Well, me, of course, and my brother Steve with the Browning auto rifle. He loved that gun, it was his baby. He'd finagled some way to exchange his old Chauchat for it, the first one in the Battalion. Then there was Mike, the other assistant gunner, Second Lieutenant Pickler, a go-getter, Sergeant Bascomb, a career man, served in the Philippines and Mexico, and 15 other guys, kids mostly. You want their names?"

"No, that's not necessary. Tell me about Steve."

"Yeah, Steve was a show boater. Back home he was something. He could sing and dance passably, but was really good with a horse and rope. And he was a looker. The girls were always hanging around him, like bees on honey. When he was 18, he lost a front tooth doing a horse trick and he immediately started saving for a gold one. Hah, even some of the girls kicked in. He accepted all donations. After graduating from high school, he lit out for New York City, said he was going to be the next Will Rogers. When he got there, he was flat broke. But he did get a job on Broadway, a stagehand at the Ziegfeld Follies. He saw ol' Will do his act. Now that brought Steve down a peg or two. So, he concentrated on the showgirls. Most of them had sugar daddies but a few liked a cowboy with rough edges. He wrote me most every week about his adventures. Then he was drafted into the 77th. I told Mom and Dad I was going to enlist and go off to war with Steve. Mom would have none of it as I was only 17, but dad understood, just as well have his sons watch out for each other. I had some money saved up and Dad gave me enough to take the train. Lied about my age and joined up. When Steve found out he wrangled an assignment for me in his platoon."

"You and your brother were very close."

"Fuck it, I loved him!"

"I understand, Private Dunn. There's no shame in crying. Just relax now. Take a deep breath, hold it, let it out. Again. Here, have a drink of water . . . can we continue?"

"Yes, sir."

"How did the river crossing go?"

"Well, nobody got drowned and the Boche must have been asleep. But pulling yourself across a strong current with a full kit is no fun. Couple of guys lost their grip. Came ashore downstream on opposite banks. Saw a dead body float by, no telling whose side he was on."

"Did that bother you?"

"I've seen lots of dead bodies. You get used to it. Doesn't help your dreams any, though."

"Please continue."

"Well, we jumped off at six. By the time we got everyone across and organized it was getting light, but still foggy. There were some abandoned rifle pits along the riverbank but no sign of any snipers, so we formed a skirmish line and advanced. The woods turned out to be only a thin strip along the bank and then a mile of open farm fields to a small village, at least that's what the Lieutenant said. Couldn't see ten feet ahead of us in that fog. We did notice a hasty wire entanglement before we tripped over it. We cut through it in no time. Well, there's no way to cut through wire without making some noise, so we were expecting a response from the Boche. But nothing. We reformed the skirmish line on the other side, making sure every man could see at least one guy on either side, which kept us sorta bunched. Just as we began advancing into the murk the world erupted. The French and American guns opened up all along the front, thousands of them. We dropped and hugged the ground. We could feel it shake. But the shells were falling along the main road a good distance in front of us. We all looked at the Lieutenant. He grinned, shrugged his shoulders like he was as surprised as the rest of us and said, Follow me. Steve cracked, 'Maybe we'll liberate that village and the mamselles will be so grateful.'"

"By this time the sun was well up and the flashes from the shell bursts added to the glow, but it was still impossible to see anything definite except the boys nearest me. Then the German guns responded. You could hear their shells whizzing overhead and exploding back over the river. It was like some weird dream, our patrol in its fuzzy little cocoon while all hell was breaking loose just out of sight. And we kept slogging along through that fucking field. We must have been advancing for twenty minutes or so when the command to halt got passed along the line. We flopped down in the mud and took what cover there was. The Lieutenant and Sarge were discussing what we should do next, couldn't hear them talking but the gist made its way down to me, Steve and Mike. Sarge said we should return to our lines, the Germans had clearly pulled out, and if we kept going, we risked getting hit by our own barrage. The Lieutenant had his map out and kept jabbing at it. Orders are to advance to contact and take a prisoner, they must be holed up in this village, he said. Then while we were lying there in what smelled like cow paddies, the fog thinned enough to make out some houses up ahead. Everyone stopped talking and brought their weapons up. Then the command came to spread out - we could see how dangerously bunched together we'd become in the fog - and advance by rushes."

"How did that make you feel, Private Dunn? Sounded like Sergeant Bascomb had the better argument."

"We were blind, now we could see, changed the circumstances. The Lieutenant was just following orders. Didn't think nothing of it, none of us did. The war was still on, wasn't it?"

"Yes, it was, any idea what time it was?"

"Likely lunch time, my stomach was growling up a storm. But I'm always hungry and I didn't have a watch. Shit, Doc, that was the last thing in the world we cared about."

"Understand, please continue."

"So, we got up and advanced Indian style. You know, half the men cover the other half who rush forward 20 yards, then they cover the other half rushing 40 yards, leapfrogging. But the Boche must have been watching us the whole time because we only made it halfway through the second rush when they opened up, machine guns, rifles, grenades, minenwerfers, whiz-bangs. The Lieutenant was about ten yards in front of us, a sniper caught him between the eyes. Sarge took over, had half of us start low crawling while the others returned fire. Steve, Mike and me found a shell hole, we dived in and Steve started blasting away. I think he got one of the MGs because they stopped firing. We thought we had a chance, some of our shells were falling short unto the Germans. Maybe it would be enough for them to retreat."

"When the other guys were close enough, they opened up on the Boche. That was the signal for our squad to dash forward to a better position. We'd done this a hundred times since August, didn't think anything of it, just second nature. We rolled over the lip of the hole and ran like crazy, zig-zagging, dropping, crawling and running again. Steve was aiming for another shell hole about 30 yards away. Steve and I made it, but Mike took a machine gun burst. I went back and dragged him into the hole. Steve put a field dressing on his chest, but it was sucking air. His lung was punctured."

"And how did that make you feel?"

"Like shit, how else was I supposed to feel? Mike was a good buddy. But in a fight, you have to carry on, regardless. No crying, you get the fucking bastard. A minenwerfer bomb exploded 10 yards away and showered us with fragments. My ears were ringing."

"Steve didn't have to say the obvious, it was up to him and me. We both scrambled back up the side of the crater. Steve fired a burst at the MG nest while I threw a grenade. But the Huns were waiting, sighted on just the right spot. A burst from the Maxim ripped into Steve's face and out the back of his head. Gore, brains, teeth, and skull fragments splattered all over me. My grenade exploded wide of the mark. I toppled backward into the crater, went kind of crazy trying to wipe Steve off me. It took me a while to calm down. When I did, I forced myself to look. Steve was sitting across from me in the stagnant water filling the bottom of the crater. There was nothing recognizable of Steve except the gold tooth he had been so proud of, protruding from his lower jaw. I lost it and vomited. I didn't hear the next mortar bomb arch through the air and into the crater. It landed between me and Steve. I reacted instinctively and curled into a ball . . ."

"Go on please, Private Dunn."

"The explosion tosses me into the air and tears my helmet off. A fragment rips through my right leg, but I stay conscious. I hear only the ringing in my ears. I see Steve again, even more mangled, lying on top of Mike. By some quirk their heads are side by side. There is movement there. How strange. Steve's jaw flexes as if trying to make words, difficult without tongue or lips or face. Mike seems to be nodding. What is Steve trying to say? I lean forward, trying to hear the words. The loose jaw moves twice, Kill . . . them. Is that an order? Mike nods. I take my .45 and shoot them both until they stop moving."

"I find the Browning, clear it and load a fresh 20 round magazine from my bandoleer, charge it and select full auto. I climb to the top of the crater and roll out, and start low crawling toward the MG nest. The Krauts are looking at me, two just sitting atop the sandbags without their helmets, another standing, talking, but I don't hear a word. I stand up, can't feel anything in my leg. My trousers are wet with blood. The standing Kraut waves to me. His lips move but there's no sound. I limp forward, stepping over the torn wire. The sitting Krauts are shouting at me, their mouths moving. The one standing smiles at me. I'm 10 yards away, I raise the Browning level and fire a burst. The Kraut splits apart and falls backward into the nest. I start running and make it to the nest before the other two Krauts grab their rifles. Two more bursts and they lie moaning beside their kamerad. I lean the Browning against the Maxim, and draw my trench knife. I carve their faces until there's nothing left human about them."

"Take a breath, Private Dunn."

"I drop to the bottom of the nest and decide to wait there until I'm relieved as ordered. I'm very sleepy, can't hear, and seeing things, a gold tooth in a pool of blood. More Krauts appear from the communication trench. They point at me and move their mouths. Some are aiming their rifles at me. One is crying like a baby and comes at me with his bayonet fixed. I'm swaying, feel dizzy. Someone in a feldgrau uniform is standing in front of me. He waves his arms and turns. He looks down at me, a Kraut officer. He kneels in front of me and stares, claps his hands and moves his mouth. There's only a roaring in my ears, like a passing train. I feel myself lifted up . . ."

"Where are they taking you?"

"Across the field, put me on a stretcher . . . excuse me Doc, I feel sick."

"Use the bed pan, Private Dunn . . . get it all out . . . here's a towel, wipe your face and have some tea . . . sugar?"

"Yes please."

"You forgot about all that but now you remember it. This is going to stay with you because it's over now, there's no danger, nothing to fear. You'll remember it all, the fog, the shells, the BAR, the knife, Mike, Steve and those Germans. But it's over. Now you're coming back to us. You're at ease and relaxed, no pain and no anxiety. You can wake now . . . Well, how are you?"

"Pretty good, Doc."

"That was excellent, Private Dunn, first time we made it through the entire event. We're making real progress understanding your neurosis. Tomorrow you should rest, take a walk around the grounds. We'll start again on Monday."

"Thanks, Doc."

Chapter 29

Monday, September 2, 1935 - The Wave

Fred parked in front of a two-story wood frame building. A sign above the door read Hospital. Numbers of veterans milled around among the rows of shacks. Many were drinking from beer bottles and hip flasks. A few appeared unsteady, stumbling. Ella was not impressed.

"Come on Dixie, meet my friends." Fred came around to the passenger side and took her hand. They entered the hospital. Two men were standing in the lobby. The older, about 60, heavy set, grey haired, dressed in white, noticed Ella, and smiled.

"Looks like you're ready for Hollywood . . . California, that is." The man laughed. The other joined in.

"Dixie, meet Doctor Main and Jimmie Conway, about the best Camp 1 can offer. Where's Razor Blade? I need his help with my car."

"Probably in his shack, packing his bag. What's the trouble?" Jimmie asked.

"Think I busted a spring. Kicks like a mule when I hit a bump."

"Might be some spare parts in the garage, let's go see."

"Doc, will you keep Dixie company? This might take a while."

"Delighted." Main smiled.

"Fred, two flags, remember?" Ella frowned. "We don't have a while."

"What do you think, Doc, how much time do we have?"

"Two, maybe three hours at the most."

"OK, Dixie, one hour and we go, ready or not."

Ella walked to the car and took out the Coast Guard bag. She watched as Fred and Jimmie drove off.

Doc Main offered his hand, "Pleasure to meet you, Miss Dixie. You're a ray of sunshine on a stormy day."

Ella smiled at that. She took his hand. Main lifted hers and barely touched it to his lips. She laughed. "The pleasure is mine, Doctor Main," she curtsied.

"Daniel."

"Daniel . . . we have room in the car, if Fred gets it fixed. Why not come with us before it's too late."

"Thank you kindly, Miss Dixie. Yesterday, friends from Miami visited. They offered to drive me out because of the storm. But my place of duty is here with the men. There have already been injuries from flying debris, there are sure to be more before the train arrives."

Water lapped at the shacks nearest the beach. Beyond, big waves broke against the reef. "The bridge across Snake Creek is sure to flood. I've already evacuated my patients to Miami by ambulance. The relief train is supposed to arrive any time now. Mr. Sheldon, the superintendent, wants to keep the men together."

"Freddie thinks the train won't get here in time," said Ella.

"All the more reason to stay."

"Going down with the ship?"

"Oh, this building was built pretty strong, not like those shacks for the men. We've already had some of locals show up to ride it out, they've seen it survive some mighty big storms."

* * *

One hour became two and entire families were seeking shelter in the hospital. Ella helped Main and his team making them comfortable. Finally, Fred, Jimmie and Razor Blade drove up in the Chevy.

"Remember Freddie, take it to the dealer in Miami and get the spring replaced and the wheels properly aligned. And drive slowly, that fix won't take any abuse," said Razor Blade leaving the car. A gust of wind nearly blew him over.

Ella and Dr. Main watched from the hospital door. Fred came running up, the others following. "Sorry, Dixie. Took longer than I thought, but we can get to Miami now. You still waiting for the train, Doc?"

"Hadn't heard anything different. So, we're all standing by."

"Everyone?"

"Well, not quite. An acquaintance of yours dropped by earlier and said he was going to a picnic of all things. Seemed very pleased with himself," said Main.

"Who?"

"Mr. Clemons, he said you slugged him Friday. You know . . . Skeeter."

"That son of a bitch, hope he drowns."

"That's hardly charitable, Fred," Ella frowned.

"Doc, I was there, saw the whole thing. Skeeter insulted that little Russell girl who works at the general store, said things I can't repeat in front of a lady. To my way of thinking, Skeeter deserved what he got."

"Well, Mr. Blade, that punch certainly had an effect, might have reformed him."

"Skeeter? Never."

"Freddie, you defended a maiden's honor? Now that's definitely in your favor."

"She's just a kid. Doc, did you say picnic?" asked Fred. Main nodded. "Any idea where?"

"Henry Russell's place, I believe."

"Damn it! Sorry pals, I have some unfinished business. Climb in Dixie, we're going back."

"You think Skeeter's going after Bernice Mae? I'll come with you."

"No thanks, Jimmie, this is between him and me."

Dr. Main raised his hand. "Hold up there, Fred. I don't think he means her any harm, and her father would never allow anything bad to happen to her."

"You don't know him like I do." Fred ran back to the car. Ella hesitated, glanced at Main, shrugged and then followed Fred with her bag.

Fred turned the car and began racing back to Islamorada. "Fred, slow down! You'll get us killed."

"Skeeter will rape her just to get back at me."

"That's crazy!"

"He knows she's sweet on me, that's why he called her a two-bit cocksucker, and that's why I hit him. I swore I'd kill anyone who messes with her. He knows I went to Key West and thinks he can rape her behind my back."

"Are you listening to yourself, Fred? It's me, me, me, all about me! The world doesn't spin around just you. Let them alone. We've got our own problems."

They were crossing Whale Harbor Fill when a gust struck the car, knocking it sideways. It skidded off the wet road and into a telephone pole. Fred's head struck the steering wheel and began bleeding above his left eye. Ella slid under the dashboard, bruised but conscious. Slowly she climbed back into her seat. "Fred, please."

Without speaking he got the car started, back on the road, now awash, and resumed driving towards Islamorada. The town was empty. Fred took the turn onto the Russell property. He reached across Ella's lap and opened the glove box. He took out the .45.

"No, Fred, you're not doing this!"

The sky erupted in lightning and thunder, the bolts landing all around them. Trees exploded, branches and pieces of tree trunk pelted the car. Fred opened his door and rolled on to the ground. He low crawled to the house through the mud and debris. Ella ran after him. She caught up and blocked his path. "Stop! Are you insane?"

He looked up and glared at her. Lightning flashes reflected in his eyes. "The fucking Krauts killed Steve. They have to pay for it!"

She knelt before him, held his face in her hands, and kissed him. "Fred, the war's over. We can go home now and make love. Give me the gun."

He sat up and pulled away. "Not until I've killed them all, you fucking yid cunt!" He whipped the pistol against her head, cutting her right ear. Stunned and bleeding, she fell to the ground and lay there. He stood and limped toward the house. There was a dim light visible through the gaps in the boarded windows of the second floor.

"Fred! Steve's not dead, he's here with me!" She got up and reached under her skirt.

He turned. "Steve? Where?"

A lightning bolt split a tree near the house, the flash silhouetting Fred. The thunder clapped simultaneously. Ella fired her PPK three times into his chest. He staggered and fell. She came up to him and felt for a pulse. There was none. She picked up the .45 where it had fallen, and then checked to see if the envelope with the letter and discharge certificate was still in his jacket. The rain washed the blood from his lips. She knelt and kissed them. Returning to the car Ella sat still, took deep breaths, and trembled. She clenched her fists until the trembling stopped. Calm now, she left the car, walked back to the body, and dragged it into the undergrowth near the road.

* * *

"Here, put this on," Bernice Mae handed a raincoat to Skeeter. "It's one of Pa's so it should cover most of you."

Skeeter tried it on. "Kinda tight but it works, mostly." He glanced out the door. It was swinging open in the wind. "Half a tree came down, must have hit the door. Rain's slowed. Storm must be nearly over. Wasn't so bad."

Bernice Mae took a look. The shattered tree still smoldered from a lightning strike. They repaired the door as much as possible and nailed an extra board across the gap. About a foot of water flowed over the ground. They pushed through floating coconuts, palm fronds, tree limbs and to the railroad grade. It was just above the water.

Bernice Mae spotted them first, two shivering key deer cowering in the bushes near the tracks. "Rosy, Snowy, come here! We won't leave you!" They came out timidly. "Skeeter, will you take Rosy? I'll take Snowy."

"Those two again. Which is which?"

"Snowy has this white patch on her head, Rosy doesn't. Makes no never mind to them, always call them with both names. There're never apart."

"I'll take both, then. You just watch where we're headed." Skeeter scooped up a wet deer under each arm.

There was an occasional break in the overcast revealing a patch of blue sky. Many trees had fallen. The houses they passed all showed damage. A truck followed by two cars drove by, throwing up a wave of water. The drivers didn't see them.

* * *

Ella stopped the car. There was something blocking the road ahead. It was on the Whale Harbor Fill, a half mile long and just wide enough for the railroad tracks and the narrow highway. She had to cross it to get back to Camp 1 and the Snake Creek bridge. It was still twilight but the storm clouds made it very dark. She turned on the headlamps. Windblown water from the bay was sloshing over the railroad embankment, onto the highway and into the ocean. It was a small house ahead, oddly sitting across the highway. As she watched, the wood frame building broke into pieces, parts drifted into the ocean waters, and floated away. There weren't any people, they must have escaped earlier, she hoped. Ella turned the car left onto the tracks and stopped, checking to see that the wheels were properly positioned. She placed the Coast Guard bag on the passenger seat and tied its strap to her right arm. "Well, let's give it a go." She began driving. The embankment was several feet higher than the highway, so she ought to make it across to Windley Key. She hoped Fred was right about the relief train running late.

To her left the bay had risen nearly level with the track bed, the rails awash. Ella found it difficult to keep the tires straight, they'd slip off and she'd struggle to find the tracks. The wind increased, and the heavy rain made it impossible to see even with the wipers going. She crept along for a few minutes more, then stopped. But the Chevy kept moving. She braked hard as the front end tipped over to the right. The car slid down the embankment and slammed into the ditch beside the roadway. The impact threw her head against the windshield. Feeling faint and nauseous, she waited for her mind to clear. Idly, she wondered if this morning's sunrise would be her last, too. It was past time to leave, but it was impossible to open the suicide door with the car pointing down. The window crank still worked and she squirmed out of the car, landing in the mud. She struggled up the embankment, against the run-off. When she reached the top, no lights were visible. Ella began walking unsteadily toward where Windley Key should be.

It was slow going, buffeted by the wind, feeling for the ties with her feet, the rain lashing her face and arms raw. She was past half-way when the roadbed began to shiver, and the familiar sound of a steam locomotive penetrated the wind noise. A dark mass was slowly approaching, a dim light behind it. She stepped off the track and slid halfway down the embankment. The tender was leading, then the engine running backward, its headlamp lighting the tops of cars coupled behind. For a moment she considered hopping aboard a coach as it passed, slow enough that she could do so safely. But the train would stop in Islamorada and that was too near the Russell place for comfort. She knew how far Camp 3 was and figured the train might never make it back. The coaches were lit and people were inside, civilians and veterans by their looks, not a happy face among them. They couldn't see the sodden, bedraggled figure regarding them.

After the train passed, Ella climbed back on the roadbed and promptly tripped over a rail. She must have pulled something in her leg and now couldn't stand. She sat there for a time then crawled to the nearest telephone pole and pulled herself upright. The pain was excruciating. She tried to massage the cramp out of her leg and work the foot around. There was a rustling sound. She looked up, the backwards facing train headlamp was gone. The sound got louder, the wind screamed, and the ocean seethed. It was climbing the embankment. Rapid lightning strikes illuminated an enormous wave rushing ashore. It was higher than the embankment, much higher. Dropping to her knees, she took a deep breath, clutched the Coast Guard bag tightly to her chest, and shut her eyes. The next moment she was lifted up. She flew through the air for a time and then splashed deep into the water. She rose to the surface in the trough of a wave, clutching the Coast Guard bag. It was the last thing she remembered.

* * *

Just past the depot Bernice Mae and Skeeter crossed the tracks and headed towards the bay side, sloshing through the ankle-deep water. The wind had returned stronger than before, forcing them to lean into it. Another turn took them into an orchard of battered lime and banana trees. Beside the road was a building set up on pilings. Bernice Mae climbed the steps to the door. She entered with Skeeter, still with the deer, following.

"Oh, baby girl, you made it! We were starting to worry." Ruby ran to Bernice Mae and hugged her. "And you found Rosy and Snowy. Thank you, Skeeter." She gave him a kiss on the cheek. He lowered the deer to the floor. The kids started petting them.

Henry asked, "How's the house holding up?"

"Well, the back door got busted in. And there are leaks. Otherwise, it's holding together." Skeeter, replied working the stiffness from his arms.

Bernice Mae looked around the crowded room. Everyone she loved was there amid the crates of limes, pineapples, sugar apples, bananas and tomatoes. She'd worked hard since Saturday, picking and packing with Pa and Cathy, saving what they could. She started crying.

"Bernice Mae, angel baby, what's the matter? We're all safe and sound now," her mother said.

"Don't rightly know, Ma. This is the happiest day of my life. Thanks for the orchid on the bed."

Ruby smiled. "No sense wasting time. It could rain tomorrow, ya know. Come on kids, let's all give Bernice Mae a big hug. She just walked through a hurricane."

The younger kids piled on. Bernice Mae's raincoat slipped off. Cathy glared. "You're wearing my dress!"

"Sorry Cathy, but the house was starting to come apart and you'd have lost it anyway."

"Still . . ."

"Hey, Skeeter, come over here, something to show you," Henry said.

On the wall was a barometer. "I brought this over from the house. It's reading 29.06 inches. That's a drop of half an inch since noon."

"Sorry, Henry, don't know much about barometers. What does that mean?"

"The lower it goes the stronger the storm, and the faster it drops the closer it is."

Skeeter studied the dial. "I can see the needle moving."

"You're right. Ain't never seen it drop that fast afore. Now it's 28.99 and falling."

"You were right to get everyone out of the house. When we left, the ocean was on the porch, the roof was leaking and the frame was shaking. Reckon it won't last if this storm gets much worse."

"What's the road like?"

"Water is flowing across it, just a few inches. Looks like the water is building up on the bay side."

"I've been through a lot of storms. 1894 was bad. Aught Five was worse. Then Aught Nine and again in 1910. 1919 was the last big one. Cathy came the next year. The kids only know what I've told them. They haven't seen what these things can do . . . I've never seen the barometer fall this fast."

"But we're safe here?"

"Used dynamite to blast out holes in the coral to set the pilings, then poured in concrete. The frame is held down with half-inch braided steel cables. Figure we're pretty safe. Nothing's blowing it down."

"Yeah," Bernice Mae interrupted. "Pa has me grease the cables twice a year to keep the rust out. Cathy won't touch them, might get her frilly frock filthy. Now it's soaked."

There came a sound just like a train coming fast, the wind so loud it hurt your ears, no one could hear anything else. When it seemed it might go on forever, the packing house began to shiver, there were sounds like gun shots. One of the heavy cross beams in the ceiling cracked, the roof sagged down, water poured in. The train moved on.

Henry grabbed a 6 x 6 post from a pile of lumber in the corner and hoisted it up under the damaged beam. It was too short. "I'll give you a hand," Skeeter shouted. He found enough wood scraps to shim the post tight up against the beam. "You can let go, now."

"Thanks, Skeeter, but we have to raise it a few inches higher."

Bernice Mae came over with a heavy mallet. "If you two can raise the post an inch I can hammer another shim underneath. Then do it again until it's high enough."

Skeeter and Henry nodded. They hugged the post. "Ready?" Henry shouted, "Now!"

The post rose. The girl drove in a shim. "Let it down, slowly," he called. It held. "OK, again." Two more lifts and the crack in the beam was closed. Water still leaked in but the torrent had stopped. Skeeter's and Henry's hands were bleeding. Ruby and Bernice Mae wrapped clean linen strips around their palms.

Henry checked the barometer then his watch. "27.84, down more than an inch in half an hour. Never seen anything like that before, and it's still dropping. We need to talk. Cathy, Bernice Mae, Sara, you mind the children." The three adults sat on packing crates in a close circle.

"We may not be able to stay here through the storm, we need to be ready to move. I think that train is our best bet. When it shows we can make a run for it. What do y'all think?" asked Henry.

Skeeter raised his hand. "Well, a rail coach floor is 5 feet above the tracks, and the roadbed is ten feet above sea level, can't get any higher on Matecumbe unless you climb a tree. And they're heavy, built of steel. If everything else gets swept away they're still be here. Tell you what, I'll go outside and watch for the headlamp. When I see the train coming, I'll high tail it back and let you know."

Henry spoke up. "OK, then I take Charlie and Willy, Cathy takes Hilton, Bernice takes Doloria, and Ma takes Carl. Sarah will just have to stay close to me."

"In the war I swam a river with a buddy on my back and then carried him two miles to the aid station, under fire," said Skeeter. "I can sure as hell carry two kids tied to my back through a storm, leastways easier than you. We'll need both arms free to get through this."

Henry stood and placed his hand on Skeeter's shoulder. "Sarah and Charlie don't know you. Bernice Mae should go along to keep them calm, and she's our best swimmer. I'll take Willie and Doloria. Now let's fix up the harnesses."

Bernice Mae had been listening. "Shouldn't I take Snowy and Rosy, seeing as I ain't carrying nobody?"

"Angel Baby," Ruby said, "the deer have lived on the Keys for centuries, they've survived all the hurricanes and they'll survive this one.

They'll follow if they're a mind to. You stay with your man and keep your brother and sister safe."

"OK, I'm going now, that train is running late," said Skeeter.

"I'm coming with," said Bernice Mae.

"No, darling, best if you stay here."

"Hey, we ain't hitched yet. I'm coming."

"Yes, dear."

Bernice Mae and Skeeter closed the door behind them and were immediately blown off their feet. Skeeter rolled over the edge of the deck and splashed into foot deep water. He waved to Bernice Mae. She crawled over. He took her under the arms and lowered her beside him. "Hang on to my belt," he shouted. The rain blew horizontal and blinded them. They struggled on towards the station. It was very dark, but they could make out that there was no train. One wall of the station had collapsed. They leaned into the wind and slowly walked toward it. Two boxcars sat on the siding. The door on the one nearest the depot was partially open. Skeeter hoisted Bernice Mae up. A hand appeared and hauled her aboard. Skeeter climbed in after her. Inside, about a dozen men sat on the floor or stood leaning against the walls, a lantern hung from a hook. "Welcome, cousin," said the man who'd pulled Bernice Mae inside."

"Thanks for the hand up, Cousin Raymond. The packing house is caving and Pa thought we should see if the train might be safer. Any word?" asked Bernice Mae.

"Yeah, three hours late and we're still waiting. The station started to blow apart so we decided to wait here. Make yourselves comfortable."

"Miss Russell? We'll have plenty of seats on the train, so bring the whole family," Ray Sheldon said.

"Thank you kindly, sir."

The wind sang as it passed the door. But then it was accompanied by a higher-pitched whistle. "That's it!" Sheldon shouted. He jumped down from the boxcar and ran splashing down the tracks. The others followed. Skeeter helped Bernice Mae down onto the tracks.

"Where is it, Skeeter? Don't see any lights."

"Wait, I hear it chugging. It didn't stop at the depot, it's still coming. Look." The rain had let up enough to see the massive form approach. The brakes squealed and the train came to a stop a little past them.

"Hey, the headlamp is facing backward."

"Yeah, that's so it will be facing forward on the way back to Miami. Come on, we need to get your folks."

Skeeter swept up Bernice Mae in his arms and headed for the packing house. The water had risen to his knees. Several times he got tangled in submerged debris but managed to wrench himself free. Bernice Mae jumped down, hooked her hands into his belt and got pulled along. When they reached the packing house, they saw that a heap of broken fruit trees had been blown up against the building. A flash of lightning revealed the sagging roof.

"Up you go," Skeeter said, hoisting Bernice Mae onto the platform by the door. He followed and they both pushed the tree limbs out of the way. Skeeter looked back in the direction of the tracks. So many trees had been flattened that the lights from the locomotive and coaches were visible.

Everyone looked up when Skeeter and Bernice Mae entered.

"The train's here, don't know for how much longer, need to move now," shouted Skeeter. "And the boss man said there was room aboard for us, don't think he knows how many us is."

"We're already harnessed up, just need to load the kids," said Henry. He came over to Skeeter. "How bad is it?"

"Well, the train made it here, but the water's getting deeper. Worst part is the wind, times we were crawling."

There was a loud snap and the entire building shifted. "That was one of the cables, Pa."

"Henry," Ruby spoke loudly to be heard, "there's water coming up through the floor." She licked her wet fingers. "Salty. The ocean has come ashore."

"Everybody got their kids? Follow me." Henry forced open the door, Willie and Doloria tied to his back. The wind stopped him for a moment, then he bulled his way out. Waist deep in the water he helped Ruby down. Bernice Mae followed Skeeter out of the packing house with Rosy and Snowy. They jumped into the water. "You skat now, y'hear?" she told them. The deer stared at Bernice Mae for a moment then swam away.

Henry saw it coming. A wall of shattered trees, the wreckage of buildings, tumbling automobiles, coral rocks and human bodies being pushed along by a mound of sea water ten feet high with waves cresting above that. Everything fell before it and was added to the wall. "Ruby!" he cried. She saw it, too, and came to his side. "Bernice, Cathy, Skeeter!" He gathered together those of his family within arm's reach. The wave struck. The screams of his children were silenced. For a moment he felt their bodies bounce against his, then a timber crushed his chest. He gasped, water and blood filled his lungs. *God save them, God save them . . .*

Skeeter, farther back saw what was happening, and started climbing the stoutest tree still standing. He scrambled up level with the top of the storm wave, wrapped his arms around the trunk and clenched his hands together. "Bernice! Hang on to me!"

The wave bent the tree over some, but it still stood. Skeeter was face down in the water. Something hit his legs. There was no feeling. He began climbing up the partially submerged tree, using just his hands. Sarah or Charlie, he didn't know which, was kicking his back. Little hands clutched his neck. His lungs were burning when his hand reached up into the air. He pulled himself the last few feet above the water. It was pitch dark, there was nothing to see and no branch to grasp. The rain pummeled his neck and ears. The kids, he thought, I must turn to shield them. But the kicking had stopped, the little hands were still.

"Skeeter! Say something. Where are you?" He knew that voice. Someone he loved.

"Over here, Darling! I'm on the tree over here." He felt a hand touch his head, then two arms were around his neck, and she kissed him. "Oh, darling, darling!" he said.

A flash of lightning revealed the horror in her eyes when she saw the lolling heads of Sarah and Charlie against his shoulders

"Skeeter . . . I think we're the only ones left. Are you hurt?"

"I think I broke something; my legs don't work. The kids, I can't feel them."

She reached over his shoulders and lifted their eyelids. "No . . ." she sobbed, ". . . they didn't make it."

"I failed you, I failed your family . . ." Blood spluttered from his lips. "I should have died, too." He coughed up more blood. "Maybe I will, something's broke inside."

"Oh, that's just your heart, Skeeter. Broken hearts heal, you'll see. The next pretty girl who swims by, you'll forget all about me."

"Bernice Mae, I don't like how you're talking, you're the one meant to live. I'm a bum, the bum who failed when it mattered. You're young and strong, you'll find someone young and strong easy." His arms slipped and he slid a few inches down the tree and deeper into the water.

"Hang in there, Skeeter." She climbed onto the tree just above him, hugging the trunk with her thighs and grabbed the harness with her hands. "Pa says these storm waves don't last very long, once they sweep over the land they don't stick around, why look, it's already gotten lower, you just keep thinking positive now, and in a few minutes, we'll just shinny down this big ol' tree onto solid ground, it'll be muddy, for sure, but we're used to that, aren't we, then we'll get back to that box car and spend the night and I'll keep you nice and warm and dry your clothes and in the morning, we'll find something to eat and drink, one of those restaurants must have survived, like the Caribbee Colony, and by then the Red Cross folks will be here and get us new clothes and help us rebuild, because you know we won't be cutting and running, 'cause we're Conchs and Russells to boot! You are too, now, you and me, Skeeter, we'll get busy, replanting the orchards and crops, fixing up the house, by God, we'll be busy! Not to mention our own kids when I get old enough, we'll make such a family together, just you wait and see, you'll love all your sons and daughters, we'll name them whatever you like, first and middle names, and I'll stay thin for you so even when you get older you can still pick me up and fuck in all kinds of fun ways, and you'll never, ever, get all floppy again, I'll just see to that. Skeeter . . . Skeeter?"

He hung there, his arms limp. "Skeeter! Say something!" She lowered herself on the tree, scraping her legs against the rough tree bark, but without him holding on she couldn't stop and they both slid down into the water. She pushed him up against the trunk and slapped him as hard as she could across the face. There was no response. She felt for a pulse in his neck and found none. She lifted his eyelids. His eyes did not see her stricken face. She kissed him, and Sarah and little Charlie. Their lips were cold. She released them and they sank into the swirling, black water. Bernice Mae started climbing, to the top of the tree, she had always been good at that, winning every race with the other kids. No more hiding this time. No running scared. If this monster wanted her, too, she'd spit in its eye. There was a thick branch near the top she used to stand upright on the slanted trunk. She saw it coming, a door or shutter, just for instant in a lightning flash. There was no pain, it split her skull too fast for that.

Chapter 30

Wednesday, September 4, 1935 – Relief

Eddie awoke on the flying bridge. It had been a warm, calm night, the boat rocking gently. In just his shorts, he carried a bucket of fresh water out to the end of the pier. Overnight, a colony of gulls had roosted there. They flew off as he approached, expressing their displeasure by leaving the planks covered with droppings. Eddie stopped short of the mess and poured the bucket over his head. He returned to the cabin, stripped and washed his privates. On Monday, Doctor Pérez had cleaned the stab wound with soap and distilled water, rinsed again, applied iodine and stitched it up. He warned Eddie to return immediately if there were a foul-smelling purulent discharge. Eddie checked. The wound was sore. He dried off, held his hand against the wound, then sniffed it. Seemed OK. He applied a clean bandage, wrapping it around his waist.

By then it was getting light outside. Los hermanos would be arriving soon. Eddie dressed and brewed a big pot of coffee. He filled a tumbler with rum and drank it down. The quantity of supplies left on the pier yesterday had concerned him, but he had worked late and was satisfied with his stowage plan. Everything was evenly distributed, Esmeralda sat well in the water with no angle of list. His passengers were another matter, it would be crowded, and if they did find Ella and Fred injured there'd be little space for them to lie down.

"Hola, Jefe," came a shout from the pier. He was confused for an instant, Emilio wasn't here. Then he understood, los hermanos were calling him, jefe. This would take some getting used to. Before Colonel Rattigan left the boat the day before, he made it clear to everyone that Esmeralda was Eddie's now. The price was $1. Eddie figured he could afford it. That afternoon he went shopping and found the perfect skipper's hat, all black with crossed gold anchors embroidered above the visor. He tried it on in front of a mirror, different poses, varied expressions, decided to take up pipe smoking. Now it was in its box on a shelf in the cabin. He opened it. "Well, new day, new look."

Eddie helped Enrique and Fernando aboard with the heavy blocks of ice they carried in duck canvas bags. Fernando noticed first. "¡Buenos días, Capitán!"

"¡Felicidades señor, bien hecho!" Enrique saluted. They all laughed, followed by handshakes and back slapping.

The blocks went directly into the ice box to cool the soda and beer. Eddie liked the brothers, they kept their heads down and knew their jobs, never complained and always cracking jokes. He didn't need to tell them what to do. Without a word they went below into the engine compartment, grooming the three Packards like thoroughbreds before a big race. He'd told them what to expect on today's trip. That sobered them, but not for long.

Sunrise was 6:09. Not long after, Colonel Rattigan and Cindy arrived. Eddie greeted them on the pier.

"Good morning, Captain," said Rattigan giving Eddie a two-handed shake.

"Fine weather we're having, eh, Colonel?"

"That it is, that it is."

"Like the look, Eddie. How long have you had that in waiting?" asked Cindy.

"Not long, Emilio gave me a heads-up Friday."

Cindy's voice caught, "Uh . . . he knew . . . how?"

"No, no Señorita Cindy, he thought it would all go well, that he'd retire and then sell me Esmeralda."

"That's Emilio, take it easy, just go fishing and . . . and clubbing." Cindy squeezed her father's hand.

"Here come the others," Eddie announced.

A taxi stopped on the quay. Emma and a young woman got out, both carrying large bags. Eddie jogged forward. "Morning, Doctor Henderson, miss," he tipped his cap to both. "May I take your bags?"

"Why, thank you, sir. But you're no red cap, I see you're skipper now."

"Yes, indeed Doctor, but we're short-handed today."

"I'll take one of those," said Rattigan, who'd followed Eddie at a more sedate pace.

"My, two gentlemen, Florence. This is starting out well."

"Yes, it is, Doctor."

"Anything I can carry, Emma?" asked Cindy.

"No, dear, that's all. May I introduce you to Nurse Florence Crane? She volunteered for this." They shook hands.

Cindy heard a bicycle bell ring, turned, and saw an elderly man peddling along the quay, in a short sleeve black clergy shirt, white collar, black pants, and white fedora.

"A fine morning to you, Miss Rattigan." The clergyman parked his bike.

"Thought maybe you wouldn't make it, Bill, such short notice."

"I know some of those men in the camps. There are souls to be saved."

"Can I help you with anything?"

"Just my Bible and Sacraments. I think I can handle that. I see I'm not the first."

"But not the last. Maybe that's him." Another cab turned onto the quay. It parked and two men exited, Renard and Cavendish.

"I'm acquainted with young Philip, but not the other gentleman."

"He's a G-man. Careful what you say."

The men walked up and tipped their caps. "Edward, this is Father Bill Reagan, he's coming with us,"

"Miss Rattigan tells me you are a government man and I should mind my language."

"Special Agent Edward Renard, Federal Bureau of Investigation, Department of Justice, Reverend Father, and you are quite above suspicion." Renard smiled and shook Reagan's hand.

"Catholic?"

"Yes, Father, Jesuit education."

"Hah! We must talk."

"Nattily attired, I see, Agent Renard," said Rattigan.

"The sport fisherman-look appealed to me. Abby suggested it."

"Well, she does have an eye for men's fashion, picks my clothes before a date. So, are we good to go, Lieutenant?"

"The coast is clear, so to speak. I have some information for the first mate." They walked to the boat where Eddie waited. "Got the report from our seaplane, weather and sea conditions are acceptable, so your relief mission may proceed. Ah, did we have a promotion here?"

Rattigan nodded. "Yes, Lieutenant, Mr. Marín is now captain and owner of the Esmeralda."

"Good morning, Lieutenant Cavendish."

"Congratulations, Captain. A well-deserved promotion."

"Thank you, Lieutenant. You have some information for me?"

"Yes, you have your charts?"

"In the cockpit, welcome aboard. Mind your step, the engine hatch is open."

Both men bent over a navigation chart of the Keys. "Recommend you take Hawk Channel to the Moser Draw then on to Lower Matecumbe through the Bay. The railroad bridges are intact, but the Channel 5 Draw is blocked by debris," said Cavendish. "All the landings and piers on the ocean side are wrecked. All buildings between Marathon and Tavernier are demolished. The ferry landing on Lower Matecumbe appears to be usable. You can safely anchor at several locations on the bay side. The State relief operation is based on Plantation Key at Snake Creek. They've set up a receiving point for the dead and injured. There's a jury-rigged foot bridge spanning the creek and they're ferrying people across in small boats. Lower Matecumbe is cut through by two trenches, several feet deep. Indian Key Fill and Whale Harbor Fill are gone but not navigable. The Danish motorship *Leise Maersk* is aground off Upper Matecumbe, about here. Any questions?"

"Heard that the *Dixie* went aground, too."

"Yes, she's stuck here, on French Reef, off Key Largo. I'll be aboard the *Saukee* today assisting."

"Survivors?" asked Reagan.

"Good news, all crew and passengers are safe."

"A blessing."

Cavendish turned to the others. "The pilot radioed that bodies were clearly discernable from Windley Key to Lower Matecumbe on land and floating offshore. There are many survivors, though. They looked pretty bad off. There's nothing left of Islamorada, just an overturned train, and the ground floor of the Matecumbe hotel. Heaps of wreckage at Camps 1 and 3, nothing of Camp 5 remains. Long Key is swept clean."

"Philip," asked Emma, "has any relief reached those poor people?"

"Just at Camp 1. A few folks have made it to Lower Matecumbe. Reports are it's very bad. There's a flotilla of motor launches leaving No Name Key this morning, carrying Sheriff Thompson and some deputies, and Major Albury with a detachment of National Guard troops. They're supposed to maintain order and evacuate the veterans, hardly any civilians live there. Hear that Mr. Hemingway is going to take a look. Maybe he'll write something."

"Best be on our way then. Thank you, Lieutenant."

"Take care of yourselves. Ladies, gentlemen." Cavendish left.

"Enrique and Fernando! Stand ready to cast off!" Eddie shouted. The brothers climbed out of the engine compartment, and leapt smartly onto the pier. Eddie proceeded confidently through the engine start routine. The Packards rumbled to life. "Cast off!"

Esmeralda moved at low wake through the crowded basin. The breeze caught the flag on the transom. Eddie sounded the horn twice. Other boats responded with their horns. There were many people about even at this hour. They let up a cheer. Eddie steered out to sea.

* * *

The smell was noticeable some ways out. "Eww, what's that?" Cindy asked.

"Death," her father answered.

On Esmeralda's right the railroad bridge appeared unscathed, but clumps of sea grass were visible on the tracks 30 feet above the water, the rails twisted at odd angles. The Channel 5 draw bridge was intact but the tender's house gone. Under the bridge every sort of debris had collected, trees, boats, buildings and their contents. At this hour the rising tide met the outflow from the bay. Enrique was stationed on the bow with a gaff to push off any floating objects that might cause damage. Eddie stood on the flying bridge piloting with the duplicate controls. "Off the starboard bow, about 20 yards," he called out, "do you see it, Enrique?"

"A log or something, Jefe. We won't hit it."

Eddie used the binoculars. "It's not a log. I'll come close. Try to hook it. We'll attach a line and tow it ashore."

"Aye, aye, Capitán."

Eddie slowed the boat and turned gradually to the right. Rattigan leaned over the side. "Shit".

Reagan joined him. "Dear God." He crossed himself.

"What is it?" asked Cindy, stepping over to see. The others joined her.

A corpse was slowly drifting toward the boat. It was impossible to tell the age or gender. The soaked clothing was stretched tight over the swollen body giving the appearance of some sea creature, perhaps a sleeping manatee. But there was no mistaking that the object was human, a hand, a foot, a face. The last was puffed up, the lips pulled back, revealing missing teeth. The eyes were empty sockets. Cindy stumbled to the port side and threw up.

Eddie maneuvered the boat so that the body came up against the bow. "Got it, Enrique?"

"Hold her steady, Jefe." Enrique leaned over the side and tried to hook an article of clothing. It took several attempts before he found a belt. "Got it."

Eddie stopped the engines. "OK, walk it back to the stern. Fernando come up here and take the controls."

He climbed down to the afterdeck, cut a length of line and fashioned a lasso. "Everyone, stand back. Now hold it steady, Enrique." Eddie sat on the transom with his legs over the edge, and considered what next. The neck would be easiest, but that just didn't seem right. He tossed the loop over a foot and pulled it tight, then tied the line's end to a cleat. "There, lift the gaff off. Good."

Emma stood beside him. "He's been in the water two days. Didn't drown though. He was already dead when he went under. See, his neck is broken. What now?"

"To the ferry slip and tie the line to something so he won't drift off again."

Fernando called down from the flying bridge, *"Jefe, tenemos otro."*

* * *

The Monroe County was aground, the upper deck a pile of wreckage beside it in the water. A battered houseboat listed half sunk between the ferry and the pier. The pier itself appeared undamaged, and the water clear of wreckage on the far side. Two men in civilian clothes waved as the Esmeralda approached. One tossed a line to Enrique. "Welcome, brother, I hope you have a doctor with you."

Eddie looked down from the flying bridge. "Yes sir, and a nurse. And food, blankets, clothes and water. We also have two bodies in tow, where do you want them?"

"I'll send some men over to collect them. But first things first. Doctor?"

"That's me, here's my bag." Emma, handing it to the man. "I'm Doctor Henderson from the Marine Hospital. Nurse Crane is my assistant."

"Pleased to meet you, ladies. I'll take your bags ... feels like you brought more supplies than the last two doctors who came here. All they had was a bottle of alcohol and some cotton swabs."

"When was that?"

"About an hour ago. They flew in on a Coast Guard seaplane from Miami, took a walk around, and left. Tourists."

"Well, we came to work mister . . ."

"Ben Davis, Doctor Henderson, I'm the camp superintendent, was rather, no camp left. This is Ed Sheeran. He's chief of bridge construction."

Sheeran added, ". . . was chief, now I'll go back to ferry operations, I guess."

"Not any time soon, Ed. Doctor Henderson, Nurse Crane, please follow me to our aid station, it's under a tarpaulin where the mess hall used to be."

Along the pier bodies were laid out on planks in a neat row covered with white bed sheets. Nurse Crane counted: "36."

"And the two you brought makes 38. There are others hung up back in the jungle. We can smell them," said Sheeran.

It was a short walk along a sandy path between heaps of wreckage. The makeshift aid station was crowded with men, lying or sitting on the bare ground. "We have 42 seriously injured, 6 of them from Camp 5."

"Mr. Davis, do you have some able-bodied men who can help us?"

"Yes, Doctor. Are 12 enough?"

"As soon as you can. Florence, let's get to work."

"Edward and I will go get the blankets."

"Thanks Cindy, we need to get our patients off the ground."

"I have to get back to work, ladies," said Sheeran and left.

* * *

Father Reagan hadn't gotten past the pier. Before each body he stopped and prayed,

Eternal rest grant unto them, O Lord, and let perpetual light shine upon them. May their souls and the souls of all the faithful departed, through the mercy of God, rest in peace. Amen.

He hadn't gone far before survivors gathered beside him and bowed their heads. Renard crossed himself as he passed by.

Rattigan accompanied Davis as he rounded up his men. He did this with authority and the men hurried to the aid station. "Mr. Davis, how many men do you have here?"

"242 on the August payroll. No telling how many now, maybe 160, including the dead. Lot of the boys spent the weekend in Miami or Key West, and didn't make it back Monday."

"That's about the strength of a rifle company, guess that makes you a Captain."

"Yeah, that's what the men call me. I wasn't in the war, you?"

"Yes. This place looks like a village in France after it changed hands a few times. How did you survive?"

"I've thought about that a lot, whether I did the right thing. I look at those bodies on the dock and doubt it."

"There were times when I've had the same feelings. You can second guess yourself forever but never change the outcome."

"Well, I'll tell you what happened. At 6 p.m. Monday the hurricane hit us with high winds, blowing in gusts. See my watch? It's still ticking. So, around seven the roof blew off the mess hall where most of us were sheltering. I told them to make their way to safety. Most of the men went to Bradford's general store near the landing. At 7:30, Bradford's roof blew off and the men sought safety wherever they could. I told them to take the lee side of the of the railroad track, some of them went in and around automobiles and rode the first storm through. The water was 12 or 14 inches deep running like a river over the camp. I reckon the wind velocity had at least reached 150 miles an hour"

"Imagine that was difficult to judge."

"I've been through bad hurricanes before and they were nothing like this. All the buildings were gone by this time and we had two dead and a small number wounded by flying debris. At nine we had a calm which lasted about an hour. The wind just stopped, and the stars came out and the wind seemed to get warm, and it was just as still a piece of paper wouldn't flutter in the air. I knew that the storm was not over and would return from the opposite direction, so we collected and decided to board the beer boat and the ferry in front of the camp and the Sarasota, a Panama dredge in back of the camp, also the water tank car about half a mile below the camp. Only places I could think of that would be safe. I told the men that it was everybody for himself and to keep cool heads, that I was going to the water tank car and the men chose to follow me."

"Chose? God man, you led them."

"Well, nobody else had a plan. When we got to the tank car you could hear the rustle of the water in the ocean, which sounded like the rustle of leaves but as it came closer it came in with a deepening roar.

At ten I watched the water coming in on us from the top of the water car, a wall of white foam. It was at least 25 feet high and completely submerged us with approximately 5 feet of water. This, with a terrible wind behind it. This was practically the worst part of the storm. Men were washed from the track as the track was completely torn down and turned over by the water, and the men on the tank car were saved by the track falling against the side of the tank car. This is where our greatest loss of life took place. We survivors were helpless to help one another. After the high wave from the Atlantic washed over the keys and land, it returned in about 15 minutes and lasted approximately 10 minutes. The water was not so high but lasted longer"

"How long did you stay on the tank car?"

"All night. At daybreak, yesterday, we got down off the tank car to rescue the injured. We released 3 men pinioned between the track and the water tank car, two were living. We made our way around the camp and piles of wreckage and also the ground surrounding Camp 3 to rescue and relieve the injured, but due to the fact that the storm had washed our ambulance away, which was located with all emergency medical supplies we had no medical attention. We took shelter from the rain Tuesday wherever we could find a place, the storm still raging but gradually decreasing. We gathered at the Sarasota that evening and had coffee and canned goods which were salvaged about camp. The storm abated overnight and this morning we went to work picking up the dead and bringing them to the ferry slip where they could be loaded on boats. About 9 a.m. a private seaplane chartered by Mrs. Bradford arrived from Miami. She was coming for her husband, a civilian, who owned and operated the store known as Bradford's. He survived. They left immediately for help and carried one of the severely injured veterans back with them to a hospital. Then that Coast Guard plane arrived with those two useless doctors. That's about it, Mr. Rattigan. Hope I didn't bore you too much."

"Hardly, Ben. The companies in my battalion rarely suffered as many casualties. You kept your head in extreme circumstances. You may not have served, but had you I'd have recommended you for a medal."

"Thank you, sir, just doing my duty. What was your rank? If you don't mind me asking."

"A major during the war. I stayed in the Army Reserves and eventually made colonel. But just call me Dan. One thing though, wasn't there supposed to be a train to evacuate your men to the mainland?"

"Yes, Dan, it was promised by Mr. Sheldon, my boss, but it never showed."

"And what became of Sheldon?"

"No idea, just hope he got as wet as we did. The train business is what's been eating me up. I was in the office when Sheldon got the hurricane warning from the Weather Bureau. He had to call his boss, Mr. Ghent, in Jacksonville to order the train. That was after 2 p.m. I waited for that train until 6 when the hurricane hit, just twiddling my thumbs. Then we were fighting for our lives. Dan, we had enough trucks and cars at Camp 3 to evacuate everyone to Homestead, in one, maybe two lifts. It would have taken less than three hours. If I had ordered the evacuation on my own by 3 p.m. we all would have survived. If Sheldon wanted to wait for the train, it was on him. I had no right to let my men die."

"Ben, you couldn't have known how close the storm was or how late the train would be. If you'd disobeyed Sheldon, you'd have lost your job."

"The Weather Bureau knew it was close enough to forecast gales Monday afternoon, and the more I think of it, the more I believe the train was just a pipe dream."

"Back in Key West this morning we got a report from a Coast Guard plane, said there was a wrecked train in Islamorada. So, there was some substance to it."

"If it only got that far, it would have taken it another hour at least to come down here, turn around and load the men from the other camps, let alone return to the mainland. It was my responsibility to know the evacuation plan, practice it, stay informed, and try something else when it all came apart."

"Ben," Rattigan placed his hand on Davis's shoulder, "You did no less than any reasonable man, and far more than most any man would. Don't be so hard on yourself."

Renard had come near and listened to the exchange. "Washington is calling it an Act of God, that no one could have predicted this, or done anything different."

"Bull shit."

"That sounds about right. Captain Davis, I'm Special Agent Renard . . ."

". . . Federal Bureau of Investigation, Department of Justice," finished Rattigan.

"Like Dan said. I was wondering if you are familiar with Fred Dunn, a veteran working in the camps?"

"No Dunn assigned to Camp 3, nor in Camp 5 as far as I know. I used to be superintendent there. Could be in Camp 1."

"He was traveling with a teenager, Ella Kaufmann, maybe passed through here Monday."

"Wait a minute. I was at a meeting with Sheldon and the camp staff Monday afternoon at the Matecumbe Hotel. Then this guy walks in, all chummy with Sheldon, like they were old pals or something. Sheldon called the guy Fred. He told some bull shit story about driving over the railroad bridges. Sheldon mentioned someone named Cindy, like she was Fred's girl. Then Fred Poock walked in and called him 'Mr. Dunn'. Then they left together."

"Do you know where I can find Mr. Poock?"

"He was antsy to get home to his family in Homestead, seems they just arrived in town."

"And what is Mr. Poock's job at the camp?"

"Office manager, and he's trustee of the veterans trust fund. The men make contributions on pay day and he deposits them in a special bank account."

Renard and Rattigan exchanged looks.

"Do you happen to know the name of the bank, Captain?"

"First National Bank of Homestead, I believe."

"Thank you, Captain Davis, you've been very helpful."

Rattigan and Renard returned to the aid station. The transformation was dramatic. All the patients were on salvaged bed frames, fitted with boards, and covered with the blankets from the boat. The beds were neatly aligned and separated at equal distances. More tarps had been added to provide shade. Emma and Florence moved purposefully among the injured. Cindy and several healthy veterans, served them food and water. Father Reagan talked calmly to a man in some distress, his leg and head bandaged.

* * *

Fernando yelled from the flying bridge, *"Jefe, tenemos visita."*

Eddie climbed up and looked through the binoculars. Two boats were approaching from the east, a large motor yacht flying a Red Cross flag and close behind, a Coast Guard cutter. *"Chicos, nos estamos moviendo."* He started the engines, the crew cast off, and Esmeralda anchored a hundred yards offshore. The yacht, Byronic, took Esmeralda's place alongside the pier and the cutter tied up beside the Byronic. Davis was there to greet the newcomers. They had come from Miami with a stop at Snake Creek. The Red Cross team was to take the injured back to Snake Creek for transport to Miami hospitals. The cutter would evacuate everyone else.

The first aid station was quickly emptied by the Red Cross workers with the help of the unhurt veterans. Emma spoke with a Red Cross doctor, while Cindy and Florence tidied up and packed the bags.

"Here's my patient list, Doctor Berrett, names, injuries, and treatments we've administered. I've marked the life-threatening conditions. I hope this will be of assistance," Florence said.

"We'll do our own diagnoses once we get them to hospital, but this may be helpful, Nurse."

He stuffed the list in his pocket. "I didn't get your name."

"Doctor Henderson, if you please."

"Really. You're from Key West, right?"

"Yes, Doctor Barrett, the Marine Hospital."

"Anything ever happen down there?"

"Everything from obstetrics to neurosurgery."

"Neurosurgery? Remarkable. Diagnosis?"

"Acute intracranial extradural hematoma."

"And the patient?"

"He survived but has not yet regained consciousness."

"A pity. It is a very complex procedure. Say, if ever you visit Miami, look me up at Jackson Memorial. Maybe we could discuss interesting cases over lunch. I know some places, Doctor Henderson."

"Yes, that would be nice" They shook hands. Berrett left with the injured.

Reagan came over. "Fine job, Doctor Henderson, you saved lives today, and certainly eased the pain of many. Don't let that fool bother you."

"I'm used to it, Father, and you can call me Emma."

"Call me Reverend Father Bill, if you don't mind." He winked.

The Red Cross finished loading the injured. Davis had checked each man off his list as they were carried or helped aboard. No sooner had the Byronic cleared the slip than the cutter took its place at the pier. Davis spoke briefly with the Coast Guard officer. "Top!" he shouted.

The top sergeant came running. "Yes, sir."

"The Coast Guard is taking the boys to Snake Creek. From there they'll be bused to Homestead. The cutter is leaving as soon as it's loaded."

"They've been ready to go since Monday, Captain."

"Yeah, well now they can. I need 12 volunteers to stay behind with me. We'll mind the store until we get instructions from Ghent over what to do next."

"I'll stay sir."

"No Top, it's on me. I need you to keep the boys in hand."

"Yes sir. Honor working with you, Ben."

"You, too, Paul."

Top Sergeant Pugh quickly assembled 104 men on the pier. Davis checked them off as they filed past the dead and boarded the cutter.

* * *

Eddie moved Esmeralda back to the pier after the cutter departed. He strapped on his machete, loaded a sack with cold drinks, and walked to where his group had gathered. "Anyone thirsty?"

"I'm parched, Eddie. I'll take a beer," said Cindy.

Nurse Crane grinned, "Me, too, Captain."

Eddie laid the sack on the ground and fished out the two beers. "Here you go, ladies. Everyone else, help yourselves."

"Enough for my men, Captain?" asked Davis.

"Sure, there's plenty more on the boat."

"Thanks everyone, you helped get us through a tough time. The cutter should be back in a couple of hours to take the dead to Snake

Creek. You folks needn't stick around for that." Davis opened a bottle and took a deep drink.

"There are still bodies back in the mangroves, Captain Davis?" Eddie asked.

"Yeah, we were going to take another crack at recovering them, maybe a dozen, all tangled up in the branches. You volunteering?"

Eddie, lifted his machete a few inches from its scabbard. The blade shone brightly. "I've done a lot of cutting in my life, figure I could lend a hand."

Davis smiled, "We could sure use your help."

* * *

Around 4 o'clock, four motor launches arrived from No Name Key. Aboard were 50 Florida National Guardsmen and a police detail, one wore a sheriff's uniform. Renard approached him.

"Sheriff, I'm Special Agent Renard, Federal Bureau of Investigation," presenting his badge, "May I have a few words?"

The Sheriff took Renard's badge, examined it, then handed it back. "You boys start patrolling, watch out for looters," he told his deputies. "So, you're Renard, Marshal Reeve told me about you. No, I haven't found your fugitives. We've been kinda busy."

"Dunn is one of the veterans working in the camps, I thought you may have crossed paths."

"Yeah, I know Dunn, smartass. I detained him for vagrancy a month ago, strayed across Snake Creek into Tavernier with no visible means of support, like some hobo, warned him and sent him back to the camps. A real piece of work. Possibly a Red. Come to think of it, it was exactly a month ago, August 4th. Now I can't prove it, but the same day he was the bum who stopped a troop train not far from here. Faked a suicide by jumping the tracks in front of the train. Called himself Huey Long. Smartass. If I find him, I'll arrest him for interfering with the railroad and consorting with a minor. And the girl, it's probably too late for her,

I heard he likes them young. Just hope he used protection. I've got some work to do, anything else Renard?"

"A Red, you say? What makes you suspect that?"

"Oh, that he was a Bonus Marcher and likes Roosevelt. That he says he has a right to go where he wants. That the Government owes him. Oh, he was all humble pie, but I knew what he really meant. Smartass."

"Well, thank you for your time, Sheriff Thompson."

"Sorry for being a little brusque there Renard, but this place reeks, and every sort of private property is just lying around for the taking."

"And the National Guard troops, what's their purpose here?"

"Pretty much the same as ours, leads to some confusion about who's in charge, me or Major Albury. The Governor ordered the Guard in, I'd be here regardless, it's my county. He's got more men than I do, but his can't arrest anyone. Once we move out the vets, we have to secure everything from looters. If you don't mind the smell, the dead are easy pickings."

"Friday was payday, the men must have had some money on them."

"You'd think so, but by Monday they'd spent most of it, gambling and drinking. That money ended up in somebody's pocket, though, you can be sure of it."

"Guess so. You've been very helpful," Renard offered his hand. Thompson shook it and left.

* * *

The man's face was unrecognizable, blackened and bloated. He'd been up high in a tree, and it had taken a while to cut him down. The clothes, what was left of them, were those of a veteran, dungarees, blue shirt, boots. Eddie began to check the pockets for something with his name on it.

"Hey, nigger! Get your thieving paws off that veteran!"

Eddie stood and slowly turned. A young soldier glared at him, rifle at the on-guard position.

"I'm looking for some identification."

"You just get your black ass outa here, or I'll have you arrested, boy."

"How old are you, son? Can't be more than 17."

"So, one of those uppity Negroes, huh? Sounds like you need a little educatin'."

"I'm a veteran myself, son, fought in Cuba. A young Spanish soldier once captured me. I was about his age, about your age now. He was armed with a Mauser rifle, almost the same as yours, a Springfield, isn't it? There weren't enough rifles for all *los guajiros*, so we brought our machetes from the sugar cane fields. I still have mine." Eddie gestured to the broad blade in its scabbard hanging from his belt. "Like I said, he was young, and a little nervous for being alone, gotten separated from his unit, sweat was dripping from his forehead into his eyes. He was carrying his Mauser low at the hip, pointing it at me. We just eyed each other for a bit. Finally, he ordered me to turn around and get down on my knees. I knew what that meant. I wasn't about to die like that. You know what? I drew my machete and charged him."

The Guardsman moved back a step. "You just stay right where you are!"

"Well, here I am. Seems that boy had the safety on, that little flag on the bolt was in the up position, just like on your Springfield. I could see it, he'd forgotten. When he pulled the trigger, nothing happened. He started running but I was faster. I disarmed him, both arms, and took his rifle and ammunition. It was taking him awhile to die, he lay their whimpering and bleeding, crying for his mama. Such carrying on annoyed me, he should have just shut up and died like a man. I helped him, chopped his head clean off, one cut, like a cane stalk."

The Guardsman took another step back.

"Boo!" Eddie said, and Guardsman double-timed away.

"Any of that true?"

"Absolutely, Señorita Cindy, but just one arm."

"You scared that one away, but he'll come back with the whole platoon. He'll have you made out to be King Kong."

"Yeah, with a little blonde hanging around. He was glancing at you. That show must have been for your benefit. Lordy, did he get you wrong. But you're right, there's a time to stand your ground, and a time to fold. I think I'll return to the boat and inspect something. That one over there is clean, no identification and the clothes seem wrong."

"Yeah, Fred liked his new clothes, don't think he'd ever go back to the way he was. Davis said Fred was on Upper Matecumbe Monday. He wouldn't come back here to die. If he's ever found, it won't be by us. And this corpse searching is making me sick. It will give me nightmares for the rest of my life."

"Why don't you come with me. I'll mix you a drink."

"I can't just walk away. This whole trip was my idea. Emma and Bill, I recruited them, what will they think of me? Just a snotty little rich girl who can't take a punch."

"Señorita Cindy, they'll understand. You have nothing to prove to them or your father. He'd rather you not be here at all."

"He said that?"

"On the boat, when the smell first hit us and we saw the bodies floating. He told me it reminded him of the war, that he was sorry you had to see it."

"I think I had to see it . . . Will you be staying in Key West after we take Emilio back to New York?"

"Haven't given it much thought. Maybe move to Bimini, plenty of charters there, and I'll be closer to my bank. Then again, me and *mis hijos* are kinda used to Key West."

* * *

Eddie and Cindy drudged back to the camp, leaving the corpse where it lay. They found Emma at the empty first aid station, seated on a crate, her eyes closed, an empty beer bottle at her feet.

"Doctor?"

She opened her eyes. "Oh, hello Captain. Something I can do for you?"

"If you please. Doc Perez told me to see him if my wound started smelling. It's itching, too, Could you take a look?"

"Show me." Eddie lifted his shirt. "Take off your shirt and lie down on your side." Cindy approached and watched.

Carefully, Emma removed the wet bandage. "Florence, bring me my bag, please. When did this happen, Captain?"

"Sunday night."

"How?"

"A knife."

"Should I ask?"

"No, Doctor."

Florence brought the bag and assessed Eddie's muscular torso, glistening with sweat. "Can I assist?"

"Watch me clean the wound and then you can stitch it up. Sorry Captain, no morphine left. Do you have anything strong to drink? This will hurt like hell."

"Time to run back to the boat, Doctor?"

"Not with your wound open."

"Eddie, would ya like some cream sherry?" Cindy said offering her silver flask.

"Jerez? Yeah, better than beer." He took the flask and emptied it. "O.K. Doctor, start carving."

* * *

About 5 p.m. the Coast Guard cutter returned for the dead. Eddie moved Esmeralda back into the bay so the cutter could tie up at the pier.

Sheriff Thompson made a list as Davis called off their names. They tagged each body with a number, the tags tied around the toe, or if they had a shoe, to the shoe laces. The bodies were then carried on planks onto the cutter by teams of veterans, police, soldiers and Coast Guardsmen. When the task was complete Thompson gave the list to a Miami policeman on the cutter.

Rattigan motioned Thompson, Davis and Major Albury together. "Gentlemen, we ought to send them off right. I believe I'm the senior officer here. We need a bugler and a firing party."

"Sir, I have both. Figured we might have some funerals here."

"Thank you, Major. Do they have blanks?"

"Yes, sir. They know the drill."

"Good. Gentlemen, please form your men in ranks, facing the cutter. To keep it simple I'll give the commands, no need to echo."

"Understood," said Albury. The others nodded.

* * *

Rattigan stood in front, facing the formation. As the cutter cast off from the pier, he ordered, "Company, TEN HUT!" The men snapped to attention. "Present, HARMS." The men saluted smartly. Rattigan about faced and saluted. The firing party fired three volleys. The reports roused some snowy egrets that had survived the storm. They took flight and circled above the cutter twice before returning to their roosts, all the while the bugler played taps. As the last note faded, Rattigan about faced and commanded, "Order, HARMS." The men brought their arms and rifles to their sides. "Take Charge of Your Units." The three commanders saluted and dismissed their men.

Cindy ran to her father and hugged him. "Oh, Daddy, I never knew!"

"Aren't we a pair. I never got through one of these without tearing up."

Reagan joined them. "Well done. Do you two need a handkerchief?"

"No thanks, Father, we're good now."

"Did you arrange the birds, too?"

"No, they were a gift."

"Indeed, they were."

"Thank you, Colonel, that was something," said Davis. "They deserved it. The boys said I didn't embarrass myself, too much. I was a little unsure what 'tin hut' meant. They gave me a nudge."

"That's something the drill sergeant teaches. The men learn quickly. Say, generally, I have a drink after sounding off. Care to join us? There's a bar on the boat."

"No thanks, Colonel, I'll just have a beer with my guys."

"You have the instincts of a good officer, Ben. The Army will need men like you in the next war."

"Hope it never comes to that."

"Hope for the best, prepare for the worst."

"Dan, a word please?"

"Yes, Edward?"

"I should apologize for misleading you and Abby back in Miami. I recognized your name immediately as Ella's sponsor, but felt it best not to reveal that my trip to Key West was to question her about a possible involvement in the Havana bombing. This may all be moot now."

"Perhaps, but she's a scrappy young lady, I wouldn't write her off just yet, absent any evidence. Why is she of interest to the FBI?"

"Anyone working at Communist Party Headquarters is a person of interest, particularly a German Jew on a visa. She agreed to be an informant. Actually, I didn't give her much choice. That she traveled to Havana without notice, in association with this Dunn character, perhaps a Red himself, who is accused of a terrorist bombing, clearly warranted an investigation."

"Edward, I've known her since she was a child, she's a good kid, and yeah, a communist, but I'm a capitalist and I cannot believe she would ever get involved in the murder of innocent people."

"I'm inclined to agree, Director Hoover may not. I wired her that I was coming Monday. But she left with Dunn. Certainly suggests she's in this with him. To clear her of suspicion I need to hear and verify her story. Otherwise, she'll be deported."

"That's a death sentence."

"I know."

* * *

Daniel sat on Esmeralda's transom, watching the storm-blasted keys pass by.

"Daddy?"

"Come sit with me." Cindy sat and he held her hand.

"It was like after a battle, collecting the dead, caring for the wounded, the funeral service. And the smell, you never forget that. You shouldn't have been there."

"Daddy, remember I asked you to come. Emma told me what to expect. I just thought it was something I needed to do if I'm to become a foreign correspondent. It made me sick. At least there were no children. That would have broken me."

"You'll see plenty of dead kids if you start covering wars. But you're a strong woman, Cindy, you'll wipe away the tears and write your story. You can start now. Put what you saw today in writing and I can help get it published. With the female angle, it shouldn't be much trouble. Just don't depend on me. Make a name for yourself and they'll come looking for you."

"Thanks Daddy." She kissed his cheek. "And the money?"

"Better it be lost than Machado get any of it. Dunn may have left some behind for the veterans trust fund. The war messed him up, but there may have been some good left in him."

"Oh, there was plenty. Are you still seeing Brooksie? When I got your wire, I thought you might come with her."

"She quit the act. Didn't even finish the engagement at the Persian Room. It's Dario and Diane now. No particular reason why, guess she just got bored."

"A shame, they were great together. And you and her . . .?"

"Same thing."

"Oh, Daddy." She rested her head on his shoulder.

* * *

Ben waited on the pier and watched until the Esmeralda vanished into the sunset.

"Davis."

"Yes, Albury?"

"Thought you'd be on that boat."

"They're going to Key West. I'm waiting for instructions from Mr. Ghent."

"Whatever. You need to get your men together and keep them on the dredge until we can evacuate y'all tomorrow."

"Where's this coming from?"

"My authority as Relief Commander. I'd hate to have any of your boys mistaken for looters. My men have orders to shoot."

"Fuck off, Major.

Chapter 31

Friday, March 3, 1933 – Verrat (Betrayal)

The black Daimler drove past Number 2 Pfleghofstrasse, the headlight beams reflecting off the wet cobblestones. Ella had expected it to stop there. She knew the address. Years before her father had taken her to report the theft of a bicycle. The officials expressed their shock and efficiently recorded all the information she could provide. A week later it was returned by a smiling policeman. He patted her head.

Ella's comrades taught her to take care, hide in crowds, walk close to walls like a mouse, and never draw attention to herself. Despite all her caution the SA thugs found her out. *"Verfickte jüdischen Fotze!"* they shouted, making obscene gestures. She wanted to kill them, instead she looked away and ran as fast as she could. It was raining, she slipped and fell hard. The leaflets she carried scattered onto the street. They laughed when they caught her, and then while some held her down, others took turns pawing her under her blouse and skirt with their filthy hands and fingers. They stopped when the polizei arrived. She thanked her saviors.

The car turned left at the next corner and left again into the alley. She counted the doors they passed. When they stopped it was at the rear entrance of a large unmarked building. There were iron bars on the windows. She knew. The door was unlocked from inside after a muffled exchange through a small opening. There were several uniformed police, they spoke briefly with her guards and then stared at her. She looked down but not before seeing the interest in their eyes. Boredom, indifference, even hostility would have been better. The rain had soaked her and mud splattered her bare legs. A scrawny, wet stray, but they were interested.

They walked her up the stairs and down a brightly lit windowless corridor, one on either side holding her arms. The floor and walls were a shiny tile which echoed their steps. There was a particularly loud clicking sound from the man on her right. The toes of his shoes were reinforced with steel plates. She'd seen such shoes used in street fights. They could break legs. Near a corner there were two doors on opposite sides, one marked Damen, the other Herren. For a moment she thought they were taking her to the lavatory, she did have to go. One of the men opened the first door. She recoiled but there was no resisting and she was hustled inside. It was an examination room. In the center was a table with gleaming steel stirrups. A large floor lamp with a big chrome reflector stood at one end. A galvanized iron barrel sat next to it, something smoldered inside. She smelled cigarette smoke. Near it were a small wheeled table and a swivel stool. On the white cloth covering the table she saw an open brown leather satchel and several shiny instruments. She felt sick.

"Ella," someone spoke near her in English. "Step behind the curtain. Remove all your clothes and put on the gown. You can do it yourself or my men will be happy to assist you. Lasst sie los."

She sagged to her knees when they released her. "I . . . I'm going to throw up."

Someone gently grasped her around the waist and supported her. He held a bed pan as she vomited. When she had finished, he offered a clean white towel to wipe her face. "There now, better? Chin up, Ella. Let's go change." Still with his arm around her, he guided her to the curtain. "Do you need help?"

"No . . . thank you."

Standing alone behind the translucent screen she took a deep breath and pinched herself hard on the forearm. Her life was nothing to these men. She resolved to survive. Ella shrugged off her wet clothing, stacking it neatly folded on a stool. Shivering, she slipped the gown over her head. There was a bed pan on the floor, she squatted and peed in it. The gown hung unevenly. Even now with everything at stake she paused to neatly adjust it, and then stepped from behind the curtain. The two guards were still there, leaning against the wall chatting. A nurse in her blue pinstripe dress, white apron and cap sat quietly in a chair avoiding Ella's glance. She saw the man who gave the orders. Perhaps it was all a masquerade, she had no way of knowing, but he was different from the others, tall and slender in a white doctor's coat, a stethoscope draped around his neck. His blonde/grey hair was thinning, dark blue eyes and thick brows, a neatly trimmed beard. He had a prominent scar on his left cheek. His smile seemed friendly. He was handsome. She fought the impulse to smile back. He flicked his cigarette into the barrel. It was filled with sand. There were several other butts lying there. His English was very good.

"It is well that you have chosen to cooperate. So many freeze. Now up on the table, this needn't take long."

She obeyed and without prompting placed her feet in the stirrups. "Do they have to be here, Herr Doktor?"

"Unfortunately, I am bound by protocol. There must be three present so no one could take advantage of the situation. The SD is scrupulous in this regard. But they will look away if I insist." He made a twisting movement with his hand and the two guards faced about. The nurse shrank lower in her chair. "Here, drink this," he offered Ella a glass. She hesitated. "Don't worry, it's just water." He took a sip and brought the glass to her lips. She drank. When she finished, he sat on the stool, raised the gown to her waist and carefully aimed the lamp. The heat from the electric light warmed her cold thighs. When he removed a camera from the bag, she started but regained control. "Again, my apologies but the SD requires a photographic record. You are accused among other charges of being an unregistered prostitute. This may work in your favor." He took several pictures and then put a rubber examination glove on his right hand with a loud snap. "I will now do a digital exam. This may be slightly uncomfortable but I'll be quick." He dipped his fingers into a jar of petrolatum and began to probe. She winced but held steady and bit her lip. She began to tear up and cursed herself silently. He stopped and stripped off the glove. "Thick, narrow, sehr gut. Still virginal."

There were leather straps on the stirrups. Calmly the doctor wrapped them around her ankles and cinched them tight.

"Was machen Sie?!"

"English please. Now we become serious." He snapped his fingers. The two guards grabbed her arms and held her down. From his bag he took a heavy revolver and held it up so she could see. "Look, a war trophy from a British officer, March 1918. I pried it from his cold dead hand, a Colt New Service, .455 caliber, 14-centimeter barrel. I modified it myself. See here? I filed off the front blade sight and rounded the muzzle, smooth as you please."

He unlatched the cylinder and extracted the six cartridges. "You work for the Russians. You should know how this game is played." He took one of the cartridges and placed it back in a chamber, relatched it, held the pistol vertically, and spun the cylinder. He dipped the muzzle of the revolver into the petrolatum jar.

"What do you want? I've been a good girl. I did everything you asked!"

"I want you to remember. You will never forget."

She cried. When he pushed it in, she shrieked. "First chance." The doctor cocked the revolver's hammer, making a noticeable click. "Quiet! Listen." He squeezed the trigger. There was another louder click. "Now what you will do is continue running errands for the Reds. But each time you will report to your contact. Simple, yes?"

Ella sobbed and shook uncontrollably. "I don't think you heard me." Again, he cocked the hammer, click . . .

"No, no!"

. . . and squeezed the trigger, click. "Lucky girl. When you make your report, you will give addresses and names. You will know these things and much more because you are a very pretty girl. You could even pass as Aryan. It will be easy for you to make many intimate friends. You understand?" He pulled back the hammer, click.

Ella recognized the sound and screamed, "Yes! Yes! I'll do it!"

He squeezed the trigger. Click.

"My, the suspense! Ella Kaufmann, born 5 September 1917, 15 years old, Auf der Morgenstelle 14, student at Wildermuth Gymnasium, honors in English, KPD Young Communist League, 6 June 1932, No. 57,649; mother, Ingrid; father, Josef, Herr Professor Doktor Josef Kaufmann. Yes, we know much about your father. We need to know everything, what he does, what he says, where he goes, his thoughts, his friends, his lovers. You are close to him, no?" Click. "He would like grandchildren, I am sure. Hold still!" Her back arched. Click. She fainted.

"Schwester, riechende Salze, bitte." The nurse stood up and came quickly to table, the bottle of smelling salts already in her hand. She held the open bottle beneath Ella's nose. After a moment Ella started, opening her eyes. She looked wildly around and started weeping again.

"Ella, dear, there is no escape that way. Do you remember the count? No? There are two chambers left, one empty, one loaded, 50/50. If the next one is empty, I will spin the cylinder and start over again. It's really a very simple matter. You are not leaving here in one piece unless you convince me. Understand?"

"I'll fuck anyone you want. I'll fuck you." Click. "I'll fuck my father!" She gasped; the thought had come unbidden. Somewhere a clock ticked the seconds. Unthinkingly she counted. On 20, she felt the pistol barrel slowly, almost languidly, regretfully withdraw. It tingled.

Involuntarily she squeezed. The sensation was thrilling, like nothing she'd ever felt, her eyes opened wide, her lips parted. Am I going mad?

"In case you wondered . . ." The doctor wiped the revolver with a cloth, aimed it into the barrel and pulled the trigger. BANG! A puff of sand erupted. The report reverberated off the tiled walls. She screamed. The guards laughed. He motioned them away and removed the straps.

"I will write a prescription, Ella. In two weeks take it to the clinic printed on the form. The doctor will fit you for a Gräfenberg ring. Wouldn't do for you to become pregnant. I've found Ernst's product to be the safest and most effective available. He is one of the few Jews still useful to the Reich." He cleaned her with an antiseptic wipe and helped her off the table. "You will need some cotton packing for a few days. Get some rest. You'll be just fine."

She dressed slowly behind the curtain. The trembling wouldn't stop, she kept dropping her clothes. It hurt to lift her leg. She felt sore inside. Pinching didn't help. She knelt on the floor and spit up a vile green liquid into the bed pan. It made her chest ache and throat burn. Bright red drops speckled the floor beneath her. Standing she willed herself to stop shaking, clenching her hands so tightly the nails drew blood from her palms.

When she stepped out the guards and nurse had gone. The doctor sat on the side of the examination table writing on a pad. He was smoking another cigarette. Looking up he smiled. "Do you smoke, Ella? A bad habit but hard to resist." She nodded. He took one from a gold case, tapped it on the lid, lit it on his own and handed it to her. She inhaled and started coughing. "Sorry, Turkish." He finished writing and gave her the prescription.

"A souvenir." He opened the cylinder of the pistol and extracted the cartridge casing. "Here."

"Thank you. May I ask something?"

"What?"

"I want you to fit me."

He looked at her for a long time. *"Warum?"*

"I . . . because you know me, now. No one else does. I don't want anyone else to touch me."

"We'll see, call first and make an appointment."

"Whom should I ask for?"

"Doktor Ludwig, they'll know." He crushed his cigarette and dropped it in the barrel. "Come with me." He led her back into the corridor to the door marked Herren. She tensed. "No need to worry. Please." He took her hand and they entered the room. It was like the one she left, white tile, bright lights. In the center a naked man sat, shackled to a heavy chair. He was bent over, he gurgled. Three muscular police stood around him. One had his shirt off, his chest was splattered with blood.

"Er ist ein schwieriger Fall, Herr Doktor."

"Macht ihn sauber."

One of the police picked up a bucket and emptied it over the prisoner's head. The man sat up with a start, gagging and coughing. The bloody water drained through a hole in the floor.

"He was arrested in a raid on a Red safe house this morning, one of your comrades. There are photographs of a meeting at Gasthaus Hirsch, you're there with him, very friendly. He looks different, I know, unavoidable. Do you know his name? Take your time, be certain."

Ella walked around in front of the prisoner, and bent low to stare into the remnants of his face. One swollen eye opened, and blinked. It filled with tears and blinked again. His pulpy lips parted. He spat out blood and bits of teeth. A croaking sound came from deep within. His mouth moved grotesquely, a parody of the smile she had loved.

"Yes."

* * *

"You did well, Ella. There's a future for you, and maybe your family. We're finished for now. Do you need a ride home? They'll drop you off around the corner."

"Vielen Dank, Herr Doktor. Ich möchte lieber zu Fuß gehen."

"As you like. I'll have the matron escort you out." He pressed a button on the wall. She faintly heard a buzzer in another room.

"One more thing, only a formality, really . . . no cause for alarm. Chin up, Ella . . . *Heil Hitler!*"

I am a whore. I am a monster. I will do anything to survive. She stood straight, brought her heels together sharply and raised her right arm to eye level.

"Sieg Heil, Herr Doktor!"

"Du bist ein gutes kleines Mädchen."

"Thank you, sir."

Chapter 32

Wednesday, September 4, 1935 – The Survivor

The sun finally reappeared, the beginning of a typical late summer day in the Keys. It baked and steamed, and the bodies began to come apart. They were everywhere among the rotting fish and broken birds, floating on the waves, washed up on beaches in windrows, snarled up in the mangroves. Crabs, flies and the occasional bird scavenged the remains. One body had not attracted much interest. The smell was wrong. It was still alive.

Ella woke to a stabbing pain in her ear. She slapped the side of her head hard, striking a bird. The blow knocked it off her head and onto the sand. The angry frigate squawked, bit her hand and then flew away. It had opened the scab over her wound. She struggled to sit upright, but couldn't feel her right arm. In terror she checked that it was still there. She found it still attached to her shoulder, but numb and entangled in something. It took a moment to remember the Coast Guard bag she'd tied to her forearm. After working the strap loose, she massaged her arm until some feeling returned. But it was thirst that consumed her. It had rained for two days. There must be fresh water collected in some hollow.

She noticed a sound, a rapid clicking and a constant buzzing. Must be water in my ears. Then the smell hit her. At first, she thought it the low tide stench when the rot of the marshes is exposed to the air. But this was far worse. Had she anything in her stomach she would have thrown it up. She saw the bloated, blackened corpses around her. The arms of one were held rigidly in the air as if beseeching mercy. She was in Hell.

* * *

For two nights and a day Ella had drifted on the waves. She'd stripped off everything, save her underpants and thigh holster. Now she reflexively patted the latter. The pistol was still there. Ella stood up, crying from the pain and looked around. The island was small, she could see across it to the ocean all around. Only scattered mirages broke the horizon. She dragged the bulky bag into a stand of battered, leafless trees. She covered it with broken branches and fronds. Something glinted on the beach. It was a can, an unopened beer can. A picture on the side showed a can opener. That's helpful. Storm wreckage was scattered along the tree line. The roof of a house leaned against a palm stump. Nails protruded from broken joints. She thought a minute, drew her pistol, and used the tang to pry one loose. Holding the pointy end against the can's lid, she whacked the head twice with the flat stone she found. The nail penetrated. She made more holes in the lid and drank. The beer was warm, she didn't mind. On her empty stomach it made her a little tipsy. Canned beer, Americans are so clever. They'll definitely win the next war.

Her skin was already burning everywhere from the sun. There were clothes on the corpses. One, a colored boy about her size, wore a pair of ragged jeans. There was no belt, only a rope with a tight knot, made tighter still by the seawater and heat. His belly had swelled, it was impossible. A naked woman was hanging head down in an uprooted tree. One of its branches had passed clear through her body, pinning her like a butterfly in a collector's box. Down the beach crabs were busy on a small lump of flesh. She came close. It was a baby, wearing blue pajamas, tiny toes peeking out. His mommy had dressed him for bed when the wave came. Did mommy wish she were dead, too? Better if she were.

Ella kept on, passing three adult men, veterans by the look of their dungarees and work boots. She paused at the last corpse, a girl, maybe 15. The dress she wore had bunched around the throat exposing her torso. The crabs were at work between her thighs. Flies were swarming around the dark sockets where birds had done their work. There was a gap in her crushed skull. "Forgive me," Ella murmured. She took the girl's stiff arms and pulled them back, then screamed when the skin came loose. Wildly, she scraped it off her hands in the sand and then stumbled into the water to wash. She came back and found the dress now easy to remove over the girl's head. She scrubbed it in the seawater. There was a small intricately embroidered name tag sewn into the collar. She tore it out and tossed it into the water. She put the dress on wet.

Ella returned to the dead girl and forced herself to look. She had collected an armful of sea grass and spread it over the body. Kneeling, she gently moved the arms to the sides, ignoring the rotting flesh, then brushed away the flies and arranged the girl's short dark hair over the wound.

There was a small leather bag on a cord around her neck. Ella removed it and looked inside, a quarter and some pennies. The pennies looked new. On a hunch she laid them out on the sand, fourteen altogether, by date. It was an unbroken sequence from 1921 to 1935. She understood and hated herself for what she must do. The coins went back inside. She wound the cord tightly around the pouch and made a knot. Then she threw it far out into the water, watching it splash and sink. She unfastened her own necklace and kissed the hamsa pendant. Choking back a sob Ella knelt, placed the necklace around the girl's neck and latched it. The gold gleamed brightly in the sunlight. It would still glitter when all the flesh was gone. "Your papi and mutti will never know what happened to you. They'll remember how beautiful and happy you were." Bowing her head, she recited,

Y'hei sh'lama raba min sh'maya, v'chayim aleinu v'al kol Yisrael. V'imru: Amen.

Oseh shalom bimromav, Hu yaaseh shalom aleinu, v'al kol Yisrael. V'imru: Amen.

[May there be abundant peace from heaven, and a good life for us and for all Israel; and say, Amen.

He Who makes peace in His heavens, may He make peace for us and for all Israel; and say, Amen.]

"I'm so sorry, that's all I remember. Forgive me."

She stood up, shaking, and clenched her fists tightly until the tears stopped. There was something else she needed to do. The beach was covered with debris now drying in the midday sun. All she required was a spark to ignite it. She forced herself to search the bodies, especially the veterans. They might have matches or cigarette lighters or maybe a knife. Instead, all she could find were a pair of reading spectacles, some damp papers, and a metal hip flask. The cheaters were in a man's shirt pocket, one of those with a button flap. She tried them on, and concluded the owner was legally blind. The papers she lay out in the sun to dry. She opened the flask and sniffed. It smelled like antiseptic. She stuck her little finger in, pulled it out and licked it. Not much taste. She took a sip, gagged and spat it out. Her mouth burned. She ran back to where she'd left the beer can and sucked out what was left. Well, should be good for something. Dampening a piece of cloth torn from her skirt with the alcohol, she applied it liberally to her scratches and wound. It stung.

Now what was that eyeglass trick Frau Fischer taught us in Wandervogel? She piled mangrove branches and palm fronds. From pieces of coconut husk, she tore out fibers and fashioned a small nest. Then she held the spectacles so that two bright sun spots appeared on a frond. She had to stand with the lenses to focus the smallest spots. It took some time before a whiff of smoke appeared and she was too far away to blow on the ambers. How did Frau Fischer manage this? It took her no time at all . . . oh, she stacked both lenses. She took the spectacles, forced one of the lenses out of its frame intact and then held them together so that their curves nestled one in the other. Now she could focus a single spot at half the distance, and twice as bright. It made her squint. Best of all she could squat. She quickly got some smoke and blew on the spot. More smoke, a hole burned through a frond, but try as she might, no flame. "This is taking too long, have to rethink this."

She removed a cartridge from the magazine of her PPK. With her left hand she held the cartridge firmly on its side against a flat rock, using thumb and forefinger to position the point of the nail she had found against the brass casing. With her right hand she struck the nail head hard with the stone. The nail slipped off the casing and bit her forefinger. Ella sucked the blood off and wiped it on the dress. She tried again this time with light taps, making a small dent. With the nail held firmly she could strike harder. The nail penetrated the casing and got stuck in the hole. She worked the nail free and carefully poured the powder grains onto a scrap of the paper. Not that much. She made a hole in another cartridge and added its powder to the little pile. She placed the paper in the center of the kindling. Then she sat, back to the sun with the nest in the sand between her legs, arms resting on her knees, holding the lenses to make the smallest possible spot of sunlight on the pile the powder. She held steady. After a few seconds the grains smoked and ignited in a flash. Startled, she fell over backward. The flame was fading. She blew on it and began adding tufts of husk, palm fronds and branches. Not satisfied, she splashed some of the moonshine from the flask on the flames. A blue flame erupted. That did the trick. It was a proper fire and she congratulated herself. She looked up and watched the smoke plume climb into the sky. Someone would notice.

The night was clear and cold, she shivered hunched near the fire. A first quarter moon was low in the west. She searched for the familiar star patterns in the sky. After moonset, in this darkest of all skies there were so many more stars visible even the constellations she knew well were lost in the mix. A shooting star crossed the sky. Its glow was mirrored in the ocean. Her stomach growled but the clicking of the voracious crabs made her nauseous. Besides there was nothing to eat. She curled herself into a tight ball and tried to sleep. Eventually exhaustion dulled her thoughts. She dozed fitfully.

With sunrise the heat and the stench returned. The fire smoldered. She doused the embers with the moonshine and got it started again. Only in the fire's smoke could Ella find some relief. But she had burned all the nearby drift wood, forcing her to scavenge further out. It was impossible to avoid the corpses. More had washed up overnight. And something else, two coconuts and four limes. She shook the coconuts and heard the water slosh inside. She carried her finds back to the fire in the hollow of her upraised dress.

"What had Frau Fischer taught us about *Kokosnüsse*?" She brought a bag of kokos to the Wandervogel camp that summer and demonstrated how to open them with large rocks.

When Ella tried, the heavy coral rock she dropped on the coconut bounced off and skinned her shins drawing blood. Four more tries and the husk was smashed enough to pull apart, using her fingers and the pistol tang. She found the "monkey face" and pushed a nail into one of the eyes. It went in some and stuck. Using her rock hammer, the nail went in easily. But when she withdrew the nail only a trickle of water came out. She punched in the other eye and mouth and got a decent flow. She sat and sipped. It tasted delicious but there was only about a deciliter. Employing Frau Fischer's technique, Ella split the coconut and devoured the meat, scraping it off with her teeth. The limes she peeled with her finger nails. She sucked them dry.

Around her the corpses' bellies split and vile fluids darkened the sand. Could she burn the bodies? Would the smoke be darker and more visible? But the flame was a sacred thing. She could not defile it. Tending it was an act of grace, a holy task. Still hungry and thirsty, she draped a wet rag she'd found on the beach over her head, and squatted beside the fire. She closed her eyes. They were too dry to weep.

If this is the second day in Hell then it must be my birthday. Was that right, or did I miss a day somewhere? If I were at the apartment there'd be a big party. I invite my comrades from Party Headquarters. There's Emilio winking at me from a wheel chair, his head bandaged, and there's Fred grinning in a sharp suit. George and Rosalind beaming, a big ring on her finger. Even my G-man shows up, he gives me a peck on the cheek. We talk politics and get into a big fight. There's a frosty pitcher of daiquiris Eddie makes with good Cuban rum, while Enrique and Fernando crack jokes. Frau Fischer brings out a steaming bowl of hardy goulash, a thick slice of Bauernbrot, bottles of Kinderbier, and an enormous Schwartzwalder tort. Abby lights the 18 candles. I make a wish and blow them all out in one puff. Mr. Rattigan with his arm around Brooksie makes a toast. Everyone shouts "Mazel Tov!" and then sings Happy Birthday dear Ella, Happy Birthday to you! I kiss them all, and eat and drink everything. Then I open my presents. Surely Mutti and Papi sent something. How much I miss them! My heart aches. Someone is buzzing the doorbell. Cindy's smiling. The buzzing grows louder and becomes a roar.

Ella opened her eyes and watched a huge shadow sweep over the beach. That sound, she'd heard it before. An airplane had just flown directly overhead. She stood and watched it curve back over the water. The pilot waggled the wings, came in low and slow, flying upside down, the top of his head visible, no higher than 20 feet. Passing above he dropped a canteen and lunch box. They landed a few feet away. Revving the big radial engine, the pilot pulled the nose up into an outside loop, climbing high in the sky, rolled and then dived back around again. It was magnificent. For that moment she was lifted above the horror on the key. Circling Ella, he pointed to himself, then out to sea and then to her. She understood, I will get help. She curtsied unsteadily. Throwing a kiss, the pilot banked the yellow-winged Cuban Army biplane, with its red cowling and black 21 painted on the silver fuselage. He did a snap roll and flew off across the bay. *"Americano loco, te amo,"* she rasped between cracked lips. "Just don't tell anyone it was me."

The lunch box contained a man-sized sandwich: a crusty loaf of white bread, roasted pork, ham and cheese with mustard and pickles. It was the most delicious thing she'd ever eaten. Hours passed. She busied herself collecting branches and sea grass to feed the fire.

Dizzy from the afternoon heat, Ella sought some relief by wading out into the shallows. She sat in the sand, the water up to her chin, a wavelet occasionally splashing her face. The sound of a motor alerted her. She stood and saw a small out-board power boat approaching. She ran to the fire, added sea grass to the glowing ambers and emptied the flask on top. The flames sprang to life. With the smoke rising in the still air, she jumped, waved her arms, and shouted, "Hey, over here! Save me!"

There were three men on board, one in a khaki National Guard uniform wearing a campaign hat, and two others, colored men in civilian clothes with bandanas over their faces. They beached the boat. The Guardsman had an Army gas mask bag around his neck. "You OK, miss?" he asked.

"Just fine . . . considering," Ella replied, gesturing to the ghastly corpses all around. "That crazy pilot saved my life. I couldn't have gone another day. Please, I really need to get home now."

"As soon as I complete my count and note any identifying features, we'll get you to Snake Creek. Here." He handed Ella his canteen. She unscrewed the cap and swallowed. He lit a long chunky cigar.

"Thank you, sir. There're eleven, all dead. I checked after I woke up yesterday morning. At least I think it was yesterday morning. A bird was pecking my ear. I took one look around and thought I was dead and gone to Hell."

"Yes, Miss, this is Hell, a part of it at any rate. We'll get the survey done as quickly as possible. Hey Joe, is there a hat in the boat she can wear? The kid's red as a beet."

"Here Miss, take mine," said Joe.

"Thank you kindly, sir."

"You're very welcome, Miss."

The Guardsman opened a small note book. "May I have your name please?"

"Is that really necessary, sir? There's nobody to notify. I'll be home before you could inform anyone who cares. Besides, I'd rather it not get around that I was in Matecumbe Monday. I didn't tell my parents where I was going. They think I'm with my girlfriend in Fort Lauderdale. I was really going to meet my boyfriend. He's with the Coast Guard in Key West, you see. But he didn't show because of the hurricane and all. It would be really embarrassing if Mom and Dad found out. They think men in uniform want only one thing from a girl. You understand don't you, sir? I could get punished!"

The three men glanced at each other, smiled and nodded. "Don't you worry, none, Missy. Us and the sergeant here will keep this on the Q. T.," said Joe.

"Thank you, sirs. I'm so very grateful."

"I have a bandana you can wear, Miss," said the third man. "Just a second." He reached into a canvas bag he carried, took out the bandana and quickly folded it into a triangle. "Here, just tie the ends together behind your head."

Ella frowned. "Could you do it sir? My fingers are so raw."

"Of course, honey . . . uh, Miss." He tied a neat knot. Then he unscrewed the lid of a small blue bottle. "And now just a dab of VapoRub on the outside over your nose. That kills most of the stink."

She took a breath. "Golly gee! That is some strong stuff. Y'all so kind to me."

"Miss, why don't you sit in the boat while we finish up here," said the sergeant.

"Oh! I need my bag. Just a sec." Ella retrieved the Coast Guard bag from under the pile of debris and returned with it to the boat using both hands. She noticed the men looking.

"My boyfriend gave it to me to keep my things dry when we go swimming. Lucky for me he did, it floats! It's why I'm alive and they're dead." She leaned over the side of the boat and placed the bag on a bench.

"Do you need help getting aboard?" asked the man who'd given her the bandana.

"Oh, please sir. I'm so weak."

He easily lifted Ella in his arms and lowered her gently on the bench beside the bag. "Thank you, sir. You're very strong, Mr. . . . ?"

"Just Pete, Missy."

"Thank you so much, Mr. Pete."

Ella sat in the boat, munching a sandwich the sergeant had given her, sipping from his canteen, and smelling Vick's VapoRub. The men were going from body to body, the sergeant puffing hard on his shrinking cigar, the others with their bandanas, wearing rubber gloves. Joe and Pete rolled the corpses over and checked the pockets. The sergeant made notes and tied a card with the body number onto a toe or shoe lace with a length of string. Then he took photos with a box camera. When they found someone who might be a veteran the sergeant took out an ink pad, a card and attempted to get fingerprints. In most cases where any skin survived it came loose. He used tweezers to transfer it to the card. The cards went into envelopes marked with the body number.

They came to the girl. Pete crossed himself.

Joe bent over and fumbled with the necklace. "Should I break it, Sarge?"

"No, I'll do it." He knelt beside the girl. Carefully, he moved her hair aside and opened the latch. "God bless you, child." He stood and placed the necklace in an envelope marked with the body number. "Pretty thing. They should have no trouble identifying you from it."

Then they found the baby. Pete ripped off his bandana and retched.

"You knew this would be tough," Joe growled.

"We can't leave him for the crabs," said the sergeant. He walked to the boat. Ella understood, she handed him a tarpaulin. He took it without a word, his lips quivering. Joe and Pete laid out the tarp in the sand, the sergeant put on his gloves and with great tenderness placed the tiny body in the center. Together the men wrapped the tarp around, binding it with a length of cord. The sergeant tied the body card, Number 11, to an eyelet. He brought the bundle to the boat. Ella took it and placed it in the bow. She didn't need to act tough, she wept.

They finished quickly after that, returned to the boat and pushed off. Joe started the motor.

"Does this place have a name? I mean, besides Hell."

"The locals call it Raccoon Key, Miss. It's about 25 miles out in the bay. It'll take us an hour and a half to get to Snake Creek," Joe answered.

* * *

The landing was crowded with men and boats. Joe helped Ella onto the make-shift pier. "Miss, the Red Cross is shuttling folks up to First Baptist Church in Homestead. You can see a doctor, wash up, get some food and clean clothes. There's a bus to Miami you can catch from there. I'll find a ride for you." A truck piled high with pine coffins came by. Joe let that one pass.

While they waited, Pete and the sergeant transferred the canvas bundle from the boat to the pier. Ella sat down on her bag and watched. After a few minutes Joe succeeded in flagging down an ambulance. "It's all fixed, Miss. Just three other riders, a white woman and her kids." Then he noticed the others staring at the bundle. Joe bowed his head and closed his eyes.

Ella stood and said to them, "You are menschen." She gave each man a hug and a kiss on the cheek. She turned and walked to the ambulance carrying her bag. They stared after her.

"Mensh-hen? Is that a good thing?" asked Pete.

"Yes," said the sergeant, "a very good thing."

Chapter 33

Miami

September 5, 1935 — Ella arrived at the Union Bus Station about ten p.m. She walked around downtown for a few blocks and found an open pawnshop. The bell above the door rang when she entered. The shop was divided by a steel grating, protecting the items on display. There was a window in the barrier for a counter where business was transacted. Behind the grating, a bald old man sat at a desk with a disassembled pocket watch splayed out on a tray before him, examining some tiny part through a monocle loupe. He looked up, removed the loupe, blinked, and put on his wire frame spectacles. He stepped to the counter and squinted. "Step closer young lady. An orphan of the storm with something to pawn?"

"How much for this?" She plumped the Coast Guard bag on the counter.

"This isn't an army-navy store, missy! I have a more discriminating clientele."

"Thirty dollars. It's in good condition and not stolen. There are plenty of yachtsmen in Miami who'd pay a hundred for a regulation Coast Guard sea-bag from the rum wars."

"Has a history, does it?" The pawn-broker picked the bag up, examined the outside and then opened it and felt around with his hand. "Well, it's dry inside." He closed the bag and tightened the seals. "Let's see how dry it is after a dunking. Come with me, dearie."

"Where to?"

"Just outside in the alley. You don't mind, do you?"

"Just don't get any ideas, buddy."

"I'm just a harmless old man who doesn't want to get rooked." He lowered and locked the hinged grating over the window.

"Fine, let's go." There was a door in the grating. The pawnbroker unlocked it and motioned Ella through, locking it behind her. He led her to a side door with two bolt locks, opened them and ushered her outside.

In the dark alley was a rain barrel brimming over. The pawnbroker dropped the bag in. It splashed, it floated. He tried to push it under and only succeeded in getting himself wet.

"It's waterproof, satisfied?"

"Now we check for leaks." They returned to the shop and the pawnbroker bolted the door behind him. He opened the window, placed the bag on the counter, and had Ella step outside the grating. He shone a light inside. "Hmm, yes."

"OK, my thirty."

"I'll give you five for it."

"That's insulting. 25."

"10, and that's final."

"I'm wasting my time here, shalom." Ella picked up the sea bag and headed for the front door, the ratty carpet bag she'd found at the refugee shelter in her other hand. The heel of her left shoe wobbled. Her dress was roughly mended. And she had such a lovely figure.

"Vartn . . . bitte, iung dame. Perhaps I've been hasty. Please allow me to examine the bag once more."

Ella turned around and landed the wet bag with a thump on the counter. "It saved my life, kept me afloat when I was too spent to swim."

The pawnbroker looked closely at her face, the stained bandage over her ear, the fatigue in her eyes, the raw sunburn. "I was mistaken, it is worth twenty-five." He reached under the counter and came back with a ten, two fives, and five ones, laying them beside the bag.

"File danken, har." Ella pocketed the bills.

"Ir zent zeyer bagrisn meyn tayer."

Ella smiled. "I'm not fluent. Did you say, You're welcome, my precious?"

"Ha! Too familiar, you think?"

Ella placed a thousand-dollar bill on the counter. He picked it up and studied it under a desk lamp. He placed the loupe in his eye and examined the bill again. "1928 Series, Cleveland Note, Federal Reserve Bank of Atlanta, very good, very good. Might even fool a bank teller."

"Don't give me that crap, it's bona fide."

"Stolen then. I don't launder money . . . What do you want for it?"

"Two fifties, ten twenties, five tens and ten fives. Clean bills, don't try to pass any counterfeits on me."

"My dear, I'm an honest man. I could hardly stay in business otherwise. So, 500 altogether. Must be hot. Two hundred."

"Not that hot. Five hundred, that's final. Do you have the money?"

"Not here, certainly." He rattled the grating with his hand. "This is just for shop-lifters. If it got out I kept real money here, I'd have break ins all the time, and this wouldn't stop the crooks."

"When then? I need it in the morning, 8:30 at the latest."

"Eight thirty? Well, uh . . . fine. Eight thirty, sharp. But you'll have to leave it with me. I can't get that much money on a promise."

"But I can?"

"If you want the clean bills by 8:30, you can. Here, I'll write you a ticket."

"Thanks. One thing more."

"What now?

"A box of 9mm ACP."

"Packing, are we? You're a very interesting kleyne meydl. As a matter of fact, I do have some in stock." He left the bill on the counter and went back into the store room. He returned shortly with a box of 50 rounds. "That'll be $5, please."

"Three."

"OK, OK. Is that all?"

Ella paid him. "I need one thing more and no haggling."

"What?"

"Your silence."

"So, I'm asking for your name already? All my transactions are private. You might want to leave before any other customers show up. At this hour the trade can be dicey. I'm a poor old man and wouldn't be able to defend you."

"Tomorrow then, shalom."

"Aleichem shalom."

* * *

After Ella left, the pawnbroker locked the front door and closed the curtains of his shop. He went back to his desk with the bill. From the drawer he removed several sheets of paper, photostat copies of a serial number list. A few minutes later, he made a phone call. "Meyer? It's Sol . . . I found her."

* * *

Ella walked back to the bus station and hailed a cab. "The Roney Plaza Hotel, Miami Beach, please."

At the hotel Ella asked the night clerk for a room. "Six dollars for the night, check out is noon, please sign the register, here." She signed as Miss Nancy Rufford from Milwaukee.

"I'd like my bag placed in the hotel safe and a wakeup call at six in the morning. Is room service still available?"

"All night, Miss Rufford, the menu is in your room. The bell hop will take you there."

After tipping the boy, Ella thought she'd lie down for a few minutes before calling room service. The menu was on the bedside table and she started reviewing the fare. She yawned.

* * *

Friday, September 7, 1935 — Ella woke to the ringing telephone beside the bed. She showered, brushed her hair, dressed, cleaned her PPK, and loaded a full six-round magazine. She opened the curtains.

Her room had an ocean view. In the morning light she considered her mirrored appearance. "Frumpy, I can do frumpy." At the hotel restaurant she downed a cup of coffee and a soft-boiled egg.

In the lobby she made a telephone call. "Hello, Pan American Airways? . . . I'd like to book a round trip ticket on this afternoon's flight to Nassau . . . 1:10 p.m. . . . yes . . . how long is the flight? . . . just two hours? . . . returning on September 20th . . . Helen Ferguson . . . that's right . . . American, from Philadelphia . . . why thank you very much . . . you, too . . . Bye now."

Ella picked up a local tourist map at the hotel and thought to check out the posh clothing stores in Miami Beach, but they didn't open until 9. Besides she couldn't shop there in her shabby castoffs. There were ads for two department stores downtown near the pawnshop. She decided to do some window shopping there. The taxi dropped her off at the Red Cross Drug Store on East Flagler Street. It was 7:30. She thought instead to go directly to the pawnshop, maybe the broker would be early for their rendezvous. A block away she could see the curtains were drawn and a closed sign placed in the window. She had approached on the other side of the street and noticed a car parked opposite the shop. Two men sat inside smoking. They didn't notice her. Their attention was on the shop. She kept walking. Two blocks further she crossed the street, and circled back to the alley. There was the rain barrel and the unmarked side door. She crossed the street and found a spot we she could still observe the alley entrance but could not be seen easily herself. She lit a cigarette and waited.

Hardly ten minutes passed before the pawnbroker appeared walking toward the alley, he was carrying a brief case. She turned her back and watched him by his reflection in a store window. When he entered the alley, she quickly crossed the street, pausing at the alley entrance. He took out his key chain. There were two locks, one above the other. He placed the brief case on the ground and opened the upper lock, then bent down to open the second. Silently she came up behind him. Grunting, he opened the bottom lock. When he reached for the briefcase, she pressed the muzzle of her PPK against his bent spine. "Gut margn."

Startled, he stumbled against the door. "Don't turn around. I have an appointment, remember? Now, let's go inside. Don't forget your brief case." They entered. Ella closed the door behind her, and slid a bolt latch shut. "Stop, don't turn." Still pressing the pistol against his back, Ella frisked him with her left hand. She found a .22 pocket pistol in his jacket, another under his belt in back, and a stiletto strapped to his left ankle. She kicked the weapons across the floor. "Take off the money belt and drop it behind you along with your wallet and keys." He grumbled but obeyed.

"Lie down on the floor, on your stomach."

"My back!"

"Get down, now." She kicked him in the butt.

"Shteyner zol zi hobn, nit kayn kinder," he muttered. She kicked him again. He slowly got down on the floor.

Ella emptied the money belt and wallet on the desk. "$156. Open the brief case."

"This is entirely uncalled for, young lady."

"Open it."

Inside was a newspaper, a sandwich wrapped in cellophane, and a clean shirt. "You owe me $344. Fork it over or I get rough."

He pointed to the wall clock. "It's only eight. We agreed on 8:30, sharp, did we not?"

"We also agreed on your silence, but there are two goons in a car across the street watching the shop. How long do you expect them to wait when the curtains stay closed after 8:30? Five, ten minutes? I intend to be long gone by then. Open the safe."

"I . . . I can't do that. I've forgotten the combination. Maybe if you'll allow me a drink I'll remember."

"Spread your legs."

"What?"

"You heard me, spread 'em." She kicked him in the crotch.

"Ow! All right, all right."

There was a broom in the office. Ella placed it on the edge of the desk and snapped off the handle. The pawnbroker flinched.

"All I want is what you owe me. I won't take anything else. You can trust me. I ask you one more time, open the safe."

"All right," he struggled to stand.

Ella whacked him hard across the shoulders with the broom handle. "Crawl."

He waddled across the floor like some bloated alligator. When he reached the safe, he asked, "May I get on my knees?"

"Yes."

He spun the dial three times, there was a click, and he opened the door.

"Take out everything and lay it on the floor. Then crawl back where you were."

There were several thick manilla envelopes, a large box of assorted jewelry and two ledgers. Ella picked up the envelopes. There was a different name written on each. The first one, Benny, contained $252 in assorted denominations. The second envelope held $300 in 10s and 20s. It was marked Meyer. She counted out $200 from the first envelope placed it in the second. "Lansky, huh? See, if you'd kept your promise, we could have avoided all this drama." She kicked his money belt and wallet back. "Here's your ticket. You can keep the $156. Now crawl back, replace everything and lock the safe."

He moved slower this time, earning him a solid whack on his backside. She glanced at the clock, 8:10. "Move it!"

There was a sink on the wall with a towel hanging from a rack. Ella wetted it while the pawnbroker locked the safe. "Lie flat, keep your head down."

"I promise not to budge until you're well away."

"Don't talk."

Ella draped the towel over the pawnbroker's head. He began to whimper.

"Oy vey iz mir!"

"Aleichem shalom." She fired three shots.

In the alley she locked the side door and dropped the keys in the rain barrel.

* * *

Ella took a roundabout route to the Mark Department Store, arriving just after it opened. She bought two ensembles of summer fashions, under wear, shoes, cosmetics, eau de toilette, sundry accessories and a sturdy travel case. A blonde wig would have helped the look she was after, but the only one she could find made her look like Harpo Marx. She'd just have to wait until Nassau and have her hair dyed professionally. It all came to $20. The salesgirl was very helpful. She removed the price tags, assisted Ella into a new ensemble, and disposed of the shabby Red Cross offerings. Everything else went into the travel case.

At the hotel she asked for the carpet bag and paid her bill. In her room she took another shower, and did what she could to conceal the wound with makeup. It stung and was maybe infected but it would have to wait for treatment. Her lipstick was a bright, glossy red. She lay out the new clothes on the bed and tried on different combinations, deciding on the lavender pants, a white blouse and blue jacket with an inside pocket just large enough for her PPK. Worn loose there was no bulge. She looked over her shoulder at the floor mirror, yes, the pants certainly flattered her derrière. She replaced the three cartridges in the pistol's magazine, and packed her purchases and money in the travel case. It was $800,000 short. She checked again. "Guess Fred took what he needed to pay those vets their war bonus . . . all of it."

She left the empty carpet bag with a note and 50 cents for the housekeeper. After dropping off the key at the front desk, Ella walked south on Collins Avenue. The new clothes and a good night's sleep had worked wonders. The business with the pawnbroker added a certain jaunty frisson to her step. It was noticed by passersby and she got the looks. She smiled under her rakishly angled sun hat.

Ella stopped at a sidewalk café bordering Collins Park. She ordered a coffee and picked up a newspaper left on the table. Just below the fold there was a photograph. The cut line read, *Gold necklace and exotic hand-shaped pendent found by relief workers in the Keys yesterday on the naked body of a white girl. Can you help identify her and solve this tragic mystery? Call Herald telephone 2-7401.* On the front page was a list of dead and missing. She recognized one name right off, Dr. D. C. Main, Veterans' Camp No. 1. The list continued on page 8, including, Jimmie Conway, veteran and Fred Dunn, veteran. Half way down the page she stopped. *Mrs. Rosalind Grooms Palmer, Key West; George Pepper, nephew of Claude Pepper, former state senator.* "Oh, no!" She bowed her head. People turned to see. The waiter approached and saw what she was reading. He looked around at his other customers and shook his head. "Hurricane dead," he said, just loud enough for the nearest to hear. They returned to their conversations and morning cocktails. The waiter placed a fresh napkin on Ella's table. She dried her eyes and read on:

Dr. Hanson, the state health official in charge of disposal of bodies, said that if by the time he arrived at the scene today, instructions were not received from the nation's capital he would direct the immediate disposal of the victims by cremation or local burial as a safeguard to public health.

She sat for a few minutes, then got up and hailed a cab. "Pan American Terminal, Dinner Key, please." She arrived about noon. Inside the lobby she stopped in front of the rotating globe. "Morgen die ganze Welt," she whispered, then walked to the ticket counter.

"Reservation for Helen Ferguson on the 1:10 flight?"

"Just a moment, Miss Ferguson . . . yes, here it is, round trip to Nassau, return on September 20th. The flight is on time. Do you have any baggage to check?"

"No, sir."

"Fine then, that will be $35, please."

"Here you go," Ella handed the bills to the clerk.

"And here's your ticket, Miss Ferguson. If you like you may wait outside on the shaded terrace or in our air-conditioned Clipper Lounge up the stairs to the right. There will be an announcement when your plane is ready to board. We at Pan American Airways appreciate your business."

"Thank you, sir. I think I'll visit the terrace. Any planes arriving soon? I've never seen a sea plane land . . . splash down or whatever the term is."

"Land is acceptable, Miss Ferguson. Actually, we just so happen to have a special flight arriving from Key West in 20 minutes. You can see it from the terrace. It will dock at Pier 2."

"Golly, that will be thrilling! Why is it special?"

"No rail service to Key West since Monday and our sea planes have been used for hurricane relief, so we're running special flights today for stranded travelers. Things should get back to normal this weekend."

"Glad the bad weather is over."

"Well, Miss Ferguson, this is hurricane season. We'll likely get another storm by November."

"Excuse me, miss," said the man standing behind Ella. "This is all very interesting, but I'm in rather a hurry."

Ella turned. "Oh dear, I'm terribly sorry. This is all so new and exciting!" She gave the man a radiant smile, "Ta, ta!" and sauntered off.

"Sir?" asked the clerk.

"Where's she going?"

* * *

Ella sat on the terrace sipping a complimentary gin and tonic, gazing across the bay through her sunglasses. She was startled when a twin-engine plane roared overhead. She stood and watched it bank around and drop low over the water. Gently, gently it kissed the surface, raising a subtle wisp of spray and leaving behind a wake of pristine foam. She clapped and squealed like a school girl. The other waiting passengers smiled indulgently at her. The Commodore taxied to Pier 2, where the ground crew quickly moored the plane and pushed a ramp up to the door. Ella watched as the twenty passengers deplaned and walked toward the terminal to claim their bags. One she recognized. Two other men, dressed like high rollers, appeared particularly impatient. They rushed past. Then one turned and looked at her. She smiled, removing her sunglasses.

"Hello miss, we haven't met before, have we? In Key West perhaps?"

"My, what an original line. I'm sure I'd remember you. How could you forget little me?" She took another sip of her drink.

He sat at her table without invitation. "You're right, Dixie, I don't forget. You were with a friend of ours in Key West, Sunday afternoon. We're kinda concerned because nobody's seen him since. That's a long time for our friend, he likes to stay in touch." The other man had returned and stood behind Ella. She could feel his shadow on her neck.

"Hmm, a friend of yours? I can't imagine who you might mean."

He placed his hand over Ella's. "Tony Conte, he was asking around about that Havana business. Spoke to Fred Dunn, a partner of yours. Then Tony met you, didn't he, Dixie . . . or is it, Ella? Monday, we trailed you to that lodge at the ferry landing. The manager confirmed you and Dunn spent the night, and left before we got there. Drove to Miami over the rail bridge, right? Quite a stunt that."

"Oh, you must mean, Goldy." She slipped her hand out of the man's grip, and put her sunglasses back on. "Cute guy. He told me all about his boss, likes the horses, family man, wife and kids. A regular mensch, according to Goldy. He was going to introduce us, maybe at Aqueduct or Saratoga Springs, one or the other. Always at Hialeah for the season, that's in January isn't? Personally, I'm not much into gambling. Now horses I do like. Beautiful animals, don't you think?"

"Maybe, you'd like to meet him now. He's waiting to hear from you about Tony and the item."

"I'm not at Dinner Key just to watch planes take off and land, mind you, although that is fun. I have a flight to catch. Maybe when I return, I can fit him in."

"He doesn't like to be kept waiting."

"Have you spoken with Meyer this morning? He may have something else on his mind."

The two men glanced at each other. "Girlie, if you know something, it would go better for you to spill it now."

"All I know is that Fred decided to stay in the Keys, some business of his." She glanced at the terminal clock. "Well, I'd better visit the powder room before my flight. If you gentlemen will excuse me." Ella shoved her chair back as hard as she could, striking the man behind her in the knees. He staggered. She screamed. Turning around she slapped him hard across the face, "Oh, you nasty man!" she shouted, everyone looked, several men stood. One was already close by. "Oh, Edward, good to see you. These men work for Meyer Lansky and just threatened me with bodily harm."

"I heard it all." Renard took out his wallet and displayed his badge. "Special Agent Renard, Federal Bureau of Investigation. Gentlemen, you are under arrest." Two airport policemen appeared from the terminal building. Renard waved them over and showed them his badge. "These men are charged with felony menacing. Frisk them and hold them inside while I get a statement from the lady."

"I want to see my lawyer!"

Renard covered his mouth and coughed. One of the cops nodded. "Well, we'll just have to see about that, Mack. What with the hurricane and the weekend coming up, telephone lines down and all, it might take a few days."

"What?"

* * *

"Smoke?"

Ella nodded. Renard handed her a cigarette and lit it with his Zippo, then lit one for himself.

They were seated on a bench near Pier One. "So, is it Dixie now?"

"Didn't make that one up, Fred did, seems to have stuck."

"That picture of your necklace was in the Key West paper this morning. The Rattigans and Abby were very upset."

"And you?"

"Disappointed. You're a survivor. Figured you'd have gotten away."

"And now?"

He smiled. "Can't deny it, very pleased."

She blew a smoke ring. "Well, if anyone knows I'm alive, glad it's you."

"My investigation hit a dead end after you two took a powder. On Wednesday we did some relief work at Camp 3. Spoke with the captain there, he remembered seeing Dunn at the Matecumbe Hotel Monday afternoon. Didn't see you, though."

"Interesting, I wondered what he was up to. Read where they identified his body."

"So, is Dunn really dead?"

"Must be, the Army is checking fingerprints. I said Kaddish for that poor girl . . . what I remembered of it."

"She was Jewish?"

"Doubt it. Because of what I did no one will mourn at her grave. She'll be just one of the missing. I thought the mourner's prayer was the least I could do . . . everyone deserves a prayer you know. It did come from my heart. I'm going to cry."

"I understand." He gave her his handkerchief. "Tomorrow they're taking Emilio back to New York by ship. He's still in a coma."

"Too bad. We hit it off. Abby, she came down with Mr. Rattigan?"

"Yeah, had the opportunity to get to know her. Remarkable woman."

"Hmm . . . well, I'm out of this Edward. Sorry about my friends, but it was necessary. I need everyone to believe Ella Kaufmann is dead. I came this close," the tips of her thumb and forefinger barely touching, "to proving honest Abe wrong. I just wanted to watch a seaplane land. How innocent is that? If I had only stayed in the lounge, no one would know I'm alive. Guess I got cocky. Can I rely on you keeping my secret?"

"They found your necklace on that girl's corpse, all the evidence I need to retire your file. The Rattigans will swear it's yours."

"I hope they send it to my parents."

"I'm sure they will. And with Dunn's body found, his case is moot."

"So, we're good. Can you keep those two jokers quiet? They know I'm on this flight."

"How long?"

"Like forever . . . no? How about a month?"

"The Miami PD will check on any open warrants. But they will eventually get to see a lawyer and their story will get out. Best I can do is maybe delay that a week, enough time for you to get a fake passport with a new name and move on. The forgers make quite good ones in Nassau and the best aren't cheap. More for rush jobs. I assume you have enough?"

"Plenty."

"Lansky's?"

"He seems to think so."

"Better get two with different names, use the second when you depart your next stop. Only way to throw them off your trail. The south of France is very nice this time of year. But it's not just the mob you're trying to fool, is it?"

"The Party will place a nice death notice in the Daily Worker, heroic comrade and such. Maybe there'll be some mention of my untimely demise in the Daily Sun, Coed takes a dive, doesn't surface. When my parents find out it will break their hearts, but it's necessary, don't you see? If I try to contact them word will get out. The Gestapo watches my father, they'll wonder why he's communicating with the dead. When Lansky finds out I'm alive, the first thing he'll do is check on my parents. I'll just have to wait until it's safe to tell them. Meanwhile I can make arrangements through an intermediary to help them leave Germany. It's not safe for them to stay there. Can't you just lock Lansky up?"

"Believe me, we've been trying for years, but he always has an ironclad alibi and never gets his hands dirty. This isn't the Reich after all. I need evidence that will stand up in court."

"Lansky had a third man in Key West, Tony Conte. Know him?"

"Sounds familiar, New York mob, an enforcer."

"On Sunday he found Fred and me. He knew everything we'd told Marshal Reed on Saturday and more. He must have flown down from Miami. He told Fred to deliver the 'item' by midnight Sunday or else. But he never showed, he disappeared, according to those two guys."

"Fred kill him?"

"Didn't tell me."

"Well, sounds like Lansky has a source at Justice. That would explain a lot of things. Thanks for the tip. Maybe I can still salvage this trip. Oh, Cindy found your camera on the boat and had the film developed. Want me to send the prints?"

"How would that work? I'm dead."

He shrugged. "There were some sunset shots at the end of the roll. I went out on the pier and found where you took them. Sunday night, right? Who was with you?"

"No one. I like sunsets. Here's another tip that might help. There's a shady pawnshop downtown, on Northeast 2nd Street. Talk to the broker, today, before he gets wind of this. He knows Lansky. They're in business together, money laundering."

"Good, I'll pass that on to the Miami office."

The public address system announced, *Pan American Airways Nassau Clipper is ready now for immediate boarding. Passengers, please proceed to Pier 1.*

"That's me Edward, gotta run. Thanks for getting me out of this jam." She and Renard stood.

"My pleasure. Bon voyage, Ella."

"Helen, Helen Ferguson. And I'm 18 now."

"Happy birthday, Helen." He held out his hand.

"Kiss me, stupid!"

He smiled and took her in his arms. "PPK?"

"In a skirt I wear it on my thigh."

They kissed; the other passengers walked by.

"OK, that's enough." Ella pushed him away. "Ha! Look at you . . . just a sec." She moistened Renard's handkerchief with her tongue and wiped her lipstick from his face. "There! Don't want people getting any ideas. I'll return this. Toodle loo, Edward."

"Solidarität, Kameradin." He raised his fist.

She saluted back. *"Oublie-moi, ô mon amour."*

* * *

The big Sikorsky S-40 climbed smoothly over Biscayne Bay and then banked steeply right. This was Ella's side of the plane and she could look straight down at the city. When they leveled off only empty ocean was visible to the horizon. It was her first flight, and more thrilling than she had imagined. It had been a good week for firsts, a really good week . . . really.

The End

Historical Notes

This novel concerns actual events. The 1935 Labor Day Hurricane is central to the plot. The Weather Bureau advisories are verbatim. The accounts of the storm and its aftermath are from contemporary news articles, official reports and the sworn testimony of survivors. 259 veterans died, and an estimated 228 civilians.

The Veterans Work Program (VWP) was a project of the Federal Emergency Relief Administration (FERA) and the Veterans Affairs Administration (VA), to provide healthy, outdoor work for transient veterans who had come to Washington, DC in search of government assistance. Many were characterized as hard cases: homeless, alcoholic, scornful of authority, lazy, larcenous and afflicted with wartime neuroses or "shell-shock". Others were responsible, hard-working men who had simply fallen on hard times. They were paid $1 a day, plus food and lodging. The VWP began in November 1934 and was terminated in November 1935. Those killed in the hurricane were posthumously recognized as Federal employees by act of Congress in June 1936, and as such were entitled to benefits under the Federal Employee Compensation Act. The initial investigation to determine responsibility for the failure to evacuate the veterans was rushed through by FERA and found no one culpable. The disaster was deemed an Act of God. A much more thorough investigation completed by the VA in October 1935 found three Florida Emergency Relief Administration officials negligent, Ray Sheldon, Fred Ghent, and Conrad Van Hyning (Florida ERA Administrator). No action was taken against them. The report of this investigation was never publicly released by the VA, nor was it presented to Congress during its hearings on the disaster in 1936. It became available to researchers only in the 1960s at the National

Archives. Until recently, 164 veterans killed in the hurricane were refused memorials by the VA because they lacked a family member willing or able to apply. The VA's case is currently before the U.S. Court of Appeals for the Federal District, Bareford v. McDonough.

The World War Adjusted Compensation Act of 1924, entitled veterans to a bonus for their wartime service. The amount was calculated on the number of days served, and whether stateside ($1.00 per day) or overseas ($1.25 per day). The bonus was payable in 1945 with interest. In 1932 during the Depression, veterans lobbied Congress for a "Bonus Bill" providing an immediate payment, averaging around $1000 per veteran. This culminated in a march on Washington DC by thousands of veterans who built encampments around the city. After the Bonus Bill was defeated in Congress, President Hoover ordered the Army to remove the encampments. Many veterans resisted. There were arrests, injuries, fires and at least one death. Veterans staged a second, peaceful march in 1933 hoping the new president, Franklin Roosevelt, would support the Bonus Bill. Congress did pass the bill but Roosevelt vetoed it. The hurricane disaster sparked renewed lobbying efforts by veterans' groups. The Bonus Bill finally became law in January 1936 over President Roosevelt's veto.

President Gerardo Machado fled Cuba on August 12, 1933. During his exile Machado was an international fugitive wanted for murder and embezzlement of government funds. The financial relationship between Machado and Chase National Bank was investigated by both the Cuban and American governments. The ABC telegram threatening his death is real. In December 1937 Cuba included him in a general amnesty and dismissed extradition proceedings. But Machado never returned to Cuba. In 1939 he died of natural causes in Miami where he had settled.

The Havana bombing is conjectural. It is based on the February 13, 1935 bombing of the U.S. Consulate in Santiago, and a truck bomb at a Havana newspaper on September 20, 1936.

The Pan American aerial observations and Leonard Povey's hurricane hunt occurred as described.

German military intelligence, the Abwehr, began spying on the United States in the 1920s. Agents infiltrated the commercial aircraft industry seeking advanced technical information. After Germany began to re-arm in 1933, the Abwehr intensified its intelligence gathering efforts. Agents recruited German-Americans in the defense industry. The fast German ocean liners, Bremen and Europa, ferried agents, propaganda and military secrets on their regular trans-Atlantic crossings between New York and German ports. Because of its large German population, Nazi sympathies and proximity to the Hapag-Lloyd terminal on the Hudson River, Manhattan's Yorkville district became the nexus of Abwehr spying in America.

The Gestapo was waiting for Lawrence Simpson when the SS Manhattan arrived in Hamburg on June 27, 1935. He had been betrayed, but by whom is uncertain. Simpson was imprisoned 15 months before his trial on September 28, 1936. He was sentenced to 3 years for seditious activities, importing Communist propaganda. But through the intercession of American consular authorities, he was released on December 22, 1936.

The Bremen incident is based on William Bailey's memoir, The Kid from Hoboken, and contemporary press reports. Bailey and his comrades were cleared of all charges. But the story did not end there. In September 1935, Hitler clarified the status of the swastika by decreeing it Germany's sole national flag. This compelled the U.S. Government to sanction its display at German diplomatic missions and on German vessels in American ports until war was declared on December 11, 1941.

Ben Davis's account of the storm in Chapter 30 is taken largely verbatim from his testimony given during the VA investigation on September 11, 1935.

Listed below are the real people depicted. Their portrayal was guided by the available records. In some cases, survivors' words are taken from sworn testimony. (†, denotes died during the hurricane):

Albury, William – Major, Florida National Guard

Bailey, William – Self-described hobo, sailor, union organizer, Spanish Civil War veteran, Communist

Brooks, Louise – Actress, dancer

Conway, Jimmie – Veteran Camp 1, former prize fighter †

Davis, Ben – FERA, Captain Camp 3

Griebl, Ignatz – Nazi agent in New York City

Hardaker, Bill – FERA, Captain Camp 1

Machado, Gerardo – President of Cuba, 1925-1933

Main, Daniel, – FERA, Doctor Camp 1 †

Menendez, Antonio – Cuban Police Chief

Obregón, José – Machado's son-in-law

Palmer, Rosalind – Key West socialite engaged to George Pepper †

Pepper, George – FERA staff, engaged to Rosalind Palmer †

Person, Addison G. – Pan American pilot

Poock, Frederick – FERA staff

Povey, Leonard – Captain, Cuban Army Air Corps, stunt pilot

Pugh, Paul – Veteran, Top Sergeant Camp 3

Reagan, William – Parish Priest, St. Mary Star of the Sea, Key West

Reeve, Guy – U.S. Marshal, South Florida District

Russell, Charlotte – Resident of Upper Matecumbe †

Russell, Henry, Ruby and their 9 children – Residents of Upper Matecumbe †

Russell, John – Postmaster, Islamorada

Sheldon, Gayle – Wife of Ray Sheldon

Sheldon, Ray – FERA Camp Superintendent

Sheeran, Edward – Superintendent of Bridge Construction

Spitz, Raymond – Florida East Coast Railway agent, Islamorada

Thompson, Karl – Sheriff of Monroe County, Florida

"Fred Dunn" is a composite of Fred Griset, Camp 3, who died in a train accident on August 4, 1935 on Lower Matecumbe Key, and Thomas Dunn, Camp 1, who died in the hurricane.

"Ella Kaufmann" is loosely based on the early life of Rose Bethe née Ewald. In the novel she is conflated with the protagonist in Friedrich Wolf's short story about a communist interrogated by the Gestapo, *Chin up, Anna!* Rose was Jewish and vehemently anti-Nazi. In 1936 she immigrated to the United States from Germany. In 1939, at the age of

22, Rose married Hans Bethe, her physics professor at Cornell University and later a Nobel Prize laureate. There is nothing to suggest she ever hurt anyone or spied for any country. In 1943, when Hans moved to Los Alamos, New Mexico, to head the Theoretical Division of the Manhattan Project, Rose came with him. J. Robert Oppenheimer chose her to manage the Los Alamos Family Housing Office. She died in 2019 in Ithaca, New York, at the age of 102.

"Edward Renard" is the name of Edward G. Robinson's character in the 1939 Warner Brothers film *Confessions of a Nazi Spy*. Renard was modeled after Leon G. Turrou, the FBI special agent who in 1938 took down the Nazi spy ring in New York City. After resigning from the FBI, Turrou was hired as technical advisor on the film.

Sources and Acknowledgements

Ideas, themes and inspiration came from many sources. I am deeply indebted to these artists, authors, historians, and Google Search.

Books, articles, short stories, magazines, newspapers, collections:

Bailey, William, The Kid from Hoboken, An Autobiography, Circus Lithographic Press, 1993

Bertelli, Brad and Wilkinson, Jerry, Islamorada, Arcadia Publishing, 2014

Best, Gary Dean, FDR and the Bonus Marchers, 1933-1935, Praeger, 1992

Best, Nicholas, The Greatest Day in History: How, on the Eleventh Hour of the Eleventh Day of the Eleventh Month, the First World War Finally Came to an End, Public Affairs, 2008

Depastino, Todd, Citizen Hobo, How a Century of Homelessness Shaped America, U. of Chicago Press, 2003

Douglas, Marjory Stoneman, September/Remember, Saturday Evening Post, 7 December 1935

Drye, Willie, Storm of the Century, The Labor Day Hurricane of 1935, National Geographic, 2002

Gallagher, Dan, Florida's Great Ocean Railway, Building the Key West Extension, Pineapple Press, 2003

Gerardo Machado y Morales Papers, University of Miami, Libraries, digital collections, https://digitalcollections.library.miami.edu/digital/collection/chc0336

Jeffreys-Jones, Rhodri, Ring of Spies, How MI5 and the FBI Brought Down the Nazis in America, History Press, 2020

Knowles, Thomas Neil, Category 5, The 1935 Labor Day Hurricane, U. Press of Florida, 2009

Hemingway, Ernest, To Have and Have Not, Charles Scribner's Sons, 1937

Hemingway, Ernest, Who Murdered the Vets? The New Masses, 17 September 1935

Hendrickson, Paul, Hemingway's Boat, Everything He Loved in Life, and Lost, Alfred A. Knopf, 2011

McEvoy, Joseph P. and Striebel, John H., Dixie Dugan – Show Girl, syndicated newspaper comic strip, 1929-1966

Nettleingham, F. T., Tommy's Tunes, Erskine Macdonald, Ltd, 1917

Odets, Clifford, What Happened to Us in Cuba, The New Masses, 16 July 1935

Okrent, Daniel, Last Call: The Rise and Fall of Prohibition, Scribner, 2010.

Paris, Barry, Louise Brooks, A Biography, University of Minnesota Press, 1989

Rhodes, Richard, The Making of the Atomic Bomb, Simon & Schuster, 1986

Scott, Phil, Hemingway's Hurricane, McGraw Hill, 2006

Sibley, Frank P., With the Yankee Division in France, Little, Brown, and Co., 1919

Somers, Robert, The Cuban Eight, Professional Aviation Services, 2010.

Standiford, Les, Last Train to Paradise, Three Rivers Press, 2002

Tannehill, Ivan Ray, Hurricanes, Their Nature and History, Princeton U. Press, 1938

Tone, Andrea, Devices and Desires, A History of Contraceptives in America, Hill and Wang, 2001

Triplet, William S., A Youth in the Meuse-Argonne, A Memoir, 1917-1918, U. of Missouri Press, 2000

Turrou, Leon G., Where My Shadow Falls, Doubleday, 1949

Webster's New International Dictionary of the English Language, Second Edition, Unabridged, 1937

Wilkinson, Jerry, Hurricane History Homepage, http://www.keyshistory.org/35-hurr- homepage.html

Wolf, Friedrich, Chin Up, Anna! The New Masses, 30 July 1935

Archives of:

Cosmopolitan

Cornell Daily Sun

Daily Worker

Havana Post

Key Veteran News, https://www.flickr.com/photos/bareford94/collections/72157633388311757/

Key West Citizen

Miami Herald

New Masses

New Yorker

New York Times

Photoplay

Time Magazine

Interviews:

Rose Bethe, June 11, 2014, Voices of the Manhattan Project, Atomic Energy Foundation, https://www.youtube.com/watch?v=IxnvcY3Medw

Rose Bethe, January 3, 2017, Ithaca Area United Jewish Community, https://www.youtube.com/watch?v=CMqq3LbEGB8

Government Sources:

The WWI Era, Part 3: On the Western Front, Chapter 24: The Last Days and Armistice, Section 1: The Final Battles; WWI Centennial Website, U.S. Army Center of Military History. https://history.army.mil/html/bookshelves/resmat/wwi/pt03/ch24/pt03-ch24-sec01.html

Glass, Albert J., Army Psychiatry Before World War II, U.S. Army Medical Department, Office of Medical History, https://achh.army.mil/history/book-wwii-neuropsychiatryinwwiivoli-chapter1

Willoughby, Malcom F., Rum War at Sea, Treasury Department, U.S. Coast Guard, U.S. Government Printing Office, Washington, 1964

Florida Hurricane Disaster, Hearings Before the Committee on World War Veterans' Legislation, House of Representatives 74th Congress 2nd Session on H.R. 9486, A Bill for the Relief of Widows, Children and Dependent Parents of the Florida Hurricane at Windley Island and Matecumbe Keys September 2, 1935, GPO 1936, https://babel.hathitrust.org/cgi/pt?id=mdp.39015049888574&seq=5

Report of Investigation, Re: Florida Hurricane Disaster Vol. I; Record Group 15: Records of the Department of Veterans Affairs, 1773-2007. National Archives Building, Washington, DC, https://www.flickr.com/photos/bareford94/collections/72157633388311757/

Films:

All Quiet on the Western Front, Universal Studios, director: Lewis Milestone, 1930

China Clipper, First National Pictures, director: Ray Enright, 1936

China Seas, Metro-Goldwyn-Mayer, director: Tay Garnett, 1935

Confessions of a Nazi Spy, Warner Brothers Studios, director: Anatole Litvak, 1939

George White's Scandals, Fox Film Corporation, director: George White, 1934

G Men, Warner Brothers Studios, director: William Keighley, 1935

Gold Diggers of 1933, Warner Brothers Studios, director: Mervyn LeRoy, 1933

Here, Prince (You Nasty Man), Warner Brothers Studios, director: Joseph Henabery, 1932

Key Largo, Warner Brothers Studios, director: John Huston, 1948

Let There Be Light, U.S. Army Pictorial Service, director: John Huston, 1946

My Man Godfrey, Universal Pictures, director: Gregory La Cava, 1936

Pandora's Box, Nero-Film A.G., director: Georg W. Pabst, 1929

Platinum Blonde, Columbia Pictures, director: Frank Capra, 1931

To Have and Have Not, Warner Brothers Studios, director: Howard Hawks, 1944

Stoopnocracy, Featuring Stoopnagle and Budd, Fleischer Studios, directors: Dave Fleischer, Seymour Kneitel, 1933

Top Hat, RKO Radio Pictures, director: Mark Sandrich, 1935

Songs:

The Big Rock Candy Mountains, Harry McClintock, 1928

It's a Long Way to Tipperary, many versions, this parody is from Tommy's Tunes, F. T. Nettleingham, 1917.

Keep Young and Beautiful, Al Dubin and Harry Warren, 1933

Horst-Wessel-Lied/Die Fahne hoch (Horst Wessel Song/Raise the Flag High), Horst Wessel, 1929

In München steht ein Hofbräuhaus (In Munich there's a royal brew house), Wilhelm Gabriel, 1935

L'Internationale, text by Eugène Pottier, 1871, music by Pierre De Geyter, 1888

Lullaby of Broadway, Al Dubin and Harry Warren, 1935

Mademoiselle from Armentieres, many versions since 1915, this one is adapted from the Key Veteran News, 1935

Manhattan, Richard Rogers and Lorenz Hart, 1925

Oh, You Nasty Man, Ray Henderson, Jack Yellen and Irving Caesar, from the film George White's Scandals, 1934

Oublie-moi (Forget me), Henri Pueca and Max François, 1945

Remember My Forgotten Man, Al Dubin and Harry Warren, 1933

Star Dust, Hoagy Carmichael and Mitchell Parish, 1929

Where the Blue of the Night Meets the Gold of the Day, Bing Crosby, Roy Turk and Fred E. Ahlert, 1931

Comedian catch phrases:

Joe Penner: "You nasty man!" and "Wanna buy a duck?"

Oliver Hardy: "Here's another nice mess you've gotten me into!"

Stoopnagle and Budd, Frederick Chase Taylor, Wilbur Budd Hulick: "Peachy ... No, Stoopnocracy is peachy!"

A special thanks to Jerry Wilkinson, Air Force veteran and historian of the Upper Keys, who generously opened his home and personal archive to me. In 2006 he applied to the United States Geological Survey to name the islet off the western end of Lower Matecumbe Key, a relic of the 1935 bridge construction project, Veterans Key. He died in 2023 at the age of 94.

About the Author

I grew up on Long Island, New York, graduated with a BA in government from Cornell University, served in the Army on active duty for 20 years, and then as an Army civilian for another 15 years. I am the grandson and son of Army veterans, World Wars I and II. My hobbies include photography, astronomy and solar eclipse chasing, often all at once. Retired now, I live in Medford, New Jersey, with Lulu, the dachshund.

In 2010 I visited the Florida Keys Memorial (AKA the 1935 Hurricane Monument), in Islamorada, Florida. I was struck by the absence of any names on the memorial, neither veteran nor civilian. Memorializing the estimated 228 civilian victims is clearly the responsibility of their families, but the 259 dead veterans are entitled to memorials furnished by the Department of Veterans Affairs (VA) at Government expense. Over the years, through the efforts of myself and many others, 95 veterans have received either private or VA headstones/grave markers and memorials. But, until recently, 164 veterans, whose remains are unavailable for burial, were refused memorials by the VA. Currently, I am the claimant-appellee in a case before the U.S. Court of Appeals for the Federal Circuit, Bareford v. McDonough, seeking to restore a VA policy permitting anyone to memorialize veterans. The inspiration for Veterans Key arose from my research on this case.

– Richard Bareford (Author Page: https://veteranskey.com)

Made in the USA
Coppell, TX
29 March 2024